Call Home the Heart

Shannon Farrell

LEISURE BOOKS NEW YORK CITY

To my family, with love.
And with many thanks to my agent Natasha Kern and my editor Alicia Condon and her staff for making such wonderful things possible.

A LEISURE BOOK®

December 2004

Published by

Dorchester Publishing Co., Inc.
200 Madison Avenue
New York, NY 10016

ISBN 0-8439-5475-2

Printed in the United States of America.

Call Home the Heart

HOMECOMING

Muireann's lips parted with a sigh, deepening the sweet kiss into something much more compelling as he raised one hand to hold her chin tenderly and explored her mouth with a leisurely thoroughness that thrilled them both to the core.

At last Lochlainn lifted his lips, knowing he couldn't hide his throbbing desire for her forever. But she seemed untroubled by the kiss, stroking her hand down the long column of his neck with her eyes closed.

"How long will it take us to get to Enniskillen?" she asked sleepily.

"We should be there by tea time if we have clear roads, but then we'll have to hope for a lift out to Barnakilla," he whispered against her silken hair, now a mass of curls which he tousled with his hands, savoring the soft feel of her all over.

Like a rose without thorns. The thought came to him suddenly, and he found the simile apt.

Muireann nodded, and stroked the hand around her as she turned her head back to the pillow. She reflected somewhere in the back of her drowsy mind how wonderful Lochlainn felt in the bed beside her. How they just seemed to fit together.

She had had the strangest sensation when she had first met him on the docks in Dun Laoghaire, and their hands had touched in greeting. She had trembled then as though the ground under her were shaking. She had felt almost as if she had come home, though of course she had never before set foot in Ireland.

I pray thee leave, love me no more,
Call home the heart you gave me,
I but in vain the saint adore,
That can, but will, not save me.

—Michael Drayton, "To His Coy Love," 1619

Chapter One

Dublin, January 1845

The gunshot echoed through the corridors of the hotel. Lochlainn dropped his water glass and dashed up the stairs two at a time.

"Mrs. Caldwell, Mrs. Caldwell, open the door! Muireann! Open up, please! It's Lochlainn Roche!" he shouted as he hammered at the oaken portal.

Lochlainn could hear nothing in the chamber apart from the sound of someone weeping. After jerking at the latch futilely for several seconds, he threw all of his weight against the solid bulk of the door.

"Muireann! Open up, please!" he demanded between blows.

At last the manager of Gresham's Hotel, stunned by the gunshot and the commotion Lochlainn was causing in the corridor, produced his master key. With a deft flick of his wrist, Lochlainn opened the lock quickly and stormed into his employer's bedchamber. There he saw Muireann, kneeling beside the body of her husband.

It was evident from the state of his head, or what was left of it, that Augustine was dead.

"God, no, please, this can't be happening to me!" the raven-haired woman whimpered as she rocked back and forth, tugging at the lapels of Augustine's coat as though she would strangle him.

"How could you! Oh God, why! What am I going to do?" she wailed, growing more and more hysterical, repeating the words over and over again.

At last Lochlainn, unsure as to what else he should do, tugged Muireann away from the corpse, and gave her a firm tap on the chin with his fist.

She crumpled into his arms like a rag doll. He caught her up before she fell to the floor and demanded of the manager, "Give me another room for Mrs. Caldwell, now!"

The little man, gaping at the carnage before him, barely heard a word Lochlainn said.

"I'll see Mrs. Caldwell's things are moved myself. She's not to be disturbed, is that clear?"

"I suppose I'd better fetch a doctor," the manager said doubtfully, shaking his head.

"For the lady, yes, Mr. Burns," Lochlainn replied grimly. "Augustine certainly won't be needing one."

The hotelier stared at the handsome, ebony-haired estate manager with something akin to horror. How could he remain so calm in the face of such an appalling spectacle?

Lochlainn's steel-gray eyes warmed a little as he tried to soothe Mr. Burns's ruffled feathers. "I'm sorry to sound so cold. It's just that everything must be handled correctly. I imagine there are certain formalities in these sorts of cases. I shall trust you to look after things."

Lifting Muireann high, he followed the little silver-haired man down the corridor to a room at the back of the hotel, far from the noise of all the carriages passing outside through the busy streets of Dublin.

"This chamber is smaller, but the bed is quite large and there is a trundle bed underneath as well. The lady shouldn't be left alone," the hotelier said, staring regretfully at the unconscious, disheveled form that Lochlainn held in his arms as though she were as light as a feather.

"She won't be alone. I'll look after her, never fear," Lochlainn reassured the worried man as he laid Muireann down on the bed. "Just ask the doctor to look in on her whenever he's finished with Mr. Caldwell, if you please."

"Yes, of course, sir. What a terrible tragedy. And to think it happened in my hotel," the little man complained, almost in tears.

"A terrible tragedy to have happened anywhere, when a man takes his own life," Lochlainn observed with a set jaw as he undid the top buttons of Muireann's gown and began to remove her boots.

"But surely, sir, it was an accident!" the dapper little man gasped. "He was cleaning his gun, and—"

Lochlainn looked up at the man in sheer disbelief, his eyes glittering dangerously. "You want me to lie, Mr. Burns?"

"Not exactly lie, Mr. Roche, more, well, give another plausible version of events. After all, his poor young wife . . . It's bad enough for her to have lost her husband on her honeymoon without being exposed to unnecessary gossip and, well, dare I say it, scandal."

Lochlainn sighed. "I hadn't thought about that. You're absolutely right, Mr. Burns. I doubt that anyone's interests would be served if the whole truth were to be revealed. Thank you for being so considerate of Mrs. Caldwell's position. I'm sure I can rely on your discretion."

The little man nodded, and stared sympathetically at the lovely dark-haired woman lying prone on the bed.

"Mr. Burns, can you stay here for one moment while I go get Mrs. Caldwell's things from the other room?"

"Yes, of course."

Lochlainn was back in a few moments with several valises and an armful of gowns. "I'll wait here while you send a maid up to look after Mrs. Caldwell," he said. "Then I'll finish clearing the room and go fetch my things from the coach."

"Thank you, Mr. Roche. I'll go attend to your, er, problem, and will see you later," Mr. Burns said before scurrying out of the room.

Once he was alone with her, Lochlainn stripped Muireann's blood-soaked gown off her limp body and hurled it into the fire, then covered her with a spare blanket he found at the foot of the bed.

Then he brought an armchair closer to the bed. He sat down heavily and cradled his head in his hands.

Why had this happened, just when he had begun to hope there might be some light at the end of the tunnel for the Caldwell estate? Why should everything he held most dear be taken away from him, just when it all seemed to be falling into place for the first time in years?

Disappointed in love, he had fled Barnakilla, the estate where he and his sister, Ciara, had grown up, longing to escape from the memories.

The old lord, Douglas Caldwell, had been alive then. Barnakilla had been a prosperous estate, elegant and well ordered, despite Augustine's extravagance, which his parents had accepted in him because he was their only child. But Douglas Caldwell had died, and then his wife, giving Augustine free rein to despoil the estate with his gambling and devil-may-care attitude.

Lochlainn had run away from the home that held such bittersweet memories for him, and had traveled the world, seeking fame and fortune. He had done well enough for himself, certainly, but in his opinion Australia could never rival the beauties of Ireland, the glories of his home. After three long years, Augustine Caldwell's summons for him to return to Barnakilla had been the answer to Lochlainn's most heartfelt prayers.

But what would the future hold for him now? And what was he to do with the delicate young beauty who lay unconscious on the bed? Poor girl. How had she come to be mixed up in all of this?

But then, she had loved Augustine—hadn't she? He recalled her hysteria in the bedroom a few moments before. *I always did have the damnedest luck,* Lochlainn thought gloomily, as he reached out to stroke her fair, petal-soft skin. He fingered her silky raven-black hair, admiring her beauty while she slept. Her complexion was so pale, she looked as though she were a visitor from another realm. Her looks—high cheekbones, long, moderately thin nose that turned up slightly at the tip, and ruby-red, full lips—might not be to every man's taste, being so ethereal, but for Lochlainn she was lovelier than words could ever hope to describe.

He had never believed in love at first sight until he had seen this tiny nymph staring at him with her incredible amethyst eyes the day before, when he had guided his employer and his new bride off the boat from Liverpool, straight from their honeymoon in Scotland and England.

Quite tall for a woman, though tiny in comparison with himself, Muireann Graham Caldwell had moved down the gangplank like a queen, her head held high, her limpid eyes moving neither to the right nor the left, until they lighted on his face. They had seemed to look into the very depths of his soul. She had taken his hand in greeting, and shock tremors passed up Lochlainn's arm until he regained his self-control, cursing himself for being so fanciful.

Now here she was, a widow, no doubt heir to the Caldwell estate, but probably completely unaware of the dire financial straits her husband Augustine had been in before he died.

But surely Muireann must have married him for love? After all, how could she not have known about all of his faults? Perhaps she was just as vain, frivolous, and addicted to gambling as Augustine had been. If so, the Lord help them all, Lochlainn thought with a shake of his head, looking at the lovely face resting on the pillow with a certain degree of resentment.

If Muireann was fool enough to have loved Augustine, she deserved whatever happened to her. He felt a twinge of guilt at the uncharitable thought as soon as it came to him. He was not normally so spiteful, but experience had been a bitter teacher.

He leapt from the chair impatiently and began to pace up and down in front of the window, until at last he stilled to watch the sun set over the rooftops of Dublin.

Damn it, how could a woman like Muireann, so lovely, so gracious, have married an idle, worthless, drunken lout like Augustine Caldwell?

And what would she do with his beloved Barnakilla now?

Chapter Two

Muireann awoke several hours later and rubbed her sore jaw tenderly. Clutching the blanket around her shivering form, she looked out the window at the snowflakes swirling, fairy-like, in the dim lamplight that glowed from the street below.

Moving her eyes slowly around the unfamiliar room so as not to jolt her throbbing head, she saw Lochlainn sitting in a low armchair by her bedside, a small case of documents open on the night table beside him. The expression in his unusual steel-gray eyes was forbidding as he toted up columns of figures, the scratch of his pen echoing in the high-ceilinged room.

The room was smaller than her other suite had been, but it seemed far more appealing to her, with a magnificently carved four-poster bed hung with flowered brocade curtains in blue and crimson. There were small tables on either side of the bed, and another low one with two chairs placed by the fire. In the corner by the large sash window was a screened-off area to make one's toilette.

The most interesting and cheering aspect of the chamber was the magnificent fireplace, with a beautifully carved oak surround. A fire was glowing in the grate, and for the first time since she had left her family home at Fintry in Scotland, Muireann felt warm and secure. It was all over, she thought with relief, then quashed the guilty thought with a pang.

Attempting to distract herself from her horrifying memories, she turned her attention to her companion.

Muireann studied him unnoticed, and not for the first time admired his arresting masculine beauty. Hard as she tried, she could find no flaw in the enigmatic Lochlainn Roche except his arrogant demeanor. His raven-black hair, which glinted with mysterious dark auburn highlights, was thick and wavy, and just brushed the edge of his collar. He was also unfashionably close-shaven. Side-whiskers would simply have detracted from his high cheekbones and firm jaw, which showed only the barest trace of a shadow. His nose was straight and narrow, with delicately arched nostrils that enhanced his haughty appearance. But the deep cleft in his chin, and the single small dimple which peeped out whenever he moved his mouth, were intriguing.

Muireann found herself wondering what he would look like if he smiled. Certainly he would look a bit more human, a bit less like a prowling tiger about to devour its prey. Lochlainn seemed to perpetually glower, his dark eyebrows lowering threateningly over his thick-lashed gray eyes whenever she had come into contact with him since her arrival in Dublin the morning before. For a man so handsome, he seemed utterly joyless.

But perhaps he has good reason to be upset, she reflected tolerantly as she saw him add up endless columns of figures over and over again, running his fingers through his ebony hair in frustration. She could remember her own father doing that many times over the years, or her brother-in-law Neil Buchanan, whenever she visited her sister Alice, now three months pregnant, at her new home in Dunoon.

Adding up had never been her father's strong point. Muireann had always helped him with his bookkeeping, though her efforts had never been taken seriously by anyone in the family, being considered "unfeminine." At least that's what her mother and sister had reminded her of often enough over the years, applying that adjective to every pursuit she had ever enjoyed.

As Muireann recalled her family's criticism of her with a faint smile, Lochlainn reached the end of his tether. He threw the pen down and rose to stretch his aching back. He stalked over to the fireplace and poked the coals vigorously, then marched over to the window to gaze out at the blizzard wrapping the city in a freezing blanket of ivory.

Muireann admired his tall physique, watching with interest as his muscles rippled through the thin fabric of his shirt. He was certainly the tallest, broadest man she had ever seen. His hard, callused hand had been large enough to take both of her own as he had greeted her and assisted her off the boat at the quay at Dun Laoghaire the previous morning. She had noticed the roughness, but had certainly not been repelled by the contact. Here was a man who had never been spoilt or pampered, who had never been afraid of hard work. Yet at the same time, he had a certain dignity in his bearing which proclaimed him no ordinary farm laborer.

Well, Lochlainn was the estate manager. That had to signify he was intelligent and good with figures, didn't it? But if his hands and clothes and his brown face, which testified to many years out in the elements, were anything to go by, he was not a man to leave all the hard work to others. She certainly admired that quality. Her own father and brother-in-law possessed the same traits. She herself was not averse to hard work, though her mother had always tried to keep her a spoilt, pampered princess, the younger of two daughters born to her very late in life.

Lochlainn heaved a huge sigh and then moved over to the bed, where he was relieved to see that Muireann was at last conscious.

"Have you been awake long?" he asked softly.

"Not very long," Muireann lied. "I've been trying to get my bearings. Where am I?"

"You're still at the Gresham, only in a different room. The snowstorm I feared has started. I'm afraid we'll have to stay at least another night," he said, being careful not to mention anything about the events of the afternoon.

"That's good. My head is pounding. I doubt I could travel all the way to Enniskillen after the terrible sea journey we had," she admitted, rubbing her temples.

Lochlainn reached down to test her forehead, and noted she had a slight fever.

"You're definitely warm, Muireann. Here, why don't I help get you get under the covers properly? Then we can see if they have any broth or soup downstairs.

"And I'll give you a headache powder as well," he offered, crossing over to search his bag, which he had placed on a low luggage holder, with their other things.

She tried to raise herself off the pillow, only to slump weakly back against it.

"Lie still, my dear!"

"I, er, I have to use the chamber pot, but I don't think I can stand," she said sheepishly.

"Here, put your arms around my neck, and I'll carry you over to the screen." He tugged the blanket down over her bare shoulders.

Muireann was painfully aware that she was clad only in her flannel chemise and petticoats, but her companion didn't seem to take any notice. She knew she simply had to accept this stranger's help. She was all alone in Ireland now. What she would do next she had no idea.

But the thought of running back to Fintry to play the part of the grieving young widow was more than she could bear. She disliked being so critical of her own parents, but hadn't she married Augustine to escape from their stifling over-protectiveness and continual disappointment that she never seemed to fit into their world or do what was expected of her?

Her one chance of satisfying them had been to marry well. They had been delighted with Augustine Caldwell when he had turned up at a ball, and taken such an interest in her. Rumors had flown around Glasgow of his great wealth, his magnificent estate in Ireland. Her mother and father had actively encouraged Augustine's suit.

Muireann, tired of letting them down, and longing for adventure, had at last agreed to Augustine's impetuous marriage proposal. They had met on All Hallow's Eve and been wed on Hogmanay, before she could really even get to know him.

"What's wrong?" Lochlainn asked, his concern evident in his tone.

"What? Oh nothing, I was just . . ."

"You're not going to be ill, are you? You made such a grimace."

"No, I'm not ill, just aching." She blushed, looking down at her bare arms, which she then looped around Lochlainn's neck.

His eyes followed her gaze. But far from looking at her leeringly, his eyes widened in alarm. "My goodness, where did all those bruises come from? I didn't hurt you carrying you in here, did I?"

"No, no, I fell on the boat a few times. It was a very rough crossing, you know, and I bruise easily," she replied hastily, trying to quell the shiver that rippled through her.

"There you are, Muireann."

He placed her gently on the floor by the screen and held on to one of her hands until he saw she could manage a few steps on her own.

"I'll go ask for more coal for the fire. You must be freezing."

Muireann marveled at his kindness and delicacy in going out of the room to talk to the serving girl in order to get more coal, and tapping on the door to see whether it was safe for him to return.

Lochlainn tugged down the covers on the bed and fluffed the pillows up against the carved headboard, then went back to the small wash area to fetch Muireann again.

He laid her gently on the bed and pulled all the covers right up to her chin.

"Shall I get you something warmer to wear? I'm sorry about your gown, but it was ruined, and . . ." Lochlainn trailed off with an awkward shrug.

Muireann paled slightly, but made no reference to the frock. "I have a heavy flannel nightdress, lilac-colored, in that small black bag there," she indicated.

He brought the valise over to her and helped her locate

the nightdress and tug it over her head. She managed to pull it down over her ankles with a bit of wiggling and some help from Lochlainn, who seemed most assiduous in his attentions, considering he seemed so manly and grim.

He tucked her in again, and after fluffing the pillows once more, stroked her tousled ebony hair back from her face and said with a small smile, "There now, better?"

"Much better, thank you," she said, lifting her amethyst eyes up to his.

Though Lochlainn Roche was a complete stranger whom fate had thrown in her path, somehow she felt at peace with him. He might be somber and arrogant looking, but he had treated her with every degree of consideration. At some point she had to start trusting someone. She was all alone here. She needed an ally desperately. Who better than her dead husband's estate manager?

"Here, now, take this draught," he said, offering her a glass of water in which he had mixed the powder from a small packet. "Your head will feel better in no time."

Their fingers touched as he handed her the glass. He retained his grip on it to make sure she didn't drop it as she drank the potion down. He put the empty tumbler down on the bedside table, then poured out a plain glass of water for her in case she was still thirsty.

"I'll just go see what's taking that girl," he said as he rose from the edge of the bed, where he had been sitting gazing at Muireann admiringly for several seconds before he had caught himself.

He brought in the tray himself a few moments later. Several seconds after that, a second tap at the door signaled the arrival of the maid with some hot water bottles. She put three into Muireann's bed and then, since it was getting late, she pulled out the trundle bed from under the large four-poster and inserted the remaining two bottles between the sheets.

Lochlainn waited until the maid had gone before answering Muireann's silent inquiry as she looked at the spare bed and then at him. He put the tray on her lap and handed her a napkin to drape over her nightgown in case of any spills.

"Because of the storm, they're short of rooms here, and I don't like the idea of leaving you on your own tonight. Not when you're obviously unwell. I hope you don't mind, Mrs. Caldwell," he said stiffly.

"No, not at all, Mr. Roche," she said with a shake of her head before taking a spoonful of the tasty broth.

"Have you eaten, yourself?" she asked after a moment, meeting his eyes once more.

"Yes, ages ago," he lied smoothly, managing to mask his surprise at her concern. In truth he hadn't wanted to spend the money and was too disturbed by the day's events to feel hungry anyway.

He continued to stare at her, puzzled by her behavior. She seemed so unaffected, unworried by what had happened. Yet she had been absolutely hysterical only a few hours before. Was this normal? Or was she simply hiding all of her tumultuous emotions, too embarrassed to let anyone see her grief?

Looking at her delicate yet well-shaped chin and nose, her candid eyes, and noting her sure movements and carriage, which he had first noticed at the quay at Dun Laoghaire, he suspected she was a spoilt, pampered society woman, but one with a mind of her own. It was probably pride, more than anything else, that would prevent her from revealing to anyone just how she felt.

While Lochlainn could not pretend to feel any grief for Augustine, at the same time he knew how harmful it was to try to bottle up all of one's misery inside oneself. He decided to broach the subject of Augustine's death as delicately as possible in order to test her reaction.

He waited until she had finished the soup and he had put the tray outside their room.

"Mrs. Caldwell, I know it's late and you're obviously upset and tired, but some decisions are going to have to be made about Augustine and the funeral," he remarked quietly.

Muireann's chin began to quiver then, and her voice cracked in several places as she said, "I've never had to deal with any of these sorts of affairs before. What would you suggest?"

He took her tiny hand in his own as he replied, "I think you have to do the whole thing quickly and quietly. There is, of course, no question of a wake under the circumstances. We might have some difficulty in even persuading a priest to bury Augustine in a churchyard."

Her hand trembled as she heard his words, but she looked at him frankly and nodded her agreement. "Ought we to bring him back to Enniskillen with us?"

He shook his head. "No, no, it would be worse there."

Lochlainn didn't want to tell her that they had barely enough money to pay for their hotel room and food, let alone the cost of transporting the coffin back to Barnakilla.

"If you'll allow me, I shall speak to one of the priests up here, Father Brennan, an old family friend who now has a town parish, and see if he would be so kind as to take care of the matter. If you're not up to it, you don't have to attend."

"It would seem so disrespectful somehow. But at the moment I feel as though I'm falling apart," she confessed frankly, starting to shudder again with cold and dread.

He felt her hand quiver in his. Though he knew he would have to tell her the truth sooner or later, for now the only thing the poor girl needed was comfort and a few kind words. So he sat down on the edge of the bed with his back resting against the headboard, and put one arm around her. As the tears began to fall, he held her close, feeling the heart-rending sobs wrack her slender body. He thought once more how lucky Augustine had been, and how foolish.

As she wept, Muireann wondered to herself how she could ever live with the immense guilt that threatened to engulf her. *I'm an evil person,* she reflected sadly. *How can I possibly feel so relieved that he is dead? How can I possibly think of myself at a time like this? But I have no idea how to cope! What on earth will become of me? What shall I do?*

These questions echoed in her mind over and over again. The past two weeks had been her worst nightmare transformed into a hideous reality that she had no idea how to confront.

She wept as though her heart would break.

He damned Augustine for having left his lovely young bride in such a state, abandoned in Ireland with no friends, no family, no estate, and no money to support her.

"It will be all right, Muireann, you'll see," he heard himself say as her arms looped around his neck.

He allowed himself to relax and even take comfort from the warmth and affection of another human being, despite her being so grief-stricken she couldn't possibly know what she was doing.

"I'll look after you. Trust me. It will all be fine, you'll see."

Eventually her sobs began to die down and she moved lower in the bed, further under the covers.

"Cold?" Lochlainn asked quietly, his lips pressed against her raven hair.

"A little."

"I'll go stoke up the fire."

"No, stay with me, please. I'm warm enough like this, really," she said in a small voice.

He didn't need a second invitation to stay put. He was so weary himself, he felt as though he could lie down and sleep forever. He moved down lower in the bed, too, and tucked the top of her head under his chin.

"There, is that better?"

"Mmm," Muireann murmured, drifting off blissfully.

"The doctor left you some medicine. Would you like some?"

"No, really, I just need to sleep, Lochlainn. The boat crossing was so awful, and there wasn't a cabin to be had."

No wonder the poor child was beside herself, Lochlainn reflected angrily. She had been pitched and tossed for three nights on the steamer from Scotland.

He tugged the spare blanket up over himself to keep off the chill as he lay there in his shirtsleeves. But despite his best efforts to keep awake to make sure Muireann was all right, he soon drifted off into a sound slumber, his arms wrapped around her as though he would never let her go.

Chapter Three

Lochlainn stirred slowly as weak winter sunlight filtered through the window. God, but it was cold, came his first thought. He snuggled more warmly under the covers and let out a soft yawn. A small movement next to him brought him fully awake as he suddenly realized he had fallen asleep next to Muireann.

He was about to ease himself away from her side quickly before she discovered his presence and took offense, when he saw that her deep purple eyes were already open.

She smiled up at him drowsily. "My, and I thought *I* was a heavy sleeper."

"Have you been awake long?" he asked, moving his hand

up to check her temperature. She seemed to be cooler and in better spirits than the night before.

"Long enough to be grateful that you don't snore."

"I'm sorry about . . ." He started to apologize as he tried to rise, but she rested a hand lightly on his chest.

"Don't be. You fell asleep. And we'd both be frozen now otherwise," she said, closing her eyes again.

Slightly less embarrassed now, he couldn't resist the temptation to linger in the bed a few minutes longer. The room was now so cold he could see his breath when he spoke, and he hadn't been with a woman for so long. . . .

Muireann's warmth and openness were too tempting. He couldn't help himself. He stroked her hair back from her delicately curved cheek and rested his head next to hers on the pillow again, deeply inhaling her clean crisp fragrance. It was soft, feminine, like roses, but with an alluring hint of musk.

Muireann was content to be held by Lochlainn, feeling no fear of him. But when he moved his hand down from her face in an attempt to rest it on her uncorseted ribs near her waist, she flinched away in agony.

"Good Lord, did I hurt you?" he exclaimed, sitting bolt upright as she sucked in a pained breath.

"Really, Lochlainn, it's not your fault. I told you, I fell on the ship. That's why I can't wear a corset."

"You should get a doctor to look at you," he said lamely as he watched her rise from the bed and walk over to the screen.

"Doctors cost money," she said over her shoulder, "and they wouldn't tell me anything I don't already know. I'll heal in time."

He recalled with a pang all the unpleasant truths he had been shielding her from since the terrible events of the day before, and lapsed into a gloomy silence.

When she came out from behind the screen, she poked the embers of the fire and began to add more coal.

"Here, let me. You shouldn't be doing that. Not when you're ill," he declared, hastily rising from the four-poster.

"I'm bruised, that's all, not ill," she replied a trifle stiffly as she tried to keep hold of the coal scuttle.

"I know, but you might be, well . . ."

She looked at him sharply, and laughed. "My goodness but you are a worrier. I noticed that about you from the first moment I met you, at the docks. You constantly scowl and look severe. You're meant to be the estate manager, not the grim reaper."

He rose to his full height and towered over her. "I take my responsibilities seriously, Mrs. Caldwell. There are many pressing concerns back at Barnakilla which, if you will forgive my saying so, you know absolutely nothing about. After Augustine's death you would hardly expect me to act overjoyed, now would you?" He again began to glower at her in his usual fashion.

She sighed to herself and handed over the scuttle. Perhaps she had been foolish to think of him as an ally after all. Like all men, he was one thing by day and another by night.

She went to her luggage and opened the first valise that came to hand. She pulled out the garment on top, a warm burgundy and black large-checked woolen gown. She tugged some fresh under things out of her smaller black bag and went behind the screen to dress.

Lochlainn searched for his own discarded clothing and looked outside the door for some hot water.

She emerged from behind the screen a few minutes later, her raven black hair clouding around her slender shoulders, cascading down to below her waist in an ebony wave.

He stared at her open-mouthed, arrested by her beauty.

She misunderstood his stare completely. "I know, it looks a fright, doesn't it? My sister Alice is always telling me I should cut it. That makes me more determined than ever not to," she admitted with a small smile as she tugged her hair into a long thick plait down her back without even looking in the mirror, and flipped it over her shoulder as though her coiffure didn't matter in the least.

"No, it's not terrible, it's lovely. Hair like that would earn you the envy of any woman," he said as he practically ran behind the screen to avoid her. What was wrong with him?

His former fiancée Tara had been beautiful—every man in the county had sought her hand. With her blonde hair and buxom good looks, she had had more proposals than any woman in Fermanagh. But she had chosen him, much to Lochlainn's surprise. One day she had caught him alone in the barn and made the nature of her interest in him all too plain.

Lochlainn certainly hadn't rejected her advances. He had been thirty at the time and had begun to think it was about time he settled down with a wife and family. Their affair had lasted two years. Two passionate, tempestuous years. Though they had been engaged almost from the first, he could never seem to get Tara to fix a date. He had hoped she would get pregnant, but no child ever appeared. And then one day she had just vanished. . . .

"Are you all right?" he heard Muireann ask.

"Yes, fine. Why?" He popped his head above the screen to look at her.

"You groaned, that's all. Here, you forgot the hot water. Stop splashing about in that cold, you silly man. You'll freeze to death."

"I'm surprised it isn't frozen in the basin," he remarked as he came out for his shaving things, then quickly tackled the bristles on his chin while Muireann tidied a few things in the room and made the bed.

She moved over to sit on a small low stool by the fire, where she warmed her hands and waited for him to get ready. She glimpsed his bare flesh as he removed his shirt to shave, and then took his clean one, draped over the top of the screen.

My, but he's handsome, even if he is always so serious, she thought admiringly. But then, as he had so rightly pointed out, there were things about the Barnakilla estate of which she knew nothing. Sooner or later, Muireann knew, she was going to have to make a decision.

But not now, not quite yet. She needed to be sure first. She needed more information, which unfortunately only he could give.

But how could she confide in him? No, it was unthinkable. She did have some pride left.

A tap at the door heralded the arrival of their breakfast.

"Could you open the door, Muireann? I'm nearly finished here."

"Yes, of course," she answered, as the enticing aromas filtered in under the door.

She took the tray and laid it down on the small table in front of the fire. She moved the two chairs up closer to it.

As she laid out the dishes and then uncovered the serving bowls, she ventured hesitantly, "Lochlainn, about what I said before, about your being so grim and serious. I'm sorry. It was frivolous of me to tease you in that way. After all, I don't really know anything about you, now do I?

"I don't usually behave so inanely. I suppose I'm just trying to block out what's happened. But telling myself it was all a bad dream isn't going to make it go away, now is it?"

He glanced at her around the screen, and came out, fastening the front of his waistcoat. He was surprised at her practicality in the face of such a loss. "Well, it is understandable that you're upset."

"I know, but there are also arrangements to be made, and decisions."

"Decisions?" he echoed warily.

Muireann looked down for a moment as she poured the coffee. Taking a deep breath, she replied, "Two weeks ago, I married Augustine and thought my life was all laid out before me. Now, just a fortnight later, I'm facing chaos. I honestly don't know what to do."

His eyes never left her face as he came to sit down across from her. "About what?"

"Well, my life now, for one thing. I'm young, inexperienced, far more ignorant than I should be, and I haven't even set eyes on Barnakilla. I know no one here in Ireland except you. One half of me thinks I should go back home to Mother and Father in Fintry. Back to the security I know I shall find there. But another part of me is too proud to go back. I would be cosseted there, wrapped up in cotton wool, and I would never, well . . ."

"Go on, never what?" he prompted.

"Get the chance to really live," she said in a rush.

Lochlainn eyed her carefully. At length he observed, "It is early yet, Muireann. You've only just been widowed. Do you have to make any decisions now?"

Her words sounded just too good to be true. He had to be cautious.

"I suppose there is that. I was thinking, though, that it's easier to travel back to Scotland from here than to go all the way to Barnakilla, only to find out that I've made a mistake.

"But I need your help, Lochlainn. I need you to tell me what Barnakilla is like. And I need your help with the funeral arrangements as well. I know it will be in the papers over here, but if we can possibly keep all this quiet, so my parents don't find out until after the funeral and I can write to them, I would be very grateful."

Lochlainn scowled. "Shouldn't you have your family, the people you love, around you at a time like this?"

"No!" she snapped, and then colored. She put her fork down and nervously folded and refolded her napkin.

He could see her agitation, and the tears that welled up in her eyes. He moved his chair closer to hers and softly held one of the hands that rested in her lap.

"I'm trying to understand, but you need to trust me. Tell me what's going on inside that head of yours. Why don't you want your family here?"

"Because I couldn't bear their pity, their kindness. I don't deserve it, nor do I want it. I would be suffocated. I do love them, it's not that. It's just, well, I'm twenty-one now. I'm not a child anymore. True, I've never organized a funeral, but if you'll help me, then I think we can get through this."

"We?" he asked in surprise.

"Well, it affects you too, doesn't it? I mean, I hope you won't start looking for another employer straight away if you wish to leave Barnakilla now that Augustine is dead," she said with a sniff.

"No, I hadn't thought of leaving Barnakilla at all," he said candidly. "I grew up there, you see. I've been away for three and half years. I've only just arrived back from Australia. Truth to tell, I would sooner cut off my right arm than ever leave Ireland again."

"Do you have a large family at Barnakilla?" Muireann asked in surprise. "Or a wife?" she added with a blush.

"No, no wife or sweetheart," he said, his handsome face darkening. "But Barnakilla has always been my home, and I, for one, think it's the most beautiful place in the world."

Muireann raised her eyebrows in surprise. "I suppose it's only natural to feel that way about the place you grew up. I'm sure I could give you glowing descriptions of my home at Fintry."

Lochlainn poured her more coffee, wondering how to answer.

She wrapped her shawl tightly around her as she waited for him to speak.

But he remained silent, brooding, avoiding her gaze as he continued his meal.

Muireann picked at her food for a few minutes longer. "Well, aren't you going to tell me about it?" she asked as the silence lengthened.

"About what?" he asked sharply, his gray eyes glittering.

She wondered at his quicksilver mood. "About Barnakilla, Enniskillen. You know—anything you think I ought to be apprised of if I am to go there."

He relaxed then, and smiled. "Anything I told you would be biased by my fondness for the place. I can tell you it was once the most prosperous estate in the northwest. The house is splendid—the grounds, the setting. The hunting and fishing are second to none."

"Are there mountains, trees?" she asked enthusiastically.

"Yes, of course, and the lough."

She frowned slightly. "The lock?"

"The lough, Lough Erne. We spell it with a *gh* on the end, instead of a *ch* as you do in Scotland. The eastern side of the property borders it, and the western side has the mountains and trees."

Muireann slowly digested this information. It sounded even more lovely than Fintry.

"And what do the people do for a living? I mean, where did my husband's wealth come from?" she asked innocently.

Lochlainn set his cup down so abruptly that the saucer almost cracked.

She jumped, startled at his violent response. "What's wrong?"

"I'm sorry, I just noticed the time. I want to see Father Brennan before he goes off on his parish rounds. You will excuse me," Lochlainn said, tugging on his great coat with evident agitation. He headed for the door, leaving her staring after him in amazement.

"Don't you want me to come with you?"

He shook his head. "I would say yes, but I think you've had a trying enough time already. The mountains of snow out in the streets that I can see from the window would be too hard for you to negotiate."

"We can go in the carriage."

"No, really, it would be faster for me on foot, given the conditions. You stay here, read or something. I'll have a good long chat with you when I get back," he promised, all the while accusing himself of being a bold-faced liar.

"How soon can we manage the funeral if the weather is so bad?"

"I don't know, Muireann. I'll see what the doctor says on my way to see Father Brennan."

"Thank you for being so considerate. Well, for everything, really."

"No need to thank me," he said with a small tight smile, avoiding her eyes as he wrapped his muffler around his neck.

Lochlainn headed out into the swirling storm to collect his thoughts. *Coward,* he berated himself soundly as he trudged through the crunching drifts. *You're going to have to tell her sooner or later, aren't you?*

But at the same time, he knew he was right. He had to get Muireann through the funeral, and then he would confront her with the dire state of affairs at Barnakilla. The last thing he needed was for her to go running back to her old life at Fintry.

Of course it would be easy enough for Muireann to give him power of attorney to sell the estate, but God only knew who would buy it. Selfish though it was, Lochlainn couldn't bear the idea of being replaced, of having to leave his home once a new landlord took over.

Muireann was young, true, but she didn't seem to be as

addlepated as most girls her age. For example, she had argued quite logically about wishing to avoid her parents' suffocating concern. She had spirit, he had to give her that. The fact that she wished to deal with the funeral was proof of it.

Of course, she could also be driven by stiff-backed pride. That was a character trait he had noticed amongst the upper classes, the ability to maintain a brave front in the face of adversity. Yet he might be able to use this tendency to his own advantage. He was certain that if he convinced her to come to Barnakilla with him, she wouldn't balk. She would have to make some hard decisions, but she would see through whatever she started, he was sure of that. And he would have the power to guide her, advise her in her decision-making so that he could look after the interests of everyone on the estate, including his own.

One other obvious point in Muireann's favor was her wealth and her experience of life on a grand estate. He had seen the richness of her dresses, the small case of jewels in her black valise. There was no doubt in his mind that Augustine had not just married her for love, but for the injection of much-needed capital she could provide. No doubt her dowry was substantial. Had Augustine put it in his bank account already? Or had it been in the form of a banker's draft? Or, due to the haste with which they had married, had the money not yet been paid out by Muireann's father?

He would have to look in Augustine's small strongbox when he got back to the hotel. Lochlainn had ordered all of his late employer's things to be put in a storage room at the Gresham so as not to upset Muireann, but if Augustine's past taste in extravagant jewelry was anything to go by, Lochlainn might at least have enough money to pay for the funeral and the hotel and livery bills if he sold everything and was able to get a good price. He only prayed Muireann wasn't too familiar with her husband's things yet. If she did ask about them, he could always lie and say he had sent them on to Barnakilla.

He stopped in the doctor's surgery first, and was informed that the body was ready to be coffined at any time. The elderly man recommended a discreet undertaker a few streets away, and Lochlainn went there to make inquiries. Not knowing where the money to pay for it would come from, he selected the cheapest coffin and arranged for a minimum of flowers: one wreath from Muireann, one from the estate workers, and one from Augustine's cousin Christopher. Christopher was currently residing abroad after having run off with Lochlainn's former fiancée, Tara, Lochlainn recollected, the bile rising in his throat.

Lastly, there would be one from Muireann's family, to at least make the thing look aboveboard in case anyone poked a nose in where it didn't belong. They had to make the funeral look as decent as possible, if only to avoid scandal for Muireann's sake, and the sake of any unborn child she might be carrying.

Lochlainn thought resentfully of Augustine as he trudged though the snow to St. Francis's Church. He couldn't help himself. Augustine had been short, fat, red-faced, loud, vulgar and stupid. Yet he had been the heir of a rich father, and had got everything his own way. Lochlainn himself was tall, dark, handsome, well educated and, he prided himself, well mannered. He was also an efficient manager. If Barnakilla had been his, he never would have allowed the magnificent estate to fall to wrack and ruin. And if Muireann had been his wife, he would have made love to her until they were both utterly satisfied. The thought made him quiver from head to toe. He certainly would never have been so foolish as to shoot himself in the head on his honeymoon.

The question had to be asked: Had Augustine known the

noose was tightening around his neck? That the debt collectors were howling at the door? Was that why he had taken his own life?

When he arrived at St. Francis's, Father Brennan was just emerging from the church after early morning mass. There were few parishioners out on such a snowy day. Father Brennan hugged Lochlainn to him jovially and dragged him into the tiny but moderately warm vestry.

"Well, my son, it's been a long time. I can't tell you how good it is to see someone from home," the middle-aged man exclaimed, beaming. He was about average height, with silver hair and sparkling blue eyes that seemed to observe everything.

"So, how are you, lad?" he asked in a hearty tone.

"As you see, Father," Lochlainn replied shortly.

"Older and wiser, by the look of things," Father Brennan commented as he glanced at Lochlainn's face, noting his gaunt features.

"I'm afraid this isn't a social visit, Father, much as I've longed to see you these past four years since you left us. No, I'm afraid I have bad news. Augustine is dead."

Father Brennan gasped. "How? When?"

"He shot himself in the head at the Gresham Hotel last night."

The priest stared at Lochlainn in horror. "Suicide?"

"I honestly don't know. It could have been while he was cleaning the gun. His wife was there at the time. She might be able to tell us, but it was a harrowing experience for her. I wouldn't like to upset her further by asking too many probing questions."

"His wife!"

"Aye, Muireann Graham from Fintry in Scotland. They were on their honeymoon, just married a fortnight, in fact. That's why it seems so unlikely that Augustine would have killed himself, and why I've come to you for help. We need to be discreet, for Muireann's sake, and for the sake of any unborn child she might be carrying.

"Also, I have to tell you now the estate is virtually bankrupt. In the years I've been in Australia, he's run Barnakilla into the ground with his gambling, drinking and hunting. No doubt womanizing, too, if the truth be told," Lochlainn said disgustedly.

"No, that was never Augustine's problem," the priest said quietly. "The drinking and gambling kept him busy enough. So you're asking me to bury him decently in my churchyard even though I can't be certain he didn't take his own life?"

Lochlainn threw himself into a small wooden chair by the fire so roughly that it groaned under the weight of his frame. "Would it be so wrong? The poor girl has gone through enough!"

"I would imagine so, being married to Augustine," Father Brennan said, looking ill at ease. "This girl—Muireann, I believe you called her. What is she like?"

"A rare jewel," were the first words that sprang from Lochlainn's lips. "I have no doubt Augustine married her for her money, but she seems to have loved him. I wouldn't wish to hurt her, or disillusion her in any way. Besides, any scandal about his death would have the creditors swarming around Barnakilla like locusts. Please, if I can convince Muireann to come back with me, to channel some of her wealth into the place, then we may be able to keep the place afloat."

"But if the estate is bankrupt, wouldn't it be best to get her to sell it?"

"We would never get a good price, not if the scandal broke. And even if it didn't, things are so bad now that we would just have to take the first offer, no matter how low. It might not be enough to cover all the debts. The new landlord would more than likely have his own tenants and servants. Where would Ciara and I go? Barnakilla has been our home all our lives."

"I did notice you keep using the word *we*," Father Brennan commented shrewdly.

"All right, I admit it! I wish the place were mine, and I don't want to leave. I've traveled around the world, but always I dreamt of coming home. I can't help it. It's in my blood," Lochlainn declared in agonized tones as he ran his fingers through his hair.

"Please, Father Brennan. Declan. You've never let me down in the past. Please, help me now. It might just buy me the time I need, and it wouldn't be harming anyone. I'm not just asking you to do this for my sake. I'm asking you to do it to protect Muireann, who's completely innocent of any wrongdoing. And for all the poor souls at Barnakilla. They need a place to live, work to do, a kind landlord.

"As estate manager, I can improve their lives," he argued passionately. "I can make a difference. If Muireann sells, they'll have nothing, and nowhere to go if the new owner decides to enclose the lands and put sheep in the fields. You know I'm right. It's happened on far too many estates recently for you to think otherwise, old friend."

"All right, Lochlainn," the priest decided at length. "If you can tell me honestly that you think it was an accident, and that you're not simply doing this for your own selfish motives, then I shall agree."

Lochlainn rose from his chair. "Thank you, Declan. I can't tell you what a weight that is off my mind."

"But one other thing before you leave, Lochlainn. How is Tara?"

He sucked in his breath, and felt as though he had been punched in the gut at the abrupt question. But he was able to reply fairly evenly, "She left me, Declan. Ran off to the Continent with Christopher Caldwell, about a year after you moved here."

"I'm sorry," Father Brennan apologized. "No wonder you look as though you've suffered cruelly."

"Australia was a pretty tough place, you know." He gave a tight smile. He moved quickly towards the door before Father Brennan could ask any more uncomfortable questions.

"But now back to the business at hand, Father. The doctor has released the body, the undertakers are coffining him now, and I've arranged for the hearse and flowers. I just need you to set a time. How soon can you manage to perform the funeral?"

"In view of the weather and the situation, the sooner the better. If we don't hurry, the ground might freeze solid, and you'd have to wait several days."

"We can't afford to wait," Lochlainn said bluntly. "I'm not even sure we have enough money to pay the hotel bill."

Father Brennan shook his head. "I had no idea things had come to such a pass. Very well then, if I get my sexton out with his son right now, can you be ready by noon?"

"Aye, I can. I just hope Muireann will be."

"Go tell the undertaker the arrangements, and I shall meet you here."

"I'll see you at noon, then. Thank you, Declan," Lochlainn said, pumping the priest's hand as he took his leave.

Chapter Four

After his visit to St. Francis's to arrange Augustine's funeral with Father Brennan, Lochlainn ran back to the undertaker's as fast as he could, and then returned to the hotel just long enough to tell Muireann the arrangements and collect all of Augustine's property from the manager, Mr. Burns.

"She couldn't bear to have any reminders of him, you know," Lochlainn lied, as he took the valises away, "so I think I'll donate them to charity."

With the cash he was able to raise by taking all of the clothes and jewelry down to a pawn shop, Lochlainn was able to pay off the undertaker and the hotel bill and other expenses they had incurred in Dublin for the previous two nights. He had just enough left over for one more night at an inn on the way back to Enniskillen, and for food and livery there.

As he counted the notes and coins one more time, he wondered how on earth he was going to manage after that. There was no help for it. He would have to tell Muireann something soon. But not now. Not until after the funeral.

Lochlainn went back to the Gresham and paid the bill. He asked if the manager would be kind enough to let him hold onto the room just until the evening, so that Muireann could rest after the service before heading into the country.

Mr. Burns was most accommodating. "So long as you're out by six, that will be fine. Once again, I'm terribly sorry about all this. I was only too glad to be of service."

Lochlainn shook the older man warmly by the hand. "You have been, sir, more than you could know."

"If you insist on coming, my dear, you'll need as many layers on you as you can carry," said Lochlainn. "Come on, take out your warmest dress, and your shawls and a good muff."

Muireann opened one valise, and took out a gown from the bottom, putting the others in a neat pile on the bed without even looking at them.

"This is my warmest dress. Will brown do? I'm afraid I haven't got anything black."

"It will be fine under your cloak," he reassured her. "It's black."

He watched her disappear behind the screen to change.

She came out only a few moments later wearing the rich sable velvet gown, with small black lace trimmings at the wrist and throat, and a lacy black jabot decorating the front. "I have a black bonnet too, in this hat box," she said, crossing over to the pile of cases.

"Good," he said, and bent to check her boots. "These are a bit flimsy. Have you anything heavier?"

"I have my old pair, which I used to use for long walks at Fintry. They're a bit scuffed, but I've just had them resoled."

"Let's see them."

She dug in one of her smaller bags, where she had packed the most precious items from her old home, and showed them to him.

"A bit of polish and they'll be fine," he said, and called down the corridor for the boot boy.

He certainly didn't want Muireann to look like an impoverished widow at the funeral, but all the same, she had to be warm.

The boots cheered him somewhat, though, for they seemed to confirm that his instincts about Muireann had been correct. His first impression of her as haughty, and his second impression of her as an overdressed china doll when he had seen her go down to supper the night she had arrived in an impossibly flouncy low-cut gown, had been the wrong assessments. She had a certain amount of steel in her character that he simply had to exploit for his own ends.

He felt guilty about leading her into a trap, but as he had told Father Brennan, it wasn't just for himself that he wished to get the Caldwell estate out of a rut. There were over a hundred tenants at Barnakilla. He knew they all owed rent, but times had been hard for everyone in recent years. He just had to find some way to make ends meet, for all their sakes.

"I'm ready," she announced a few moments later as she straightened up and tested her boots to make sure they were tied securely, and then looped the ribbons of her bonnet under her chin.

Again, Lochlainn found it odd that she dressed so rapidly and didn't seem the least bit interested in her hair or clothes. She wore virtually no ornaments apart from her wedding ring.

"Let's go." He put on his hat and took her arm. He escorted her down the stairs hurriedly, hoping to avoid the prying eyes of members of the public as they crossed the lobby. He hoped the carriage was waiting for them outside as he had ordered.

The cold weather continued unabated, making it dangerously icy underfoot. Lochlainn felt Muireann slip, and he steadied her quickly as she began to slide.

"Thank you," she said breathlessly as she at last scrambled safely into the seat he propelled her towards. She offered him a hand up as his boot skidded on the iced-over metal stair. Her grip was strong and firm, he noted, as he hauled himself up and sat next to her.

He knew he should have gone to sit above on the box with the driver, since by rights he was little more than a servant. But Muireann had made it quite clear by offering her hand that he was to sit inside with her.

At any rate, it was bitterly cold outside. It would do no one any good if he got pneumonia. She certainly seemed to need his warmth as she nestled closely against him under the traveling rugs and observed, "It's freezing."

"Aye, that's why Father Brennan wanted to take care of the matter straight away," he said as he tucked her into the corner of the carriage. He draped the folds of his cloak securely over her lap before once more settling the rugs over them both.

He pointed out several impressive-looking buildings as they traveled through the snowy streets, such as Trinity College and Christ Church Cathedral, and Muireann had to admit to herself that despite her difficult circumstances, she enjoyed the impromptu tour of the city. She looked with interest at all the things Lochlainn pointed out to her, and was certainly pleased with what she saw.

Ireland had often been ridiculed in her hearing as a troublesome, backward sort of place, but certainly Dublin seemed a fairly modern European capital.

"And Australia, what was it like?" she asked conversationally as the coach lurched to and fro on the icy streets, occasionally throwing them intimately together.

"Very hot some days, freezing the next, all of that and rainy in Melbourne. I worked all over, mainly with cattle, but also doing some carpentry and blacksmith's work, which I picked up over the years at Barnakilla. Some of the country is like a desert, no green for miles. After Ireland, well, I just couldn't get used to the bleakness. That's why I had to return. When my sister wrote to me and said that Augustine was begging me to come back and look after things as I had done when his father was alive, I jumped at the chance," he told her. "I'd made some money, enough to keep myself and my sister comfortably but not enough to set up my own place, as I had once dreamt."

"What about your sister? Tell me about her, unless of course it's too personal," Muireann said shyly, recalling how brooding he had looked earlier that morning when she had mentioned Barnakilla.

But Lochlainn smiled now. "Ciara is a very talented young woman, bright, intelligent, excellent at sewing, cooking, cleaning. She kept house for Augustine for a time, though of late she's been taking in sewing and laundry."

"Oh, why is that?"

Lochlainn neatly avoided the subject by saying, "Almost there."

He absentmindedly tucked a stray lock of hair back into Muireann's bonnet, his long, warm fingers stroking her petal-soft cheek lightly.

He smiled. "There, pretty as a picture."

Then he nearly kicked himself as he realized he had blurted out something so suggestive to the lady just before her husband's funeral. But she seemed to take no notice of his compliment, and merely thanked him as she tugged on her gloves.

He got out of the carriage first, and lifted Muireann down, holding onto her under the arms, close to his long lean body, until he was certain she had her feet firmly planted under her. Then he took her arm and escorted her to the graveside. There he wrapped her in the voluminous folds of his cloak, pressing her close enough against his front for her to be acutely aware of his masculine strength throughout the ceremony.

Really, Lochlainn was the most extraordinary man—kind, tender and smiling one moment, brooding and arrogant the next. She was glad, however, that he couldn't see her face, for it was almost as though the bitter weather had frozen up her tears. She remained dry-eyed throughout the funeral, so that Father Brennan kept casting anxious looks at her as she stood numbly, no trace of emotion apparent in her face.

As she knelt to put the first handful of soil on the coffin, Father Brennan caught Lochlainn's eye and indicated he should come into the vestry for a moment afterwards.

"Muireann, would you like to come inside, while they fill

the grave?" Lochlainn asked softly, bending his head towards hers.

"No, really, I'll be fine in the carriage," she said, the tears beginning to well up as she wondered what she was going to do now.

He conducted her to the carriage and helped her into it.

"Settle yourself in there. I'll be back in a moment. I just have to give Father Brennan a bit of money for the poor box for his troubles."

"What's wrong?" he asked without preamble as he entered the vestry.

"I'm just a bit worried about that poor young girl, that's all. She seems to be holding all of her grief in, trying to be brave. It's not good for her."

"Well, grief takes all forms," Lochlainn said with an uncomfortable shrug. "I can tell you she certainly cried herself to sleep last night."

"I know, but all the same, don't let her overdo things."

Lochlainn scowled blackly. "I'm hardly in a position to be telling her what to do, now am I? After all, I'm only the hired help."

"You know what I mean, so don't be disingenuous. Make sure if she does decide to go back to Barnakilla with you that you don't allow her to overtax her strength."

Lochlainn sighed. "I'll look after Muireann, Father, I promise. She doesn't deserve any of this. I'll do everything I can to help her if she does decide to come home with me."

"Very well. Go now, before she freezes out there. Good luck to you both then, and may God be with you."

"Amen to that, Father," Lochlainn assented wholeheartedly, crossing himself. Then he headed back to the waiting carriage.

That unpleasant duty done, he had a far more distasteful one to perform. Lochlainn knew he would have to do it as soon as they got back to the Gresham if they were to be out of their room by six.

Watery January sunlight filtered though the coach windows as they rode back together in silence.

"It looks like more snow," she observed forlornly as she huddled against Lochlainn for warmth.

He put his arm around her. "I was thinking, you know, that we really ought to consider heading back to Barnakilla. After all, the weather could get worse, and you might be more comfortable there than at a hotel."

This was a complete fabrication, of course, but it was one way of broaching the subject of their leaving soon without disclosing the whole truth before he was sure Muireann was ready to hear it.

She still felt uneasy about the magnitude of her decision to go to Barnakilla. After all, it would be like cutting her last tie with the past if she ventured into the complete unknown with this enigmatic stranger. At the same time, she knew beyond a doubt what waited for her back at Fintry.

She sighed and rested her head against the squabs of the seat. For a time she stared up at the ceiling.

At length she replied, "I suppose you're right. There's no sense in putting off unpleasant things, is there? I have to be an adult about all this, accept my responsibilities to Barnakilla as Augustine's wife."

"You're doing fine so far."

Muireann looked up at him and gave an uncertain smile. "I know this might sound odd to you, Lochlainn, but I've always felt I was destined for important things. I mean, I've never spent all my time dreaming about who I would marry, the house I would have, balls, parties. I always dreamed of adventure, of doing something on my own, without my parents or anyone else dictating to me. I must sound rather dull, to you—or arrogant."

"No, not at all. Go on," he urged.

"Well, Augustine never told me very much about Barnakilla, just that he needed a good wife to run his household. I mean, I'm not saying I was being mercenary, that I married him for the estate. You mustn't think that."

"I don't." *If you had, child, you certainly would be in for a big disappointment,* he thought sardonically.

"It was the challenge. I mean, here was a man who swept me off my feet, who said he needed me, *loved* me. It all seemed too good to be true for a girl like me, plain and silly as I am. I should have known my happiness wouldn't last. But having seen this rosy vista laid out for me in my mind's eye, how can I go back to Fintry, to my old life? I married Augustine for a whole welter of reasons, not simply because I thought I might be falling in love. Those reasons still hold true. So I need your honest opinion now," she stated as she looked up at him searchingly.

"About what, my dear?"

"Am I making a mistake in thinking that a foolish girl like myself could make a difference to Barnakilla? Is it just stupid pride that makes me believe I might actually be able to run an estate, if you were willing to teach me, and pick me up when I stumble and fall flat as I shall no doubt do?"

The coach pulled up in front of the hotel just then. Lochlainn looked at her earnestly. Taking one of her delicate hands in his own, he vowed, "You're not ugly, foolish or silly. I *know* you can make a difference, Muireann. I'm certain of it. And I promise, I'll never leave you, not for as long as you ever need me. I give you my word."

Her amethyst eyes gazed up into his steel-gray ones which stared down at her so pierçingly, and all her doubts melted like snow in the sunshine.

"Then let's go upstairs and pack. Tell Paddy the driver to get a few items ready for our journey."

Lochlainn swung her down from the coach and trailed

after her up to their room. Once inside, she immediately moved to pack her case, but he took her gently by the arm and asked her to sit down with him for a moment.

Muireann blinked in surprise. "If you're worried about my having made my mind up too abruptly in the coach . . ."

"I am, but not for the reason you think," he said as he seated her by the rapidly dying fire. "I have to be honest with you. I want our relationship to be completely candid if I'm to help you through this."

"Fine," she agreed, suddenly feeling a prickle of unease at the base of her spine.

"All right. I hate to have to tell you this so soon after Augustine's death, but the truth of the matter is that Barnakilla is nearly bankrupt."

Muireann's eyes widened and she began to laugh bitterly.

He was too astonished for words at her strange reaction. He had expected horror, dismay, but never amusement. "It isn't funny, you know! The estate is in desperate shape. If you don't try to help us, Muireann, we'll all be turned off the land!" Lochlainn rose to pace the floor in his agitation.

"I'm sorry, I didn't mean to laugh." Muireann shook her head. "It's just that, well, I couldn't see how things could get any worse than they were just a minute ago. Now I know. You see, I'm penniless as well. My father gave Augustine thousands for my dowry, and he went on a gambling spree and frittered it all away as soon as we were married. I have virtually nothing in my purse. I hate to even think where I'm going to get the money to pay for the funeral."

"I've taken care of that," Lochlainn said quietly, trying to ignore his churning stomach and the bile which had risen to his throat. If Augustine hadn't already been dead, he would most assuredly have strangled him with his bare hands.

"And the hotel bill?"

"That as well, but we have to be out of here by six."

"I knew it was too good to be true, like a fairytale." She sniffed. "And to think that all my life, my father tried to protect me from fortune hunters, only to let one walk right through his door and carry me off to God only knows where!" She began to laugh again, shaking her head ruefully.

"Muireann, I'm sure that Augustine . . ."

"No, Lochlainn, don't even start to try to make me feel better about all this," she practically shouted, hugging her arms to herself as she gazed bleakly into the fire.

"Well, what did I expect," she sighed after a few minutes. "I made my bed, I'll have to lie in it. I wasn't blind to Augustine's faults. I married him, and I'll just have to suffer the consequences."

"No, you don't. You can go back to Scotland, admit you made a mistake."

"That's the *last* thing I would ever consider doing!" she said in exasperation as she rose and moved to look out the window at the snowy streets below.

Suddenly the room began to close in around her. And Lochlainn had said they would have to leave that night.

As he came to join her by the window, she asked him bluntly, "What did you use to pay for the funeral?"

"All of Augustine's clothes and jewelry."

"I see."

"I would have told you, but you seemed so devastated," he apologized lamely, spreading his hands wide.

"I can't blame you. You did what you felt needed to be done. You were only trying to protect me. Did you at least get a good price for them?"

"There's a fair pawn broker in Sackville Street who gave me a good price."

"Is there any money left?"

"Enough to put us up in a modest inn on our way back to Enniskillen, but no more."

She digested this information for a few minutes, drumming her fingers on the window pane, like a tiny bird futilely trying to peck its way to freedom.

After a few more minutes' contemplation, she said, "Tell me, is there a good livery stable here in town?"

He looked down at her inquiringly. "Aye, there are two or three that I know of personally."

"And is there a public coach to Barnakilla?"

"It goes as far as Enniskillen; the estate is another nine miles from there."

"How does the coach travel to Enniskillen?"

"It goes through Virginia Town, where the passengers spend the night."

She gave a last look out the window, and moved to where her trunks stood. "What time would it go?"

"There are two each day. The last one is at two. But why?"

"Never mind that now, come help me with these bags," Muireann said.

"Why, what are you going to do?"

"Sell it all."

"But Muireann, your clothes," he protested, shocked.

"They're all new, my trousseau. I didn't even want them, but my mother and sister insisted. I don't need so many dresses. All of my most important items are in these two small bags here. I have this dress I'm wearing, so if I take two or three more warm practical ones out of the bags, and my more personal items, we can sell the rest."

"I can't let you come to Barnakilla with nothing!"

"I won't have nothing," she said as she tugged a heavy black watch tartan woolen gown and a dark navy one out of the bag, and several white lacy items. She moved over to the screen to take the burgundy and black checked gown as well, and her nightdress.

"All of these things are new," she said with a sweep of her hand, putting the neat pile of dresses back in the larger valise. "And those, and those," she added, clicking each bag open for a quick scrutiny of their contents. At last she fished into her black bag, and removed her jewel case.

"I won't have nothing," she repeated as she perused the contents of her jewel case and closed the lid with an abrupt snap before she had the chance to change her mind.

"I'll have four dresses, a warm cloak, some books and small trinkets of sentimental value, and above all, I'll have you, Lochlainn. That is, unless you've changed your mind about helping me now that you've discovered I'm penniless as well."

He shook his head. "I'm not going to change my mind. But I think perhaps I should try to change yours, if you're going to have to sell everything you possess to go to Barnakilla, when you could just as easily go home."

"And I've told you, I'm going to my new home. Now I'll just finish packing these bags. Then we'll head for Sackville Street first, and see what we can get for these. Here, help me."

He loaded himself down with her cases, and she followed along, checking the room one last time before she left. She took her two small bags, now crammed full to overflowing, and Lochlainn's small overnight bag. She helped load all the cases into the back of the carriage, and climbed up unhesitatingly.

"Drive on, Paddy, to Sackville Street," she said in a commanding voice, and sat back in the carriage stiffly, trying desperately not to break down and howl her misery and disappointment in front of Lochlainn, who did nothing but look at her pityingly.

Chapter Five

Lochlainn would have tried to talk Muireann out of her drastic course of action on the carriage ride to Sackville Street, but he could see from the glint in her eyes and the set of her jaw that she was angry. Angry and determined. Besides, she was right. What else could she do?

All the same, he was terribly conscious of the fact that he had been economical with the truth. Not only was the estate bankrupt, but the mansion was virtually uninhabitable. God knows how they were to make a living to support everyone. She might get a good price for her trousseau and jewels, but the money would only last so long, encumbered as the estate was with debt.

But Muireann had no doubts. This was a test of her character, of that she was sure. She had grown weary of her easy life at Fintry. Had hoped for adventures. *Well, I've certainly got my wish,* she thought wryly. Since she had taken her marriage vows on New Year's Day, her entire life had changed.

Lochlainn was astonished as he watched her haggle for the best prices possible, giving the owner behind the counter, Mr. Murphy, a spurious story about how her sister had died before her marriage and no longer needed the clothes and jewels of her trousseau. The hardened pawnbroker had actually found himself moved by the young beauty's affecting tale of woe. Since all the items were of the highest quality, he offered her what under any other circumstances would have sounded to Lochlainn like a small fortune.

But Muireann held out for a higher price. Suddenly

Lochlainn's heart was in his mouth. He was convinced that she had overplayed her hand. That the old man would tell her she was asking too much, and to go elsewhere.

But at last Mr. Murphy gave in, and began to pay the whole sum out in crisp bank notes and gold.

"Would you have anything smaller?" she asked sweetly.

The shop owner gave her smaller denominations. Her purse fairly bulged as she left the shop. Far from being despondent, she felt a curious sense of freedom.

"There, that wasn't so difficult," she said with a satisfied smile, glancing up at Lochlainn's forbidding expression. "Now I need Paddy to take these things to the coach depot while we go see that livery stable you were telling me about."

"What on earth for?"

"To sell the carriage, of course!" Muireann replied in exasperation as she crossed the street and made a beeline for their conveyance.

"But Muireann, how will you manage without one?" he shouted to her as she trotted ahead.

She reached the other side of the street safely and turned to face him. "By walking, like everyone else."

"And the team?"

"We'll have to sell the horses as well. You know we have no choice. We can get on the coach to Virginia tonight if we hurry."

Lochlainn stared at her in astonishment as she practically skipped up the stairs of the carriage and called out to Paddy to hurry.

Once they arrived at the depot, Paddy took their bags and traveling rugs, and agreed to wait for them there. They quickly checked the coach times and saw that one was supposed to be leaving at quarter past two, despite the harsh weather.

"Come on, Lochlainn, we'll need to hurry!" she urged as she climbed up onto the box and took the reins.

Lochlainn gaped as she whipped the horses up into a trot and, with his instructions, expertly negotiated the narrow cobblestoned streets of Dublin.

"How on earth did you ever learn to drive a coach, Muireann?"

"A sign of my wayward youth. I used to sneak off all the time, and I was friendly with the servants. That was an unpardonable offense in my sister's and mother's eyes. But I've always felt that servants and workers can never really look up to you if they don't see you prepared to get your hands dirty yourself. Besides, it's far more fun than embroidery or tatting," she added as she clicked to the horses.

"I'm beginning to wonder just what sort of other hidden talents you possess, Muireann Graham Caldwell."

"Well, I shan't tell you any more of them for now. It's always nice to be able to surprise people."

"You certainly astonished me," Lochlainn said truthfully, trying to reconcile this Muireann, with her long plait of hair bouncing down her back, her cheeks glowing with the cold, laughing and smiling, with the delicate-looking society dame he had first met only two short days before.

She never failed to amaze him utterly. He had to admit his fascination for her increased with every passing moment. It was as if she had taken control of his every waking thought. She was completely mesmerizing, like no woman he had ever met. Certainly a far cry from his fiancée, Tara.

Lochlainn clung to the carriage by bracing himself with one hand against the side of the box, and curling the other around Muireann's waist as they careened up Abbey Street and at last reached their destination.

Once at the stables, she told Mr. Bradley such a convincing story about breaking up her establishment to go to warmer climes for her health, that the owner of the livery stables bought the carriage and team for an excellent price. Muireann put the large wad of notes in her purse and staggered out of the shop leaning heavily on Lochlainn's arm as though needing his support.

Once outside in the street, however, she grabbed his hand tightly and broke into a trot.

"We'd better hurry! The coach will be leaving soon, and this snow is freezing over."

They walked, ran, and skated along the streets breathlessly as they hurried to the coach depot. At one point Muireann tumbled in the snow, having lost her footing.

Lochlainn ran over to kneel down by her, his concern apparent on his handsome features.

"I'm fine," she laughed up at him. "I love the snow!"

He lifted her and held her close, feeling the warmth radiating from her soft body through the voluminous folds of her gown and cloak. She might just as well have been naked, he was so painfully conscious of her alluring form.

She reached up and stroked his cheek. "Don't look so worried. I'm fine. Let's go."

She tugged him along until at last they made it back to the depot. Once there, Muireann marched up to the counter, where Paddy gave them some welcome news. While he had been waiting for them, the man running the coach had announced that it would have to be canceled because the second man who usually helped to drive it had come down ill. Paddy had immediately offered his services.

After confirming with Muireann and Lochlainn that he was definitely an experienced coach driver, the manager accepted his offer, thus waiving his coach fare and giving Muireann and Lochlainn a discount on their two inside seats.

Paddy, middle-aged but very grizzled, skipped up onto

the box like a young goat while Muireann went inside to pay for their places. Lochlainn began to protest at the expense and impropriety of allowing him to ride inside with her, since he was only her servant. She waved his argument away airily and counted out the necessary coins.

"I will not have you freezing to death on top of the coach. As for propriety, anyone who would object to your accompanying me would not be a person with whom I would choose to associate, or whose opinions I would value. You are a human being, not an animal. I wouldn't even want the horses outside in weather like this, if it were my choice!" she argued stoutly, daring him to protest again.

Muireann climbed up into the already nearly full coach and found herself sandwiched in between Lochlainn and a rather portly elderly woman. She smiled shyly at her new traveling companions and then took the rugs which Lochlainn handed up to her. Muireann asked him if Paddy had enough cloaks and blankets to keep him warm up on the box, and he replied in the affirmative.

Lochlainn stowed their three small bags safely up top and disappeared for a few moments. He only entered the carriage just as it was about to leave.

"Here. You didn't have any dinner. It was the best I could do," Lochlainn said as he offered her a paper wrapper with some hot muffins in it.

Muireann saw he was shivering after having been outside in the cold for so long. She tugged the robe off her lap and tucked it around his legs as well, before looking up at him and offering him one of the muffins.

He shook his head, but she whispered, "You haven't had anything either. From now on we share everything, Lochlainn, even starvation if we have to. Is that clear?"

Chapter Six

It seemed as though he had only been asleep for a few minutes when he noticed the coach had halted. It was pitch dark outside the window, and Muireann was standing over him with all of their traveling rugs draped over one arm.

"Where are we?"

"At Virginia, sleepy head. Come on, it's very late. They're getting our room ready for us, and some supper."

"*Our* room?"

He had no time to press the matter further, for several porters came to help Muireann get their luggage down. She skipped out of the coach, and lifting her skirts high, entered the lobby of the inn, where she ran over to the huge blazing fire. Lochlainn was left alone to follow along behind.

When he came inside, the servant boy said, "This way, please," and led them up to a pleasantly decorated, wood-paneled room with a huge oaken four-poster bed. Other servants began to parade up and down the stairs with cans of hot water. Another maid took Muireann's food order for their evening meal, which she requested should be served in their room.

Only when the tub was full and the servants had disappeared did Lochlainn have the opportunity to ask with a disconcerted frown, "Our room? And a bath?"

"Well, what do you want to do, spend money we really don't have on another chamber? And if the estate is as bad as you say it is, this might be the last decent bath and meal I'll get for a while. So I'm going to enjoy it," Muireann said a trifle impatiently as she stripped off her cloak and shawl, and then began to unbutton the top of her gown. "What did you want me to do, tell the manager that we weren't married, and cause a scandal?"

"No, of course not, I just thought that—"

"I've told you before, we're in this together. We share everything, unless of course you object with regard to the bath water. We did it all the time at Fintry to save the servants trouble. You can go first if you like. And as for false modesty, you've already seen me in my underclothes yesterday. I think I can trust you."

Lochlainn, astonished at her forthrightness, shook his head. "Never mind, Muireann, forget I said anything. You're right, of course. I'm sorry. But you should go first. Get into that bath now, before it gets cold, and I'll go downstairs."

"Please, Lochlainn, I'm not that modest," she answered with a withering look. "There is a screen, you know. If you're still sleepy, go lie down on the bed. If not, then here's a copy of today's paper. Read me the items while I have a soak, and then it will be your turn. Unless of course you don't wish a bath."

"I'd love one," Lochlainn said enthusiastically, looking forward to the prospect of his first full bath in over a week. Muireann had been absolutely right about the primitive conditions at Barnakilla. In the summer the lake was fine, but in the winter, hot baths were an unheard-of luxury for him except when his sister took the trouble to set up the tubs for washing day and boiled them a few extra cauldrons for a hasty, tepid dip.

Muireann tugged out the lilac nightdress and matching robe from her valise and went behind the screen. Soon Lochlainn could hear her happily splashing, and the sounds of her lathering herself all over.

"Go on, read to me," she encouraged.

Lochlainn did as he was told.

She sat back in the tub with a satisfied sigh and soaked,

adding a bit more hot water from the cans the servants had left, until at last she felt cleansed after her terrible journey from Scotland and the dreadful ordeal she had endured the day before at the hotel.

It's like it all happened in another lifetime, she reflected in surprise. She decided that that was as it should be. It was better for her to pretend her past life had never happened if she was to face the hardships of Barnakilla.

She was no fool. Lochlainn had been very sparing with the details about circumstances there, but she had got to know him well enough over the past three days to sense the fear lurking just below the surface. She certainly couldn't blame him for being frightened. She had learnt for herself about the tragedy caused by a bankrupt estate when her Uncle Arthur had made some unwise speculative ventures.

Her father had bailed Uncle Arthur out, but not without issuing a stern lecture about his foolishness, and frequent reminders ever since about his own largesse in having helped, for which her father felt Arthur should be suitably grateful.

Muireann was determined that that would never happen to her. She loved her father, but his smugness from his superior position as a person who had never known a day's want would be more than she could bear. All the same, Muireann knew she would have to tell the truth to someone back home, if only to prevent her family from coming over once the news of her widowhood reached them.

The only effective ally who she was convinced could be trusted was her brother-in-law, Neil Buchanan. Over the years he had always defended Muireann's actions while her mother and sister had denounced them as unfeminine. Neil had four sisters, all talented, beautiful and well educated. Neil had always been impressed with her head for figures, and had carefully explained investments and other financial matters to her. He had been pleased at how apt a pupil she had become.

As their family's lawyer after the early death of his father, Neil would be as familiar as anyone with her father's affairs. He would be able to tell her whether there might be money she could get her hands on easily without her father discovering that Augustine had frittered away her entire marriage portion. And as a landlord himself, he might have a few good ideas about the estate.

Neil was also a fine judge of livestock. He had taught her a great deal about that, as well, during her visits to his family's estate at Dumbarton, and lately at his new home just by Dunoon on the Firth of Clyde. He had always loved living near the water, and had purchased the estate from a bankrupt laird. He would no doubt sympathize with her plight and admire her for trying to do the right thing by the poor wretches who were dependent upon her prosperity for their own.

Neil and Alice had been married the previous year and had been insistent that Muireann visit often. Muireann knew it was because Alice wished to show off how well she had done for herself in the marriage stakes. Though Neil was fairly handsome in an earthy sort of way, his deciding point had been his wealth. Muireann sometimes felt sorry for Neil for having made such a poor bargain. She was certain that the only person her icy sister loved was herself. Muireann's stays at Dunoon House would have seemed interminably long if Neil and his much younger brother Philip, a few years older than herself, hadn't taken it upon themselves to entertain her. She had been allowed the run of the estate, and there had been a conspiracy of silence regarding what she had got up to whenever she hadn't been under the sharp eyes of Alice or her mother.

Muireann was an excellent horsewoman, a good cook, and had assisted at the births of many calves, lambs and foals. She had little fear of men, for she had practically grown up with Neil and Philip as part of her family, and her Uncle Arthur and his large family of six boys had come to live in the gate house at Fintry many years before. Muireann had been a terrible hoyden in her younger days, she knew. But at least the boys had been given a good education. Her father had emphasized this as the only way the penniless lads would ever be able to make a living for themselves. Muireann had insisted so intently that she be allowed to take lessons with their tutor that she had eventually been allowed to join them in the school room, and possessed Latin, French, German, and an excellent grasp of mathematics.

Three of the boys were now in business in London, Paris and Edinburgh, in jobs with financial institutions and trading houses. Muireann wondered if they might not be able to give her some advice. The three youngest were still at Fintry, working in various positions to help their uncle run the mighty estate.

Neil's brother Philip might also prove a potentially useful ally, since he was the owner of a fleet of small trading schooners that plied the coast of England and Scotland. But Philip was in Canada at the moment, although Neil was looking out for his business interests while he was gone.

"Are you all right in there?" Muireann suddenly heard Lochlainn inquire.

"Fine, fine. I'm sorry, I was just making some plans in my head, that's all," she replied quickly. Giving her hair a last rinse, she put down her flannel and stood.

"Anything for me to worry about?" Lochlainn teased, for in truth, he wondered what went on in her mind all the time.

"Not at the moment, though you'll probably worry anyway," Muireann called as she rose and began to towel herself off. She wrapped the towel turban-like around her dripping tresses and hastily rubbed herself down before pulling the nightdress over her head. Then she did up her robe and came out from behind the screen.

"Do you have a pair of scissors handy?" she asked as she towel-dried her hair and then ran her brush through it quickly, impatiently tugging out the worst of the knots.

Lochlainn nodded and then watched in horror as she took her wet hair in a huge handful and snipped off nearly three feet of it, until it waved over her shoulders. Then she looked at herself in the mirror and trimmed the remainder until it was completely even.

"There was no need for that!" Lochlainn protested when he was finally able to speak. "Your lovely hair!"

Muireann waved aside his objection with a flourish of her delicate white hand. "It will grow back in time. Besides, it will be easier to keep clean, and it's still long enough to wear up, so no one will know, now will they? I can even sell it to a wig maker." She smiled up at him, and enjoyed the shocked look on Lochlainn's face.

He scowled. "Really, Muireann, this isn't some sort of game!"

Her eyes flashed. "I know it isn't! I'm doing the best I can to maintain my optimism in the face of such terrible circumstances, Lochlainn, that's all. I'm sorry you don't approve. But frankly, I don't need your approval, just your loyalty to me as your employer!"

Muireann marched across the room stiffly and sat down by the fire to dry what he considered to be the pitiful remnants of her once glorious ebony hair.

Lochlainn had been stung by her words and stood uncertainly in the center of the room, staring at her as she deliberately ignored him.

At last he approached her chair, and knelt down next to

it. He raised one hand tentatively and stroked her hair down to her shoulder. "I'm sorry. I had no right to criticize or complain. But your hair was so lovely."

"It still will be. It gets very curly when it's this short. Mother and Alice used to complain about it being like a bird's nest all the time. They have completely straight hair, you see. And don't worry about the criticism. I'm accustomed to never doing anything right," she said quietly.

"That's a sad thing to say," Lochlainn remarked as he stroked her tresses again and sat down in front of her, curious to learn as much about Muireann as possible. "Why would that be?"

"Because my mother and sister are incredibly beautiful. I'm the ugly, unfeminine one in the family. I have dark curly hair, dark heavy brows, my skin is too pale. I'm too tall for a woman, not shapely enough where it matters, and I have large hands and feet. Even my eyes are a funny color." Muireann recited by heart the litany of criticisms she had been subjected to.

Lochlainn laughed long and loud until he saw Muireann's eyes fill with hurt tears.

"Is that what they told you?" he guffawed, unable to help himself.

"Well, it's true. They have blonde hair and blue eyes, and are small and dainty. Why, their rings couldn't even fit on my little finger."

"My dear girl, not every man admires blonde hair and blues eyes, you know," Lochlainn found himself saying, making an unconscious comparison between Muireann and his former fiancée Tara, and discovering that he was suddenly unable to recall what Tara looked like all that clearly.

"As for being too large, well, you're certainly quite small compared to me," he said, pulling her out of the chair so that he towered over her by at least a foot.

Then he took Muireann's hands and placed both of them in his own. He had a signet ring old Douglas Caldwell had given him as a young man. Tugging it off his own little finger, he placed it on her thumb, where it hung off and nearly rolled onto the floor.

"Now, no more nonsense about there being anything wrong with you, do you hear?" Lochlainn scolded, playfully chucking her under the chin.

Then he sighed as he looked at the ring. "I suppose I should have sold it," he said, squeezing her hands tightly before putting it back on his own finger, then moving to get his things ready for the bath, which was rapidly growing cold.

"Not if it had sentimental value. It looks very old."

"How can you say that to me when you sold your wedding band?"

She shook her head and sat back down by the fire to dry her hair. "I don't need any reminders of Augustine. Now go on, get in that tub before it all goes cold."

"Will you read to me?" Lochlainn asked, not wishing to argue with her again and wondering why he felt as though he had been punched in the guts. He picked up his toiletries, a fresh shirt and pair of trousers.

"Of course, if you like."

Lochlainn poured the rest of the hot water into the tub, quickly stripped off his clothes and sat back with a sigh as the steam swirled softly around him.

Muireann read aloud the latest agricultural prices, which Lochlainn assumed she would find very boring.

"What about something more exciting, like the court circular?" he suggested. Then he thumped himself in the head soundly with the heel of his hand. Idiot! The last thing she needed was to be reminded of her aristocratic lifestyle back in Scotland.

"No, thank you, the price of wedders and lumpers will do me just fine."

"How much for the wedders?" Lochlainn asked quickly in an effort to cover up his silly blunder.

"Seven and a half shillings per pound at the moment. I must say, that seems very expensive. At my brother-in-law's estate, when we went to market last, they were only six shillings the pound for top pedigree beeves, let alone sheep."

"It's transport costs, isn't it, as well as people trying to get as much money as they can for their cattle," Lochlainn explained.

"The lumpers are two pounds per tonne. That's not too bad, but it's still more expensive than we're accustomed to."

"Everyone eats lumper potatoes here. They have the best yield from the seed, you see, though I myself think they're very watery. Pinks or Queens, now they're a fine spud. But the people eat nothing but potatoes here because it's so hard to grow grain, with our harvest season being quite late here compared to the rest of Europe."

"So what do you eat, then?"

"As I said, plenty of potatoes, plus a bit of milk and butter if we can get it, and vegetables."

"It sounds a pretty poor lifestyle. Why so many potatoes?"

"It's the only crop that will feed a whole family in a growing season on the small pieces of land that the tenants get in exchange for their rent. The potato is also easy to grow, being underground, so that the crop doesn't require a great deal of tending. The men can work at other things like hunting, building and fishing."

"Or go to work elsewhere, and then go home to their families," Muireann remarked.

"That's right."

"It's beginning to make sense to me now. We've had Irish laborers working at our harvests before. I always did wonder how they were able to manage to be spared by their own families at harvest time.

"But why are their landholdings so small?" Muireann ventured to ask a few moments later.

"Because people in Ireland value land as wealth. Everyone wants his or her own wee plot. A man will pay the most exorbitant rent to get one to support his family. Then he'll subdivide the plot amongst his sons, so the holdings over the years have become smaller and smaller.

"And I have to say, the landlords have become much more greedy. They rent out to middlemen, who subdivide, and thus make more profit from people who can ill afford the exorbitant prices. Even if you deal directly with a landlord, he may rent the property at a lower price, but charge for improvements. So if you build a cottage on the property, you immediately owe more rent. Thus the vicious cycle of debt starts and continues, tying the people to the land and the landlord like serfs from the Middle Ages. It traps them on the estates and they end up facing debtor's prison if they don't pay up."

"My God, I had no idea!"

"That's all right, Muireann, there's no reason why you should know," he said before ducking down to rinse his hair. "Many people do know and simply don't care. I'm convinced that Ireland will always have unrest until the system is more fair. But with absentee landlords who don't worry about their estates, and simply bleed them dry to support their extravagant lifestyles in England and Europe, the problem has only become worse. Greedy agents can rob both tenant and landlord blind, and no one is any the wiser."

"I see."

"I suspect that's what happened after I left Barnakilla. My predecessor became ill and eventually died. While he was ill, Augustine asked my sister to send for me. I left Australia as soon as I got the letter. By the time I got back, the old man was dead. I haven't yet been able to make heads or tails out of the accounts that have been left."

"Well, we'll just have to try to sort them out together when I get there," she said in a firm tone.

Muireann lapsed into silence as she digested the information she had gleaned from the paper and Lochlainn's replies to her questions.

Lochlainn, thoroughly refreshed after his bath and feeling much more optimistic, dried himself and then dressed behind the screen, emerging clad in his trousers and shirt.

"I do have Augustine's small strongbox in my bag," he informed her quietly.

"We could look through it then," she said, averting her gaze before she stared in too obvious a manner. She remarked to herself how handsome Lochlainn was when dressed less formally.

A tap at the door signaled that supper had at last arrived. Muireann rose from the chair and threw a shawl around her shoulders. The maid put down the tray and left.

"Do you want to dress before we eat?" Lochlainn asked suddenly.

Muireann glanced up at him in surprise. "There's no need, is there? I mean, it's late, and I'm warm enough like this. If you don't mind—"

"No, not at all." He shook his head, thinking how curious a woman she was. Tara had never allowed him to see her at anything less than her best. Though their relationship had been remarkably passionate for the first month or so, in the ensuing two years Tara had always complained about him mussing her hair or gown, and their acts of intimacy had become fewer and further in between until they had finally stopped altogether.

Later, Lochlainn had put it down to her infidelity with Christopher Caldwell. Now he wondered if there hadn't been more to it. That Tara had been essentially a cold woman who didn't really relish physical contact.

She had come from a good family fallen on hard times.

Above all else she had made sure the little money she did have from her work as seamstress in Enniskillen was spent on her own appearance. It had certainly got her what she wanted in the end—a rich if frivolous lover, he thought bitterly, once again unconsciously comparing Muireann to his former fiancée and finding Tara sadly wanting.

"Come and eat, Lochlainn," she coaxed, taking his hand when she saw he had become distracted.

She heaped his plate and then took smaller portions of everything for herself and sat down. All the dishes were simple but tasty. Lochlainn could see that while she had ordered the cheapest things on the menu, they were nourishing. They finished the vegetables and most of the potatoes. With the remaining bread and meat, Muireann made sandwiches for them to eat in the coach the next day, which she wrapped up in a clean napkin along with the leftover potatoes.

The warm baths, hot food and late hour made them both sleepy. They pushed the table away from the fire so they could huddle up closer to the hearth, and sat back sipping their coffee, which Muireann admitted was her one weakness. They contentedly gazed into the crackling flames, their knees just touching.

Lochlainn stared at Muireann's lovely face in repose from under hooded lids, and then remarked, "I must say, Muireann, you've coped with all of this amazingly well."

"I haven't had much choice, have I, Lochlainn?" she replied with a shrug.

"Yes, you have, my dear. You could have gone back to Scotland today, washed your hands of Barnakilla completely. Perhaps tomorrow you might wish you had."

"You've coped well too, Lochlainn. I mean, all of this must have been very hard for you."

"It has been, but I have to be strong. My sister is counting on me, you know. Well, they all are, really."

"And now they're counting on me," she said sadly. "I only hope I'll be up to the challenge."

"I am sure you will be, Muireann. I feel it in my bones."

Muireann rose and stretched. "The only thing I feel in my bones is a perpetual ache after that rattling carriage ride. If you don't mind, I think I'll go to bed."

She called down the corridor for hot water bottles and a warming pan, and tidied the supper tray while the servants looked after the bed and took the used dishes away. Muireann busied herself laying out her warmest under things and stockings. She put the food parcel near her bag and hung her sable woolen dress on the peg for the morning.

When they were alone again, Lochlainn gathered up some cushions and took the spare blanket off the bed.

She stared. "What are you doing?"

"I'm getting myself comfortable in this chair for the night."

Muireann took the blanket out of his hand and threw it back on the bed with a flourish.

"Now I've told you, Lochlainn, we share everything, and that includes the bed."

Lochlainn blushed a furious red. "Muireann, you don't know what you're saying!"

"Oh, for heaven's sake, I'm not going to have you freeze to death in this chair or on the floor. The bed is so big, you won't even notice me in it. And if it will make you feel better, we can run a line of hot water bottles down the center to shield your virtue," she said with a small smile.

Lochlainn blushed again, but laughed in spite of himself. "Really, you're the oddest girl I've ever met!"

"I thought we said we would be honest with each other. I'm tired of pretense, of worrying about what is and isn't the proper thing to do. I'm twenty-one, a married woman, who has lived on a farm all her life. I have no illusions about what happens between a man and a woman. I also happen to know it usually has to be mutual. I trust you, Lochlainn, so just stop arguing. I'm tired and cold, and we have to be up early in the morning."

"Why?" Lochlainn asked, raising his eyebrows.

"Because I've booked us two seats on the earlier coach, so we'll have to breakfast and be out of here by seven."

Lochlainn rubbed his eyes wearily. "May I ask why? Look at you, Muireann, you must be done in, poor thing," he said in a too tender tone as he stroked one riotous ebony curl back from her face and tucked it behind her ear.

"Because we need to get to work at Barnakilla. There's no sense in remaining here in Virginia all day, then getting to Enniskillen late and probably having to stay there overnight because we can't get a lift out to Barnakilla."

"You do seem to think of everything, little miss," he said, suddenly stooping to kiss her on the cheek before he could stop himself.

"I do try, Lochlainn, I really do."

"You succeed, clever girl. Right, we'll share the bed, then, but I'm sticking the pillow in between us, and this blanket, to protect your virtue."

"Alice would say I was a hoyden who had none," Muireann giggled.

"Why?" Lochlainn asked, astonished.

"She liked Augustine, but she loathed my other suitors. She accused me of trying to make up for my ugliness by encouraging men to pay me unsuitable attentions."

Lochlainn frowned, suddenly feeling unaccountably jealous. "And what unsuitable attentions might those have been?" he asked sharply, his eyes glittering.

Muireann shrugged. "Oh, dancing, riding horses, hunting, talking."

Lochlainn visibly relaxed. "I can't see that there's anything wrong with any of those things. My sister does the same all the time, and her virtue is without question."

"I'm glad to hear it. It's nice to know I'm not abnormal after all. You're a good person to talk to. Very, well, understanding. Sympathetic. Alice doesn't talk, she issues orders," Muireann said, lifting her nose in the air in imitation of her sister.

Lochlainn laughed as he unfastened the top of his shirt and then rolled the blanket into the center of the bed. "I knew someone like that once myself. But I think I'm beginning to see why Fintry isn't as attractive as it might be. Though you are. Certainly not ugly." He reddened and turned his full attention to the blanket.

"Very kind, I'm sure. I suppose it's a question of how strict one's family is," Muireann explained as she unbuttoned her robe. "Believe it or not, being wealthy does have its disadvantages, though I don't expect any sympathy. It's like . . ." She paused for a moment to gather her thoughts.

"Like what, Muireann?"

"Like being asked to perform the same role in a play day in and day out," she said as she got into bed. "I don't want to play that part any more. I just want to be myself. I accepted the marriage part because I met a man who made me feel like I was someone important when he courted me. I thought I was the most precious object in the world to him. But it was all an act, wasn't it?"

Lochlainn swallowed past the lump in his throat, and it took all of his self-control not to reach out to kiss and comfort her. "I'm sure you were, Muireann. It couldn't have been an act."

"Nay, Lochlainn." Muireann shook her head bitterly, spreading her black tresses across the pillow in an ebony cloud. "Barnakilla was and always will be more important, wouldn't you say?"

"Muireann, I don't think—"

"Let's go to sleep, shall we?" Muireann said as she pulled the covers up to her chin and turned her back on him.

Lochlainn paused just long enough to turn down the oil lamps, then got into the bed and at last closed his eyes. But he was haunted by images of Muireann laughing, weeping, in despair, and for a seemingly endless time, sleep eluded him.

Chapter Seven

It grew bitterly cold during the long winter's night. As the blazing fire in their hearth gradually died down, both Muireann and Lochlainn instinctively moved towards one another in the bed, seeking each other's comforting warmth.

By the time they awakened groggily in response to the maid tapping on the door at six to give them time to get ready for the seven o'clock coach, the dividing blanket between them had been pulled over their bodies. Lochlainn opened his eyes to find himself lying on his side with Muireann on her back tucked tightly against him.

Again, her face in repose was an arresting sight. Her lips curved in a small smile. Lochlainn could never remember having seen Tara in the cold light of morning. They had always met furtively, briefly, in the outbuildings or in the woods during the summer months. Tara had said it was all part of the excitement of being in love. Lochlainn, now in his mid-thirties, wondered as he soaked up Muireann's warmth, if there were more important things than the thrill of sensuality. There was tenderness, and affection, too; things he had never known since his mother had died many years before, when he had been only two and his sister a newborn.

"Mmm, I smell coffee," Muireann practically purred. She opened her eyes and gazed up at him.

His head lowered then, and he kissed her on the lips, forcing himself to be gentle as his emotions nearly spiraled out of control. He recalled her pain the morning before when he had touched her midriff, so he simply stroked her face and hair.

Muireann's lips parted with a sigh, deepening the sweet kiss into something much more compelling as he raised one hand to hold her chin tenderly and explored her mouth with a leisurely thoroughness that thrilled them both to the core.

At last Lochlainn lifted his lips, knowing he couldn't hide his throbbing desire for her forever. But she seemed untroubled by the kiss, stroking her hand down the long column of his neck with her eyes closed.

"God, it's cold," she murmured, seeking his warmth again as he tried to pull his lower body away from hers before he shocked her. "I wish we could stay here a bit longer."

"We can have another five minutes," he suggested as Muireann sleepily rolled over onto her side, putting her back to him. She stretched, her full length pressing up against him.

His hand moved down under the covers to hold her gently around the waist. He warned himself to be careful, to just enjoy the moment, for he would never get another like it again. A moment later, she turned her head to look at Lochlainn sleepily.

"How long will it take us to get to Enniskillen?"

"We should be there by tea time if we have clear roads, but then we'll have to hope for a lift out to Barnakilla," he whispered against her silken soft hair, now a mass of curls which he tousled with his hands, savoring the soft feel of her all over.

Like a rose without thorns. The thought came to him suddenly, and he found the simile apt.

Muireann nodded, and stroked the hand around her as

she turned her head back onto the pillow. She reflected somewhere in the back of her drowsy mind how wonderful Lochlainn felt in the bed beside her. How they just seemed to fit together.

She had had the strangest sensation when she had first met him on the docks in Dun Laoghaire and their hands had touched in greeting. She had trembled then as though the ground under her were shaking. Strangely, she had felt almost as if she had come home, though of course she had never before set foot in Ireland.

"I hope we get a lift out to the house as soon as we arrive," she murmured. "It'll be good to be home."

Lochlainn looked down at her, wondering if she was asleep, so little sense did her statement make. She had never been to Barnakilla. Nor could she possibly imagine a run-down and bankrupt estate as home.

Also, her response to his kiss and his presence in the bed began to worry him. Was she a complete wanton, or had she somehow lost her wits? Or worse still, had she somehow confused him with Augustine in her mind?

Lochlainn's unease grew as she rolled over onto her back again, and his arm came into intimate contact with her breasts. Struggling for control, he knew he had to test her.

"Muireann, are you awake?" he asked a trifle too loudly, moving away from her a short distance in the bed.

Muireann opened her eyes and glanced up at him with some irritation. "Of course I am, Lochlainn. You said five more minutes." She wondered why his tone seemed so sharp.

"But I suppose you're right," she sighed as she planted a peck on his cheek and swung her long legs over the edge and onto the floor. "We have to go, and breakfast will be here soon."

She padded across the room to the screen. In a few minutes she emerged fully dressed. Gathering up her discarded hairpins, which she placed between her ruby lips, she hastily brushed her cloud of raven hair and tugged it forcefully into a severe roll at the nape of her neck, jabbing her hairpins into it as though attacking an enemy.

Lochlainn watched her from the bed and noted that the whole procedure took less than a minute.

She went to the door and fetched the can of hot water, and for a minute splashing sounds could be heard. She emptied the basin into the slop bucket and went over to the door to fetch the breakfast tray, which the maid had just placed outside.

Muireann turned to Lochlainn and said, "Right, lazybones, your turn. I'll lay out the breakfast while you shave."

There was porridge, toast, bacon, eggs and sausages. Again Muireann made sandwiches out of the meat and bread they didn't eat, and wrapped them in another clean cloth. She then packed her things, placing the food parcels in her large purse, which she laid next to her cloak and the traveling rugs.

All this time Lochlainn had been watching her warily whenever he had the opportunity, popping his head above the screen to keep an eye on her every movement. As he finished shaving he remarked to himself that if Muireann were indeed mad, she was certainly the most practical insane person he had ever come across.

Muireann could see he was in one of his odd moods again. She had grown quite used to his frosty demeanor and was bold enough to observe softly, "You're awfully quiet this morning, Lochlainn. A penny for them?"

"They're not even worth that, my dear." He smiled as he fastened his shirt and waistcoat.

He fussed with his stock for several moments as she watched him, a puzzled frown marring her lovely face.

At last Muireann reached up and brushed his fingers

aside, and offered, "Here, let me." She tied it expertly with her small nimble fingers, explaining, "Papa used to have trouble all the time too."

Lochlainn couldn't resist her nearness as her amethyst eyes shone up at him. He kissed her on the lips fleetingly before releasing her to put on his jacket. Odd she might be, he commented to himself, but really, she was the most charming woman.

But there was little time for further reflection on Muireann's behavior. Not when the coach was about to leave. Lochlainn gathered up his things while Muireann checked the room to make sure they had left nothing behind.

Then she paid the hotel bill while Lochlainn loaded their bags on top of the waiting coach. She stepped out into the bright crisp morning air. Lochlainn stared at her as a ray of sunshine lit her up in the hotel entrance. She was a most arresting sight, he thought as his heart turned over. Every man in the quiet street turned to look at the illuminated figure, standing above the throng like an angel from on high.

Muireann, completely unconscious of the effect she was having on Lochlainn, hopped up into the carriage, where she made a small nest for them with the traveling rugs. She assumed there would be other passengers, but due to the early hour and the poor weather conditions over the past few days, they ended up with the whole carriage to themselves.

Lochlainn wondered if he should sit across from Muireann rather than next to her, but it seemed ridiculously formal. After all, they had shared a bed, and it was certainly very cold. So he sat next to her, with both of them tucked securely under the rugs. Lochlainn passed the time by regaling Muireann with tales of his experiences in Australia. He also asked her about her life in Fintry.

The information that she gave Lochlainn about the

things she had been accustomed to doing back home made him feel terribly inadequate. Not for the first time he wondered what her reaction would be when she arrived at Barnakilla. Would she hate him for having been so economical with the truth?

He wanted to warn her, and debated doing so in his mind whenever there was a lull in their conversation. But it was just so good to talk to someone about the things that mattered to him, the things he was interested in, as if he were someone important in her life. Even their silences were comfortable; while Muireann gazed out the window admiring the view, for example, or when they ate side by side, washing down their sandwiches with some milk they were able to purchase at a small farmhouse when they made a brief rest stop to change horses.

Whenever Muireann laughed, she sparkled like a rare jewel. Not for the first time, Lochlainn compared her to Tara, who had remained cool, aloof, and had seldom smiled, let alone laughed. She had been incredibly alluring, but in a frustrating sort of way.

Muireann was also enticing, Lochlainn had to admit. It was amazing to him that she was full of joie de vivre even after all that had happened to her. Or was she simply trying to block out all she had endured, pretend it had never happened?

"You're doing it again, Lochlainn," Muireann remarked at one point as they neared Enniskillen.

"What's that?" Lochlainn asked, puzzled, his steel-gray eyes glancing down at her lingeringly.

"Going off into that grim dark little world of yours, where I can't reach you."

Lochlainn stared at her for a brief moment before looking away. He told himself he simply couldn't kiss her again, though every fiber of his being yearned for her.

"I'm sorry, there are just so many things on my mind."

"I know. I can see that. I just wish you'd tell me what they are. A problem shared is often a problem halved."

"I'm not sure what the problem is myself," Lochlainn admitted honestly. "I'm very confused."

"I know I'm young and foolish, Lochlainn, but I do want to help Barnakilla as much as I can. And you did promise to be honest with me," she reminded him, taking his hand for a moment.

"I did indeed. I promise I shall keep nothing from you about Barnakilla," he replied, neatly sidestepping the issue. He scolded himself inwardly. In future he would simply have to keep his mind on his work and not on his new employer.

"We'll look over the papers whenever you feel up to it, Muireann, I swear."

Muireann lapsed into silence again, until Lochlainn reached out and took her hand in both of his own, enjoying her spontaneous gesture of affection and wishing to prolong the pleasure.

"You're very good with people, you know," he said suddenly. "You notice things about them. You, well, charm them might be a good word, if it didn't sound like something deliberate or coquettish. You're so natural, it just puts people at their ease."

Muireann blushed. "I'll take it as a compliment, though I'm sure I don't deserve it."

"But you do. That's the other odd thing about you. You're perhaps a bit too honest and open in your dealings with people."

"Oh dear, didn't I drive a hard enough bargain with the man in the shop and the owner of the livery stable?" she joked.

"No, I'm not talking about that. I just mean that you and I only met each other three days ago, and here we are conversing like old friends. And you, of course, are my employer, and Paddy's, yet you treat us as your equals, members of your own family."

Muireann blushed and avoided his gaze as she declared, "Well, you are my family now. I have no other here." She paused for a moment and sighed. "People are dishonest with each other all the time. I try to be honest, and I think you do as well. Just because I've been badly disappointed, though, doesn't mean that I'm willing to stop trusting everyone entirely. I'll trust you for as long as you prove yourself to be trustworthy, Lochlainn.

"But if I find you've betrayed me as well, our friendship will be at an end. But that's better than always being suspicious of people and fearing the worst. I find if you expect the worst from people, they inevitably live up, or down, to your expectations."

"Beauty, intelligence, and a philosophical disposition as well." Lochlainn smiled slightly, kissing her hand. "What more could a man ask for?"

She suddenly looked desolate. "I don't know."

Her pained expression snapped Lochlainn's resolve, and he pulled her to him for a real kiss on the lips, which deepened as the carriage lurched on the road. Muireann looped her arms around Lochlainn's neck and pressed herself against him. Her whole body arched toward him like a flower opening itself to the vibrant rays of the sun. Though his hands on her ribs hurt terribly, she needed to feel his strength and warmth flow through her.

Lochlainn twisted his mouth against hers, devouring her lips, his tongue exploring the moist cavern of her mouth, mingling with her own. It was like sipping a heady wine. Lochlainn's heart hammered in his chest as Muireann hugged him to her, and ran her fingers through his hair. *Tara certainly never kissed like this,* he reflected as his loins tightened alarmingly.

Finally Lochlainn knew he couldn't hold back any

longer. If he didn't stop now, he knew he would try to lift her skirt. That was completely unthinkable. Muireann was his employer. She needed his help, not his lovemaking. And if he offended her, she could dismiss him from her service any time she liked.

Suddenly Paddy called down from the driver's box that Enniskillen was within view. Lochlainn moved away from Muireann to open the window.

A blast of icy cold air quenched his passion for a moment, and he let the freezing wind cool his flushed face. Turning to Muireann, who sat now with her hands pressed tightly in her lap, he said, "There it is!"

Muireann rose to look out of the window. Despite her mixed emotions about the kiss she had just shared with Lochlainn, she smiled.

It was lovely. The whole countryside was like a sparkling blue-green jewel. For a brief moment she was distracted from her worries. But she knew the kiss had been wrong. Her only excuse was that the fiery sweetness had carried her away utterly.

However, her duty lay before her now all too clearly as the coach pulled into the depot. She was responsible for Barnakilla. Though it felt like a heavy burden on her shoulders, she knew she would have to carry the load herself. The utter powerlessness she had felt after her marriage to Augustine, when she had discovered abruptly just what a monster he was, had been enough to make her cautious about putting herself in the hands of any man ever again.

Of course she longed to be held, and comforted. The kisses she and Lochlainn had shared had been nothing like those she had encountered before. She had been kissed a number of times in the past, but never had she felt she was missing out on anything when the kissing had ended. With Lochlainn, his lips held all sorts of unspoken promises which she could only guess at.

But to wonder about him in that way would be to court disaster. Lochlainn was the most handsome, exciting man she had ever met. But he was her estate agent. She had to trust him with her business matters. Her growing feelings for him couldn't be allowed to get in the way of the work that was ahead of them. At any rate, he would probably be horrified if she admitted that she wanted him desperately. What would he think of her?

She was certainly aware of the stereotype of the young widow. The last thing she needed was unnecessary gossip. He had just been trying to cheer her up, to comfort her in her time of loss and confusion. She shouldn't be foolish enough to read anything more into it.

Besides, she had to be strong. Muireann vowed that no matter what, she would never show how weak she was, and never, ever admit the awful truth, which she mournfully tried to push to the back of her mind: she was falling in love with Lochlainn Roche.

I have to leave the past behind. This is my future now. I have to succeed on my own, she vowed as she folded the rugs up into a bundle and stepped out of the carriage decisively.

Chapter Eight

Muireann and Lochlainn unloaded the carriage together and walked to the west end of the town in the hope of getting a lift on a cart bound for Donegal, which would at least take them part of the way to Barnakilla. They left Paddy with the coach driver to make the trip back to Dublin. Muireann gave him permission to stay away for as long as he was needed.

"And make sure they pay you good wages," she advised as she waved goodbye to him.

"I will, miss. Thank you!"

The sky was darkening rapidly. Muireann began to shiver, but she refused to let Lochlainn see she was suffering. So she simply wrapped her cloak more tightly around her and said, "Come on, let's walk."

"But it's freezing!" he exclaimed, shouldering his own bag.

"It will be worse if we stand around doing nothing," Muireann said as she began to walk.

Fortunately, most of the snow had melted, so the road was slushy but not too dangerously slippery. After about a mile, a cart coming along the road shone its beams on them, and for a few pennies the man agreed to take them straight to Barnakilla.

Since it was a bright moonlit night, Muireann was able to see Barnakilla from the bottom of the long avenue as the cart neared her new home. The trees were completely bare, giving her an unimpeded view of the mansion.

At first it didn't look too bad. Quite grand, in fact. The front entrance was large, with a portico held up by four stout pillars. Muireann could see it had once been a traditional early Georgian house, square, with tall, elegant windows, but had been added to over the years.

There was a small terrace running down one side of Barnakilla, accessible by a pair of French windows, and a long wing at the back. A second terrace led down to what no doubt had once been a magnificent lawn, now wildly overgrown, which was evident despite the winter weather blighting most of the Irish vegetation at that time of year.

As she drew closer, however, she could see moss and lichens clambering up the dingy walls. In some places she wasn't even certain the roof was still on. The stable and outbuildings were also dilapidated. The whole house and its surrounds gave Muireann the impression of something from a Gothic horror novel—grim, deserted, isolated.

"You'll have to stay with us at our cottage for the night. It will be freezing inside the house, and I must say I've not had much time to look through it since I got back a few weeks ago. I've done nothing to the estate except battle with creditors because Augustine didn't leave me any instructions before he left for Scotland."

"There's no need to apologize, Lochlainn. I'm sure you've done your best," Muireann replied in an even tone, trying to conceal the fact that her heart had sunk into her boots. "Do we at least have lots of firewood?" she asked with a shiver.

"I had plenty chopped when the weather was fine last week, so we should be in good shape for a while. There's also lots of turf."

"And where are the estate papers?"

"In the study, and in the estate office. But it is too late to start working on that now! You must be exhausted."

"I'm fine, really. Can you show me where the office is?"

"This way," he indicated, lifting the bags and leading her around to the back of the house.

The rusty old key turned in the equally rusty lock, and he ushered Muireann in. She looked at the mountain of papers and said, "I think I see what you mean."

Lochlainn put his arm around her shoulders. "Why don't you just come home with me now and meet Ciara?"

"I'll just take some of these ledgers to read by the fire, if I may."

"You may do as you like, Muireann. You're the owner now," Lochlainn reminded her.

Once again, she got a sinking feeling in the pit of her stomach.

Lochlainn's cottage was near the stable block, a small

three-room structure divided into a large kitchen and living area and two reasonably sized bedrooms at one end.

Lochlainn's sister Ciara was immediately at the door to greet her brother. After patting him on the shoulder, she shook hands with Muireann quite formally.

Ciara was a very small, reserved woman, with dark brown, auburn-streaked hair, and green eyes. At thirty-four, she was two years younger than Lochlainn, but she looked even older, and her rough hands testified to the hard work she had carried out over the years. She was cordial and polite, but not friendly. She eyed Muireann with obvious curiosity and mistrust. Lochlainn smiled in a forced manner as he introduced Muireann.

"This is Muireann Graham Caldwell, Augustine's wife."

Ciara slammed down the bowl she had been spooning potatoes into, and stared at both of them, shock etched on her sharp, weary features.

"The landlord's married?"

"The news is more astonishing than that. Augustine is dead. I've asked Muireann to stay with us until we can get the house in better order for her."

Ciara continued to stare, and at last she reached for Muireann's cloak and began to make her feel more welcome.

"You poor child! But how? I don't understand. . ."

"Please, Ciara, not now," Lochlainn urged futilely.

"No, Lochlainn, tell her. Or better still, I will. There was a gun accident in the hotel in Dublin and he was killed. We buried him yesterday, and came up here."

"My goodness, how horrible!" Ciara shook her head as she tried to recover herself.

She moved over to the fireplace and uncovered a small black pot-bellied cauldron. She divided the potatoes from it onto three plates before opening another small pot hanging suspended over the turf, and ladling some rabbit stew over them.

Lochlainn blushed at the simplicity of his cottage and the poor fare. He was relieved to see that Muireann seemed to take no notice and began to eat the food hungrily once she had said grace. *At least the cottage is clean,* he thought to himself. All the same, he felt completely inadequate.

"I shall move my things out of my room in a minute," he said. He put another mouthful of the now seemingly tasteless stew into his mouth and tried to swallow it.

"Don't be silly. I can sleep out here by the fire, or share with Ciara. There's no need to put you out."

"But there's only one bed in my room," Ciara protested sullenly, earning a sharp look from her brother.

"It doesn't matter. I can have a pallet on the floor," Muireann said calmly.

"Muireann, you're an aristocratic lady. It's bad enough that you have to stay here, but for you to sleep on the floor is unthinkable," Lochlainn rasped, his color rising.

"Well, I've just thought of it, so that's what I shall do. Please, Lochlainn, I thought we had this discussion last night and ironed out the difficulties."

Lochlainn blushed at the recollection, and almost wished he could contrive for them to share a bed again.

You mustn't think of it! he scolded himself roundly, and avoided Muireann's amethyst glance.

He rose to take the bags into Ciara's room, and went out of the door of the cottage, coming back a few minutes later with a mattress, which he had fetched from the stables.

"This one is quite clean. I found it in the barn. It must have been for the stable lad, but the last boy left before I arrived. I suppose once the horses had gone, there was no point in replacing him. So it's all yours."

"It will do perfectly well," Muireann said. She took one

end and helped him lay it down on the floor of the room while Ciara fetched some clean sheets out of the press.

"What did happen to the horses?" Muireann asked as she maneuvered the mattress into a corner.

"I suspect Augustine must have sold them all to get the money to go over to Scotland, but knowing the way the Caldwells liked to spend money, it could have been for anything," Lochlainn speculated, the disgust all too evident in his voice.

"And are there any other family, people who might be willing to help Augustine's widow, if I appealed to their better sensibilities?" Muireann asked.

Lochlainn's features clouded over with anger at Christopher's past insult to him. "There's only his cousin Christopher from the neighboring estate, Duchara. He's been in Europe on and off for quite some time, or so I believe. He's as much of a spendthrift as Augustine ever was."

Just then Ciara came into the room, and upon hearing her brother's words, dropped the sheets and blankets she was carrying.

"What's the matter?" Lochlainn demanded impatiently, embarrassed at his sister's clumsiness.

"N-n-nothing," she replied. "I was just careless, that's all."

"Really, Lochlainn, there's no harm done," Muireann said reassuringly as she picked up the bed linen while Ciara scurried from the room.

"There now, you've hurt her feelings. And all because of me," she accused Lochlainn angrily. "This can't be easy for her, you know. I'm a total stranger taking over her home, after all."

"I know, I know. It's just that of late she acts so strangely sometimes. She should have married, had children. It would have been an outlet for all her, well, fussiness, her attention to details. She likes everything to be perfect, you see, now more than ever."

"Well, perhaps the right man never asked her to marry him?" Muireann said with a sharp look as she began to make up the bed quickly and efficiently.

"That's just the point. She used to be very beautiful. In the last three years she's changed so much, I barely recognized her when I returned home. Plenty of men have asked her over the years, but she's always said no. Even my best friend, Robert, who was the blacksmith on the estate, asked her. She refused him and he went away broken-hearted," Lochlainn revealed, shaking his head at the waste of it all.

"And where is Robert now?" Muireann asked. She stooped to lay the blankets down one by one, forming a cozy resting place for herself.

"I'm not sure. On one of the estates hereabouts. He moves around a lot."

"We might use his services some time, if you can find him," Muireann offered kindly.

"Well, we have few horses now, just two farm animals for the plough, but for repairs around the estate he would be excellent."

"Is he married?"

"No, he never wed."

Lochlainn disliked talking about his sister's odd behavior with an outsider. Before Muireann could ask any more probing questions, he went out into the kitchen and moved towards the fireplace. There he filled the hot water bottles and put one into each of the three beds.

Muireann finished making her bed and sat down with Lochlainn and Ciara at the table again for a cup of tea. She could feel her head getting heavy.

Lochlainn looked at her pale face and tumbled hair, and suggested, "Why don't you go to bed now?"

"No, no, I think I should look at these ledgers first," Muireann said as she took her cup and went over to sit by the fire.

Lochlainn decided to leave her alone for a while to digest the information in her own time. He went into his room to unpack his bag and put away his things while Ciara cleaned up the supper dishes.

She clattered them so loudly that Lochlainn occasionally looked out to make sure she wasn't smashing every bit of crockery they owned. She was scrubbing at them so hard it was almost as though she were trying to wash the floral patterns off each dish.

In the end he went over to the basin and, taking up a cloth, removed the dishes one by one from his sister's hands. He dried them thoroughly before putting them back in the oaken sideboard, which was the most impressive piece of furniture in the room, though all of it was of remarkable quality.

Muireann glanced up for a moment to look at the pair, and remarked, "I must say, all of the furnishings are lovely here. Did your father make them?"

"We never knew our father, or our mother. We lost them both when we were very young," Lochlainn said shortly, in a tone which indicated that she had blundered into an area of his life in which she was not welcome.

"As for the furniture, I made it myself. I originally trained as a carpenter, until I decided a proper school education was far more important and began to learn book-keeping and so on."

Ciara shot her brother a sharp look. Without a word to him or Muireann, she went into her room and shut the door.

Muireann blushed. "I'm sorry, I had no idea." She turned her attention back to the ledgers quickly when she saw Lochlainn's eyes had grown as hard as granite.

He finished drying the dishes, all the while reproaching himself for having been so rude to Muireann and for having not revealed the whole truth about his parents. He excused this omission by telling himself that he didn't want her to think any less of him than she already did as a result of the poverty of his existence. The word bastard was such an ugly one . . .

But however hard he tried, he couldn't stay annoyed with her blunder, and couldn't keep away from her. He was like a moth compelled to hover around the candle flame. At length Lochlainn approached the hearth and asked, "Can you make heads or tails out of them?"

"Not quite yet, but I think I'm getting a pretty good idea of just how bad things are," Muireann said, glancing up from the book briefly.

"I think we're going to have to hurry up making sense of all this. Once everyone knows Augustine is dead and that you're very young and inexperienced, the creditors will be lining up on the avenue screaming for payment," Lochlainn predicted.

Muireann shut the book with a snap, and returning to the table in the center of the room, took up paper and pen. "Unless I go see them first. I shall make a list of them tomorrow. But first I shall have to write to my family to tell them the news and prevent them from coming here on the next boat."

"How do you rate your chances of success in fobbing off any of them?"

Muireann smiled thinly. "I can be very persuasive when I wish to be."

In the end she wrote a quite cheerful letter to her parents, claiming that Augustine's family had welcomed her into their bosom despite the tragedy, and that all the necessary formalities had been arranged discreetly after the terrible accident. She was stunned to find that the lies rolled onto the paper so easily, but she knew she was fighting for her very survival. If a few falsehoods here and there would help her, fine.

Muireann also wrote to her brother-in-law Neil, telling him of the dreadful state of affairs at Barnakilla but making him swear not to tell another living soul, especially not Alice.

She knew she was taking a risk, but someone had to know how bad things really were. She found this unbridled outpouring of her heart cathartic, as if a huge weight had been lifted from her shoulders. Neil would help her keep the place afloat, she was certain.

But though she longed to confide everything in him, she knew she simply couldn't. If she did, Neil would be over in an instant, insisting on her coming home. No, Muireann could never tell another living soul the sorry truth about her dreadful marriage and the terrifying events that had taken place behind the closed doors of the Gresham until that one pistol ball had at last ended the nightmare. Muireann herself certainly never wanted to think about any of it ever again.

In a final paragraph, she asked about the stocks and shares, and any financial investments in her name, then signed off the letter with a cheerful message to take care of himself and Alice and reply quickly.

She was just sealing this letter when Lochlainn came out of his room.

She glanced up at him nervously as he loomed over her.

"It's very late."

She answered tensely, "I'm just off to bed. Will you show me the house tomorrow? Afterwards we can go into town and see the accountant and the lawyer."

"Of course. But are you sure . . ."

"There's no sense in postponing the inevitable. I'm not a fool, Lochlainn. I've seen Barnakilla in the moonlight, and that was bad enough. Now I need to face up to it in the cold light of day. Besides, you're the one who just finished telling me time was of the essence."

"You're very brave," he said, stroking one curl which tumbled down over her brow.

Muireann stepped away, terrified at the nearness of him, the way she seemed to melt every time he touched her, however gently.

"Not so brave, Lochlainn. I admit I'm frightened at times. But I can't afford to be weak. I can't allow myself to lean too heavily on you. Do you understand?"

Lochlainn stiffened and dropped his hand.

"Yes, Muireann, I do. But you know where to find me if you need me."

She smiled tentatively. "Good night, Lochlainn."

"Good night." He nodded, his eyes never leaving her face until at last he shut his door.

Muireann went into Ciara's room. After unbuttoning the top of her gown, she lay down on the pallet and forced herself to relax by taking deep breaths. She had wanted Lochlainn to hold her, kiss her. Was it so wrong?

But she sensed Ciara's disapproval of her friendship with Lochlainn, which was obviously growing closer. Lochlainn had touched her hand, arm, or shoulder, sat next to her closely on the bench, indeed, barely ever taken his eyes off her at the meal. Sooner or later people were bound to notice, to gossip.

Muireann could also see how embarrassed he had felt about his poor home, how desperate he had been to make a good impression on her. The worst of it was, she didn't care about any of those things. But of course to even mention his unease openly would be to risk offending him. She could see he was very proud.

Sadly, Muireann reflected that Lochlainn seemed to assume his accommodations and food weren't good enough. But there were plenty of worse things than a small thatched cottage and rabbit stew—such as being homeless and starving, which was what they would all be if she didn't pull everything together soon.

Muireann rolled over onto her side and forced herself to think of all the lovely scenery she had passed though on the way from Dublin. All the blue and green of the Fermanagh lakelands. Surely there could be a lot worse places to live. She had seen far bleaker spots in her travels in Scotland over the years. She would succeed. She *had to.*

Though she tried to block Lochlainn out of her mind, her last waking thoughts were of the torrid kiss they had shared in the coach, and Lochlainn's glimmering gray eyes gazing intimately into her own.

Chapter Nine

After a restless night, during which it seemed she did nothing but toss and turn, Muireann rose early in the morning. After dressing, she went to the pump for water and built up the fire with turf from the stack outside the cottage.

She busied herself making porridge for the three of them, and also washed her face and hands once the water was hot.

Lochlainn came out of his room first and scolded Muireann for not staying in bed longer.

"I'm fine, really. I had a very good night," she lied. She was sure if she admitted she hadn't had a good rest that Lochlainn would think it was because she had been sleeping on the floor.

Ciara overheard the conversation through her bedroom door, however. When Muireann had gone to fill another creel of turf, she came out of her room and remarked, "She had a terrible night last night, tossing and turning, moaning in her sleep."

"I know, I heard," Lochlainn admitted, his expression one of deep concern. "But she seems calm enough this morning, and not at all tearful."

"I suppose it must be because it's all so strange for her, being here, so far away from home."

"It's odd, though. She didn't have any nightmares at all the last two nights," Lochlainn remarked absent-mindedly as he ate his porridge.

He only looked up to see his sister's disconcerted face when she exclaimed, "*What* did you say?"

"After Augustine died, we shared a room so I could keep an eye on her. Besides, it was cheaper, and you know how bad our finances are. It just seemed to make sense at the time," he answered quickly and seemingly innocently, though he could feel an uncharacteristic blush rising to his cheeks. "Muireann appeared fine, but perhaps she was too fine."

Ciara frowned. "What do you mean?"

"I saw Father Brennan while I was in Dublin. He was kind enough to take care of the funeral even though Augustine had died under peculiar circumstances. After the ceremony he warned me that Muireann might try to block things out, overdo things. Make every effort to try to appear normal. He was afraid she might get in over her head here at Barnakilla once she found out the appalling state of affairs, and asked me to be extra vigilant. So now I'm asking you the same thing. Will you keep an eye on her, try to befriend her? After all, if Muireann crumbles, we'll be walking the roads with only the clothes on our backs, every single one of us."

Ciara looked gloomier than ever, but she promised her brother she would try. "Poor thing. How she ever married Augustine Caldwell I have no idea." She shuddered, then rose from the table and began scrubbing the dishes frenetically.

"It would be better for her if she had never come here. This is an unhappy place, Barnakilla," she remarked, looking appraisingly at her brother for a few more seconds.

Lochlainn rose from his chair and went into his chamber to wash and shave, wondering what on earth had got into Ciara now. He came out dressed in a clean shirt, waistcoat and trousers a few moments later, and put his used linens in the laundry pile.

Muireann at last came in with the turf. He didn't approve of her hauling the creel, but he decided to hold his tongue, and simply took one end to help her carry it across to the hearth.

She sat down to eat her cereal. He could see her face was clouded over. She had no doubt walked around some of the cottages and seen for herself the poverty and squalor many had to endure.

He tried to cheer her by declaring, "Well, we'll have lots to do today, won't we? And Ciara here is going to help you get the big house in order once again. After all, she was housekeeper there for many years." Lochlainn smiled at his sister.

The bowl Ciara had been washing flew from her hands and smashed into pieces on the floor. Ciara began to weep then, and ran into her room and slammed the door.

Muireann and Lochlainn stared at each other across the table.

Lochlainn made to rise from his seat.

"No, don't! Just leave her," Muireann said, her hand shooting out to grab his wrist.

"But she's . . ."

"Yes, of course she's upset. We all are. I know it's bad enough for me, having to come here like this and confront the reality of poverty, poverty such as I have never known, and which will get much worse for you all if I can't do something to improve matters here. How much more terrible it must be for you, Lochlainn, remembering this estate when it was once prosperous. So consider how difficult it must be for Ciara, who stayed behind and watched Barnakilla decline while you were away in Australia. Everyone here has suffered. Surely you can see that? So please be patient with her. You probably just reminded her of all she has lost."

"You never got upset yesterday when you sold everything you owned."

"All people are different, and respond in different ways to a crisis. After I buried Augustine yesterday, I determined to force myself to let go of the past. There is no sense in regretting mistakes, or things we can't change.

"You mentioned the things I sold, the gowns, the carriage. In a sense, Lochlainn, none of those things were really mine. They were all new, for one thing. And in another sense, they belonged to Muireann Graham, new bride. Now I'm Muireann Graham Caldwell, poor widow. I have to learn how to fit this new role somehow. So those things don't matter, except for the money they have given us to start again. I'll do my best to wipe the slate clean and rebuild my life as well as Barnakilla."

Lochlainn silently fed the fire again while Muireann cleaned up the broken shards of pottery and finished the last of the washing up. Then she called to Ciara through the door, "I'm going up to the house now. I'll see you there whenever you're ready."

Lochlainn looked down at Muireann, his gray gaze mingling intimately with her own. "Thank you for being kind to her."

"Not at all. She looks like she could use a friend, and so can I."

The sun shone brightly as she stepped out into the lane

that led from the cluster of cottages to the mansion. Lochlainn followed along behind, and Muireann commented fairly enthusiastically about all she saw.

"There are some very old trees here, and the land looks quite fertile. There aren't nearly as many rocks and not as much bracken as we would have around our way. How's the pasture land?"

"Good, if we had any livestock, but all of it went. There isn't so much as a chicken around the place, just the two cart horses."

"That means we can get into town at least," Muireann said with evident relief.

Lochlainn took her around to the front of the house and let her in through the huge creaking wooden portal with a massive key.

A scurry of mice and evidence of various nests were the first things to greet her in the foyer. She stared in the semi-darkness at the cobwebs, which were about the only furnishings in the place. Going from room to empty room, her heart sank into her boots. There was nothing left of the once great Barnakilla except filth and squalor, as though Augustine had simply left his rubbish wherever it had landed.

The only rooms which were distinguishable were the small office, which had a sofa with some grimy blankets on it, indicating to Muireann where Augustine had slept during his occasional visits to Barnakilla. The library was crammed full of books, but there were only one or two rickety chairs and a very old sofa remaining. Other than that, all of the reception rooms downstairs were completely empty. Every stick of furniture had been sold.

The kitchen was full of mice and rats as well, but Muireann saw some distinct possibilities for it. It was huge, and in Barnakilla's better days had been bustling. It had several ovens for baking and roasting, a bread oven, and even one for smoking attached to the far end of it. There was a huge copper cauldron with a spigot which hung suspended above a grate and a large tub. Muireann saw it was a water boiler for doing the laundry, with several large sinks nearby, no doubt for the same purpose. Best of all, there were two water pumps close by.

The larders were exceptionally large, stretching from floor to ceiling, and there were some baskets of vegetables and canisters of flour, oats and sugar on the shelves.

Judging from the glass-fronted pantry cabinets, Muireann guessed that at least Augustine hadn't got around to selling any of the kitchenware. There were simple sets of plain earthenware dishes, wooden as well as steel forks and spoons, and some good knives. There was even some china in a glass-fronted wooden cabinet inserted into the wall of the corridor between the kitchen and what Muireann assumed must have once been the dining room. No doubt the silverware had all been sold long ago.

In the cupboards under the ovens were some huge cauldrons and pans for cooking and baking, and some more potatoes and vegetables, and even a few bottles of wine. Of course, everything was coated with dirt and grime, but all the same, at least Muireann felt she had something with which to start her new life.

She opened the back door of the kitchen, and was glad to see a small pile of wood outside.

"We'll need plenty of hot water first of all, so you get the fires going under the boiler while I fill the cauldron," Muireann instructed.

"But it's such hard work for you!"

"Well, get some other people in here to help, then. We can't clean anything without hot water. In any case, it's about time we let the people here know that I'm now in charge and that I'm serious about getting this place on its feet again."

Lochlainn assented to her plan, and went off to find several of his old friends and their wives while Muireann went into the scullery. Rolling up the sleeves of her black and burgundy gown, she began to pump the water.

At first it came out an appalling brown color and smelt foul, but soon it began to run quite clear. She noted there was still a brownish tinge to it. Lochlainn explained when he got back a short time later that the color was due to the large amount of turf in the area.

She began toting buckets back and forth to the boiler. "I've seen turf before back home, but I don't think we use it nearly as much as you do here."

Lochlainn stacked the wood in the burner underneath. "That's probably because you have coal readily available. But here it is very expensive, so we exploit the woods and the bog."

"I see."

Soon three couples arrived at the back door and Lochlainn introduced them.

"This is Patrick Martin and his wife Siobhan, who used to do carpentry and weaving before we fell on hard times. This is Mark McManus and Sharon, who used to grow potatoes and take in the washing. And this is Colm Maguire and Brona, who also farmed and looked after the livestock. They are some of the best workers we've ever had, born and bred on this estate, as were their mothers and fathers before them."

They all looked at the beautiful young girl quite warily.

Muireann gave them her warmest smile. After shaking each of them by the hand, she asked for their help with the water, fuel and cleaning.

"We'll need more wood soon enough, or turf if it's handier. We need to get lots of buckets of hot soapy water to scrub this place down and get rid of the nests and close up the mouse holes. Can you help me?"

They all nodded, and for a time all eight of them labored away in the kitchen until Ciara joined them and made a ninth.

As soon as the water was hot, the women filled the sinks with the grimy dishes and pans, and began to scrub them, while Muireann scoured all the tables and work surfaces, which were caked with grease and dirt. Lochlainn got the other ovens going, and Muireann asked him to send out some men to hunt for deer or pheasant.

"And we'll need some rabbit snares as well, if you haven't already got them out," she said with a wink, knowing full well that in such a badly run estate, poaching would be rife. "Tell them to get as much food as they can. We have a break in the weather at the moment, but who's to say that it won't turn cold again soon."

Lochlainn nodded his agreement, pleased at her foresight. He summoned the best marksmen on the estate. He went into the gun cabinet in the study and issued them arms and ammunition.

He reported back to Muireann, "At least there are plenty of guns and cartridges. Let's just hope they hit everything they shoot at."

"We'll cook some of the meat, because I'm sure everyone here could use a decent meal. But we can also smoke some of it if you will get the smoke oven going and I can find some salt."

"That's an excellent idea. I hope they catch a mountain of food."

"But we will need some other women to do the preparation," Muireann reminded him.

Lochlainn grinned, suddenly feeling his spirits lift. "I'm sure there will be many willing for a decent bowl of stew in return."

She was successful in her search for the salt, and by midday the kitchen looked a bit more habitable. The work surfaces gleamed, and wonderful smells were issuing from the ovens and the cooking pot Ciara had put on the stove.

Ciara and the other women had picked through the several baskets of rather wizened vegetables and potatoes, and had thrown the best of them into a stew pot with some of the rabbits the men had brought back. The rest of the vegetables were scrubbed and thrown into a vat of boiling water.

"They'll make good stock for soup or stew, and we can keep the pulp for a pig. We'll need to get more animals here, and soon," she said, wrinkling her nose at the rancid butter she found in the cool press. She stood looking at it silently for a moment and then declared, "There must be an ice house here somewhere."

"Aye, there is, though I must admit, I doubt any of us have gone on ice-cutting detail on the lough for a long time," Patrick said. He was a pleasant-looking dark-haired young man with sunken cheeks and piercing blue eyes.

"Well, perhaps it would be a good idea to get it going again. If we bought some cows, we could make butter, and sell it. The same with eggs. We can get some laying hens and do a milk, egg, butter, and bread round for the townspeople."

"All of that costs money, Muireann," Lochlainn reminded her.

"I know that, Lochlainn, and I know we have terrible debts. I'm just planning ahead. If the bank and our creditors see that we have a definite plan for getting Barnakilla up and running again, they might be willing to wait for their money just a little while longer. A few cows and pigs and hens won't set us back that far, now will they, compared to the huge sum that must be owing," Muireann argued logically.

Lochlainn had to admit he couldn't find fault with her reasoning. But he was unwilling to discuss money matters with her in front of the others. He and Muireann had to restore confidence in Barnakilla. There was no way he could do that if they seemed to be at odds with one another.

He could see she was quite distressed by what she had discovered, though she had never once complained. Again he felt an acute sense of having betrayed her. He watched her closely for any sign of weakness as she moved about, scrubbing, organizing, and making an inventory, until at last she made a face at him, and then smiled, which reassured him somewhat.

After they had eaten their dinner, a bowl of stew apiece, Muireann went upstairs with Ciara to see if she could find a suitable bedchamber for herself.

At the back of the house was a room with flowered blue and white wallpaper, now yellowed with age. The chamber had an eastern exposure, and was small enough to be kept warm easily. In it were a large tester bed, a small dressing table, and a chair. So far as she could see, no tiny visitors had made any nests anywhere, so she decided to claim it for her own.

"Can you clean this one out for me? The mattress looks sound, if a bit damp, so we can put it outside in the sunshine for a while. In the meantime I can use some straw from the barn. I would scrub it out myself, Ciara, but Lochlainn and I need to go into town to see the accountant."

"That's fine," Ciara said stiffly. "I'll take care of it."

"Well, if you have something else to do, it can wait," Muireann said, trying desperately to warm to Lochlainn's sister, who seemed as though she went out of her way to be unpleasant to people.

"No, Mrs. Caldwell, I'll do whatever you say. You are, after all, the owner now."

Muireann sighed. "Ciara, I know all of this must be upsetting for you. I would feel the same way if the home I had come to love over the years fell to wrack and ruin as this has. But I'm trying to help, and am quite humbly asking for your assistance in this endeavor. I know I'm young and inexperienced. It was a pure quirk of fate that I've ended up here as heir to a bankrupt estate.

"I'm not asking you to be loyal to me because I'm your mistress and owner of the estate. I'm asking for your help and friendship because we will all need to work hard to restore Barnakilla to its former glories. I'm prepared to work as hard as any of you. Nay, harder. But my first priority has to be to see whom we're indebted to. There's no point in our slaving away to renovate the mansion and the estate if we're going to have to sell anyway because the debts are too high."

At length Ciara replied with obvious reluctance, "All right, Mrs. Caldwell, you have my loyalty for as long as you need it, so long as you deserve it."

With that she bent to strip the bed of its dirty linens.

Muireann saw there was little point in forcing her friendship upon someone so completely unreceptive to any well-meaning overtures.

"Thank you, Ciara. I suppose that will have to do. And please, try to call me Muireann from now on," she requested stiffly as she left the room.

Chapter Ten

When Muireann had finished organizing the bedroom upstairs to her satisfaction, she began to head back to the kitchen. She found Lochlainn waiting for her at the bottom of the stairs.

"Come sit down inside the study for a moment, Muireann. You're tired and I think we need to talk," he said, taking her arm and noting with a thrill that it was still bared to the elbow. He felt the silky soft flesh under his fingers, felt the pulse throbbing through her. The contact was both thrilling and terrifying.

Muireann leaned upon him wearily and accompanied him down the corridor. Once inside, he shut the door, and waited until she sat before doing so himself.

They reclined in their chairs in silence for a moment before Lochlainn asked quietly, "Well, what do you think of your new home?"

Muireann glanced around the room like a trapped animal. "God, this is all such a mess! How on earth could things have come to such a pass?"

"I honestly don't know, Muireann. Augustine must have run wild altogether once he inherited. I'm sorry. I should never have persuaded you to come. Not without knowing the full facts," Lochlainn apologized, though he knew he was being insincere.

He had needed her help, and knew deep down in his heart that he would have said and done anything to get her to come to Fermanagh to save Barnakilla. Or said and done anything to prevent her from getting on a boat back to Scotland and going out of his life forever.

Muireann gazed at the dingy wallpaper, the mountain of ledgers and correspondence on the desk, the chairs fit only for firewood. Then a thought struck her.

"Tell me again why you left Barnakilla?" Muireann asked suddenly, as she rose from the chair and began to flip through some of the ledgers, glancing over at him from time to time.

Lochlainn blushed and avoided her gaze as she waited for an answer.

"I suppose you're bound to find out sooner or later, so I might as well tell you now to get it out of the way. Then we never have to discuss it again. My fiancée Tara left me for another man. Plus, the old man, Douglas Caldwell, was dying. I pretty much figured it was time to pull up stakes and go. I knew Augustine and I would never see eye to eye on how to run the estate. I suppose I fancied a change anyway.

"So I went out to Australia. I was there up until about eight months ago, when I got a letter from Ciara saying Augustine was asking for my help. I came back the shortest route I could, working my passage to save money.

"I'm not completely penniless. I made some good money out there working on a cattle station. But nor do I have the kind of money we are talking about to get this place back on its feet. Whatever I have is yours to do with as you like. I want to help in any way I can."

"So you dreamed of owning a place like this?"

"As it was at its height, yes, of course. Who wouldn't? But let's not talk about me. Let's discuss the estate, please," he said uncomfortably. "I'm sure you're wondering how things could have got so bad in such a short amount of time. It wouldn't have been so bad if the tenants had at least been paying their rent. But the potato crop failed in the autumn of 1841, a few months after I left, so people got into arrears, and Augustine allowed things to drift."

"And what are the possibilities of our recovering some of those losses?" Muireann asked, though she was pretty sure she already knew the answer from what she had seen of the estate and its tenantry so far.

"I really don't think we could possibly ask these people for back rent. If we held them to it, they would starve, I'm sure of it."

Muireann patted his shoulder, and sat back down again close by him. "Don't be so defensive. I agree with you. Apart from you and your sister, most of the people I've seen only have what they stand up in, and the little potato plots they tend for themselves, which are hardly going to be so productive that they can sell their surplus for a profit. It's pretty obvious, too, that they have nothing worth selling.

"But think of this from my point of view. I don't know how I'm meant to make the estate a going concern if no money is coming in. But neither will I evict them, so don't look so worried. You and I both know that would be unconscionable." Muireann stared into the empty fireplace thoughtfully.

Lochlainn reached over and took her hand. "I'm sure with that sharp brain of yours and the reputation the Scottish have for being clever with money, you'll work something out."

"Thank you for the vote of confidence, but I can't produce things out of thin air. I can't even make sense out of these accounts!" she admitted, her exasperation all too evident. "There are gaps everywhere! We shall have to visit the accountant and lawyer in town later and see if they can shed any light on the matter."

"Why don't you come outside for a breath of fresh air?" Lochlainn suggested, worried she might be overdoing things.

"The books aren't going to do themselves, you know!" she said sharply, and then apologized. "I am sorry. I didn't mean to snap at you."

"I would probably do worse than snap if I were you. I feel like I've betrayed you. Convinced you to come here to this!" He indicated the chaotic pile of papers with a sweep of his hand.

"You didn't know. Not really. How could you? You've only been back a short time. Augustine was in Scotland with me anyway. You couldn't consult with him then, and he died shortly after we arrived in Dublin. So there was no chance for you to discuss any business matters," she said, squeezing his hand for a brief moment before she rose.

"If you'll excuse me, I need to write another letter home now so I can post it in town later. And I want to note down a few more ideas before I go to Enniskillen."

"Very well then, I'll leave you. Is there anything you wish done?"

"Start cleaning out all of these downstairs rooms. Get rid of the rubbish, and the nests. We may have to get a cat to catch all these mice."

"Or a dog," Lochlainn said thoughtfully.

"What did you say?" Muireann asked, distractedly.

"Nothing. I just had a splendid idea, that's all. But I can't tell you. It would spoil the surprise. When is your birthday?"

"My what?"

"Your birthday," Lochlainn repeated.

"At the end of April. Why?"

"Perfect." He grinned, and refused to say any more, hurrying out when she tried to press him for an explanation.

As soon as Lochlainn had left, Muireann penned a letter to her cousin Michael, one of the estate stewards at Fintry, asking for his help and advice, and telling him the basic facts about the appalling state of Barnakilla. She knew he would help her with the livestock problem without her father finding out, and would be full of good ideas for running the estate and turning a profit.

Then she wrote to Neil again, informing him of her letter to Michael, and asking the two of them to work as allies on her behalf. Soon she turned her attention back to the books, and at last she knew what had been eluding her all along. She was grim-faced as she mounted the cart beside Lochlainn an hour later, and quite thoughtful as she asked Lochlainn about market days in Enniskillen.

"They're on Mondays and Thursdays."

"Are there any other big towns nearby?"

"Sligo is roughly forty miles away, and Donegal Town is

about the same to the northwest. There is also Cavan, which we drove through, and Clogher, about twenty miles away due east."

"What days of the week would they have their markets?"

"So far as I recall, Tuesdays and Saturdays for Sligo, Wednesdays and Fridays in Donegal, Mondays and Thursdays I think for Virginia. I am sure it's Thursdays for Clogher."

"And who is the resident magistrate in Enniskillen?"

Lochlainn looked at her in surprise. "It's Colonel Lowry, our neighbor on the northeastern side of the estate. Mr. Cole is on the southeastern end, and Christopher Caldwell, Augustine's cousin, is on the southwestern side. The lough of course takes up the whole eastern edge of the estate, so no one to worry about there. We have unrestricted use of the waterways."

"Is there anyone to the northwest of our estate?"

"Aye, Mr. Malcolm Stephens, but we haven't had anything to do with his family since Augustine started a feud over the pastureland and timber up there ages ago, as well as access to the lough, which our lands prevent him from using," Lochlainn informed her as they neared the outskirts of Enniskillen.

She lifted her chin, a picture of determination. "Well, perhaps it's about time that feud ended?"

Lochlainn gaped. "But they've been the Caldwells' enemies for years!"

"It doesn't matter a jot to me! I didn't start the feud, but it might be beneficial to us all if we finished it."

"It's a huge step, Muireann."

"Well, we don't have to decide right now, Lochlainn. We have more pressing matters here at Mr. Blessington's."

Muireann went into the accountant's office like an avenging angel. Lochlainn accompanied her, carrying the mountain of books and papers Muireann had brought with her from Barnakilla. She insisted he remain in the room as the oily little accountant tried to explain the expenses.

It wasn't long before Muireann confirmed her suspicions that Mr. Blessington had been skimming a substantial amount of money off the top, and stated quietly, "Well, sir, if you can't satisfy me as to the veracity of the accounts, I shall have to go to every single one of these creditors and ask them to produce their copies of these bills."

She rose from her chair. Mr. Blessington tried to waylay her by declaring, "Perhaps there has been some small error. I tell you what, I won't charge you for my service for this quarter and we'll call it quits."

"You will not be receiving wages for any quarter, Mr. Blessington. The only thing you will receive is a court summons from my solicitor," Muireann threatened as she stormed out.

Going on foot, Muireann and Lochlainn wove in and out of the narrow streets of the town, going to each shop on the lists she had jotted down. It took Lochlainn and Muireann the whole afternoon to see the various shopkeepers and obtain copies of the Barnakilla accounts. Even then their information wasn't complete, but at least Muireann was at last able to determine to some extent the level of Mr. Blessington's thievery.

In the course of the proceedings, however, the shopkeepers all discovered that Augustine had been tricked, and revealed that even though some of the sums owing were actually less than had supposedly been paid out, few of them had actually been paid at all. Mr. Blessington had therefore robbed the estate blind. Many of the shopkeepers were facing ruin if they didn't call in the debts soon. It was the same story everywhere, at the butcher's, the baker's, the smith's, everywhere that Augustine had done business.

Armed with the money from the clothes and carriage she had sold two days before, Muireann paid out half of what was owing to each shop owner, until her purse was empty.

She got receipts for the money paid out, an updated account for each, and she entered all the figures in a new ledger which she set up and vowed she would always keep herself.

Then she went to the local magistrate, Colonel Lowry, to present the evidence she had gleaned from her visits.

"I want the man arrested!" Muireann declared angrily when she had finished her tale.

Colonel Lowry, tall, distinguished, with silver hair and deep-set sherry-brown eyes, listened to her plea tolerantly before replying, "My dear, it will give me great pleasure to arrest the toad. I'm only too glad you have the proof against him in black and white. But if you will forgive an old man presuming to offer you some advice, I would suggest you get rid of your lawyer as well. They've been in each other's pockets for years."

Muireann and Lochlainn both stared at him openmouthed.

Colonel Lowry offered, "I'll give you the address of my son Anthony in Dublin. I'm sure he will suit you better, and not take you for every penny you're worth."

He wrote down the name and address on a slip of paper, and issued a writ seizing all of Mr. Blessington's assets. He said to Muireann encouragingly, "I'm fully booked up at the moment, but I can see you're desperate. I'll make sure it gets on my calendar of cases for March.

"If we can tally all the accounts, we shall make sure the shopkeepers are paid, and shall get back some of the money he has stolen from you. But it will take time. From what I can see, the fraud goes back years. God only knows what he's done with all of the money."

"I know it will be difficult, but I'm sure you will do the

best you can, you and your son. Thank you, sir. Thank you very much for all your help!" Muireann replied gratefully, shaking his hand as she made ready to leave.

"Good to meet you, Mrs. Caldwell. I'm only too happy to be of assistance. Nice to see you again, Lochlainn. Glad to see you looking so well. And make sure she looks in on Mr. Henry the lawyer, won't you?"

"Of course, Colonel," Lochlainn agreed, shaking the older man heartily by the hand. "We're both very grateful."

"The wee lassie has spark, that's for sure," the colonel said, directing a wink at Muireann.

They took their leave of the magistrate. Then Muireann marched determinedly after Lochlainn as he led the way to the lawyer's office.

As Colonel Lowry had warned, Mr. Henry had abused his position of trust most blatantly, having paid out all sorts of false legacies to himself on Augustine's property as soon as he had heard Augustine's father had died. He had read about Augustine's death in the morning newspapers the day before, and had wasted no time in drawing up false papers for fake bequests for himself and his partner in crime, Mr. Blessington.

He tried to invent all sorts of excuses as to why he couldn't hand over the will to Muireann. Lochlainn's large and brooding presence soon persuaded him otherwise.

Looking at the widow in her rich brown sable velvet gown, Mr. Henry attempted to present his false bequests for immediate payment, but Muireann laughed in his face. "I know those papers are forgeries, and not only because they're very poor imitations of Augustine's signature, which was quite distinctive, as I can prove from my marriage lines. I also know he couldn't possibly have signed them here in front of your notary, as it states here, in December and January, because he was with me in Scotland.

"At any rate, since he was marrying me, why would he want to leave anything to you? He would have a new family to consider, would he not?" Muireann argued logically.

"Well, with the New Year, and all that, perhaps he thought it was a good time to take stock of the estate? Maybe wanted to get some of his affairs in order. No doubt marrying you might have prompted it," the fat little bald man said desperately. "He sent me the orders from Scotland already signed."

"Don't take me for a fool. I know he sent no papers. He was otherwise engaged," Muireann hissed angrily. "At any rate, you know as well as I do how unreliable the postal service to Ireland is at the best of times. Even if he had signed these on the most recent date indicated here, which, by the way, was the second day we were traveling on board the steamer, they still wouldn't have arrived here in time for you to have them in your possession now. So stop wasting my time. I want all the papers relating to the estate this instant, do you hear me!" Muireann stamped her foot.

Lochlainn loomed over the tiny man threateningly, sending him scurrying into an inner office, where at length he produced a huge dusty trunk and several other folders. Muireann looked at some of the papers on the top of the trunk while Lochlainn went to fetch the junior magistrate of the town, Mr. Clarke, who had an office two doors down from Mr. Henry. All of the legal documents were entrusted into his safekeeping pending the trial. With a last withering glance at Mr. Henry, Lochlainn escorted Muireann to the cart.

"Is there anything else you wish to do before we head back?" he asked softly.

"Nay, without money, there isn't much we can do," Muireann said, dejection at last creeping into her voice.

"Well, it was a trifle foolhardy, my dear, but you did the right thing. It will make the shopkeepers feel confident that you will pay the other half of what you owe. It will stop them panicking once they find out that you have had Mr. Blessington and Mr. Henry's assets frozen and property seized because they cheated you. Well done."

They lapsed into silence then, and remained quietly huddled up against one other as the evening dropped down dark all around them.

At last Muireann said, "I suppose it could be worse. We'll have to get by somehow for the rest of the month, but at least we don't owe as much money as we had at first assumed."

"Not to the shopkeepers in Enniskillen, but there might be gambling debts all over the place," Lochlainn warned. "And there's still the mortgage to be paid out. God only knows how far behind that is."

"They'll just have to wait until the court case in March is heard. In the meantime we shall have to convince them we can keep Barnakilla afloat. I shall take over the accounts from now on. I've got the whole thing off to a start by paying the butcher and the others. But now we're going to have to try to wipe the slate clean at home."

"What do you mean?"

"I want us to tally everything we have on the farm, down to the last cup, spoon, stick of furniture, and farming implement, no matter how old, or dilapidated. Once we see what we have to work with, we can decide what to do with the surplus, and what we need to buy."

"But we haven't any money now that the magistrates have taken the books, and you've spent every penny you had."

"I know. That's why I'm going to start collecting the rent first thing tomorrow morning."

"What do you mean? The tenants at Barnakilla have no gold or coins!"

Muireann looked up at him calmly. "You told me to trust

you in Dublin, Lochlainn. Well now you'll just have to trust me, won't you? Can we use Patrick, Mark, Colm and their wives, and four or five other trustworthy men, as well as yourself and Ciara?"

"Yes, but . . ."

"Good. Inventory tonight, rent tomorrow."

"But I don't understand . . ."

"I know how much they have paid, how much they owe. If they have no money, they can pay me in other ways. I'll know better once we've carried out that inventory," Muireann replied, refusing to say more.

After a hasty supper of stirabout and a thin slice of bread, Muireann began with the kitchen storage area, and with Brona, Sharon, Siobhan and Ciara helping, they tallied up the food down to the last sultana.

Lochlainn, eager to be of help, and deeply impressed by Muireann's business acumen, went through the outbuildings with Patrick, Colm and Mark, and began to count all they possessed, down to the last nail. He prayed Muireann knew what she was doing.

Chapter Eleven

At about midnight, Lochlainn went in search of Muireann. He found her at the top of the house, organizing a chain of workers from the cottages to bring down all the items from the upper stories.

"Surely you can't mean to throw all of these things away!"

"Not throw them away. Sell them at the market in Enniskillen, if anyone is willing to buy them. These won't fetch much, which is probably why Augustine never bothered to sell them himself, but whatever price we get is better than nothing. Besides, these rooms haven't been cleared out for years." She grimaced, wiping her forehead with the back of her hand. "I need to see just how bad the house really is. I can't do that until I move all these things out."

"But how will you live? What will you use?"

She shrugged. "So long as I have a bed and a dresser, and a nail on the back of the door to hang things, what else do I need?"

"But Muireann, you weren't brought up like this! There are some sacrifices you shouldn't be expected to make."

"It's only furniture. You can't eat it, or pay taxes with it," Muireann pointed out casually, as if the matter weren't of the least concern to her.

Lochlainn watched her march down the stairs with an old chair. In the end he gave up and decided it was fruitless trying to fight Muireann once she had made her mind up. It was like trying to wrestle with the wind.

They labored all night indoors, and in the cold morning light, at half past six the next morning, Lochlainn began to supervise the loading of the cart to take to the market in town.

"We should repair the two-seater carriage and the small dog cart soon, so we can sell them too," Muireann said as she came up behind him.

"But Muireann, you're a genteelly brought up lady. How can you pay social visits without a carriage?"

Muireann laughed then. "I haven't got the horse to pull them! Besides, how can I have anyone here when I have nothing but empty rooms and crumbling walls!"

She marched back into the house and headed up to her small bedchamber, where she splashed some water on her grimy face and hands before drying herself with a towel.

Then she went back down the stairs to begin searching inside the trunks which the workers had placed in what Muireann guessed must have once been the drawing room.

Lochlainn, alarmed at the cold which seemed to creep into every crevice of the old house, checked the chimney first to make sure that it wasn't blocked, then brought in some wood and lit a fire for her.

The trunks were full of old and rather expensive clothes. Muireann soon determined that Patrick and Siobhan, who had experience trading in the markets, should take them into town to sell as well.

"But someone might need them here!"

Muireann shook her head. "They're too rich. Look at the brocades and velvets. No, sell them all. When more of my things arrive in a couple of weeks, we can see what's needed then."

"More of your things?"

"Well, what I had with me was for the wedding tour, supposedly of the Continent, and those clothes were my trousseau. I've asked my cousin Michael and his mother to supervise the removal of the rest of my things from Fintry. I've told them no matter how small it is, they are to send it.

"The wedding presents also haven't been sent here yet. Due to the suddenness of the wedding, not everyone in my family was able to send me something. I've told Michael to sell what he can in Glasgow, and post me a banker's draft for the money. Anyone who hasn't sent a present is to be told to send a banker's draft. There is no sense in shipping a million toasting forks over here, now is there? But I do have some clothes suitable for daily wear, and some elegant ball gowns and so on that I can sell."

Lochlainn scowled again at her getting rid of all her things so easily, but decided that complaining every two minutes wasn't going to get the work done. Muireann was headstrong, true, but his admiration for her grew with every passing moment. She certainly had a good eye for detail, and seemed to think of everything.

So instead he brought up the subject which had been troubling him ever since their chat on the way home from Enniskillen the previous evening.

"What was that you said about collecting rent today?"

"As soon as we've had some breakfast, we shall start," she said, dusting off her hands as she finished searching another trunk, and pushing it off to one side to be sold later.

"Muireann, you've been up all night. Please don't overdo things," he begged, stroking back a damp tendril from her forehead.

"Lochlainn, I haven't got time to stop. If I sat by idly and thought about this whole mess, I should probably crumple with despair. Now, will you join me in a bowl of porridge or not?" she asked, stepping away from him quickly to head for the kitchen.

"Aye, if I may."

Muireann poured some warm water into the sink and scrubbed her hands and face yet again, hating how filthy she became every time she moved in the house. Lochlainn needed a wash before eating as well, and dipped his hands in the basin. Their slippery fingers mingled intimately under the water, sending delightful tingles coursing through their veins. They indulged in a few shy but intense caresses, until Muireann moved away from the sink and went over to the stove.

There she ladled out two bowls of porridge from the vat Ciara had prepared for the workers that morning. Then she called everyone in the house to come wash and eat. The kitchen was now quite spotless and very cozy. The workers all began to chat quietly among themselves in quite a cheerful way about all they had done that night. Muireann sat down on one of the long benches in front of the fire, and ate her oatmeal hungrily.

Lochlainn sat next to her on the bench, slightly crushed because of the others. He couldn't help feeling acutely aware of Muireann's softness whenever he brushed against her. Their legs were practically touching, and the contact for both of them was utterly thrilling. At the same time, it was comforting huddling close together in the kitchen, and Muireann began to feel as if she belonged for the first time since she had arrived.

But Lochlainn was worried about this new state of affairs. He disliked the fact that Muireann was not eating in the dining room. All the laborers helping to ready the house came in and went out, availed themselves of the porridge, and no longer seemed to be in awe of the unusual Scottish woman who had come into their midst. But since Muireann herself seemed to be completely at ease with the circumstances, he remained silent.

After finishing her last mouthful of cereal and taking a small sip of black tea so thick she could nearly stand a spoon up in it, Muireann took her cloak off the peg in the hall and strode outside towards the stable block. Lochlainn trailed along behind her, and waited for her instructions.

"If you could gather our helpers and your sister together, we can get started."

"What do you want us to do?" Lochlainn asked a few minutes later, as Mark, Sharon, Brona and Colm arrived, with Ciara bringing up the rear.

"We'll need a few more men, and then I want you to knock on every cottage door and tell the tenants to come out," Muireann said.

Lochlainn called on three other reliable workers, Conn, Kevin, and Niall, and then they all set to work rousing the tenantry.

Soon about eighty men and women were assembled in the courtyard of the stable block.

Muireann looked at each one of them before she declared aloud, "I am Mrs. Muireann Caldwell. You probably know by now that I recently married your former landlord, Augustine Caldwell, and that he died suddenly in Dublin.

"I have decided to come here because I have been told by my estate manager, Mr. Lochlainn Roche, that Barnakilla is in a desperate plight, and will have to be sold if something isn't done to halt the decay. I have been looking into the books, and see that none of you have paid any rents at all for the past two quarters. In fact, some of you owe as much as two years' back rent.

"I'm aware that times have been hard, but they will get harder for all of us if drastic steps aren't taken to try to pull this estate out of the quagmire of debt. So I am here to collect your rents now. What I say is that we will pool our resources together. I want you to give up everything you have, down to the last needle and thread, and cast in your lot with me," Muireann announced to the assembled crowd.

There were gasps of astonishment and grumbles of resentment. She could see Lochlainn gaping at her, horrified by what he had just heard.

Muireann raised a hand for silence, "Please, listen to me! We will go through each family's property, and it will all go into a group store for the whole farm. Apart from your most intimate articles of clothing and children's nappies, I even want us to count down to the last baby booty and bib. I want all your farming tools and even your furniture.

"You can keep the beds inside, but I want everything else brought here into the courtyard. Then you will go back and clean your houses from top to bottom with hot water, which you can fetch from the kitchen. I will count all the work you do today at a fair day laborer's rate against the rent you owe. I will also give you a fair valuation for everything you put on your piles, and deduct that from the rent you owe.

"From now on, you will be given chores to do around Barnakilla, according to your talent and our needs here. If you work hard, you will be fed and clothed, and have your daily wages go towards paying off your rent. I promise you, I will look after you. Once your rent is paid, if you wish to go elsewhere, you shall be free to do so.

"But in the meantime I want us to start by looking after what we have. That means scrubbing the houses and improving them. It also means keeping ourselves neat and clean. Those of you with skills like carpentry and building, or cooking and sewing, can also make extra money by undertaking that work for those who can't, and by passing on your skills to others. So I want you to go away now and start bringing your things out. I shall start making my calculations."

Everyone looked at each other sideways.

Muireann warned, "I'm no fool, ladies and gentlemen. If I catch you trying to hold things back, I will fine you, and hand you over to the magistrates for non-payment of rent. Debtors' prison won't be half as nice as here, however awful Barnakilla may be at the moment."

The people continued to grumble and gossip.

Muireann waited patiently for the noise to die down.

But there was at least one doughty soul prepared to challenge her authority and position. "What gives you the right to tell us we have to give up everything, make these sacrifices? You rich people never suffer when the estates fail. You just put up the rents to try to squeeze more out of us! How do we know those rents are accurate? And how do we know if, even after we give everything we have, you might not turn around and evict us anyway?" one older man with broad shoulders and a haggard look declared loudly.

Lochlainn stepped forward. "If I may, Mrs. Caldwell?"

"Of course, Mr. Roche," Muireann assented.

"I'm the estate agent, and you know me of old. I admit I've been away for the past three years, but the rents I set when I first took over about ten years ago were fair. They haven't increased substantially over that period, or at least not according to these ledgers, which Mrs. Caldwell has here and which I have gone over fully. As for Mrs. Caldwell being rich, I'm afraid to say that Mr. Caldwell used her dowry to pay off some of his own gambling debts, leaving her completely penniless and alone when he died.

"I admit that we had to sell Mr. Caldwell's things to get enough cash to pay for his funeral. Mrs. Caldwell herself willingly sold every garment she had and her carriage to pay off some of the debts. So apart from a couple of dresses, she has nothing but what she stands up in. She has no way of counting on any outside support. I'm asking all of you to trust me, and I can tell you that I trust her.

"Muireann came here, even knowing how poor the estate was, because she sincerely believed she could make a huge difference to all of our lives. I think she can do it, but only if you're all willing to support her. After all, isn't it better to stay here with me and Mrs. Caldwell than force her to sell, and run the risk of having a far worse landlord, who might evict you as soon as he bought the place?" he argued persuasively.

Lochlainn looked round at the sea of worried faces, and knew he had won this round at least.

"Will you support Muireann?" he demanded of the crowd.

"Aye, we will!" several of the men and women declared stoutly. The crowd dispersed to start organizing their cottages.

"Can you and your sister start making inventories of the piles?" Muireann asked Lochlainn. "I want one pile for each cottage, is that clear?"

Lochlainn nodded, and set to work. Though he was stunned at her idea, he was unable to see any other way of doing things. She was absolutely right. They would sink or swim together, all of them.

Muireann went to inspect each cottage, and made sure all of the tenants threw out their filthy mattresses and took some straw from the barn for clean ticking for all the beds. She even had them bring every last piece of turf and every potato and the few remaining privately owned animals to the stable yard, and she and her helpers began to busily calculate all of the 'wealth' of the estate. Soon there were small mountains of vegetables and even a few pigs, geese and hens.

Muireann consulted with Lochlainn about fair market prices for each of the items. The livestock were put in the appropriate pens, and the vegetables brought to the larders in the kitchen.

Muireann instructed the women there to take some of the vegetables and some of the meat from the day before to make enough stew for a hundred people. Once the cottages were all empty and the women began the cleaning, she told the men that anyone who wished to hunt could take the guns out, and she would give a bonus off the rent to the three men who brought home the most.

"Anyone who is too old or too ill to work, or expecting, can look after the children, and we will make someone come around to clean your house. And I want to think about having slate floors instead of mud ones."

"There's a slate quarry up at the northwestern side of the estate, and Thomas MacMahon over here knows all about cutting it," Lochlainn informed her.

"Good. If we have enough skilled workers, we could even think about having slate roofs instead of the thatched ones, once we've repaired the big house. Some of these look rotten through and through."

Everyone on the estate put in an exhausting day's work, while Muireann filled out a new rent ledger with the names of the head of each household, and how much credit they had against their back rent. She then had the men not out hunting take all the farming implements into the storage sheds. All of the clothes went into a huge pile to be redistributed to those who were most needy, especially some of the elderly women and young children on the estate.

She supervised the transfer of the kitchen goods and then added the figures to her inventory from the evening before. Lochlainn did a new inventory of the farming implements. Muireann and he worked out exactly how many items they would need, and how much surplus they could sell.

"Patrick and Siobhan can take them to the market in Donegal tomorrow if the weather is good, and sell them there along with the clothes and the other things we didn't manage to fit in the cart," Muireann outlined as she redid her figures one last time, and sat back in her chair satisfied.

Just then they heard Ciara's voice calling them to supper. After scrubbing their hands in the scullery sink, they waited in the line in front of the stew pot like everyone else, and gratefully received a bowl of rabbit-and-venison stew and two freshly made oatcakes.

"Well, what now, Mrs. Caldwell?" Lochlainn asked wearily, as he sat down beside her on the bench to eat his supper.

"The next thing is to find out what talents the tenants have, if any. Some of the women must be good at cooking, sewing and so on. As for the men, hunting, fishing, carpentry, and suchlike. We need to draw up lists and keep track of what everyone is doing each day so we can pay them fairly.

"Even the old can work, if they're willing to look after the children and mend. The older children can work if we can find them some simple chores. I don't want anyone lying idle. I certainly don't want them to think I'm some rich snooty heiress. If they are going to work, then I shall as well."

"What will you do?" Lochlainn asked between mouthfuls.

"I can cook, bake, sew, teach them how to read, do the accounts, oversee the foodstuffs and all the purchases, milk the cows when we get some, muck out the stables—"

"But you were brought up with dozens of servants!"

"I won't say I didn't have a great deal of leisure time growing up. I was spoilt and privileged, and lucky enough to be well educated, I know that. But I lived on a big estate. I'm not completely ignorant as to the daily workings of a farm. I just have to take all the responsibility on my own shoulders now. I only hope I make the right decisions."

Lochlainn was unsure what to say, so they remained silent, eating the last of the rather tasty stew, until at last Muireann looked directly at Lochlainn and said, "About today. You looked very worried, uncomfortable even, when I made my announcement. Do you think I made the wrong decision?"

"No, no, I was just surprised, that's all. But what you said makes sense. What's the point of everyone farming the potatoes and so on upon his own small plot, when a few can do that for everyone while the others do useful tasks like hunting and fishing, or carpentry."

"Do you think I can strike a bargain with the victuallers in town to take the extra game and fish?"

He considered in silence for a moment. "It's worth a try, especially with the smoke oven working again."

Muireann stood up and brought her bowl over to the sink to be washed and dried by Sharon and Brona, who had adapted very well to working in the house. She strolled out the back door into the deepening twilight.

She watched silently as the tenants tidied away the rest of the items still in the stable yard. Lochlainn came up and stood beside her. She looped her arm in his and moved closer to him, sharing his warmth and strength for a brief moment.

"Thank you, for everything, Lochlainn."

"I haven't done anything," he replied, embarrassed.

"You did. Your speech made a big difference, I'm sure. You supported me right through this even when you were unsure of what I was doing. It counts for a great deal, you know."

"So does your faith in me, Muireann."

"Well, I never would have come here if it hadn't been for you."

Lochlainn laughed. "Somehow I think it's early days for you to be thanking me for bringing you to Barnakilla."

Muireann grinned as she gazed up at his broodingly handsome features. "I'll astonish you all, just wait and see."

Suddenly his face lit up into a broad smile that took Muireann's breath away. "I think you've already done that."

He stroked her hand briefly until, afraid of his feelings for her, he moved on to a more neutral topic of conversation.

"You know, I do have some carpentry skills. I'm a bit rusty, but perhaps we might consider making our own furniture here and selling it. There are some good stacks of well-seasoned timber Augustine obviously never got around to selling. We could also get the men on tree-cutting detail to get more timber. We could even sell some of it. But let's make sure we have enough firewood for ourselves before we branch out into any enterprises like that."

"I'll help too. I've done woodcutting myself once or twice, and hunting and fishing as well."

"Just what sort of parents did you have?" he asked, surprised.

"Ones who didn't really take the trouble to keep an eye on me too closely, I must admit," Muireann said with a small smile. "They couldn't help it if I was willful."

"Willful? You? I wonder that makes you say that?" Lochlainn teased.

Muireann frowned slightly. "You don't think I'm just doing this all for myself, do you?"

"No, of course not," Lochlainn hastened to reassure her, hugging her to his side briefly as he escorted her back into the house. "I think what you're doing is incredibly brave and selfless. I saw you sell all your clothes and jewels in Dublin, remember? You could have gone back to Scotland, never set foot here, never had to sell all your lovely things.

"But you did it without even pausing to consider the consequences or the sacrifice you were making. You gave whatever you could to the shopkeepers to help them protect their livelihoods yesterday, even though it left you penniless. How could I feel anything other than admiration for you?" Lochlainn said candidly, stroking her cheek with his free hand.

He accompanied Muireann into the study, where she began loading more books into the boxes, keeping count of them in a small ledger. Lochlainn took down the ones on the highest shelves, laughing at her fondly when she tried to reach and nearly lost her balance. He caught her by the waist, and it took every ounce of willpower not to kiss her.

Muireann thanked him for his help, but he noticed she looked thoughtful. Finally she admitted, "It wasn't that much of a sacrifice. I didn't want to go back. I've always been spoilt and petted, I know, but I want my life to be different. I want to be of some use in the world. I felt restless, anxious until I came here.

"Men have careers, jobs and roles in society that take them out of the home. What would I have done in Scotland except attend dull tea parties and endless balls? More often than not I used to make excuses and stay at home with a good book," she confessed. "That's why I used to sneak around the estate learning how to do things."

"You're a rare woman, Muireann."

"And you're a rare man. It must have been hard coming back from Australia to this, this ruin. . . ."

"This ruin, as you call it, is my home," Lochlainn said stiffly.

"I know, I didn't mean . . . I'm sorry."

"No, it isn't your fault. I can admit the truth even if it is painful for me to bear. But you've allowed me to dream again. I'll admit that I was in utter despair when I first met you, but now, things seem to be a great deal more rosy."

"I was in despair when you looked after me in the hotel in Dublin," Muireann said with a shudder.

"Let's not talk about it, if it upsets you."

"I think we should forget about the past and look to the future," Muireann said as she moved across the room to where Augustine had left a pair of decanters on a small dilapidated table.

"Let's drink to new beginnings, shall we?" she suggested, picking up the two small glasses that stood there and checking to see they were relatively dust free after the rigorous cleaning the room had received that day.

"That sounds like an excellent idea."

Muireann poured two glasses of the amber liquid. "To a whole new life, for both of us."

"To a fresh start," Lochlainn toasted. They clinked their glassed lightly together and smiled.

Each took a sip of the liquor, and she forced herself to swallow.

"Ugh! Augustine certainly had rotten taste in brandy!" Lochlainn gasped, coughing.

"It's like fire," Muireann wheezed, the tears streaming down her cheeks.

She hastily poured them glasses of water from the jug Ciara had left there, and then began to giggle. "I think it will definitely have to be for medicinal doses."

"For whom, the bulls?"

Muireann laughed aloud then, and Lochlainn, unable to resist her sparkling beauty any longer, bent and gave her a peck on the lips.

She stopped laughing then and blinked in puzzlement before putting down her glass and going back to her book count. Lochlainn was too near, too enticing. Why did she respond like this to him whenever they were alone?

"Well, I think I'd better clean up and get to bed," Lochlainn said hesitantly when he saw her withdraw from him.

"Aye, that sounds like a good idea. And speaking of cleaning up, I've arranged for laundry and washing day tomorrow. I will not have the people in my care living in squalor if I can help it. So if you're first up, you can get the hottest bath. The men are going to go first, before the women, who will no doubt need longer soaks."

"I'll look forward to it," Lochlainn said, looking at his grimy hands, which he was sure would get worse tomorrow when he began the timber cutting. "It will certainly be a luxury compared to a quick dip in the lough."

"What, you mean you actually bathe in Lough Erne in this weather?" Muireann asked, aghast.

"Well, the cold does have a few useful purposes," Lochlainn remarked somewhat cryptically, giving her one last longing look before he left her alone with her ledgers.

Chapter Twelve

By the end of her first month at Barnakilla, Muireann began to feel that things were on a much more even keel at the estate. Though the court cases against Mr. Blessington and Mr. Henry were still pending, at least she had a specific date, the thirteenth of March. She hoped the estate would be fairly solvent once some of Barnakilla's money was returned to its rightful place.

Even more gratifying was the fact that all of her work schemes and enterprises seemed to be bearing fruit. They had meat and fish in plenty from the hunting, and the butcher had increased his order steadily over the past weeks. The fresh and smoked fish and meat were also selling well in the market stalls. Colonel Lowry and Mr. Cole had also decided to help the feisty young widow and fill their bellies at the same time with her high-quality produce.

The timber business was going very well, with the trees being cut and rolled down to the dock without very much difficulty, to await eventual transportation to Scotland and abroad. Deliveries to the town of turf and wood had also increased steadily since they had gone into business, so that Muireann eventually ordered Patrick to buy two more carts if he could get them at a good price.

Lochlainn's furniture was exquisite, and he and Ciara had made the ultimate sacrifice by selling off all of the pieces he had made from their own home.

"But Lochlainn, that sideboard. I love it! Please, don't sell it!" she had argued, tears pricking the back of her eyes inexplicably.

"You sold everything you had," Lochlainn reminded her, and ordered all the furniture to be loaded on the cart.

Though Muireann knew Lochlainn would be cross when he eventually found out what she had done, she waited until Lochlainn's back was turned later and asked Patrick to take the sideboard off the cart and put it in her room upstairs. It was so lovely, with its carved acorns, she couldn't bear to let it go.

Many of the women had proven themselves excellent hands in the kitchen and at sewing and knitting, and were educating the others. They all gathered in the kitchen at night after supper, and stitched together huge quilts from any scraps they had, or made bibs and baby clothes. Their baking was also particularly fine, and many Enniskillen residents said it rivaled that of the bakery. Muireann had little chance to judge, since they couldn't afford to eat any of what they made themselves at the farm.

Lochlainn instituted woodworking classes, which he held in his own cottage, though Ciara complained about the bits of wood and sawdust everywhere, so much so that Muireann made room for the men in the bright warm kitchen as well.

Once a week they did the wash and made candles, and waited for some warmer weather to herald the arrival of spring. The cottages were all being repaired one by one, and some of the more experienced builders looked over the mansion and made a list of the most urgent repairs.

The women with no specific skills did the laundry, washing up, and child-minding tasks, and also scrubbed the old house from top to bottom. It seemed odd to Lochlainn that Muireann was content to be living in a nearly empty house, but Muireann was too busy and often too tired to care. In truth, she was hardly even sleeping, for as much as she hated to admit it, she was terrified of the nightmares she experienced whenever she shut her eyes.

Lochlainn became concerned when he found her dozing in her chair early one afternoon.

"I'm sorry," she said with a yawn, looking around the study blearily. "I just can't seem to settle down at night. It's a strange place, I suppose, and with so much going on in my mind, I can't really rest."

"Are you unhappy about being alone?" Lochlainn probed gently.

Muireann looked up at his handsome face, and wondered if he recalled the nights they had spent in Dublin together as vividly as she did. But that time seemed so long ago now. It was ridiculous to assume that he could possibly remember it after all they had been through since.

"There is that too," she admitted reluctantly. "This house is so big and draughty, and it certainly rattles."

"Would you like to come back and stay at the cottage with Ciara and me for a few days? You'd be more than welcome. I'm sure my sister would love the company."

Muireann smiled tightly. "I wouldn't like to inconvenience you. I'm sure your sister would *not* be delighted with an unwanted house guest, especially me."

So far, the two women had managed to be civil to one another, but no more, despite all of Lochlainn's efforts to get them to be friends.

"Would you like me to move up here for a few days, just until you feel a bit more settled?" Lochlainn offered, secretly looking forward to the chance of being alone with Muireann again.

"No, really, it's very kind of you to offer, but I'm a grown woman. It is silly to be uneasy in my own house. At my age I shouldn't be afraid of a few nightmares."

This was the first time she had mentioned nightmares. He recalled the night she had spent at his cottage, tossing and turning.

"You never had nightmares in the hotel or the inn."

"I know. But I doubt it's anything to worry about. Probably just something I ate before bed." She gave a wan smile and turned her attention back to her ledgers.

Lochlainn detected her nervousness, but decided not to pursue the matter for the moment. "The next time I'm in town, I shall ask Dr. Fredrickson for a sleeping draught for you."

Muireann blushed. "No, really, I'll be fine. I'm sorry I even mentioned it."

Lochlainn replayed the conversation over and over in his head as he went out to the sheds to work on a table Colonel Lowry had commissioned. When he stopped work for a short rest, he went over to his cottage and took some blankets and a pillow off his bed.

He crept into the kitchen, and seeing Muireann wasn't around, he tiptoed up the stairs and opened the door of the room next to Muireann's own. It was a large lofty chamber with peeling gold-flocked wallpaper. He made up a small pallet for himself in the room, and asked Sharon and Brona to light a fire in it to help take the chill off.

Next he headed into town to get some flour, salt, sugar and vegetables. But his first port of call was the doctor's surgery. There he managed to get some sleeping powder by explaining to the doctor just what a strain Muireann had been under recently.

"I know people shouldn't take too much of this sort of thing, but she's been overdoing it lately. She needs her rest. She hardly eats or sleeps, and she does as much work as any man on the estate."

Dr. Fredrickson frowned. "If she's working that hard, it's a wonder she doesn't fall into bed exhausted every night."

"I suppose you're right. She probably just has far too many things preying on her mind."

Lochlainn brought the medicine home, and managed to slip it to her in her stew when she wasn't looking. He was relieved to see her with her head down on her desk an hour later. He gently lifted her and carried her up the stairs to her own bedchamber. He laid her on the four-poster and pulled the covers up over her, desperately resisting the temptation to get in beside her as he had done in Dublin. What would she think if she woke to find him there?

He kissed her brow softly, and crept out. He went into his own room to stoke the fire, and looked over some estate papers there rather than down in the study, in case she should need him.

Lochlainn did hear whimpering sounds in the middle of the night, but Muireann quieted after a while, so Lochlainn didn't feel it was urgent for him to go in to her. At length he gave up his vigil, satisfied that his little plan had worked, and slept the sleep of the dead for the rest of the night.

Muireann awoke the next day feeling far more refreshed, and went down to breakfast almost skipping, she felt so cheerful. Lochlainn was relieved to see her looking so much brighter, and resolved he would give her more sleeping powder that night as well.

Just as she was finishing her morning chores, Mark came running into the kitchen.

"Muireann! Muireann! There's a ship pulling up to the dock!"

Muireann dropped her axe, which she had been using to chop firewood despite Lochlainn's protests that it was not a job for a lady. Throwing a shawl over her dark navy gown, she ran to the shore.

There her cousin Michael was just disembarking. He hugged her tightly and swung her around as she flew into his arms.

"I see you got my letter," she laughed, as she noted all the animal pens which had been lashed to the decks.

"I did indeed, though of course your father had already

promised to send over your stallion and mare just as soon as you got yourself settled," Michael replied easily, taking in his cousin's thinner appearance. "I'm very sorry for your trouble."

Muireann waved his condolences away. "He's gone. There's nothing more to be said. I just have to get on with my life. This place is going to thrive now that we have more livestock," she said as she strode up and down the pens and counted the cows, sheep and hens.

"You haven't left Fintry without a single animal, have you?" she giggled a short time later, viewing the menagerie with delight.

"Not at all. Neil and I skimmed a few of the animals from each of our estates. You paid for them with the money from the stocks and shares Neil could liquidate for you at such short notice. I didn't tell anyone anything, I swear. But some of the old aunts and uncles sent you the hens and geese as wedding presents, and many of the rest sent cash without having to be told anything."

"Mother and Father and Alice don't suspect there is something amiss?"

"They did want to come themselves, of course. But with Alice expecting, and your father's gout beginning to trouble him again, it didn't seem a good idea. You know full well how rough the sea can be at this time of year, though I must admit we did have a remarkably good crossing.

"Neil would have come himself except that he has a mountain of papers to go through on your behalf, and several very important court cases pending which prevented him from getting away even for a few days. But he sends his love and promises to contact Anthony Lowry in Dublin over your lawsuit on the thirteenth of March," Michael told her.

Muireann sighed. "I do feel awful about deceiving them all into thinking that everything is fine here. But what else can I do? You know what they're like."

"I know Uncle Alistair, at any rate." Michael laughed bitterly. "He's completely intolerant of failure, and he always did have very set notions about how you were to be brought up and to behave. He would take one look at your dress, your hands, and he would insist on your coming back to Fintry, even if he had to drag you back on board the *Andromeda*."

"I don't look that bad, do I?" Muireann asked worriedly.

"All things considered, no. But I can see these are not the hands of a genteel Graham sister," he said as he took her hand in his own briefly before tucking it into the crook of his arm to escort her around the ship.

"Neil took the liberty of ordering you some essentials if you're to start your spring planting soon. And he also provisioned you with staples—oats, flour, sugar and so on."

"His idea of staples seems quite odd," she laughed, as she spotted several crates of wine and a chest of strawberry preserves.

"He's only trying to be kind. He has no way of knowing how bad things are here."

She grinned as she espied a huge container on the top. "Well, at least there's lots of coffee, so not all is doom and gloom."

"Neil said if the ship sank, that was the only thing I should trouble to save," he joked.

"That's very kind of him. He knows what I'm like without at least three cups of it a day." Muireann chuckled. She romped playfully around the deck with her old school fellow, chasing after the canister, which he dangled just beyond her reach.

Just then Lochlainn came on board, and she introduced him to her cousin. She noticed Lochlainn was looking particularly gloomy, and he seemed to eye her tall, handsome, young brown-eyed cousin rather suspiciously.

"Look at all the things Neil has sent out of my share money."

Lochlainn stared at the coffee and preserves, and her cousin Michael, so suave and sophisticated in his expensive clothes, and felt that Muireann was suddenly slipping away from him.

"How nice," he said noncommittally.

"Well, playing hide-and-seek won't get the work done. Lochlainn, muster all the men to get the animals off and into the stables. Then we can prepare to load the timber."

She turned to Michael. "How long can you stay?"

"We'll have to go by the end of the day, I'm afraid. This is one of Philip Buchanan's ships. Neil could only get hold of it because his brother left him in charge while he's away in Canada.

"We would have come sooner, only the ship's been busy bringing supplies to the Western Isles. We have to get back for another regular run. Neil says to let him know what else you need, and it will be sent when we pick up the next load of timber.

"Here are all the ledgers for the cargo, and the sums from the shares. And this is the money left over," he said as he handed her a small leather pouch. "Neil also says you're to keep track of the timber in this book, so that everything is decent and aboveboard."

Muireann flipped the books open and consulted Lochlainn about them for a moment.

"It all looks very impressive," Lochlainn said, unable to take his eyes off the splendid livestock coming down the gangplank.

Muireann's stallion, Bran, was jet black, and easily the largest horse Lochlainn had ever seen in his thirty-six years. The mare, Misty, was remarkably similar, and it didn't surprise Lochlainn to discover that they were both one-half Arabian. Then there were the ordinary dray horses, all very heavily muscled and extremely well built, with glossy coats that bespoke lavish care.

The cows were mainly Friesians, but there were also a pair of Simmentals and two Charolais.

The sheep were all Leicesters or Cheviots, and there was even a pair of goats and a large Berkshire boar and sow.

As for the poultry, they were also of the highest quality. Lochlainn was certain the estate would double its egg production in no time.

"Can you supervise the livestock getting good homes, while I take care of the timber?" Muireann requested of Lochlainn.

"Aye. Patrick, you help Mrs. Caldwell with the timber over here. I'm going up to the stables."

Lochlainn tried not to feel as though he were being left out, but all the same, he was worried. What if Michael tried to persuade Muireann to go back with him to Scotland, and leave things in the hands of her estate agent? He felt his chest constrict so that he could barely breathe.

He knew it was wrong, but he simply couldn't help himself. He and Muireann had worked side by side night and day ever since they had met in Dublin. The more he got to know her, the more he knew he desired even the slightest touch of her hand, or glance from her incredible amethyst eyes.

He had long ago ceased to think about Tara except as an unpleasant reminder of how fickle women were generally. He knew Muireann might prove to be the same. But for the moment he could find no flaws in her, and the attraction between them was growing by leaps and bounds.

Once all the animals were safely penned, Lochlainn went down to the dock to help supervise the rest of the timber loading.

He came up behind Muireann and put his arm around her.

"Why don't you go up to the house to get warm?"

Muireann smiled up at him, and took comfort from his large form beside her. She breathed in the musky male scent of him, and felt herself go weak in the knees. An uncontrollable wave of desire surged through her as she had a sudden recollection of their kiss in the bed in Virginia that fateful morning when she had just buried Augustine and vowed to start a whole new life for herself.

Here she was, a little over a month later, and this enigmatic man had been at her side every step of the way, arguing, true, but also supporting and encouraging. Backing up her every idea even when she could tell he believed her to be wrong. Part of her longed for the old comforts of Fintry, the beauties of her childhood home. But the other half told her that though it had been a difficult path so far, she was on the right road. With Lochlainn by her side, how could she fail?

But there was more to life than hard work, wasn't there? There should be time for love, too. Muireann stiffened slightly as that word suddenly soared into her mind. She examined it carefully in the context of her relationship with Lochlainn, and thought perhaps it was not so strange a word to use after all. What did marriage mean for her? Her ideal was a meeting of equals, a partnership, a special closeness and comfort shared with the beloved.

She had seen enough failed marriages, experienced one for herself briefly and horribly, to know she wanted something different from what her parents and Alice and Neil seemed to share. Alice had taken great delight in warning Muireann about the terrible things one was required to do in the marriage bed. Muireann shuddered again briefly, causing Lochlainn to tighten his arm around her and offer her his jacket.

"No, really, I'm fine. It was just someone walking over my grave," she said quickly.

She tried to distract herself by moving forward to help

with a particularly stubborn log, which suddenly swung into her arm with a crunching blow. She grabbed it and cried out in pain. Lochlainn came running.

"Here, let me see!" he commanded, taking her hand and gently baring her arm to the elbow. "Well, you'll certainly have a good bruise there, but I don't think it's broken."

"I'll be fine. I don't bruise easily," Muireann remarked unthinkingly.

Lochlainn frowned at the remark, puzzled. When he had first met her . . .

But Muireann had colored furiously, and stalked away up to the house. "Come up for something hot to eat and drink as soon as you're all finished here, Michael," she said over her shoulder. "You and the whole crew."

"We'll be up in a minute," Michael called after her.

"Patrick will watch the boat just to make sure it doesn't sail away without you."

Lochlainn could see the strain in her expression. Worried that she was overdoing things again, he determined she would get another good night's sleep at least, and made plans to smuggle the sleeping powder into a cup of coffee later in the evening. Bringing it to her in the study would give him a good excuse to be alone with her.

The *Andromeda* crew and the Barnakilla workers all crammed into the benches together, chatting amiably, and ate their fill of the hearty stew with suet dumplings that was put before them.

Once they had finished their meal, Michael asked for a small tour of the house and estate. At the end of it, when they had returned once more to the warmth of the kitchen, he admitted, "You certainly do have your work cut out for you, cousin. At the same time, I know you can't resist a challenge. You probably love every minute of this, even the scrubbing, cleaning, and living as though you're camping out under the stars."

"It's certainly not been fun." Muireann shook her head. "But now, with all these things you've brought me, and Neil's help, I think I'm beginning to see some glimmer of hope. My only worry is the sum owing to the bank, which is huge. But they've agreed not to do anything until after the court case against the old accountant and lawyer. All the same, things will still be pretty tight if my businesses don't thrive."

"Neil says he will take as much timber as you can give him, and I'm sure Philip will have no objections to a couple of trips each month. We'll get to see each other pretty often."

"You mean so you can all keep an eye on me," Muireann accused a trifle angrily.

"No, of course not," he said indignantly. "I know you well enough to know you'll be fine. For what it's worth, I'm certain you have a good man in Lochlainn. I like him very much."

"I'm glad. He *is* a good man," Muireann replied warmly. "Give my love to your parents and brothers, and Neil and my parents too, of course. Anything you can do to dissuade Mother and Father from coming over will be greatly appreciated."

"I understand, Muireann. Never fear, I shall present everything in the most glowing terms possible."

"Not too glowing, I hope. If I do have to sell this place because the bank forecloses, they will definitely find out what a bunch of liars you, myself and Neil really are."

"You won't fail. I'll bet you anything you like."

"I haven't any money, and I don't gamble," she said sharply.

"I'll bet you a kiss, then," Michael joked.

"You can have one of those without having to make a bet," Muireann laughed, and kissed her cousin on the cheek.

"Take care of yourself."

"Aye, and you."

She walked him down to the dock, and watched the boat as it cast off. Wondering why she felt so alone, she waved as the *Andromeda* rowed away, then became a mere speck on the horizon before vanishing altogether in the glimmering twilight.

Chapter Thirteen

Lochlainn found Muireann in the study about an hour later. He sat down in front of the desk, but she never looked up from her column of figures.

"Are you all right, Muireann?" Lochlainn asked softly.

"Yes, of course. Why shouldn't I be?"

His gray eyes rested upon her intently. "You look a bit sad, that's all."

"There is no reason to be, is there? With all the livestock and other items Michael has brought, things couldn't be better," she said in an optimistic tone.

"Well, with the court case still pending, and the problems of the mortgage repayment, I thought you might be getting a bit despondent."

She shook her head.

But Lochlainn saw her pinched white face and the dark circles under her eyes. "Did you manage to sleep well last night?"

"I've been sleeping quite well," she lied.

Lochlainn knew for certain she was lying now. From his vantage point in the room next to her own, he had heard her whimpering on and off all night. Why was she behaving so oddly? Was her sleeplessness and dullness over the past few days symptomatic of grief, or was something else weighing on her mind?

He went into the kitchen and brought her back a cup of coffee, which he had laced with the sleeping mixture. Soon she was nodding off, and Lochlainn carried her up to bed. Loosening her dress, he tucked her in. He kissed her on the lips lingeringly, but berated himself for taking advantage of her. She would no doubt be horrified if she knew what he had been thinking. . . .

Again that night he heard her moan and cry. Holding his head in his hands, he forced himself not to go in to see her. To get into bed with her again would be completely wrong. She trusted him. He simply couldn't break that trust. He went into the room and spoke to her quietly from the doorway, not daring to move closer for fear of touching her, loving her. . . .

The next day was relatively uneventful, except that Muireann's payments for all her various enterprises came in when Patrick returned from town. She immediately paid off the other half of her debts to the creditors in town, wiping every slate clean, and then made further bargains for her produce and timber.

When Lochlainn saw her that night, she looked more contented than he had seen her for a while, but she was so weary her eyes were black with shadows. He knew she still got up at five or six every day. Even with the sleeping powder, she wasn't getting very much rest.

"Come now, my dear, you're absolutely done in," he said, taking her hand and leading her away from the shed where she had been helping with the milking. "I've got some sleeping powder for you. I want you to take it and get a good night's sleep."

Muireann's eyes widened in alarm. "No, really, I mustn't!"

"Muireann, this is ridiculous. You'll be no good to any of us if you collapse. Now please, for me, take the draught."

Muireann still looked disturbed, but in the end she obeyed his command and swallowed it in one gulp.

"Good girl," Lochlainn said, kissing her on the forehead.

Muireann put her arms around him briefly. She didn't dare admit how terrified she was of her nightmares. It would sound so silly, and she would have to admit the truth, which she wasn't even prepared to acknowledge to herself.

She was just about to let go of Lochlainn when her knees began to wobble, and his whole face swam before her eyes.

"God, I'm so tired," she murmured drowsily.

He swung her up into his arms and carried her up the stairs. He tugged down the covers with one hand before laying her down. Then he loosened the top buttons of her dress and tucked her in under the quilt.

"Sleep now, my dear."

She gazed up at him tenderly, stroking his lightly bristled cheek. "Thank you, Lochlainn."

"Don't mention it." He kissed her gently on the lips, then rose from the bed to close the shutters, and left her alone slumbering peacefully.

It seemed to Lochlainn that he had only just fallen asleep himself when he heard a shout from the next room. The nightmares again, he thought as he grabbed his trousers and shirt, yanking them on as he ran into the bedchamber next door. Muireann was thrashing about on the bed wildly. Lochlainn was terrified she might do herself an injury.

"It's me, Muireann, Lochlainn. Wake up!" he urged, shaking her by the shoulders.

But she continued to thrash about, so that he pinned her body down as she shouted, moaned and wailed like one possessed.

"No, don't! Don't! You can't! You'll be sorry, you'll see!" she shrieked over and over again.

At one point she even shouted, "Let me go!"

For a moment Lochlainn took her literally at her word, but then she jumped off the bed wild-eyed, and began tugging at the door handle as though she were trying to escape from some unseen terror in the room.

She didn't waken, but eventually, with Lochlainn's comforting arms around her, her wailing began to subside. She gulped and sniffed a few times, and soon her ragged breathing grew more even.

Lochlainn laid her down and got into the bed beside her, but for him sleep was elusive. He was stunned by her behavior. Why was she so disturbed by nightmares? Could it be she was reliving the horror of the hotel incident?

Despite himself, Lochlainn now began to wonder if it truly had been an accident, as he had told Father Brennan. Muireann had said the same, at the time. Surely she had nothing to hide, to reproach herself for, did she?

Ridiculous, he berated himself as he rose from the bed restlessly. It simply wasn't possible to think she had been to blame. Had shot him . . .

He went back into the chamber he had been using and removed the blankets from the straw mattress. He wrapped them around himself before pulling up the chair by the window. He sat down heavily and stroked her tousled hair back from her face.

As he looked at the young beauty in the dim glow of the fire, he knew she had to be completely innocent. It must have been the shock of seeing her beloved husband dead which had affected her mind. No doubt she tried hard to block out the vision of the gaping head wound during the day, but at night, it came back to haunt her.

Lochlainn now grew furious with himself for having ever thought that he might one day win her hand. How could he possibly wipe away the love she had obviously felt for Augustine? Not that the lout had deserved it, curse him, but Augustine and Christopher Caldwell always had had the damnedest luck. Alas, it hadn't rubbed off on him or his sister Ciara, who had begun acting strangely again, he recollected wearily. She'd been moody and odd ever since he'd told her he was going to stay up at the house for a time to keep an eye on Muireann.

Lochlainn must have eventually dozed off, for he awoke as the first rays of dawn were just filtering in through the cracks in the shutters. He straightened and found he had slumped forward, and been sleeping with his head next to Muireann's on the pillow.

Stiff as a board, he rose from the chair and dragged his blankets away. The last thing he wanted was for her to find him in her room.

For the next three days, Muireann seemed more rested, and appeared to be her normal calm self. But every night, he insisted she take the sleeping draught. And every night she turned into a wailing banshee. Lochlainn would run in and hold her until she calmed, and at last lay back on the pillow and slept soundly and peacefully.

He always forced himself to sit in the chair by her side. What if she should wake up and find him in the bed with her? It would be bad enough trying to explain what he was doing in her room.

He always made sure he left her chamber before she could waken, so that she would not feel embarrassed about his presence there. She seemed determined to deny that anything was wrong the few times he had tried to broach the subject. If anything, she grew more distant from him the closer he tried to get to her.

Muireann struggled desperately to pretend things were normal, but the more concerned Lochlainn got, the closer he got to her, the more she wanted him. She tried to tell herself it was wrong, unseemly. But they were such close companions in every other way. Surely hugging and kissing couldn't be so wrong? She had been brought up to believe that women who desired men that way were hussies, but her heart told her a different tale.

She looked at Patrick and Siobhan and the other married couples around the estate. They all seemed to be so happy, affectionate and loving towards one another. Why did she have to deny herself just because she had been deceived, and because of ridiculous class divisions? Muireann had met many men over the years, but never one with whom she could behave completely unreservedly. With Lochlainn, she could talk about anything, and usually did, but she made sure that they were seldom if ever alone, as they had been in the past.

I mustn't give in to the temptation, I mustn't, she thought with a shudder, as his hand rested on her shoulder perilously close to her breast at one point when they were out in the farmyard. *I want him, but what would he think of me?*

"Are you homesick?" he asked her, at a loss to explain her puzzling behavior. "Are you tired of Barnakilla already?"

He looked so sorrowful, Muireann quickly denied his suggestion, "No, not at all!"

"What is it, then?"

"What do you mean?"

"I can't understand you. You go off for hours at a time by yourself. I hardly ever see you, and then it's only in the kitchen with half the estate there. Please, I know there's something on your mind. Won't you confide in me? Perhaps I can help."

Muireann shook her head. "I have to do this on my own, Lochlainn. I told you, I don't want to be dependent upon you. I'm very grateful for all you've done, of course I am, but I need to be strong. Mr. Blessington's trial will be over soon, and then perhaps I'll feel more settled."

"I'm not doing it for the sake of your *gratitude*!" Lochlainn spat. "I care, Muireann, you know I do!"

"I know, or else you never would have come to Barnakilla to help out your sister and all of your old friends," she replied, mistaking his meaning.

"Damn Barnakilla!" he muttered under his breath, and stalked away before he made a complete fool of himself.

It was absurd. She felt only gratitude towards him. It would be a mistake ever to try to get close to her romantically. He wanted Muireann to want him for himself, not for the estate. But as soon as he framed these thoughts in his head, he realized how absurd it sounded.

"How could she ever want me? I'm the estate manager, nothing more," he muttered aloud.

Lochlainn went down to the timber cutting and took his frustrations out on a large number of tree trunks, until he was absolutely numb with exhaustion. Then he headed into town for some provisions, and stepped in at the doctor's on the way back to Barnakilla. He explained Muireann's odd behavior, and asked for Dr. Fredrickson's advice.

"It is a potent drug. It isn't really meant to allow the patient to dream, but perhaps Muireann is reacting to the narcotic. It might be giving her sick fancies. Give her less this time, just enough to make her drop off to sleep, but not enough to render her unconscious all night," Dr. Fredrickson advised.

"All right, doctor, I shall do as you say. I just hope she starts to improve soon. I'm very worried. I don't think she can take much more of this."

* * *

That night Lochlainn obeyed the doctor's instructions, giving her a small sleeping draught before seeing her safely upstairs to bed.

Totally exhausted himself by the hard work he had been carrying out during the day in the forest, as well as the long vigils he had been keeping every night, Lochlainn stripped off all his clothes wearily and collapsed onto his pallet.

At about two in the morning, Muireann's sleeping draught wore off, and she experienced the worst nightmares she had ever known.

First Augustine stood before her dripping gore, pointing an accusing finger at her.

Her next vision was of herself alone at Barnakilla, but it was more of a tomb than a mansion, dark and foreboding. She felt as though she had been buried alive in a desolate grave.

She called for help, and could sense movement in the shadows. It was Lochlainn, but he was abandoning her, leaving her alone with the terrible threatening presence she sensed but could not see.

Muireann shouted loud enough for all the county to hear as she was gripped by the terrifying dream.

"No, don't! Stop it, please!" she shrieked, struggling desperately against the tight grip which held her prisoner.

"No, I won't let you!" she bellowed as she twisted and turned, wrenching the covers off the bed as she tumbled to the floor, dragging her assailant with her.

"For God's sake, Muireann, it's me, Lochlainn! You're safe. There's nothing to fear. You're safe with me!" Lochlainn repeated over and over again, until at last she opened her eyes and saw her own little room, and Lochlainn's concerned face hovering over her.

"I thought I was . . . Oh, thank God you're here. I thought you'd left me," Muireann wept. She threw herself into his arms and kissed him full on the mouth.

Lochlainn stiffened for a moment. Was she really awake?

But as the kiss deepened, he decided he simply didn't care. His arms looped around her, hugging her tightly. His brain suddenly became acutely aware that the two of them had landed on the floor in a tangle of bare limbs. The kiss and the feel of her in his arms was simply too enticing for him to resist. His body, so long deprived, took over of its own accord.

Lochlainn struggled to control himself, but it was impossible. He had wanted her in his arms like this from the moment she had stepped off the ship from Scotland. He had been tormented night and day with fantasies of having her beg him not to leave her.

If anything, the reality was even more exciting than his imaginings. Though he might be damned for it on the morrow, he simply could not give up this one chance of making her his own. His mouth deepened the kiss possessively as he lifted her back onto the bed, and began to fondle her all over.

Muireann was fully awake by now, and aware of Lochlainn's every move, his every touch. Far from being dreadful or repellent as her sister Alice had described, this was the most thrilling experience she had ever encountered. Every kiss, every tender caress only left her wanting more. God knows she had struggled against her passion for Lochlainn desperately, but she wanted him. She didn't know why or how he had come to be in her room, but she was certain that this was what she desired above all else, even if she paid for it eventually. So much pleasure couldn't be so wrong, could it?

The merging of their minds, bodies and emotions was a cataclysmic one. Each strained with the effort of trying to get as close as possible to the other. Lochlainn tugged the top of her chemise down to her waist to feel her full feminine softness, and Muireann caressed his bare chest boldly.

In his hurry to reach her when she had begun to scream, Lochlainn hadn't had time to pull on anything more than a pair of breeches. She reveled in his smooth skin, and admired it as it gave off a creamy glow in the moonlight pouring in through the open shutters.

The seams of her gown began to strain as he fondled her, until she broke off the kiss long enough to disrobe. She then fingered the waistband of his trousers boldly, until he yanked them off impatiently and stretched out his full length on the bed beside her. He was sure she was awake now, and despite his compelling need for her, he wanted to hold back a bit longer, to savor the moment. He kissed her neck and breasts. She laced her fingers through Lochlainn's thick lush hair and sighed softly. He teased each rosy peak in turn, until she pulled him up for another kiss. Then, placing both her hands on his hips, she guided him to her.

They paused briefly to revel in the moment, kissing, stroking each other tenderly, until Muireann felt a moist burgeoning inside of her, an ache in her deepest core which only Lochlainn could satisfy. She ran her fingers through his light downy chest hair, marveling at its silky softness, before moving her hand lower until he gasped and positioned himself above her.

Muireann thought briefly about warning him of her untouched state, but the last thing she wanted to do was to have him treat her like a fragile doll. She had been a burden to him, a delicate porcelain figure, ever since they had first met in Dublin the month before.

But she was flesh and blood, with a mind of her own, and desires which, though unspoken, had raged inside of her ever since she had beheld his arrogantly handsome features at the Dun Laoghaire docks. So Muireann arched up to meet him, and bit back her cry as he pressed into her with one long hard stroke.

Muireann could sense Lochlainn struggling for control as he pressed ever deeper, the pleasure almost unbearable. Not since his fiancée had run off over three years before had he trusted himself to get so near to a woman. Now he wished he could hold back the tide, give her as much pleasure as she was giving him.

Muireann's gasps as he moved inside her proclaimed that she was certainly more than satisfied. Lochlainn tried to still his movements, but she tugged her lips away from his questing ones and begged, "Now, Lochlainn, please!"

She dug her fingernails into his back. Then he gave her his all, throbbing into her until he nearly shouted his joy for all the world to hear.

Afterwards, he pulled her over onto her side as he rolled over in the bed, and reached down to tug the covers up over them both. His huge hands, warm and firm, continued to stroke and explore her, until Muireann could feel all of the excitement building up inside herself again.

Lochlainn tried to hold back, stunned, never having experienced such passion before. But Muireann persuaded him otherwise, wrapping one leg around his waist, leaning into him until they joined again as one. Lochlainn stroked the long graceful curve of her back, and toyed with the luxurious fall of wavy hair that tumbled down Muireann's back in glorious disarray as he made love to her.

Muireann stroked his cheeks, planting kisses on his eyelids, before once again darting her tongue in and out of his mouth in imitation of what he had done to her. Nibbling his earlobes playfully, she felt Lochlainn began to shudder out of control again. She didn't wish to appear too eager, but she was perceptive enough to realize Lochlainn frequently felt inadequate around her. She wanted to give of herself, to show how important he was to her. She wanted to be powerful and alluring not only because of her wealth and social status, but also because of her attractiveness as a woman.

Lochlainn certainly couldn't seem to get enough of her, as he pulled away once or twice to prevent himself from giving in to his own pleasure. He turned her onto her back gently, and covered her body with his hands, stroking her gently, almost as though trying to memorize her every curve.

"Are you disappointed?" Muireann eventually worked up the courage to whisper, nervous at his intense scrutiny of her bare body and painfully aware of her own inexperience.

"How could I be? I've never seen anything lovelier in my life than you, Muireann. You ought to know that," he said sincerely as he bent to kiss each breast in turn.

He trailed hot molten kisses down her midriff, and gently turned her onto her stomach. Lochlainn began to stroke her back, and rubbed his lightly bristled cheek against her soft skin. He drank in her scent and warmth and softness like a parched desert flower drinking in rain.

Muireann shivered with the intensity of the pleasure his slightest touch gave. As his hand slipped between her thighs to caress her, she almost lost control.

Turning over into his arms, she pleaded, "Lochlainn, now! I need you now."

Lochlainn was shocked by her ardor, but was unable to resist her plea even had he wanted to. He stroked assuredly inside of her, until Muireann's face flushed and her breathing grew ragged. Lochlainn could see her struggling to subdue her emotions. Suddenly changing the rhythm to more powerful strokes, he urged in her ear, "Let it all go, Muireann."

Muireann's body responded to his new tempo of its own accord.

"Oh, Lochlainn!" she gasped, her eyes flying wide open as the miraculous sensations flooded through her from top to toe. She raked her fingernails down his back as she rode the crest of her passion, taking Lochlainn soaring with her.

At last, both lay completely fulfilled in each other's arms, and drifted off into a dreamless sleep.

Chapter Fourteen

With the cold light of day came the realization of what she had done. Muireann awoke to find herself alone in the bed. She would have almost thought the night of lovemaking she had shared with Lochlainn had been a dream had she not seen with her own eyes the ruined sheets, and smelt Lochlainn's unmistakable woodsy fragrance on the pillow she hugged to herself when she woke up. A pleasant ache between her thighs and in the pit of her belly reminded her of the incredible sensations Lochlainn had filled her with the night before.

But what would he think of her now? Surely he couldn't love her, could he? His heart had sustained irreparable damage when Tara had gone away. He had told her so himself. Muireann had allowed their friendship to deepen, knowing in what direction it had been heading. She had tried to resist treading the path of temptation, but had grown tired of denying her own needs and desires. Yet now that she found herself at her expected destination, what was she to do next?

In the end she decided to take her cue from Lochlainn. If he was cold, aloof and distant, she would be as well. If he showed the least sign of regret, they would simply have to pretend that none of it had happened. But what if he wanted more?

Muireann was no fool. The thought of an unwanted child filled her with cold dread. She padded over to her dressing table to tug on her robe, which she had left on the back of the chair, then took her brush and sat back on the bed with it. As she brushed her tumbled locks into some semblance of order, she reflected that although she would be delighted to have a child some day, this was certainly not the right moment.

What would her parents say? Or Alice? Enough time had elapsed for people to suspect the infant couldn't possibly be Augustine's, unless she said the child was very late. On the other hand, she might not even be pregnant at all, she thought.

"But then, of course, if the damage is already done . . ." she wondered aloud wistfully, but pushed that notion firmly to one side.

She rose from the bed to tug the bloodstained sheets off it, and rammed them into the bottom drawer of her dresser. The last thing she wanted was for Lochlainn to find out she had been a virgin and either reproach himself or pity her. It was bad enough he had had to look after her ever since he had arrived, she reflected as she went down the hall checking each room, and found his pallet.

So he *had* been keeping an eye on her. The knowledge rankled. The last thing she wanted was for Lochlainn to treat her like a child or an incompetent. She certainly didn't want to be a burden to him. She also knew a relationship based upon pity would never succeed in the long run.

No, Muireann wanted to prove to Lochlainn that she could stand on her own two feet, be independent. But did that necessarily have to exclude a romantic relationship with him? Did they even have enough in common to have a future together?

It was all so confusing, Muireann sighed as she began to remake the bed. The clock in the steeple of the nearby church struck eight, and at last she shook herself from her torpor. There was no need to make a decision right now. She would just have to see how things progressed. She was completely unsure what Lochlainn wanted, and it was not exactly the sort of question one came right out and asked.

When she saw him next, she would be politely friendly, but not terribly intimate with him, Muireann determined as she finished tucking the sheets under the mattress. At any rate, she and Lochlainn had far too much work to do to be spending time billing and cooing with one another. With the weather growing warmer, the planting season would progress apace. There was also the tree cutting, bread making, milking, egg rounds, trips to market, sewing, and all of the other chores they both did around Barnakilla.

Lochlainn, too, was distant, unable to believe he had had the temerity to take advantage of Muireann's desperate plight when she had turned to him for comfort. He prayed she wouldn't send him away for his disgraceful conduct.

Even worse was the knowledge that he still wanted her. Making love to her had been like trying a new, addictive, powerful drug. Every time her amethyst eyes gazed at him, he wanted to kiss her senseless. His relationship with Tara had never been like this, he thought with alarm, wondering if what he felt for Muireann could be true love. He had been fascinated by Tara, yet now he could barely even recall what she looked like.

It was awful to have tasted the joys he and Muireann had shared together, yet never be able to have her for himself. He was convinced he would one day wake up to find she had gone, just as Tara had disappeared. Worse still, she might wake beside him full of regrets and tell him she never wanted to see him again. He had risked everything because of his uncontrollable desires: his home, his friendship with Muireann, his livelihood.

Thus Lochlainn, full of guilt, shame, and fear, avoided Muireann, even when other people were around.

He thinks it was a mistake, she reflected miserably, and in turn began to avoid him as well.

How could I have been such a fool, she groaned in the privacy of her own room later that day, and shed a few bitter tears into her pillow. Muireann had never known desire could be so acute, so compelling. The more she told herself it was impossible, the more she seemed to want him. She had opened a door within herself, had experienced a burst of freedom such as she had never known before, only to have her desires and needs curbed and shackled once again, as they had always been.

A busy week at the farm prevented Muireann from brooding, however, and she knew it would serve no purpose to look downcast in front of the others. She tried to maintain a cheerful front, and worked harder than ever to get Barnakilla back on its feet.

As February turned to March, the days lengthened and the weather improved. Muireann found herself restless, and kept taking on more and more new projects. She knew it was because she was filled with the joys of spring, but it was also to avoid any chance of seeing Lochlainn unless absolutely necessary.

One bright sunny afternoon Muireann decided to check her prize horses and perhaps take one of them for some exercise herself.

She was just finishing loading oats into the feeding troughs when Lochlainn came into the stable.

"Oh, sorry, I didn't know you were here," he apologized, about to beat a hasty retreat.

"That's all right. Stay here and talk with me for a moment." Muireann smiled timidly as she sat down on a bale of hay.

Lochlainn looked at her warily and then shook his head. "No, no, I mustn't stop. I'm just about to finish that sideboard for the colonel, and I was coming to harness the horses to take it over to him, if that's all right with you."

"Of course it is. You don't need to ask permission to use the wagon, you know."

"I thought you might have needed it yourself."

"To pay all my social visits?" she laughed.

Lochlainn colored. "I know this must be hard for you, not what you're used to at all, of course, Mrs. Caldwell," he said stiffly, and fled the barn.

Once she was alone, Muireann wondered if that perhaps was Lochlainn's whole problem, why he had been avoiding her. Perhaps he couldn't get around the fact that she had been genteelly brought up, and had doubts as to how she would cope at Barnakilla. *He thinks I am going to disappear back into that vain and empty world, doesn't he? After all, Tara did.*

Determinedly, Muireann lifted a rake and began to muck out one of the stalls. She did some serious soul-searching there amongst the piles of steaming manure. Did she really want to revert back to her old lifestyle, a never-ending round of parties and soirees full of dull people who were only interested in meaningless small talk, and in puffing up their already inflated opinions of themselves?

I'm happy here, she suddenly realized, and laughed aloud. Despite all the hardship, trials and tribulations she had undergone, all the hard work and sacrifices, she was indeed happy.

And I have Lochlainn to thank for that. He had faith in me, he guided me, looked after me. . . . So now it's up to me to make sure I make this place a success, she reflected, as she finished in the stables and then went up to the house to begin the evening meal.

Brona and Sharon were already in the kitchen when she

arrived. She began cutting up vegetables and peeling potatoes as though she had done it all her life.

The two women exchanged glances with each other behind Muireann's back, but said nothing. They would have liked to voice their newfound admiration for the woman whom they had first believed would be vain and spoilt, but somehow it seemed rude. At least they were not reluctant to praise her amongst themselves when the tenants all gathered together at the end of the day for a cup of tea and a gossip.

Most evenings, Muireann finished up her share of the sewing and wisely withdrew, stating that she had to update the books. She liked all of the people she met at Barnakilla, and had grown very fond of Brona, Sharon, and Siobhan and her husband Patrick. All the same, she could sense their reserve in front of her.

Wiping her hand on her apron as she suddenly recalled she was meant to be helping to churn the butter that night for market in Clogher early the next morning, Muireann scurried out of the kitchen, almost barreling into Lochlainn's broad chest.

He grabbed her by the elbows as she brought herself up short and slipped, and held her to him tightly for a moment before apologizing gruffly and releasing her.

Muireann glanced at his retreating back and ran on to the barn, trying to suppress the desire coursing through her veins.

Lochlainn entered the kitchen unobserved, and overheard Brona commenting to Sharon about how handy Muireann had become in the kitchen.

"I never would have thought she would have stuck it a day, let alone a month. And she seems to be deft at everything she turns her hand to."

"And she can read and write," Sharon remarked enviously. "I wish I could do my letters and suchlike as easily as she."

"I'm sure she'll teach you if you ask. She's been talking about setting up a proper school for the children as soon as things are a bit more settled. You know, I always heard Scotchy people were very cold and haughty, but she isn't, now, is she?"

"Not at all. She has us call her Muireann at the sewing circles, and though we none of us are very good with a needle, she's very patient with us."

"What do you think of her making us all new dresses for the summer?" Brona asked excitedly. "Have you got measured yet?"

"Not yet, but you should see the pattern she drew for me. It's like something out of them social papers about what the queen and all get up to," Sharon marveled.

Lochlainn listened pensively to their praise of Muireann, and then moved closer to the fire.

"So you think she is happy here? That she would want to stay?" he asked the two women.

"Heaven help us if she doesn't," Brona said. "I've heard tell that with the new government taxes, a great number of the landlords won't be able to keep up. That they are going to evict all their tenants. If Muireann goes, we'll be walking the roads just like the rest of them poor souls."

"Where did you hear that rumor?" he asked sharply.

"I heard it the other day at the market when I went to sell some of those wooden bowls and things you and the other men have made. They said the English government had increased the taxes and were expecting the landlords to pay by head. The men and women were to be charged one rate, and two children would make a grown-up rate," Brona informed him.

Lochlainn frowned as he did some quick calculations. "There are a hundred of us here. If that is true, Muireann will have to come up with a very large amount of cash quite soon."

Brona and Sharon exchanged alarmed glances.

Lochlainn stood up from his chair by the fire and declared, "Well, there's no sense in talking about it now. We'll just have to wait and see, won't we?"

The two women nodded, but suddenly the kitchen had turned unaccountably gloomy. The women called the workers into dinner a great deal less cheerfully than was their wont. The rumor went around quickly despite Lochlainn's charge not to worry. It cast a pall over the whole room.

After supper was finished, rather than lingering to do sewing or carving, one by one they all began to drift back home to their cold lonely cottages, to lie down and sleep until the rooster would summon them to another arduous day's labor early the next morning.

Lochlainn noticed Muireann had not come in for her stew. Against his better judgment, he went in search of her. He knew she had made a great many sacrifices to try to make her plans work, but what of these new taxes? Had all their efforts been in vain?

And more to the point, was Muireann happy? Lochlainn had admired for a long time how she turned her hand to anything that needed doing on the estate without a word of complaint, no matter how difficult or disgusting the task.

But she was young, wealthy in her own right. If she were ever willing to go back to her father in Scotland and confess her financial woes, she would most certainly be taken back into the bosom of her family. She could marry well, leave all of this behind, or perhaps even marry someone who would be willing to take over Barnakilla for her.

The thought of Muireann marrying again suddenly filled him with inexplicable dread. He hurried down to the milking shed, anxious to see her again.

Muireann looked up in surprise as Lochlainn declared, "I need to speak with you about the estate."

"Fine. I was just finishing here. Give me a moment," she said, hoping her voice didn't betray the strain she felt. She completed the churning and handed over the butter paddles to Siobhan, who had come in to check that everything was ready for the trip to Clogher in the morning.

Then she led the way up to the house, untying her apron and tugging her kerchief off to shake out her raven tresses. She felt nervous around him and wished she could go back to the long, easy chats they had always had with each other before that fateful night which now seemed so long ago.

Only a few short days before, they had been able to work side by side compatibly for hours on end, in tune with each other's thoughts. Now he was like a stranger.

Are all men completely untrustworthy? Muireann wondered sadly.

She led him into the study and sat at the desk. "Well, what's wrong? Is it a problem with the ledgers?"

"No, not really. It's more to do with a rumor I just heard in the kitchen about new taxes."

"It's not a rumor, it's true," Muireann said, looking away from his blazing steel-gray eyes.

Lochlainn exploded. "Why didn't you tell me?"

"We haven't exactly been on speaking terms recently, have we?" she said quietly, the hurt evident in her voice.

Lochlainn ran a finger under his suddenly too tight neck cloth. "I've been busy."

"As have I. Besides, there didn't seem much point in making a fuss at this point in time. With the trial set for the thirteenth, there's just a little more than a week until we get a clearer picture of what will happen to us. I suggest we wait until then before we panic."

"But the trial could go on for weeks. You know that as well as I do!"

She sat back in her chair wearily. "I'm sorry, Lochlainn,

but the taxes are so high, I can't really give you any good news. We could sell some of the livestock, and try to get Neil to liquidate any more shares I might own. Of course, we could always sell a field or two to Mr. Stephens."

"You can't be serious!"

Muireann waved aside his objections impatiently. "I know all about the long-standing feud between the two families, but really, it doesn't concern me. We can't eat the grass ourselves, can we? And what good will it do if the government arrests me for debt? So I'll sell the field if I can't find any other way around the problem."

"We could sell the tree plantation on the northeastern side of the property," Lochlainn suggested almost desperately.

"Aye, but what will we live on if we curtail the timber business? It's the same problem with the animals. If we sell them, we haven't got anything to keep the estate profitable. I'd get a good price for the mare and stallion, but wouldn't it be better to keep them, and sell their offspring?"

"You're right, of course, but everything seems to take time, which is the one thing we don't have very much of at the moment."

She gave him a tight smile. "I know. But I don't want to hamstring myself further down the line by making a snap decision on the basis of only a few suppositions. Look, I know you're tired, Lochlainn. You and I have been working all sorts of ungodly hours ever since we arrived back here. Now to be told it might all have been in vain, well, it's insupportable."

The pair lapsed into silence for a moment, until Muireann remarked quietly, "There is one other possible solution, though it is no good getting our hopes up at this point."

Lochlainn frowned. "I'm not sure what you're trying to tell me."

"I'm not sure myself."

"What do you mean?"

Muireann sighed. "I've found some property deeds for a house Augustine bought a couple of years ago in Dublin."

"A *house*? In Dublin?"

"So you know nothing about it either," Muireann said uneasily.

"No, not a thing," Lochlainn admitted, not caring how inadequate it made him seem.

"Well, I think it should be sold. The current tenant is listed as a Mrs. Barnet. If she is willing to take a first option out on it, the money we get would not only help us with the taxes, but also towards realizing the sum the bank is demanding as back payment on the mortgage."

"It is better than selling the fields, certainly, but—"

"Yes, I know—even if Mrs. Barnet were in a position to buy the place straight away, we still wouldn't get the money for quite some time. Besides, how do we know it hasn't been mortgaged already, and I just haven't been able to find the documents somewhere in this mess of papers?"

"It will all get sorted out eventually," Lochlainn reassured her, trying to sound cheerful despite the leaden weight on his heart.

She leafed through the papers once more. "Well, I think I should go up to Dublin to investigate the matter and see what can be done."

"Surely you don't have to go now, Muireann," Lochlainn argued, loath to part with her. "Why not make preliminary inquiries by post first?"

"Aye, I will. I wouldn't like to be away from the estate too long. Not when there is so much to do. But in the meantime, there's no need for you to worry too much, Lochlainn. We're just about keeping our heads above water at the moment."

"That's so long as no unforeseen disaster occurs," Lochlainn grumbled.

"Touch wood as you say that," Muireann said superstitiously, tapping her finger on the desk. "It will be a struggle, but with the livestock, which will no doubt breed, and the occasional useful wedding present coming in, I think we'll do fine."

"Muireann, about selling the house in Dublin . . ."

"Well?" she asked, raising her eyes from her papers to look at him.

Lochlainn had to swallow hard past the lump in his throat to get the words out. "Do you not think you might be better off selling Barnakilla, and living in Dublin? Look at the life you're leading here, with nothing but hardship and toil. You could be the belle of Dublin society if you sold this place. After all, it's only a burden to you."

Muireann sensed he was testing her. She rose from her chair and went over to where he was sitting and put her arm around his shoulder. She sat in his lap and declared softly, "I'm the one who's been a burden to you. I'll try not to be anymore, I promise. You've been a huge help. I'm so grateful I can't even begin to tell you how much. So don't ever talk about me going to be the toast of Dublin society. My family and friends are all here now."

Lochlainn longed to believe her, but he couldn't quite suppress his doubts. Nor could he suppress his desires as he took her lips in a soul-stirring kiss. He nuzzled her ear and murmured, "Are you finished with business for tonight?"

"Aye."

"Then what about some pleasure?"

Muireann met his eyes, and melted. She rose from his lap, kissing him lingeringly, then took his hand to tug him to his feet. Blowing out the candles on the desk, she and Lochlainn walked up the stairs with their arms around each other's waists. Once in her room, she turned to face him, and they tumbled into each other's arms, barely able to make it to the bed, so overwhelming was their passion for one another.

"Muireann, I'm sorry about—" Lochlainn began, stroking the petal soft skin of her stomach.

Muireann silenced him with a kiss. "No more words, Lochlainn. When we talk, all we ever seem to do is disagree."

"But surely you'll regret this one day," he sighed, pressing his cheek against hers as he held her tightly and felt desire burning within him.

"I don't want to think about the future. When I'm here like this with you, Lochlainn, I just want the here and now," she breathed, rolling him onto his back and lying atop him.

Desire raged within them both, and Lochlainn wondered how it was possible to yearn for Muireann even in the throes of their passion. Their devouring kisses, ardent strokes, all seemed so satisfying, yet frustrating at the same time.

He had been passionately involved with Tara, or so he'd thought. But this went beyond passion, to near obsession. He rolled her over onto the sweat-soaked sheets and tasted every inch of her flesh, until her head rolled from side to side. She clutched his hair and cried out his name, arching up off the bed so violently that she nearly hurled him onto the floor. He hung on hard, and joined with her at last. Their climax was explosive, all-encompassing, a plea for love and understanding, and above all for a future they could hardly dare to guess at. But knew they could never endure without the other.

When at last she had calmed, he held her close and felt tears on her cheeks.

Muireann laughed then and kissed him, opening her arms like an enveloping blanket to warm the dark chilly night, and they settled down to sleep. Lochlainn told himself it was too good, an incredible dream that was bound to come to an end sooner or later. Like Tara, Muireann would fly, too.

* * *

He struggled hard to keep away from her the next day, but the following night, unable to sleep, he paced up and down the cottage floor until at last he flung open the door and made his way to the kitchen of the big house. Taking a candle from a holder by the door, he searched for Muireann in the study and library, and at last made so bold as to ascend to her room. There she was just banking the fire, clad only in her nightdress. Her heavy hair fell loosely about her shoulders, and she smiled invitingly as he entered.

"I was hoping you'd come," she said with a soft smile. She ran into his arms, and wrapping both her arms and legs about him she tumbled him onto the bed joyously.

Chapter Fifteen

The affair between Muireann and Lochlainn continued unabated throughout the whole of March. Both wondered how long it could endure without their having to face the consequences, but neither was willing to give up the other. It became an unspoken rule between them never to talk about the future.

As the days passed, Lochlainn realized that he was a little intimidated by the daytime Muireann, so cool, calm and rational. He wanted, nay, needed to keep that Muireann separate from the woman he held in his arms during the night when, unable to help himself, he went to her room to seek a few hours' solace in her company.

Muireann, too, wanted to treat the Lochlainn who came to her in the night differently from the daily companion with whom she shared all of her triumphs and trials. They had to deal with a million and one problems during the day. Together they ran the businesses and tried to balance the books, but the night was a magical time for them as, hovering between sleeping and waking, their lovemaking took on a life all its own.

Nothing was too daring or shocking as they explored each other, laughed, and loved unreservedly until the first rosy rays of dawn came to flood their secret retreat from the rest of the world. But all too soon, the rooster would summon them to their never-ending round of chores. They would give each other one last warm kiss, then have nothing but their memories to hug close until the next time they were able to snatch a few precious hours alone together.

Lochlainn tried not to think about the future, but he felt he could never be certain of Muireann always being there by his side. A ship might come from Scotland with her father on it, and she would vanish without a trace. Yet while she was with him, he was determined to enjoy every second they could be with each other. Often he made love to her desperately, almost as though it were the last time.

Lochlainn waited for her to tell him it was over, that she had made a mistake, without realizing that through his mistrust, he might help to bring about the fulfillment of his own prophecy and one day drive her away.

Muireann also tried not to think about their future, but she wondered how it would all end. She loved Lochlainn, she was sure. But how on earth could they ever be happy together? No sooner did they manage to surmount one problem when another took its place.

Moreover, Lochlainn always seemed so sure that he wasn't good enough for her. And she was sure he compared her to Tara continually. Muireann's awareness of her inexperience, and the insecurity that resulted, also served to drive a wedge between them. She believed Tara had been the one great love of Lochlainn's life, and that she was merely a friend, a companion, someone for Lochlainn to pass the lonely nights with.

Muireann dealt with the crisis of the tax money by selling every single luxury item that had come in the shipment from Scotland. She even parceled up the coffee into brown paper wrappers to sell at the various markets. Lochlainn gave Patrick the money for two of the packets, and gave one of them to Muireann as a present, saving the other for her birthday on the thirtieth of April.

"Really, you shouldn't have," she said, kissing him warmly.

"Now we're even. You shouldn't have kept the sideboard," he said with a grin, pointing to where it stood in her bedroom.

She smiled shyly. "It was too beautiful to sell without a second thought. You made it with your own two hands, and it reminds me of you, and the first night I ever came here."

"I would hardly think you needed a reminder of that horrible time. As for reminding you of me, isn't the real thing good enough?" he teased, tickling her so that she wriggled in his arms and laughed up at him.

"More than good enough," she said, kissing him lingeringly.

Ciara came into the chamber at that moment looking for advice, and they separated abruptly.

His sister frowned her disapproval of their behavior, and did whatever she could to discourage her brother from spending time alone with Muireann.

Muireann couldn't blame her. She was simply worried about her brother getting hurt again. All the same, though, it didn't bode well for their relationship if his only living relative didn't approve of her. What her own family would say if they knew about Lochlainn, she didn't even dare contemplate.

* * *

By the end of March, some of the money Mr. Blessington had stolen was returned to her. Muireann spent most of it on paying off part of the mortgage and most of the taxes, and the rest went for new livestock, especially sheep for wool. They were sturdy beasts and could graze even on the worst ground on the estate. For a time she began to feel optimistic that things were finally starting to take a turn for the better.

But stunning new developments occurred in the middle of April, when Mr. Cole, her neighbor to the southeast, announced that he would be converting all his farmland to sheep pasture, and served eviction notices on every one of his tenants.

Even worse, Colonel Lowry, her neighbor to the north, was prepared to pay the passage money for all of his workers to go to Canada, so that he could avoid paying the high taxes which the government had imposed. The taxes were based upon large numbers of tenants who were supposedly paying vast rents for their tiny cottages and minute potato plots.

"The Devon Commission calculated the rents coming in early in 1841, before the potato crop failed that October," Lochlainn explained to Muireann as she sat at her desk trying to make sense of their own tax figures.

"They added up all the rents that were on the books then, without even taking into account the amount of arrears owed. Some of the people have left, some have died since, and of course, more children are born all the time, which boosts the tax figure even higher. Unfortunately, the women and children don't bring much money or wealth into the family, so there are more and more mouths to feed, and thus less cash. That's why the colonel and Mr. Cole are cutting their losses now, before the situation reaches crisis point in another few years' time."

"But where will their tenants go? What will they do? Sheep are all very well and fine, but you need people to work with them, shear them, card and dye the wool, and spin it into cloth!" Muireann exclaimed. "Or herd them and slaughter them for food."

Lochlainn advanced from the doorway where he had been standing. He looked more grim than she had ever seen him.

"I can't believe this is happening!" he declared as he flung himself into a chair dejectedly.

"I know this must be hard for you, Lochlainn. I'm sorry."

He sighed and rubbed his eyes wearily. "I've known many of those people since I was a boy. Some of them are far too old. They can't emigrate. Most of them would never survive the passage! It's like signing their death warrants. Even if they do survive the passage, what then? They'll have to try to make a fresh start in a land very different from their own. It is too horrible even to think of. I certainly know how hard it was in Australia. I wouldn't wish that fate on anyone."

"But you were successful," Muireann pointed out.

"I worked damned hard, but a lot of it was luck, as well. How lucky are all of them going to be? More and more emigrants are heading for the New World all the time."

Muireann listened carefully to Lochlainn's bitter tone, and looked down at the figures in front of her pensively. Then she put the ledger to one side, and laid a fresh sheet of paper on the blotter.

"How many are there on the colonel's estate?"

"A hundred or thereabouts."

"And on Mr. Cole's?"

"About the same, maybe a few more."

"Out of these people, how many of them have any skills, you know, carpentry and so on?"

Lochlainn scratched his head thoughtfully. "I don't know.

My guess is most of them are farmers, but there must be some carpenters and builders, I'm sure."

"From both estates?"

He frowned, puzzled. "I think so. But why are you asking?"

Muireann checked her calculations carefully before replying. "Because I want them to come and live here."

He half rose from his chair. "Are you mad? We could never—"

"I know what you're going to say, Lochlainn. Please hear me out before you fly off the handle completely. I know it won't be easy for us here at Barnakilla, but in a few weeks' time those poor people will either be homeless on the road, or dying on the long trip over to Canada. These are men, women and children we are talking about. If we take them in—"

"We couldn't even begin to feed them all with the way things are at the moment!"

"I'll find a way, even if I have to beg, borrow or steal."

Lochlainn rounded on her angrily. "Why should you care? You could just go home to Scotland tomorrow!"

Muireann blinked in surprise. "That's not fair, Lochlainn, and you know it. I could run away, of course, but I'm not going to. Barnakilla is the first real home I have ever had, and all should be welcome here if they wish to come. The estate will thrive. It just takes time. I'll go to Dublin, get the house sold, and we will just have to keep on making sacrifices until we get the money those men stole. Then we'll thrive even more, I'm certain of it.

"Please be patient, Lochlainn. It's not an easy decision, but you just said it yourself. To send them to Canada would be like signing their death warrants."

"But how will we feed them all?"

"The first thing we will do is calculate the wealth they

bring with them, if any, the same as we did with the tenants here. Then we set a fair rent for them and chores to do. I still have a tiny bit of the money Colonel Lowry awarded us from Blessington's holdings. We can buy some oats, vegetables, potatoes, and corn meal with it. We'll have to cut down on the butter to increase our milk yield. If there are as many children as you say, we'll need the extra milk.

"We also need more turf, more firewood, more meat and fish. I know Neil will send more food from Scotland as soon as the timber ship comes for another load. We can sell any luxury items like coffee, tea or wine and brandy immediately to buy staples. We'll have to think ahead to harvest time now as well.

"Forget the crop rotation scheme we devised. I want you to start plowing up all the fallow fields and planting more turnips and beets. They will get the animals and people through the winter. Clear the land of tree stumps where we have already been timber-cutting, and put it under cultivation also," Muireann outlined for Lochlainn.

He sat there numbly shaking his head. This was yet another burden for them to face. How much longer could they survive like this? How much longer would it be until she gave up and went back to Scotland?

Muireann made a few notes on her paper, and looked at him hopefully. "Now if Colonel Lowry and Mr. Cole have really made up their minds about enclosing their lands, I'm going to go see them both to make a deal to sell their wool to me. You and your carpenters can make some spinning wheels and looms, and we are going to make cloth, lots of woolen cloth. All of the women will pitch in, while the men will carry on with the farming, hunting, fishing and carpentry. We'll also need to quarry more stone for new cottages to be built straightaway. Once the new people arrive, they can rotate into the chores system."

"What else do you think we need?" he asked quietly, feeling slightly piqued that she seemed to have worked out everything without even consulting him or listening to his objections to the whole scheme.

Muireann continued jotting down her ideas, one hand cradling her head. "I want to clear more trees now so we can season the timber. We can use it for furniture, or a new load of wood if Neil is willing to buy more. And I want some strong sturdy rabbit and pheasant pens built. We'll start breeding them ourselves from now on. And if you see a big stag, try to trap rather than kill it, and capture some does as well. We could begin to breed them."

Then she sighed. "There are probably a hundred other things we will have to take care of once they're here. But in the meantime, that is enough for everyone to be getting started with. The only other thing is to get more fertilizer from somewhere. And I think perhaps it is possible to start working around the clock on the estate. You know, divide the workers into three or four groups, get them to work eight or six hours each. But we will have to wait and see what skills and talents they possess before we make any decisions about that."

Lochlainn stared at Muireann as though seeing her for the first time.

"What is it? What have I said?" Muireann said sharply.

"Nothing, nothing. I just can't believe you would do all this for people you don't even know."

"The wealth of Ireland is in her people, in the land. I won't let those men, women, and children be made homeless due to the appalling greed of their landlords and the government, any more than I would have let you all suffer for Augustine's mistakes."

This was the first time in a long time that she had mentioned Augustine's name in Lochlainn's hearing. She stood up suddenly and began to pace the room.

Lochlainn watched her uncomfortably for a few minutes, wondering why she was so disturbed.

Suddenly she ordered, "I want a detail of people to come in here now to make these rooms habitable. Get the carpenters to make as many bedsteads as they can. We can get some oyster shells to burn to make whitewash for the rooms to help keep the damp out. The weather has been fine, so I want to make sure all the holes in the roof are patched, and the chimneys cleared. Hire a proper sweep from Enniskillen tomorrow so he can get started.

"I also want the library and the study cleaned, and I shall give up my room upstairs as well. And we will need more long benches and tables for the kitchen. We'll have to work day and night, but we can take the first of the new arrivals at the end of the week."

"I don't understand. What are you talking about? Why give up your room? Where would you go?"

"If they come here, we're all casting our lot in together, are we not? So they will come live here, in every spare room we can find. I'll move into the small storeroom next to the agent's office at the back of the stable block. We shall leave the big house to the newcomers."

"But think of the sacrifice, my dear."

"I don't care. They need somewhere to stay, and we could fit a whole family in each of the rooms I use by myself."

"This is meant to be your home. I will not have you living like a pauper!"

"It is my decision, Lochlainn," Muireann snapped back. "You aren't making me do anything I don't want to do."

Lochlainn rose from his chair then and pulled her to him. His blistering kiss sapped their fury instantly, and within seconds they had tumbled onto the small sofa and begun stripping their lower clothing off in a frenzy of desire. For half an hour the only sounds that could be heard were their moans and sighs of contentment, but all too soon Lochlainn recalled his resolution not to take advantage of her in this way, not to impinge upon her daytime self.

He hastily adjusted his clothing, embarrassed, and with a last kiss, fled from the room. Lochlainn prayed Muireann hadn't noticed his hands shaking as he reached for the catch to let himself out.

She pulled her skirts down over her knees and sat on the sofa staring after him as he ran.

His sister noticed something was amiss almost as soon as he got home. After revealing his momentous news about the evictions and Muireann's offer to support the other estates' tenants and make arrangements to have them live in the house, she asked, "What's really troubling you, Lochlainn?"

He sat down at the kitchen table and put his head in both hands. "I'm afraid that this is all a dream. That Muireann is too good to be true. After all, she married Augustine, didn't she? What if all this is just a passing fancy for an idle rich girl? What if she grows bored with it? Abandons us for the bright lights of Dublin, London, or beyond?" Lochlainn wondered, his frustration evident on his handsome face.

Ciara digested this information in silence, and then looked at her brother directly. "That isn't what's really worrying you either."

"All right, all right, I'll tell you. I'll go mad if I don't tell someone. I just can't get the thought out of my head that I'm going to lose her. I'm obsessed by her. No matter what, I can't get Muireann out of my mind. Every moment of the day and night, sleeping or waking, I think about her. I can't help myself, Ciara, though God knows I've tried."

His sister looked at him stonily for a few moments, but then began to relent, moving closer to him to hear him out.

"But it would never work! It is ridiculous to ever imagine she could be happy here living in a hovel. I worship the ground she walks on, but it's completely absurd to imagine she could ever care about someone like me."

"We don't really have any control over whom we fall in love with, now do we?" Ciara observed bitterly.

"Love? Who said anything about love? I was in love once, remember, and she betrayed me," Lochlainn growled.

Ciara sighed, and sat down beside her brother on the bench. "First of all, Lochlainn, the only person Tara ever loved was herself. I never did understand what you saw in her. She set her sights on you one day, and you never even knew what hit you until she was gone. It was all an illusion. She liked power, but she never loved you, trusted you, gave of herself. You say you loved her, but I think she held you in thrall with her feminine wiles. I think you're in love with Muireann, deeply in love, but you're afraid of being betrayed by her because of the terrible experience you had with Tara.

"But don't assume all women are the same. Compare the two of them, and ask yourself if there are any similarities, any warning signs that would cause you to fear," Ciara advised. "If you have no reason to mistrust Muireann, then just accept what you have together and be thankful for it, without trying to analyze it all the time. Enjoy it while it lasts, without being fearful all the time that it's going to come to an end. Besides, how do you know she couldn't care about you, unless you asked her?"

"Don't be silly. I couldn't talk to her about something like this! At any rate, I know how Muireann feels. I saw her hysterically weeping over Augustine when he died. She loved him, though God knows why. She's grateful to me for my help and support. But love? It's impossible."

Ciara shook her head. "All right, I'm not going to argue with you about words. I just want to ask you one question. Imagine yourself in five years' time, or ten. Where would you like to be, and what would you like to be doing? If you can see Muireann being at your side as part of it, then you belong together, and you do love her. If not, then you're better off letting her go on without you. If you don't really care about her, don't trifle with her feelings and lead her on. Just stay away from her."

Lochlainn propped his chin up on both stacked fists. "I do care. I care too much. I can't bear to have her lose her house because of my ideas. I convinced her to come here in the first place. Things have gone from bad to worse ever since. If we can't keep our heads above water, we'll lose everything, and all of Muireann's hard work and sacrifice will have been for nothing."

Lochlainn outlined for his sister the plans Muireann had for the house, making his disapproval of her scheme all too clear.

"Please, Lochlainn, be practical for a moment, won't you? Even if everyone here at Barnakilla were willing to double or triple up in their cottages, how would all the new tenants fit in?"

Lochlainn scowled silently, but finally he shrugged. "I suppose it is only bricks and mortar. We'll build cottages and give all these people new homes."

His sister smiled encouragingly. "Barnakilla is nothing but a draughty old place, isn't it?"

"Thank you, Ciara. I'm glad you're such a sensible creature. You've always stopped me from doing rash things."

"Falling in love is rash, but I think she'll be good for you if the two of you really love each other," Ciara said, a strange expression crossing her wan features.

"But she doesn't love me. She's only just been widowed. She's just turning to me for comfort, that's all."

Ciara shook her head. "You make Muireann sound weak and feeble. She's proven herself strong time and time again. She isn't leaning on you because she has to; it's because she wants to be with you."

She paused and blushed to the roots of her hair. "I've noticed what time you've been getting in each morning recently, Lochlainn. Just remember, a woman never gives herself where she doesn't love, unless she's forced to do it because of his brute strength or her financial desperation. There is no obligation for her to spend the night with you, now is there?"

"No, you're right about that, but again, I just think it's because being a young widow . . ."

"I'm not going to continue this conversation," Ciara said, coloring to the roots of her hair as she stood up and began to fold some sheets. "All I'm saying is, if you want Muireann to move in here with us, you have only to let me know."

"I couldn't possibly ask her," Lochlainn said with a shake of his head. "She plans to move into the stable block."

"Well, perhaps it's best to let Muireann do it her way. She has a rather annoying habit of always being right."

"I know you and Muireann aren't exactly the best of friends. . . ." he said tentatively.

"That's been all my fault. I'll try harder to like her."

Lochlainn wondered why she looked so nervous. But he was also relieved that at last his sister was starting to act a bit more like her old self. She was far less moody and prone to strange spells of odd behavior now that she was working for Muireann, overseeing the running of the kitchen and the purchasing of provisions. Muireann had encouraged her gradually to take on more and more responsibility around Barnakilla, and Lochlainn prayed that she wouldn't suffer any setbacks.

As Lochlainn trudged over to the nearby row of cottages to put the work details together to start preparing for the new arrivals, he wondered for the hundredth time that day why his life had to be so complicated, and what he would ever do without Muireann by his side. He might have disagreed with her in the study about the extra burdens she was imposing upon herself to help Colonel

Lowry's and Mr. Cole's tenants. At the same time, he knew if their roles had been reversed, he would have done exactly the same thing. Pray God they didn't all suffer for it in the long run.

Chapter Sixteen

By the end of the week, all of Muireann's preparations for welcoming the new residents to Barnakilla were well under way. Though many on the estate had reservations about what Muireann was doing, they saw that she had made the offer to the homeless people out of the kindness of her own heart, rather than with any intent to exploit them. With Lochlainn's encouragement, they all decided it was up to every single one of them to make it work, for all their sakes. They had cast their lots with their new landlady, and would see the thing through to prosperity or ruin.

For her part, Muireann had a new scheme in mind to build up the estate.

Her first call was at Colonel Lowry's estate, Castle Lowry. The property was a farm similar to her own, near to the shore, but much more hilly, and with no easy access to the lough.

The house itself was quite gloomy, the original seventeenth-century mansion having been remodeled as a Gothic castle in 1803, according to the colonel, who gave her a small tour of the downstairs before ushering her into a splendid drawing room. It was oak-paneled, with burgundy flocked wallpaper and a variety of leather sofas and fine occasional tables dotted all around the room. Muireann noted the splendid view of the grounds from the mullioned windows with a touch of envy. But certainly the most impressive features of the room were the dozens of magnificent pictures on the wall.

Muireann tried to subdue her anger as she looked at each old masterpiece. Why, the sale of one painting alone would have paid the taxes, without the eviction of any of his tenants. But she needed this man's help. Venting her spleen at his injustice was not going to secure it for her.

"I'm just back from the courts, so you will forgive me if I go freshen up and look through my letters for a moment, won't you, child."

"Yes, of course, Colonel. I shall have plenty to keep me occupied here," she said in a brittle tone, seemingly turning her attention back to the paintings to conceal her distaste for the selfish old man.

After he had left the room, she paced up and down in front of the fireplace, rehearsing all the arguments she had formed in her head. He might be much older than herself, but the magistrate was certainly not in his dotage. Greed was a powerful motive, but it alone would not be enough to carry the day. No, she needed logic and persuasiveness on her side as well.

The colonel reentered the room several minutes later, followed a short time afterward by a servant with a tray groaning with cakes and sandwiches, which Muireann had to force herself to eat for the sake of politeness.

"Well, my dear, and what can I do for you?" the silver-haired old gentleman said patronizingly as he waited for her to take command of the tea tray. "Milk, two lumps."

Muireann handed him the cup with a sharp look in her eyes which the blustering old colonel failed to detect.

"Well, first of all, sir, I was going to ask you how the court case is coming along. I'm sure that Anthony is doing his best for me, but with all the new tenants I have now, and the taxes and mortgage to pay, things are starting to get a bit tight."

Colonel Lowry smiled slyly. "I find that hard to believe, a woman with your business acumen."

Muireann smiled at him prettily. "It's a case of continuous outgoings, and not many incomings at the moment. But I would think it would be in your interests to get the matter settled as quickly as possible in the courts, for I should like to buy your tree plantation and lower pasture."

Colonel Lowry nearly gagged on the tea he was sipping. "Who on earth told you they were for sale!" he spluttered, outraged.

"No one. I'm here to make you an honest business proposal," Muireann replied calmly.

"But I have more sheep arriving any day! Why would I want to give you my pasture land?"

"Because you and I both know that the pasture in question, the one bordering my estate, is divided by the huge forest running along the bottom of your estate from east to west.

"If you sold me the whole forest, along with the pasture, you would have a much smaller but better organized and maintained holding. You also wouldn't have to worry about the sheep straying off into the woods and getting lost or injured. We can redraw the boundaries, and you can enclose the whole with fences to protect your investments. My men will even help build them, so there will be no misunderstandings, and no inconvenience to yourself."

"How do you know I might not want to go into the carpentry or timber business myself?" Colonel Lowry asked gruffly.

Muireann's eyes glinted hard in the firelight. "Forgive me, sir, but may I remind you that you have dismissed all your workers. You have even contracted with me for the shearing of the sheep by my tenants. Where would you get the people to perform the labor? Plus, the trees are mostly Scotch pine and fir, not suitable for furniture at all.

"Even if you wanted to use them for timber, your trees are so high up, it would be impractical for you to transport them by land or water. I'm the only one with a dock convenient to you, and I would hardly let you load them if you were going to try to set yourself up as a business rival to me."

The colonel looked dumbfounded.

"But if I were to allow you to use the docks for your sheep at particular dates during the month, would you be willing to let me purchase the forest and pasture for a reasonable price, to be paid to you as soon as further monies come through from the case against Mr. Blessington?"

Colonel Lowry pondered her proposal silently, and began to see the wisdom of her suggestion.

"It is true, I would have a smaller property, but that would mean lower taxes, less unproductive land for me, and the chance to ship the sheep by sea via your dock would mean I could trade in England, Scotland or even further abroad."

"It wouldn't just have to be livestock, either. It could even be sheep skins, meat products, and so on," Muireann said.

"Well, I would have to consult my son, not only as the eventual heir to the estate, but also as my lawyer. But I think he would agree to it, provided the price were right."

"As I said, you would have to wait for the money from the trial, but if I give you, say, two years' passage rights to my docks, effective immediately, and you work out the dates with my estate manager, Lochlainn Roche, can we say this figure would be suitable?" she asked, jotting down a sum on a piece of paper with her pencil.

Colonel Lowry read the slip of paper and tried to bargain her up a bit, but Muireann remained firm.

"After all, Colonel, I do have a great number of mouths to feed," she reminded him, fluttering her eyelashes and simpering like a mindless society beauty.

The colonel laughed then, and gave in. "All right, I agree, so long as Anthony does as well. It would be churlish of me to refuse so pretty a lady. And you did, after all, save me the trouble and expense of shipping those no-good tenants of mine to the New World."

Muireann tamped down her rage at his callousness as she shook him firmly by the hand. "It's a bargain then. How soon would you like to fence in your estate?"

"Well, er, as soon as you like, I should think," the colonel blustered, wondering why he suddenly felt as though he had been tricked in some way.

"I'd like the papers all drawn up and brought to me as soon as possible. I shall tell Lochlainn to get the men on work detail first thing tomorrow morning."

"Whatever you wish, Mrs. Caldwell," the colonel replied amiably, convinced by her charming manners into thinking he had nothing to worry about. "I'll contact my son and get the whole process under way immediately."

"Thank you, Colonel. You are too kind." She smiled graciously, resisting the temptation to crow her triumph for all the world to hear.

She accepted his offer to escort her to her mount, and nodded her agreement when he insisted she should buy herself a sidesaddle immediately, though behind his back she rolled her eyes in exasperation. With one last wave, Muireann spurred her horse, and headed off to tackle her next victim.

Chapter Seventeen

As Muireann rode down the avenue of Castle Lowry, she was overjoyed at how easy her negotiations had been.

She had not only deprived the colonel of his best hunting land and timber, she had also cut off Mr. Stephens's access to the lough through the colonel's property. She would now be in an excellent bargaining position with Malcolm Stephens. Though Lochlainn had warned her that he was a lying snake in the grass and someone to be avoided at all costs, she was certain she could gain the upper hand if she played her cards right.

As she rode up to the front door of Malcolm Stephens's house, the Grange, she saw a tall man of about forty, slightly stout, with ginger hair, standing on the steps of the mansion, removing his gloves and mud-bespattered coat while the groom led his horse away around the left-hand side of the house to the stables.

He paused on the steps to look at his visitor. He did not recognize Muireann, and since there was no groom about, he descended the steps and offered her a hand down.

Muireann was slightly embarrassed to have been caught riding astride, but there were no ladies' sidesaddles at Barnakilla. She was damned if she was going to waste money on one just for the sake of not shocking the neighbors. So she swung her leg over the pommel with a flurry of skirts, and rested her hands on his shoulders lightly as he held her waist and made sure she reached the ground safely.

"Well, Miss, er . . ."

"I'm Mrs. Muireann Caldwell," she said, extending her hand by way of greeting.

Malcolm Stephens stepped back as though he had been bitten, and snapped, "Then you and I have nothing to say to one another. The groom will be around in a minute, and he will help you onto your mount." He turned on his heel and strode up the steps again.

Muireann was nothing if not persistent. She ran after him and grasped his elbow. "Please, sir, I know you had differences with my husband, but I run Barnakilla now, and I've come here to discuss business with you!"

"I vowed I would never speak to another Caldwell until

my dying day!" he muttered, trying to shake her off as he marched into the drawing room where his wife, a small dark-haired woman of about thirty-five, was occupying herself with two small boys.

"Well, then, I'm not a Caldwell. How do you do, Mrs. Stephens? I'm Muireann Graham." She smiled broadly.

The children could see their father was upset, but the lady was so pretty, they couldn't resist being friendly to her. They both ran up to her shyly, and chorused, "Do you want to see our toy soldiers?"

Mrs. Stephens scolded the boys for their boldness.

Muireann simply smiled down at the two dark-haired boys kindly.

Malcolm Stephens gaped in surprise as she disappeared out of the room, one boy having taken each of her hands to escort her up to the nursery.

His wife's eyebrows lifted several inches, but she was a kind woman at heart, and if the boys, usually shy and retiring, had taken to the strange young woman so quickly, she trusted their instincts.

"Surely it won't do any harm to listen to what the girl has to say, dear," she said mildly, picking up her knitting once again.

"I suppose not. God only knows how that bastard Augustine ever got a wife like her."

"He probably deceived and tricked her the way he did the rest of us," his wife sniffed, jabbing the needles in and out of the wool as though she were stabbing them through Augustine's heart.

"But whatever we do, we mustn't mention it. She looks very young and innocent. It would be too horrible!" Malcolm shook his head.

"Please, dear, don't get yourself upset."

"I can't help it. My own brother! I should have killed him with my bare hands!"

"I know it's no consolation, my love, but Jonathan never sustained any lasting damage, though the memory must be terrible of what might have happened if you hadn't saved him."

"Thank God Caldwell is dead. The man was a savage. I can't tell you what a funny turn it gives me to see little Jon and Robin talking to his widow. It's all too strange."

"Perhaps it's fate. Maybe she's come here to heal all the old wounds. I've only seen her for a brief second, but she seems genuine. All I know is she took Colonel Lowry's and Mr. Cole's tenants to stop them from being evicted," Priscilla Stephens said in Muireann's defense.

"Maybe she did it so she can take advantage of the poor devils," Malcolm snapped bitterly, pouring himself a large drink from a decanter on the sideboard.

"Really, dear, there's no call to be so boorish. Now, if you will go up and tell Nanny to give the boys their tea upstairs tonight, you can go fetch Mrs. Caldwell, er, Miss Graham down, and invite her to have a drop with us," his wife instructed.

When Malcolm reached the top of the stairs and popped his head in the nursery, Muireann and the two boys were hard at it recreating the Battle of Waterloo.

"Who's winning?" he asked quietly, looking at the young beauty stretched out on the carpet with his two small sons on either side of her leaning their heads on her shoulders affectionately.

"The English and the Allies, of course, Daddy," piped Robin, the youngest of the pair, who was only six.

"Excellent," he said, rubbing his hands together. "But now Mummy says it's time for tea, and I have to take Miss Graham downstairs to meet Mummy properly."

"Can't we come?" John asked with a pout.

"After you've had yours. I'm sure Miss Graham will be here for a while, and she wouldn't dream of leaving without saying goodbye."

"Where do you live, Muireann?" Robin asked her sweetly.

"Just to the south of you."

"In that case you can come see us lots!" he exclaimed delightedly. "We can do the Battle of Trafalgar with our wooden ships next time."

"I'll look forward to that. And you can visit me, and see all of our animals on the farm."

"Can we, Daddy?" Jon asked excitedly.

"We'll see. Only good little boys who drink up all their tea and eat all their nice food get to go visiting." Malcolm smiled down at his sons, tousling their hair playfully.

Muireann rose from the floor and tidied her black-watch tartan woolen gown.

"May I wash my hands before tea? That is, assuming your invitation was genuine," she said in a low voice, gathering up her cloak from where she had draped it over the back of the chair.

"My wife Priscilla and I would be most pleased if you could join us, Miss Graham," Malcolm said stiffly.

He offered her his arm, and escorted her to a small boudoir, where a servant brought some warm water a few moments later. Muireann tugged her unruly hair back vigorously and reinserted the pins, and then descended the final flight of stairs to rejoin the Stephenses in their drawing room.

"So, tell us my dear, how long were you and Augustine Caldwell married?" Mrs. Stephens asked curiously.

"A little over a fortnight," came the prompt reply.

Both the man and woman stared at Muireann, and Priscilla shook her head.

"You poor thing."

"I don't expect any sympathy," Muireann said directly. "I deserve none, and it would be hypocritical of anyone to offer it. No one here in this part of the world liked Augustine, that's for certain. So please, spare me the platitudes."

"You are very direct for one so young," Malcolm commented uncomfortably.

Muireann made a deprecating moue. "It saves time in the long run, and time is a commodity I have very little of at the moment. So if you will forgive me, I shall get straight down to business.

"I've come here today because your land adjoins mine. Since I have over three hundred tenants now, I need to plan for the future, to be able to provide food and shelter for them. I know you've always been interested in buying my most northwesterly pasture. But surely you can see that now, with the number of mouths I have to feed, it would be impossible for me to sell it. I've come to offer to buy your adjacent pasture instead. I also wish to negotiate for giving you reasonable access to the lough shore, and the use of my docks for the loading and unloading of your wares."

Malcolm stared at her, and snorted.

"From what I hear, you're penniless! How on earth could you be in a position to buy my pasture, even were I willing to sell it? Moreover, what makes you think I would be so eager to want access to the lough? I've done without full access for long enough."

"Yes, but you see, my brother-in-law Philip is a wealthy merchant and ship owner, always interested in expanding his business interests. I have been successfully trading with him since I arrived here. And since I have also bought the southernmost pasture and the whole forest on Colonel Lowry's estate, you will not be able to use the lough at all once those lands are enclosed if you don't make a deal with me now." She smiled sweetly, but her steely determination was evident in her amethyst eyes.

Malcolm sat down on the sofa with a thump, too stunned to respond.

"You're as ruthless as Augustine ever was!" he eventually accused angrily.

His wife tried to lay a restraining hand on his arm.

Muireann stiffened visibly, and she strove to defend herself. "Not for myself, Mr. Stephens. Surely you must see that! I've done everything I can to get Barnakilla back up on its feet. I refuse to throw those people off their land, to allow them to be forcibly removed from Ireland against their will, simply because of the greed of a few shortsighted landlords. I can make Barnakilla strong again, give those people a decent home, and even a degree of comfort, if they're prepared to work hard.

"I've worked hard!" she declared, holding out her hands palm upwards so he could see her blisters and calluses. "I've done it all for them! All those people were strangers to me, but they're my family now. You would do anything for your family, your two boys. I saw it in your eyes. Certainly you would be selling part of their land, their inheritance, to me. But you would become very wealthy indeed if my brother-in-law's ships could give you access to foreign markets, and you were willing to give me a good price on the land. Rather than money changing hands now, would you be willing to take the price of the land out of a small percentage of your monthly profits over a period of time, with another sum set aside for a contract for my workers to load and unload the ships?"

Malcolm looked uneasy, but she added reasonably, "At the moment the pasture we have been talking about is lying fallow, and the woods above it have always been an inconvenience, dividing the property as it does."

Malcolm responded, "You could take them both off my hands, so long as you allowed me a corridor on your property to go through to the lough."

"And I will set aside special days for loading and unloading, allocate you skilled workers, and will oblige you with meat, timber, workers at harvest time, or for doing the shearing and making yarn from your fleeces, whatever trades you are willing to make with me, so long as we can put all past hostilities behind us," Muireann said enthusiastically. "I'm not too proud to beg for my people if I have to."

Malcolm rose from his seat and paced up and down in front of the fireplace. "You won't have to beg, Miss Graham. I'll discuss your ideas with my lawyer and my estate manager in the morning. You and the two gentlemen can settle a fair price, to be taken out of the profits starting in say, six months time, since you are in straitened circumstances at the moment. One day, perhaps, when you are less busy, you might care to join us for dinner," he offered.

"I would love to, but I am indeed hard pressed to find a spare moment of the day. In any case, I'm afraid I have nothing to wear, no evening gowns, no jewels, not even a carriage. I sold everything after I was widowed, and have literally started from scratch with what I stand up in."

Priscilla Stephens exclaimed sadly over her misfortunes, and the three of them discussed her various adventures since her arrival in January as they sipped their tea.

In the end, Malcolm was glad he had decided to bury the past and befriend this extraordinary Scottish woman.

"But of course you can visit us," Muireann suggested. "You could come in a few weeks' time to see how the new tenants have settled, and bring the boys. I'm sure they'd love to play with the lambs. There are a few that need bottle-feeding. They could help me look after them."

"Well, Malcolm is very busy, but I'd love to come," Priscilla said warmly. "It sounds like you've done wonders with the place."

"Thank you." Muireann was relieved that she seemed to have won the older woman's approval.

When the carriage clock on the mantelpiece struck six, Muireann started up. "Heavens, is that the time? I must get back. I'm afraid I've taken up far too much of your time already, and the estate manager will be wondering where I am."

"Aye, we had heard you'd taken on Lochlainn Roche. An excellent head on his shoulders, I'm pleased to say, though the rest of the family was so wild."

"The Roches?" Muireann asked, puzzled.

Malcolm opened his mouth, but Priscilla stepped on his foot and ostentatiously declared, "Here, let me help you with your cloak. I'll walk up with you to say goodbye to the boys. And please, do write and tell us a convenient day to visit you."

"It will have to be after Easter, but yes, I promise." Muireann looked from one to the other in confusion. She had no idea why they were both acting so strangely. All the same, they seemed genuine enough, and so she went up to have a final romp with Jon and Robin.

Then she shook hands with both Mr. and Mrs. Stephens in the foyer of their stately home, and without waiting for Malcolm to come help her, she swung up into the saddle and headed straight back to Barnakilla.

After a hasty supper of rabbit stew, she strode into her office and found Lochlainn waiting for her.

"And just where the hell have you been all day?" he snapped, as she threw off her cloak and went over to warm herself before the fire.

"I told you, I had some deals to make. I went to see Colonel Lowry and Malcolm Stephens. Why, did something happen while I was gone?"

"Damn it, Muireann, you swore to me that you wouldn't sell the pasture to Stephens!"

Of course he couldn't tell her that his own insecurities made him fearful that she would be seduced into longing for the wealthy lifestyle she had sacrificed, once she went visiting around the neighborhood and witnessed first hand the luxury of the Grange or Castle Lowry.

Muireann smiled, infuriating Lochlainn still further. *Why does she always have to be in such complete control?* he wondered resentfully.

"I didn't sell our pasture. I bought his," she announced proudly. "His and the colonel's and their forests on the southern end of their estates as well."

Lochlainn's mouth dropped open. "You did *what*?"

"I told you, I've bought more land, to be paid for out of my share of Malcolm Stephens's trade profits over the next few years. And the colonel has agreed to wait for his payment until we get more money from Mr. Blessington's estate, which he assures me will be soon."

"But how the hell are we going to plant and fertilize the fields?"

"We'll put in more turnips, beets and carrots, and we'll use manure and seaweed."

"Seaweed?"

"It's what we always used in Scotland."

Lochlainn threw himself down in a chair and looked at her thoughtfully for a few moments before declaring, "I'll tell you what we also use around here: sea sticks. You dry them out and burn them, and use the ashes for fertilizer. Also fish bones, ground up fine, depending upon the type of soil you have."

Muireann said excitedly, "It sounds good to me. We can use the sea sticks for fuel for heating things, and then rake up the ashy residue carefully to put on the fields."

"If you give me a couple of days to supervise the new timber cutting, we could go to the beach in Donegal and get ourselves a load."

"What, go on another little excursion?" Her delight was evident from her expression.

"You've been working so hard, you deserve it. I must say, I quite fancy a trip to the beach. There is a lovely sandy one at Rossnowlagh. We would have to stay overnight, and camp out in the dunes." He grinned lazily, already looking forward to having several days alone with Muireann.

But Muireann shook her head. "I don't know. Perhaps one of us should stay behind if it will take that long."

Lochlainn protested, "You just said this afternoon that you would start trusting everyone to run the place in your absence. Isn't it about time you started delegating responsibility? You can't keep on like this forever, you know. Besides, your birthday is coming up soon. Don't you think you deserve a little treat?"

Muireann weighed the pros and cons in her head, and at last agreed. "All right, I'll go. We can head up on Wednesday, return on Friday, and combine it with a trip to the Donegal market, can't we?"

"Clever woman, that's exactly what I was thinking. We'll get the first cart loaded, and get the other two to come up on Friday for market, load them, and come back home on Saturday or Sunday."

Muireann turned back to her papers to make some new calculations concerning the bargains she had just struck with Malcolm Stephens and Colonel Lowry. She tried to focus her eyes on the column of figures, but Lochlainn was a distracting presence. He certainly was in a strange mood, and seemed to fill the room, overwhelming her senses.

Suddenly he reached out to stroke her cheek tenderly. "Muireann, I'm sorry if I was angry with you before. I know you're only trying to do what's best for everyone. Augustine always warned me never to trust a word that Malcolm Stephens said, but if you liked him . . ."

"And his wife and little boys. I thought they were lovely people, very genuine," Muireann said, giving her honest assessment.

"I have no idea what could have provoked the fight between them so many years ago. Since I trust your judgment implicitly, I shall have to work with the man from now on, and I'm sorry if I doubted you."

"He certainly seems to think very highly of you as an estate agent, from what he said. So your apology is accepted. I understand your frustration. I suppose it all gets to us in the end, this feeling of, well, confusion—of powerlessness at times."

"You? Confused? Powerless? You seem to have all the power you need at your fingertips," Lochlainn said, astonished.

"I wish I did sometimes. But I must admit to you, Lochlainn, I'm tired of all these deals, of living by my wits, struggling for every penny, trying to pay the mortgage and feed everyone. Sometimes I would just like things to be on an even keel for us all."

"Our situation is bound to improve, you'll see. It's been a long three months, but things will get better, I promise. You've already done so much. You can't afford to let yourself get despondent now," he said, kissing her on the cheek.

Inwardly he worried about her. She did indeed look absolutely exhausted. He might have even wondered if she were expecting had she not been so pale. Moreover, she had complained to him shyly of monthly cramps only a few days before, and he had advised her then to rest.

Muireann looked down at her ledger again. "They'll really improve no end if I can tally up these sums," she sighed, desperately trying to concentrate. But she could smell Lochlainn's clean, sharp, woodsy fragrance, and couldn't seem to take her eyes off his long lean hands.

"Are you going to be much longer poring over those papers?" Lochlainn asked abruptly.

Muireann looked at him. "No, why?"

He reached over and snuffed out the candles. Taking her by the hand, he led her into her bedroom and began to

make love to her with a slow, leisured thoroughness which took Muireann's breath away.

"Wouldn't it be lovely if it could be like this all the time," she murmured, before drifting off to sleep contentedly.

In truth, Lochlainn had been thinking the same thing himself. But with so much to do all day, every day, there just never seemed to be enough time for the two of them to be alone with each other, to laugh and love. He had never shared a relationship like that with Tara. He had desired her, surely, but every moment he spent with Muireann left him aching for more.

But he couldn't reproach Muireann, demand more of her time. For one thing, their feelings for each other were something they never dared talk about. For another, he certainly couldn't complain when she had willingly chosen to help all those poor unfortunates from Colonel Lowry's and Mr. Cole's estates. If they never had enough time together, it was because Muireann had shouldered so many responsibilities. As her estate manager, he had to take on those burdens as well. They were his own people after all, weren't they?

They certainly weren't Muireann's. Perhaps they would be one day, but he still couldn't help thinking of her as the beautiful young girl in the incredibly elegant gown he had first met in Dublin all those months before.

He was terrified she would go back home to Fintry. But to reveal his fears would be impossible. She would only laugh at him for having dared presume to fall in love with her. He could only try to make Muireann happy, support her, and pray she would decide to stay.

Chapter Eighteen

Several mornings later, Muireann rolled over in the bed sleepily, feeling a warm presence beside her. A smile curled her lips and she cuddled up against the warm body. It was only when it stuck its fluffy wet nose in her face to kiss her that she opened her eyes and sat bolt upright.

Lochlainn laughed heartily at her stunned face as she exclaimed, "What is it?"

"It's a puppy, you silly woman. Surely they have dogs in Scotland," he teased.

Muireann reached out a tentative hand to stroke the auburn and black creature, which had the longest legs she had ever seen, and a fine coat that only waved slightly between its two tiny, high-set ears.

"No, Lochlainn, I mean what breed is it?" she giggled. "It looks a bit like an Airedale terrier, but the coat is wrong."

"It's an Irish terrier, in fact. You're right, they're similar to Airedales, but his black bits will disappear from his back and beard when he's older, and his whole coat will become the same auburn color, and stay straight, instead of becoming wiry," Lochlainn explained, stroking the affectionate creature as it snuggled up between the two of them.

"He's so beautiful, and so playful," she marveled as the pup played with her fingers like a kitten. "But why is he here? Where did he come from?"

"Colonel Lowry's bitch whelped shortly before you arrived. When you mentioned the rat and mouse problem, I thought one of the puppies would be perfect for you. Irish terriers are terribly loyal, and you can even train them as gun dogs. They have very soft mouths and are very gentle, medium-sized dogs. They're also wonderfully sociable and love children, so there's no worry about him being unruly around the farm."

"What about the livestock?"

"You'll probably find he'll follow you everywhere, but as I said, with the right training, he won't bother to chase sheep."

"So he's *mine*?" she asked with astonished delight.

Lochlainn grinned. "I know it's early, Muireann, but happy birthday. He's only just weaned, so I want him to become part of our little family straight away. Do you really like him?"

"He's gorgeous. Thank you," she said, kissing him warmly on the lips and getting another fond lick from the puppy.

She giggled again and asked, "What should I name him?"

Lochlainn thought about it for a moment, and then replied, "Well, there is a famous Irish terrier in *The Book of Leinster* called Tadhg. You could try that for a name."

"How do you spell it?" Muireann asked.

"T A- D- H- G," Lochlainn told her. "It was a name given to the poets and storytellers in Ireland centuries ago."

"Tay-g," she intoned, experimenting with the name. "I like it. It suits him."

The pup friskily romped on the bed and she observed, "Look at him. He prances like a racehorse."

"It's in the breed to do that. They can be very proud and haughty with other dogs, and are completely game for anything."

"You seem to know a lot about them. Did you ever have one yourself?"

"No. I must admit I always wanted one, but my aunt who raised us never let us have dogs. Working so much, I never really had time to train one. Christopher Caldwell always had a pack of them though, which is how I know of them. Unfortunately, his were allowed to run rather wild. You have to be firm with this little chap," he warned.

"You'll just have to help me train him. I've never really had a dog of my very own, either."

"I'll do my best to give you advice, but I think you'll do fine. Happy birthday, Muireann, even if it is a bit early."

He bent to kiss her, and the dog jumped up and licked him on the chin as well.

"Thank you, Lochlainn. He's just what I needed to cheer me up."

"I hope you're not sad, Muireann," he said worriedly.

"Not really. I'm just taking stock of my life, I suppose. I'll be twenty-two soon."

"And I'll be thirty-seven at the end of the year. Where does the time go? I'm nearly old enough to be your father," he sighed.

"You would have had to have been a very precocious adolescent." She grinned cheekily, before lying back down with the pup, looking more weary than he had ever seen her.

"I'm sorry we woke you early, but I couldn't wait to see your face. I'll leave you and Tadhg to have a little nap, shall I?"

"No, not at all. I'll just have a small stretch for a second, and get dressed. There's plenty to do today if we're going to Donegal for the seaweed tomorrow."

Suddenly he thumped his forehead with the palm of one hand. "I nearly forgot. I've got one more birthday surprise for you."

Lochlainn came back a few minutes later with a steaming cup of coffee.

Thrilled, she asked, "Oh, Lochlainn, wherever did you get it?"

"I bought a second pack out of the items you sold back in February, to save for your birthday. I know you were careful, but ran out the other day, so you might as well have this now."

"Thank you for a lovely surprise, both the pup and the coffee," she said, kissing him full on the lips.

"Not sad anymore?"

"How could I be, looking at those sweet brown eyes, and that adorable little beard?" she laughed, stroking Tadhg fondly as he squirmed under the covers to hunt her toes. "He is far nicer than the Scottish terriers or West Highland white terriers we have."

"These are meant to be the dogs of kings," Lochlainn told her as he stood and buttoned up his waistcoat, then put his jacket on. "But now, I'd better go. Tree cutting, you know."

"You certainly know how to make me feel like a queen."

He blushed. "I do try."

"You succeed. Thank you. Have a good day."

"And you, darling."

Muireann stood and kissed him one last time, then waved at him as he left for work.

Lochlainn was delighted to see that Muireann and Tadhg took to each other right away. He followed her everywhere, went up and down the stairs, even tried to climb trees when she swung from a low-hanging branch on her way through the woods to see Lochlainn later that day.

"There's a ship sailing up to the docks. Do you want to come down to greet it?" she called.

Lochlainn swallowed uncomfortably, and declined. "No, no, I need to finish here today if we're to go first thing in the morning."

"All right." Muireann shrugged, disappointed that he never seemed to take an interest in her family or the letters she received from home, mainly from her sister and mother inquiring after her health and well-being.

Muireann prayed they hadn't suddenly taken it into their heads to come over. She was relieved to see it was her cousin Michael on deck, with his youngest brother Archie, a playful, spirited, red-headed lad a couple of years younger than Muireann, who admired the new pup and instantly declared he wanted to see Colonel Lowry about getting one for himself.

"If I get a good bitch, we could start our own kennels," he said as he romped with Tadhg on the dock.

"They look like each other, red hair, long legs," Michael joked, but soon they got down to business.

Muireann was delighted to see another shipment of staples, all purchased for excellent prices, according to the ledger, as well as Neil's usual luxuries. There was a huge number of parcels for her birthday as well.

"I know they're early, but everyone wanted to cheer you up. And this is the biggest present of all, the *Andromeda*."

"Present? I don't understand." Muireann stared at her cousin.

"Philip Buchanan and Neil are giving it to you as your very own ship. The only thing you have to do is feed the crew. Any deals or trades you make are your own, though it will fly as a Buchanan flagship in order for you not to have to pay any taxes and duties yourself," Michael explained.

She gaped. When she could find her voice again she declared, "I couldn't accept! It's far too generous of Philip! He can't just *give* me one of his ships!"

"Neil says it is a good investment for you, and the price of it has come out of your stocks and shares. Philip doesn't need the ship anyway, since he's on his way back from Canada with another three to add to his fleet."

Muireann was so overwhelmed she could only gaze at the ship in awe. Hers?

"And you, how will you all get back?"

"We'll just wait until you have a cargo of your own to send to Scotland, and go home then."

"We were going to go up to Donegal tomorrow to gather seaweed for fertilizer, so if we can get the timber loaded, you can take us up there. We'll come back on the carts, and you can head back home," Muireann proposed.

"That sounds fine. I'll get things unloaded and organized at this end, and you can give Archie here a tour of the estate."

Muireann said proudly, "A lot has changed since you were last here. We have three times more tenants now than before, and we're pretty crowded in, but I think you'll find the workshops impressive."

"I find everything you do impressive, little coz. You should have been a man, with that head on your shoulders."

"It's too much fun sometimes being a woman." She winked conspiratorially.

"Ah, yes, and how is the stunningly handsome Mr. Lochlainn Roche? Is he well?" Michael asked, tousling her hair affectionately.

"Wonderful as always." Muireann smiled up at her cousin, and then turned away to give orders for all the men in the cottages not already working to come out and lend a hand.

Muireann went up to the house to see if there would be enough dinner for the hungry crew as well as the workers. Entering the kitchen with the faithful Tadhg at her heels, she stopped short when she heard Ciara drop her knife on the cutting board, sending chopped vegetables flying in every direction, which of course the pup began to chase and devour enthusiastically.

Ciara stared in horror. "Where on earth did you get that thing!" she shrieked, jumping up onto the table.

Thinking it was a game, Tadhg clambered up on the bench after her, and tried to reach Ciara on the tabletop.

"Help me! Help me!" Ciara screamed hysterically at the top of her lungs.

Muireann and Archie, who had tagged along behind his cousin, both ran after the puppy and dragged it away.

"Did it bite you? Let me see!" Muireann insisted, as Ciara huddled up, grasping her legs.

"Get away from me! Don't touch me! Don't touch me ever again, you bastard!" she hissed, her wild eyes darting around the room as if trying to focus on something.

Muireann stepped back from the table, stunned, while the other kitchen workers stared at Ciara in dismay.

Archie, who was kneeling with the pup on the floor, looked at the two women in confusion.

Muireann tried again. "Ciara, it's me, Muireann. I won't hurt you. I won't even touch you if you don't want me to. I just need to know if Tadhg bit you. If you're all right."

Ciara visibly shook, and suddenly unfolded herself and stepped down off the table.

"No, no, I'm fine. Really, I'm sure he's a lovely dog. I'm just afraid of them, that's all," she said in a forced tone.

"I'll try to keep him away from you as much as possible from now on," Muireann promised, but she was talking to thin air, for Lochlainn's sister had already disappeared out the door.

Archie finally released his breath with a loud whoosh. "I say! What on earth was all that about?"

Muireann shook her head. "I have no idea."

"I swear to you, Muireann, I didn't lay a finger on her. I just grabbed the dog."

She shook her head. "No, I don't think she was talking to you, Archie."

"Well, she couldn't have been speaking to you. She said 'you bastard.' "

"She probably meant the dog," she muttered, lost in thought.

"Well, dogs and bitches hardly get married, now do they," Archie said with an uncomfortable laugh.

With the usual high spirits of youth, he shrugged off the whole incident, and investigated the entire estate from top to bottom with Michael and Mark, while Muireann made some room in the new loft above the barn for her overnight guests.

When Lochlainn appeared in the kitchen for his dinner, Muireann managed to pull him over to one side and asked, "Have you seen Ciara?"

"No, why?"

"I'm a bit worried about her, that's all. She was terribly upset when she saw Tadhg. Is she usually terrified of dogs?"

He frowned. "Not that I know of. She was quite fond of them as a child, though we never had one ourselves."

"Well, don't mention it to her. She's probably already embarrassed enough. But just keep an eye on her, will you?"

Lochlainn nodded. "Thanks for being so concerned."

"And another thing. Neil and his brother Philip have given us the use of the *Andromeda* to make our own trades. So we'll be going to Donegal by ship tomorrow, and the carts can follow along behind after the markets."

"That's wonderful news." Lochlainn tried to smile, though it cost him a great effort. He knew he had to stop bristling every time she had contact with Scotland.

But with every new letter, or every time a ship arrived at the dock, he became more and more certain he was going to lose her. And jealousy burned within his heart for the man who could give her such riches, when he himself had nothing to offer.

He tried to pay attention to her next words, but he was lost in a welter of misery.

She said more loudly, "It is wonderful news, isn't it? So why do you look so worried?"

"I'm not at all. Just thinking," he lied.

"We do have a small problem, though. I don't want Michael to find out that all the luxuries he's taken the trouble to bring over will have to be sold at market. Can you make sure the coffee is parceled up, and the crates opened? We can put a variety of things into the carts for Donegal, and for Clogher and Enniskillen on Thursday."

"Do you really need to sell it all?"

"I think so. The little birthday presents too. I just need to open them all so I can write the appropriate thank-you notes to everyone."

"But Muireann . . ."

"No, really, I have Tadhg, and a packet of coffee. Who could ask for more wonderful presents than that? What do I need with baubles, jewels and gowns?"

"But your family wanted you to have them."

"They wanted Muireann Graham to have them. I'm Muireann Graham Caldwell now, landlord, and I have no time for such fripperies."

Reluctantly Lochlainn acceded to her wishes. "All right, I'll see to it they're all loaded on the carts before we go in the morning, with not a word to Michael."

Muireann went off to write her letters, and then prepared for her excursion to Donegal the next day. She packed a small parcel of clothes, food and other necessaries for herself and Lochlainn, and Patrick and Siobhan, who would drive the first cart up the following day. Lochlainn and Muireann would sail on the *Andromeda* to Donegal Town, and start gathering up the sea sticks and laying them out to dry. She was looking forward to her trip to the seaside, not least because she would have nearly a whole day with Lochlainn all to herself.

The ship set off at first light, and made good progress with favorable winds. Soon they sailed into Donegal Town harbor, where Michael dropped them off at the dock.

"Don't forget to give them all my letters," she called.

"As if I could! Any more of those packets would have sunk the ship!"

Muireann stuck her tongue out at Michael and then called, "Bye, Archie! Take care! And remember, not a word to Mother or Father!"

Archie waved his new puppy's paw by way of reply. He had managed to secure a lovely bitch from Colonel Lowry, which they named Earc. Lochlainn told them the name meant "red."

The *Andromeda* cast off then, and headed for Scotland. Muireann watched it wistfully for a time, and then turned to Lochlainn, who had been standing behind her, waiting for the ship to disappear and leave him alone with her once again.

Her amethyst eyes glimmered with unshed tears, but she forced herself to smile. Taking Lochlainn's arm she declared, "Well, Lochlainn, it's time to show me the sights."

Donegal was a lovely market town built around a diamond-shaped green, with an impressive castle built of tawny-colored stone.

"Isn't it lovely," Muireann admired.

"It was originally owned by the O'Donnell clan. Donegal, or Dun na nGall, 'fort of the strangers,' in this case Vikings, who founded it in the tenth century. It was the capital of the O'Donnell territory, which was known as Tír Chonaill. But the English forcibly settled the area, and the castle was rebuilt in 1610."

"I like all the turrets. Very fine," Muireann commented as they strolled past.

"There are also the remains of an old Franciscan monastery over by the seawall. It was built in 1474, but it was pretty much destroyed by Hugh Roe O'Donnell in 1601 when he was besieging his cousin Garbhan and the English garrison there. He was trying to ally himself with the English, you see, though he didn't get anywhere. They put him in prison until the day he died in 1629," Lochlainn informed her as they strolled along the Diamond, looking in the shop windows before moving on to the market.

"How do you know so much about your own history? I must plead ignorance of Scottish history generally," she said, impressed with Lochlainn's knowledge.

"There were several great historians known as 'The Four Masters,' who undertook to write a history of Ireland in the seventeenth century," he explained.

He led her over to a corner of the Diamond, where there was a curious-looking stone carving. "They were from here, and this is a small monument commemorating them. They wrote the history at the abbey, where this hotel now stands."

"Fascinating. I would love to be able to read it some time," Muireann said as she took his arm and strolled into the hotel with him, where they had some refreshment. Lochlainn made some inquiries about who might be willing to take them out to Rossnowlagh to get started gathering sea sticks.

Half an hour later he announced, "I've got a lift."

They managed to get a ride on the back of a furniture cart heading back out of the town after having sold all its wares early at the market.

After a few miles, Lochlainn declared, "Now we have to get down and walk."

He lifted her off the back of the cart, his hands lingering on her slender waist intimately for a blissful moment. They trudged about three miles overland until at last they reached the most exquisite beach Muireann had ever seen. It stretched for miles, a golden strand, with seaweed, the valuable sea sticks, and some seashells the only items marring its smooth surface.

Muireann took off her boots and stockings, and hitched up her skirts to above her knees, enjoying the cool, smooth feeling of the sand between her toes. Tadhg, who had accompanied them, sitting on her lap obediently for almost the whole journey, sported himself by chasing the surf, and after a time, he even copied his mistress and began fetching sea sticks to drop on the pile.

He also proved to be an excellent winkler and whelker, for as the sun rose high in the sky and the tide began to go out, Lochlainn suggested they collect some shellfish for their meal. Using her shawl tied around her waist as an apron, she and Lochlainn collected winkles, cockles, whelks and mussels. Lochlainn set a small fire going with some of the flotsam that had been cast further up the beach. Muireann had had the foresight to bring a small saucepan and some fresh water, and the three of them shared the meal, with Muireann and Lochlainn chatting about all they had seen so far that day.

"The *Andromeda* is a fine ship."

"It is indeed. We'll be able to do wonders with it. You know, Lochlainn, I really am beginning to feel as if our luck might be changing after all."

"I certainly hope so." He smiled down at her, and patted the jolly little pup on the head to hide his emotions.

After they had finished their meal, they gathered sea sticks for another hour, but as the weather turned warmer, Muireann suddenly stripped off her black and burgundy checked gown, and all of her underclothes except her petticoat and chemise, and charged into the surf. Tadhg the terrier charged after her, wondering what new game his mistress was playing now.

"Muireann, it's freezing! Come out of there!" Lochlainn called, standing at the water's edge in his bare feet.

He was afraid Muireann would drown, but a few strokes told him she swam as well as she did everything else. He watched the graceful naiad in the water for a few minutes until, with a sigh, he stripped off all his clothes and thundered naked into the chilly surf.

"I was wondering if you could swim," she laughed.

"Only with great difficulty," he admitted, as he stopped at the point where he could still comfortably touch bottom with his feet if he needed to.

Muireann swam up to him and kissed him. It wasn't long before they were scurrying for the privacy of a sand dune, leaving Tadhg playing contentedly on the beach in the tide.

Their lovemaking was urgent and desperate, full of the fear of discovery, and enhanced by the excitement of their being able to see each other's responses clearly in the broad daylight. The sand and icy water had set their skin tingling, and every caress of their hands was like sweet torture. He stroked her breasts and belly and rolled her under him, entering her with one sure thrust. More eager than ever, Muireann climaxed almost instantly, with Lochlainn following just behind.

"This is bliss," she purred when she had calmed. She rubbed her cheek against his damp chest, snuggling up to him like a contented cat.

"That's one of the things I always hate about the beach."

"What, making love in the dunes?" she teased.

"No, getting sand all over."

Lochlainn blushed as she tried to dust off his more intimate areas, and felt his arousal burning within and without.

She kissed him, but much as she wanted him, duty called.

"Come on. We'll go for another swim to wash ourselves off, and get back to the sea sticks."

"But you'll freeze in those wet things," Lochlainn worried.

"I have my very own bundle of tricks. I got some clean linen from your sister for you, and brought some myself. So let's get washed and changed, and go gather up another few bunches. After all, we need the fertilizer. And remember, the others will be here soon enough."

The joy of the moment was thus lost, and though Lochlainn tried to recapture it with a warm, rousing kiss, there was work to be done. He loved being alone with her, chatting to her about her childhood memories and experiences, and her life in Scotland. At one point she remarked as she stooped for more sticks to add to her pile, "But you never talk about yourself, your childhood. Was it so bad?"

Lochlainn thought carefully before replying. "It was hard, I have to say. My aunt sewed for a living. It was a nightmare for her to try to feed the three of us at times. I also know she never got married because no one wanted the responsibility of looking after us."

"It must have been terrible, that sensation of being unwanted."

"It was. Ciara and I were close when we were younger, but once we were both marrying age, well, she changed."

"In what way?" she asked, looking at him directly.

His gray eyes reflected the pain of the recollection. "I don't know. She acted like I wasn't good enough for her anymore. She put on all sorts of fancy airs and graces. She lost her happiness somehow, her joy of living."

She was surprised at his description of his sister. "I must admit it's very difficult to imagine her happy, if even something as simple as a little puppy like Tadhg can send her into fits."

Lochlainn shook his head then. "We seem to do nothing but talk about things that cast a pall over the day. Why don't we play a game instead?"

"What would you like to play?"

"Authors to start with, and then perhaps quotations?" he suggested.

"All right," Muireann assented. They passed the rest of the afternoon agreeably playing games and singing songs.

"You've been practicing," Muireann said at one point, as Lochlainn sang "Tá mé mo shuí" and a few others.

"I'll admit I did ask around for some of the words." He grinned, and ran his fingers through his hair to see if it was dry yet.

"Go on, sing one of yours," he requested as he started on another bundle of sticks.

"All right, but I think it's about time we got the supper started, don't you? It'll be getting dark soon, and we'll need more firewood and a nice place to bed down for the night."

"You go gather the winkles. I'll get the firewood and set up camp."

Muireann was able to produce a sumptuous meal with what she had gleaned from the sea, and the items she had brought in her small bag. They ate bathed in the rosy light of the setting sun, and she had never felt more content. They even finished off their meal with a cup of coffee each.

"My little contribution to the supper," he said, offering her the brown paper package. "I bought another pack out of all the things going to the market today."

"I hope they got a good price for the other things."

"Well, you can ask them yourself," he said. "It sounds like they're on their way."

Patrick and Siobhan saw the cooking fire glowing in the distance, and pulled the wagon right up onto the beach in front of them.

"It will help act as a windbreak to keep the sea breezes off us," Patrick explained as he jumped down off the box.

"There's some supper here if you want it," Muireann offered.

"It smells good," Siobhan said with an appreciative sniff, shaking her auburn hair back from her face as a gentle wind tossed it to and fro.

"Well, you'd better hurry before the whelks turn too chewy, or Tadhg eats every last one of them." Lochlainn laughed as the dog's bearded muzzle probed the saucepan.

All four of them discussed their different experiences in Donegal Town, until Lochlainn rose and stretched.

"Well, if you'll excuse us, I'm sure Muireann has had a very long day, so we're going to bed down behind that sand dune."

Muireann blushed, but took the hand he held out for her. With Tadhg bounding along behind, they sought their own private corner of the beach. They lay on their backs in each other's arms watching as the millions of stars came out. Lochlainn impressed her with his knowledge of the names of the different constellations.

Muireann thought she had never spent such a perfect day. As Lochlainn's mouth found hers, she melted in his embrace, surrounded his body as he surrounded hers. *Wherever he is,* she thought at the back of her mind, *is my home.*

Chapter Nineteen

Muireann's four days and nights on the beach at Rossnowlagh did her a world of good, but it seemed as if the time just flew by. All too soon they had to return to Barnakilla with the carts laden with their valuable cargo.

Gathering the sticks and seaweed had certainly been hard labor, but working by the sea in the fresh air, and eating the bounty they took from the ocean, had at least put some color back into Muireann's cheeks. The fresh air had allowed her to sleep more soundly than ever before, and Lochlainn was delighted that she never seemed to have her nightmares anymore.

Muireann stood by the water's edge, letting the surf lap between her toes as she watched the breakers roll in.

"We can always come back, you know," Lochlainn said softly as he came up behind her and wrapped her in his enveloping cloak, protecting her from the chill wind with his warm, strong body.

"I know. It's just sad that it has to come to an end," she sighed. "Tadhg loved the beach, and it was fun, swimming, playing in the dunes, sleeping under the stars, wasn't it?"

"For you perhaps. You could teach a mermaid how to swim."

"You're getting better all the time," she said sincerely. "We can continue your lessons once we get back to Barnakilla. But Lochlainn, I've been thinking . . ."

Lochlainn's face fell. He knew what she was going to say before she even said it. She was leaving him.

The catch in his voice seemed painfully obvious to him as he asked, "Thinking about what, my dear?"

"I know we're doing well, but I really think I should go to Dublin to investigate this house at St. Stephen's Green."

His heart pounded in his chest. She was going back to the city. Then back to Scotland. "Do you want me to come with you?" he dared to ask, though he was certain of the answer. No. She didn't want him. Not anymore.

"No, because I would have to be away for some time, consulting with Anthony Lowry about the legal documents and so on, and—"

"I understand," he said curtly. He couldn't bear listening to an excuse. Not now, not after the most perfect four days. It seemed an even more cruel betrayal than the one committed by Tara. "Where would you stay?"

"Anthony's kindly offered to put me up in his house in Harcourt Street."

Lochlainn scowled. "And is he married?"

"He's engaged to be married. It's all perfectly respectable. He has a housekeeper to look after things for him, so we would be chaperoned."

"I see. You seem to have all the details worked out perfectly. I imagine you've been planning this trip for some time."

"No, not exactly," she denied, wondering why he suddenly seemed so gloomy. Offended, even.

Lochlainn swallowed audibly. "When would you leave?"

"Soon enough. The end of the month, perhaps."

"After your birthday?" Lochlainn asked, allowing himself a small glimmer of hope. Perhaps if he had enough time he could convince her to stay?

"Aye, after my birthday."

"You'd also have to preside over the May Day festivities. And there's the shearing coming up," he reminded her, trying to think of any excuse to keep her with him a bit longer.

"Yes, of course." Muireann smiled. She herself was not terribly anxious to go, and she hated leaving any unfinished business behind. "There's no hurry. The middle of May will be time enough, won't it?"

"Aye, it will be, indeed," he replied, hugging her close, glad she couldn't see the haunted expression in his eyes.

Then he released her, and took her by the hand. "Come, my dear. Barnakilla beckons."

She cast one last wistful look down the strand, and allowed herself to be led away.

He lifted her onto the box beside Patrick and clicked to the horse as he turned the cart around and headed for home.

Ten days later Muireann celebrated her birthday in grand style. She put on her favorite black watch tartan gown and tied an old red hair ribbon around Tadhg's neck to remind everyone that he had been a present. Lochlainn roused her early for a long ride on the mare she seldom got to exercise anymore, and admired her superb horsemanship.

When they got in, he laid before her bacon, eggs, and

sausages for breakfast, and made her eat every mouthful. While she sat eating, she received dozens of bunches of wildflowers and some homemade gifts such as embroidered handkerchiefs and a new apron with her initials on it from her closest friends.

Then he took her for a walk in the woods, and hugged and kissed her frequently, enjoying being away from the ever-watchful eye of his sister for even a short while. She was the only person who didn't seem to enter into the festive atmosphere. He wondered why she always looked so disapprovingly at them. But no one was going to spoil Muireann's special day, not if he could help it. He even got a small rowboat out and took her onto a little island on the lough.

"We should have brought a picnic," she commented, swirling one hand languidly in the water as he pulled at the oars.

"A good idea for another time. But I'm afraid there's a special surprise awaiting you when we get back to the house. We'll have that picnic another day though, won't we?"

"Soon, please. But it's so difficult to find the time."

He grinned lopsidedly. "If it's important, my dear, we'll just have to make the time."

Priscilla Stephens had organized a small party for Muireann in the kitchen after dinner. He had agreed to get her out of the way so that everything could be set up. Since it was a glorious spring day, they arranged the kitchen benches outside and set out the food, all sorts of meat pies and pastries which Sharon and Brona had baked. Priscilla had brought cake, some wine, beer and whisky, freshly baked scones, and strawberry jam for all the workers. Everyone tucked in heartily and personally offered their new landlord many happy returns of the day.

Muireann blushed to the roots of her hair as she expressed her gratitude to Priscilla for the kind gesture. "Really, it's so kind of you to have done all this for me."

"It's the least I can do. You deserve it, with you being so far from home, and after everything you have done for all these people," Priscilla said shyly.

She desperately tried to restrain her two sons, who insistently tugged at Muireann's hands begging to be shown the horses and lambs.

"There was no need, really. I *am* home," she said, as she went out into the bright sunshine to show the boys around the estate.

She introduced the Stephens boys to some of the children their own age on the estate, and they all played blind man's bluff in the fields, and held three-legged races. Some of the workers also brought out their musical instruments, and the singing and dancing began.

Since the following day was May Day, and she could see they were all in high spirits after their special treats, Muireann declared a half-day holiday for all the workers for her birthday, and the whole day off the following day.

"It's the least we can do after they've tried so hard to fit in with my plans," she told Lochlainn as they stood on the lawn at the back of the house and watched all the women dance a reel.

"They were happy to do it. You're their landlord now, and certainly the best one I've ever seen," he said sincerely.

She laughed. "Well, I couldn't have done much worse than some people we could mention."

"A damn sight better, as well you know. Most landlords are ruthless. But you gave these people a home. You trained them, had faith in them. They'll never forget that, Muireann."

"I wouldn't be so sure I'm not ruthless, Lochlainn." She smiled up at him, though the expression in her eyes was anything but cheerful. "Barnakilla is my very own home now, that I've made into something beautiful and worthwhile with my own two hands. Now that I've made it my own, I mean to make it stronger every day. I'll fight tooth and nail if I have to, do whatever it takes to keep it," she warned.

Lochlainn shuddered then, and prayed she would never be forced to put her words to the test.

He tried to cheer himself by offering his arm and whisking her down the dance set, noting how light and graceful she was on her feet. He thought he could detect a note of false gaiety in the proceedings, and knew in his heart that Muireann was right. Things were going well, but they would need to get a lot better if her plans for the future were ever to bear fruit.

Once they were finally alone that night, Lochlainn gave her the present he had made for her specially, a small carved box inlaid with a huge variety of veneers. On the box was a picture of a waterfall, with a heron, made out of inlay and brass.

"Oh, Lochlainn, it's exquisite!" she breathed, tears shimmering in her eyes. "I've never seen anything more lovely in my life. It's just like the waterfall at Glencar. Not that I needed reminding, but now I shall be able to treasure the memory always."

"I'm glad you like it," he murmured, planting a kiss on her forehead.

"I'm only sorry I haven't got anything valuable to put in it," she sighed.

Lochlainn stared at the floor silently. He cursed himself for being a clumsy fool. The gift had only served to remind her of all she had lost.

"But you needn't have gone to so much trouble. Tadhg was a wonderful present, and the coffee, of course." She kissed him full on the lips.

"I have one more gift for you," he said with a grin.

"Oh, and where might it be?" she teased as she put her hands in his pockets suggestively.

"Well, then, that makes two more presents," he said with a grin, "but you have to have the first before I'll let you have the second."

Just then there was a tap at the door, and Brona and Sharon brought in one of the large bathtubs from the scullery while several other of the kitchen women brought a number of steaming kettles of water into the room.

"My very own bath?" she exclaimed. "No, really, it's too much trouble for you all."

"Not in the least," Sharon reassured her. "Happy birthday, Muireann, and many more. Enjoy the bath without having to take it in the draughty old kitchen with one hundred women screaming to get their turn."

"Oh, Lochlainn, it was kind of you to have thought of it," she said, stretching up to kiss him on the cheek once they were alone again. "Will you share it with me?"

"Of course. You might even bathe that smelly brute as well, while you're at it," Lochlainn laughed, looking at Tadhg, who gazed from one to the other in confusion with his big sherry-brown eyes, wondering what interesting thing he had done now to please his master and mistress.

Lochlainn toyed with the idea of trying to fit himself into the large tub at the same time as Muireann but he wanted her to enjoy the special treat as much as possible. Restraining his passionate urges, Lochlainn read to her from a book of Renaissance poetry Muireann had found in the library and kept, while she soaked for ages in the tub until she was completely wrinkled.

Muireann was pleased to discover they had similar taste in poets, and they discussed their favorite authors as she lay back in the tub drowsily.

Eventually he rose from his chair and reached for a ewer

on the small table by the bed. He poured some hot and some cold into it from the buckets, and then told her to lean forward in the tub while he washed her hair.

"I've always wondered what it would be like to do this," he said softly as he rubbed her scalp with lingering, sensual strokes of his strong fingers, before requesting, "Sit up."

His sudsy hands continued up and down her back until she sighed with absolute abandon. Her blood felt as though it were on fire, and his every touch, every kiss, threatened to set her soaring. He rinsed her hair carefully, making sure no soap got into her eyes, and wrapped a towel turban-like around her head.

Knees trembling, Muireann rinsed herself off one more time and then hauled herself out of the tub. She pulled on her dressing gown and added more hot to the tub from the containers the women had brought.

"Your turn," she said huskily, with a glint in her amethyst eyes.

She lathered his head and back in imitation of what he had done to her, though Lochlainn protested, "It's your birthday. There's no need to fuss over me."

"Oh, but there is. You deserve to be spoilt now and again as well, you know," she whispered in his ear as she rinsed his hair and began to scrub his back and then his chest.

Her hands dipped lower down in the tub, fondling him boldly until he was certain he would lose control.

"My love, it's wonderful, truly, but I want you to have a special night. That will be impossible if you don't stop now," he said in a tight voice, tugging at her wrists urgently.

Muireann kissed him lingeringly on the lips. "I've already had a wonderful day and night. Every night with you is special. You should know that."

Once again Lochlainn began to wonder whether she had a wanton nature as he rose from the tub and she moved to dry him off. She led him to the bed by the hand,

and patted it invitingly, before moving away from him slightly to remove her robe and place it on the back of her chair. He reached over to snuff the candles but she urged, "No, I want to see you, taste you."

Lochlainn was mildly shocked, but was soon carried away on the whirling eddy of his own desires as Muireann led him down avenues they had never explored before. He struggled to match her kiss for kiss, stroke for stroke, with every caress of hand, mouth and tongue heightening his desire to fever pitch, until at last they joined as one.

Their cataclysmic conclusion shook both to the very core of their beings. They collapsed exhaustedly onto their backs and lay there with the chill spring air cooling their naked bodies. Muireann eventually moved to pull the covers up over their glowing flesh, and she gathered him close, so that his head rested on her chest.

"Thank you for today, and tonight. It's been marvelous," she said, stroking his thick dark hair back from his brow lovingly.

Lochlainn felt himself drifting off into a deep sleep. "It's been wonderful for me too."

"I love you, Lochlainn," Muireann declared softly.

But Lochlainn never heard the words he had been longing for ever since he and Muireann had first met. He was already sound asleep in her warm embrace.

The sheepshearing commenced on the second of May, and it was certainly backbreaking work for the many who weren't used to the dipping and cutting. Muireann and Lochlainn worked side by side, and for a time he hoped that she might have relinquished the idea of going away.

But three days after the shearing was finished, he found himself riding on the cart with her to Enniskillen, where she was to board the coach for Dublin.

"Have you got everything you need?" he asked quietly.

"Aye, I do, but you'll have to look after Tadhg for me while I'm gone. I'll miss the little tyke."

"And he'll miss you. We all will," he said, forcing himself to smile, though his eyes remained serious.

Muireann stroked his cheek tenderly.

"I'll be fine. Don't look so worried."

"I know. I just think perhaps I should go with you, to look after you," he said, chewing his lower lip nervously. He tried to ignore the voice inside his head that said he would never make love to her again. He had done so passionately, desperately, the night before. He tried to block out the persistent thought that he would never again see Muireann.

"No, Lochlainn, really. Anthony Lowry will be there to look after all my business interests in Dublin. I need you to do the same for me here. I'll be home as soon as I can, I promise." She squeezed his hand tightly.

"I'll be counting the days. Write to me?"

"I will," she said for the hundredth time.

He helped her up into the interior of the coach. He wrapped her traveling rugs around her legs as if she were the most precious treasure. He held her hand tightly as it rested on the ledge of the door, and then impulsively jumped onto the step and gave her one last kiss through the open window.

Muireann blushed to the roots of her hair, but she was fairly sure no one had noticed.

"Goodbye! I'll see you soon," she called.

The coach moved off from the depot.

He waved seemingly cheerfully until the carriage went out of sight, then released a ragged sigh. Lochlainn wondered how he would live without her by his side day and night. He knew he would count the hours until she once more returned to his arms.

If she ever returned.

Chapter Twenty

Return she did, but the Muireann who returned home to Lochlainn and Barnakilla five weeks later in the middle of June proved to be a very different woman from the one who had gone away on that idyllic May morning.

Muireann arrived back in the middle of June, thinner and paler than ever, with a young man and an even younger woman in tow. Both of them were quite attractive in an earthy sort of way. Muireann simply introduced them to the rest of the workers as Emma and Sam.

"They're going to be teachers," she announced to everyone at dinner on the day she arrived home. "I want schools for all the children, and even reading and writing classes for the adults. The time you spend in class will be charged at quarter rate against your rents."

Lochlainn, delighted when he heard Muireann had finally returned to Barnakilla, had envisioned a romantic reunion. A chance to be alone with her, to greet her warmly and intimately. His hopes were soon dashed completely. Since so many people were crowded into the room to hear her surprise announcement, there wasn't a chance of a quiet word.

When Muireann finally did take the trouble to look at him directly, it was a hollow, vacant stare, almost as though she were looking through him. And over the next few days, as she organized and set up the new school in two of the cottages that had just been built near a small wooded glen, she seemed to avoid Lochlainn and take an inordinate interest in Emma and Sam's welfare.

Sam was a very good-looking young man, only a couple

of years older that Muireann. Lochlainn felt jealousy burn furiously within him, yet he could see nothing wrong with the quiet, withdrawn chap. He behaved circumspectly at all times, and certainly did not seem flirtatious in the least. Since Lochlainn always noticed the three of them together, conversing so no one could overhear, he told himself he was being absurd. Muireann couldn't possibly have taken this poor emaciated young man as her lover, could she?

All the same, he felt left out. They had always used each other as a sounding board, yet now she was setting up the school without even troubling to consult him.

When he finally did get a chance to ask her how she had fared in Dublin a few days after her arrival home, on a sultry June evening, she said curtly, "Everything is fine. The house is sold, and I've paid off a large portion of our mortgage. Those high interest payments were crippling, but I think we've solved that problem now."

"I'm glad to hear it," Lochlainn said quietly, trying to subdue his rising temper. "But that still doesn't tell me what the house was like, or Mrs. Barnes, or any of it. You've been gone for weeks, with not a single letter to any of us, and now you come back with money and these two schoolteachers. What's the matter, are we not good enough for you? Too lacking in education?"

She turned sideways to avoid his blazing gaze.

Infuriated, he took her by the shoulders to get her to face him.

Like lightning, Muireann knocked his hands away roughly and stepped back. "Let go of me, damn you!"

Lochlainn stared down at her in stunned surprise. The very words he had dreaded hearing for so long now echoed in his ears like the death knell at his own funeral.

"I'm terribly sorry, Mrs. Caldwell," he said in his most crisp accent. "It won't happen again."

Turning on his heel, he stalked out of the office.

"No, Lochlainn, wait!" Muireann tried to call him back to explain, but he kept on going and soon disappeared out of sight.

Muireann sighed and let him go. After all, there was work to be done on the farm, and in truth she couldn't really explain it all anyway. He was better off not knowing.

Besides, it was much better to block out the truth even from her own mind, than to face all she had seen, all she had learnt since that fateful day when she had exchanged vows with Augustine Caldwell. Her two trips to Dublin had both been a test of her character. She judged herself harshly, and found herself lacking.

She wanted to make up for what she had done, channel the bitter experiences she had endured into a positive force for the future. There would be time enough to mend fences with Lochlainn when she felt she was ready, or so she believed.

In the meantime there was more than enough to keep her occupied at Barnakilla. For example, the sheep shearing at the start of May had gone quite well. It was the washing, dyeing, carding, spinning and weaving that were causing trouble. She managed in the end to find more experienced weavers, knitters and crocheters, who produced a wide variety of socks, stockings, mufflers and shawls, which were added to an ever growing pile of clothes for the estate workers.

Muireann's sewing circle, too, proceeded to make dresses out of the woolen cloth the looms were producing slowly but surely. At first Muireann hadn't believed it possible to dye the wool, but with her experts' knowledge of lichens, mosses and so on to get the right colors, some of the cloth was proving to be quite attractive.

"You know, we might even be able to sell our surplus soon," she said optimistically to Sharon. "That is, once we all get kitted out for winter ourselves."

Everyone on the estate noticed that she never smiled anymore, except when she played with Tadhg, which wasn't very often. The poor puppy followed her devotedly everywhere. His long spindly legs helped him keep up with her stride as she went restlessly from building to building. He also sat on her lap comfortingly when she was at rest in a chair, but this happened rarely.

"Why is she working so hard? What's the matter with her?" Ciara asked Lochlainn late one evening when she heard the familiar light crunch of gravel as Muireann went past their house.

Lochlainn paused, listening expectantly, hoping she was coming to see him. When the footsteps had disappeared off into the distance, he replied bitterly, "We haven't spoken since she returned from Dublin. I have no idea what she's thinking these days."

Ciara looked gloomy and observed, "Well, perhaps it's for the best. It will save you worse disappointment in the long run if you end it now."

"That's the last thing I wanted to hear," he snapped.

He stormed out of the house and headed in the opposite direction from the one Muireann had taken. He knew if he met her on the path on a balmy moonlit night, he would only end up making a complete fool of himself.

Day after day, Muireann laboriously kept track of all the finances, tallying up the hours everyone worked, and how much each family owed for rent and food. She had made it clear from the start that the workers were not to consider themselves servants, but neither was she running a charity. Not when her own finances were in such desperate shape with the mortgage and other expenses every month. Some people even worked two or three shifts in an effort to pay off their arrears, and Muireann prayed they were all succeeding in keeping the wolf from the door.

Her brother-in-law Neil continued to support her endeavors by buying more timber, which they cut from the new forests she had bought from the colonel and from Malcolm Stephens. It was hard work clearing all the trees, but Muireann wanted them all out to conserve her own hardwoods for Lochlainn's carpentry enterprise, and in order to consolidate the estates. With the trees gone and the stumps dug up, she would have more pastureland for her expanding herds, and could convert her current pastures into fields for crops.

As June matured into July, she began to feel more content with the way things were going on the estate and more at ease that she had done the right thing, despite the horror she had felt at her own acts in Dublin in May.

Her only worry now was that she knew she had to mend fences with Lochlainn, who had continued to avoid her, and never spent time alone with her for more than a minute since they had exchanged heated words. She had missed him desperately, but he was so good, so decent, as were all the people at Barnakilla. She was almost afraid of contaminating them, or being punished for what she had done, even though she knew it had been for the best.

Lochlainn had immediately jumped to the conclusion that their relationship was over. He was certain that the trip to Dublin had triggered her seeming depression because she pined for her old life.

His theory couldn't have been further from the truth, but Muireann had no idea what he was thinking. She tried feebly to explain her odd behavior to him without revealing everything. At the back of her mind she knew perhaps one day he might find out the truth if he quizzed Emma and Sam about their past life too deeply, but for the moment they were following her orders and keeping to themselves, teaching but not socializing with the tenantry except at meal times.

One evening toward the end of July, Muireann went to

look for Lochlainn in the carpentry workshop, and was relieved to find him there.

"Please, Lochlainn, we need to talk to each other without arguing," she said quickly when she saw him moving to leave.

It crossed his mind to tell her he was busy, but over six weeks of this impasse had certainly been long enough. He needed her. He only prayed she was going to tell him something he would be glad to hear.

He laid down his tools. "All right."

She went ahead of him up the path to her office, and poured them both a glass of the vile liquor Augustine had always drunk. Lochlainn noticed her hands shook but said nothing, merely waited for her to start.

"I wanted to speak to you about when I first came home, about how I shouted at you. I'm terribly sorry if I upset you. It was the way you grabbed me. It hurt. It made me feel helpless. I know you didn't mean to hurt me, but on top of everything else, well, I just sort of snapped."

"Everything else?" Lochlainn prompted softly.

She came to sit down beside him. "The bad dreams came back as soon as I left here. I think it must have been because I went back to Dublin, and had all sorts of terrible associations with Augustine's death. I hope you can understand that I was distraught. Forgive me if I upset you or seemed to reject you.

"It's just that so much has happened since January. I've been trying to get things more settled, plan for our future. I'm not used to any of this. I led a sheltered, protected life until I came here. I know it's no excuse for the way I've acted, but I'm asking you to try to be patient with a foolish young girl, and forgive me.

"I've missed you, Lochlainn. I want us to try to get things back to the way they were between us before I went away. It may be wrong of me to want you, to rely upon you so much, but I can't do this on my own anymore. I don't *want* to do it on my own anymore, Lochlainn."

At her words, Lochlainn simply opened his arms wide and she ran into them and hugged him tightly. He stroked his hands down her back soothingly, but was unable to trust himself to speak at first. He had grave misgivings as to the wisdom of resuming the affair, not least because she was apparently admitting to him that she was still completely distraught over Augustine's death.

"If that's what you really want, Muireann, of course we can try to get back what we once had. But as you say, you're young. That isn't a criticism. You've coped far better than people twice or even three times your age. But what I'm saying is, you have your whole life ahead of you. I'm so much older than you, Muireann. You might change your mind about us one day.

"With so much having happened, I do think you need time to ponder the situation a bit more first. You yourself said when we started all this back in January that you wanted to be strong. I've been here for you by your side since. But there may come a time when you find you don't need me any longer."

"I do need you, Lochlainn, truly," Muireann said tearfully.

"No, you don't, Muireann, not really. You went to Dublin on your own, and you coped. I'm sure it was hard, but you did it on your own. You're strong, Muireann, but you don't have to be strong all the time. You've worked so hard in the past few weeks since you got back. Let me share the burden with you now. But if there ever comes a time when you don't need me any longer, I'll understand."

Muireann slumped back into her chair wearily, shattered by his rejection of any future for them together. She sat there silently, feeling utterly defeated.

He relented at once. "Please, my dear, I hate to see you looking so wan and pale. It isn't like you." Taking her by the arm gently, he helped her out of the chair and led her to her room. He urged her to lie down on the bed, and sat on the edge.

He held one hand tenderly and asked, "Where's the woman who drove the coach and four and had a snowball fight with me in Dublin, or who used to climb trees with Tadhg?"

He reached down then and patted the pup fondly on the head as it wrapped itself around its mistress's feet.

Muireann lay there silently. In her heart she was disappointed. If she had expected any declaration of love from Lochlainn, certainly none seemed to be forthcoming.

When Lochlainn got no response, he began to rise from the bed. Muireann's hand shot out, and she clung to him. "Please don't go. We haven't finished talking. You haven't told me you forgive me."

Lochlainn gave a bitter laugh. "There's nothing to forgive. Not really. People can't help the way they feel, can they? I'm sorry I upset you. I didn't understand. I pushed you too hard. But I don't own you, my dear, any more than you own me.

"I must admit I don't always agree with your decisions about the fields, the school, the trading. But I want you to have your own thoughts and ideas, your own emotions and feelings, even when I hold you in my arms like this." He kissed her forehead. "Sometimes caring for someone means knowing when to let them go."

Muireann looked up into his steel gray eyes and saw no trace of the light that had once shone in them. Lochlainn had almost given up hope. It was hard for him to accept that Muireann was sincere in wanting him back. Even if she were, how long would they be able to go on like this?

He never seemed to know what she was thinking anymore. Had he ever? There were all sorts of hidden places within her that he didn't dare explore for fear of losing her as he had once lost Tara. Now he simply felt lonely and worn out, and unsure of his ability to ever make her truly happy.

He pulled the covers up to her chin and then moved to snuff out the candles.

"You're not going already, are you?" she asked, disappointment evident in her tone. "We haven't had a chance to discuss anything yet."

Lochlainn shook his head. "We don't have to decide about this right now, do we? I have to get back to work, and you look exhausted, Muireann."

"Don't leave me," Muireann pleaded tearfully.

Lochlainn hadn't seen her cry since the early days after she had been widowed. He relented at the sight, and offered, "I'll sit with you until you fall asleep, all right?"

Muireann stroked his cheek and reached up to kiss him passionately on the mouth.

Despite his best efforts to keep his hands off her, Lochlainn couldn't resist her rousing kisses forever. Soon he found himself naked, making love to her so gently he almost thought he was dreaming. Muireann sighed and moaned under him, and after her long, gasping climax, she suddenly began to weep.

Lochlainn asked her worriedly if he had hurt her, but she denied it, eventually crying herself to sleep in his arms.

He lay sleepless for hours by her side, with her wrapped around him like a clinging kitten. His misgivings grew as the hours ticked by.

Finally he eased himself from her side as the early morning light filtered through the curtains, got dressed, and let himself out silently.

Lochlainn saw over the next few days that the resumption of their relationship did not seem to do anything to improve Muireann's mood. Gone was the joy he had seen on her face on the beach at Rossnowlagh and when she had run about the estate on her birthday with Tadhg skipping at her heels.

He was sure it was only a matter of time before Muireann returned to Scotland, a suspicion which seemed to be confirmed as July made way for August, and yet another crisis for Muireann at Barnakilla began to loom on the horizon like a dark thundercloud.

Muireann had prayed that no more emergencies would arise, but rumors began to spread in early August that the potato crops in Europe were not doing well because of the unusually cool spring and very damp summer weather.

Being quite far north, Muireann knew they couldn't start harvesting their crops until the end of August, and their potatoes until the end of October, and prayed for good weather. But a murky cold fog seemed to settle on the entire country, accompanied by a strange odor, not unlike rotting vegetables.

Muireann looked out of her window one gray August morning, and then turned back into the warmth of Lochlainn's arms.

"It certainly looks grim out there," she said sleepily, her breath tickling his shoulder.

"Maybe you should have a day off for a change," Lochlainn suggested. "It would do you the world of good, Muireann. You've been working like a slave ever since you arrived here seven months ago. Go into Enniskillen to do some shopping, or go visit Priscilla and the boys at the Grange. I'm sure they would be delighted to see you."

"It is tempting, but no. I have too much to do today. Besides, if I had one day off, I would just lie in bed. Not that I ever really did that back home. I always found things to occupy my time, but I would often sit in bed reading, writing letters, and so on. So one day in bed would be absolutely splendid. But not today."

"Why not?"

"Because I happen to know that *you* have a huge long list of things to do as well."

Lochlainn frowned down at her.

"What, you didn't expect me to want to spend the whole day in bed by myself, did you?" She smiled up at him. "Where would be the fun in that?"

Lochlainn, overwhelmingly relieved that she had at last smiled again, hugged her close.

Muireann planted a kiss on his mouth, and despite the nagging voice at the back of his mind reminding him to get to work, that it was daylight, that their special time together had to come to an end, he made love to Muireann in the glowing sunlight that suddenly lit the bed as a ray pierced through the gloomy clouds, until they both lay exhausted.

With one last kiss he tore himself away from Muireann. Donning his clothes hastily, he fled the room. He didn't want to linger long enough to see the look of regret on her face at what they had done in the bright light of day.

As she watched him go, Muireann looked anything but regretful. With each passing day, she knew she loved Lochlainn more and more. But how could she bring herself to tell him? All the secrets she had kept from him weighed on her heart like lead.

How could she be sure he really loved her? She was grateful for all his help, of course. But how did she know he hadn't begun their relationship to help himself, his family and friends? Had he in fact been using her? *Everyone uses people,* she thought cynically. *Even me.*

Chapter Twenty-one

Over the next three months, the dreaded potato blight, which had started as only a wild rumor spread about by scaremongers, suddenly seized the land in its deathly grip. The first reports of the crop disease were printed in the English newspapers, when ruined potatoes were harvested in the Isle of Wight and Kent on the eleventh of August. The news reached Muireann a few days later, and she discussed it with Lochlainn one evening as they sat in her small office while the rain pattered down on the roof.

"I have a bad feeling about this," she said, showing the newspaper to Lochlainn. "Call it my Scottish superstition, but I think we should take this seriously. If the best land in England has been infected by this blight, what will happen here?"

"I don't know. Surely it might only be a small local incident. The Isle of Wight is tiny, and the land in Kent could be isolated to stop it spreading, you know, by preventing the carts from trading further afield. The disease might never get this far. Those places are hundreds of miles away across the sea, after all," he sought to reassure her.

"I think we would do better to be prepared, than to do nothing now and then have to deal with yet another crisis here on the estate in another six weeks' time when our lumpers for the winter are meant to be coming out of the ground."

"What do you suggest?"

Really, she never seems to be content with anything these days, he reflected with a touch of impatience.

"I think we should buy oats, wheat, and seed potatoes,

and turnips, carrots, beets. We should cut down on milk consumption, or use more sheep and goat milk, and lay up lots of cheeses. We will also need to fish a lot more. We can smoke it for the winter. I'd like to do another seaweed run to Donegal as well. It can be dried and is apparently very nutritious. Not to mention all the shellfish, which can be smoked.

"Also, let's see if we can get a good price for some more pigs, and I want the men to go onto the islands in the lough and hunt for wild goats. They can capture a few she-goats, and shoot the others. I've heard the meat is quite tasty. Both pigs and goats eat scraps, and will be cheap enough to keep if we're careful. Let's also build more rabbit and pheasant pens. I want the best men to go hunting as soon as the season starts again. And a few more chickens, geese, and ducks wouldn't go to waste."

"Shouldn't we just wait until the *Andromeda* comes?"

"No. It isn't due back here for several more weeks. If people start to panic, it will drive the prices up."

"What will we use to buy these things? I thought money was a bit tight at the moment until the accounts come in at the end of the month."

"I still have a little money set by from the sale of the Dublin house. We also have all the woolen bolts of cloth, which I was going to use for the women's and men's clothes this winter. Now I think I'll trade it and get flannel and some heavy cotton and see what money is left after the sale."

In the end, Lochlainn gave in. "I'll buy everything you've listed for me, but I do think you're being a bit gloomy."

"I know, Lochlainn, and I'm sorry. But ever since, well, for the past eight months anyway, every single time I think I see the light at the end of the tunnel, something comes to darken our already desperate situation."

Lochlainn pulled her to him then and kissed her tenderly, stroking back a stray curl from her temple.

"I have faith in your judgment and will do as you say, my dear. But let's just hope you're only having morbid fancies."

He knew she wasn't sleeping as well as she had been before she had left for Dublin. Though she never spoke of her nightmares, even when he demanded she tell him about them, they were terrifying enough to make her wake up screaming sometimes.

"And if I'm not being morbid?" she asked quietly, staring up at him.

Lochlainn held her close, propping his chin on the top of her head. "Then God help us all."

On the fifteenth of October, after a particularly rainy autumn, Muireann could bear the uncertainty no longer. Assembling all the men by the side of the potato beds, which she had already noticed had begun to emit a rancid odor, she ordered them to start digging.

As the first batches came up, she sagged against Lochlainn in relief. Though the potatoes were quite small, they still seemed to be edible.

"Thank God!" she sighed, hugging him to her, heedless of who saw.

Lochlainn had patted her on the shoulder in embarrassment and proceeded to help with the digging.

But about three days later, as the women were preparing the dinner in the kitchen for everyone, a huge commotion broke out, and Muireann came running from the turf cutting as soon as she heard the news.

"They were sound only the other day, and now look!" Sharon shrieked.

"Patrick, Mark, saddle the two horses now and ride into Enniskillen. Take whatever money I have in the strongbox. Buy as much rice and Indian meal as you can with it, and hurry!" Muireann ordered, as she stared at the black putrescent mass oozing all over the floor through the wickerwork basket.

Lochlainn came running in a short time later, having heard all sorts of weeping and wailing going up around the estate, and curious as to why everyone was standing there stock still.

Muireann pointed wordlessly as Lochlainn gazed at the black ooze on the floor, uncomprehending.

He gaped. "What on earth is it?"

"Our potatoes."

"Oh no, God, no!" Lochlainn ran his fingers through his hair as he stared in horror at the ruination of all his dreams.

Muireann shook her head, and then squared her shoulders and looked around the room commandingly.

"Right, I want everyone out at the potato storage pit now, and I mean everyone. The men will dig, the women will fill the creels. Get all the knives out, will you, Brona? Sharon, fill up every cauldron in the house, the washtubs too. We need to dig all the potatoes up and cut them in half. Any potatoes that look all right, we boil them now. Hopefully they will keep for a few days cooked. God knows what would happen if we just left them lying. Any other potatoes go into the laundry tubs. We will boil them up for starch, which we can sell to the laundry in Enniskillen."

Everyone continued to stare at the floor, until Muireann exclaimed impatiently, "Come on, don't just stand there! We haven't a moment to waste!"

Muireann reached for a knife and stalked out, and began the heart-breaking task. Lifting the first shovelful herself, she almost gagged at the smell and then began to pick through them with her knife. Lochlainn came up to stand beside her a short time later, and took the shovel wordlessly.

The tenantry all came out to lend a hand then, digging, cutting, filling the creels, and carrying them back and forth to the kitchen. Only about an eighth were salvageable, and even then Muireann was not so sure they should be eaten.

She put plenty of salt in the boiling water, and then tasted one herself.

"It seems fine, but we won't overdo it. We will just have to eat them warmed up in the stew for the next few days until they run out. Everyone gets one hot one now, but no more. If these still have traces of the disease, the last thing we need is to all get ill."

Lochlainn agreed with Muireann's assessment of the situation, and oversaw the handing out of the rations at dinner. It was a gloomy meal at best, eaten quickly and silently as they knew they would soon have to return to their soul-destroying work at the potato bed.

After most of them had gone, she remarked to Lochlainn, "We're complaining because the few we do have to eat will be rationed and served up in stew. We ought to be thankful that we have any at all. I just hope we've laid in enough stores, and that we can get more. Otherwise we're all going to have a very hard winter."

Muireann went into the storerooms then to do some calculations. "I know what you're going to say, that the *Andromeda* will come. But they're probably facing the same disaster we are. Also, they'll have to stop sailing soon anyway because of the winter weather. We'll be lucky if they fit in another run. I say we shouldn't get our hopes up that they will make it through again this year, not with all the terrible gales we've been having recently. So we have to begin making other plans. If we ration the food we have here at the moment, how long could we survive until the next crops are ready?"

Lochlainn took out his small pocket notebook and began to scribble down some figures hastily. "There are still onions, beets and turnips to come. If we have oatmeal and rice, and cornmeal . . ."

"We need to think about the milk and eggs as well. I

mean, I know I've paid off all the arrears on the mortgage, and a bit extra, but we still have to make the monthly payments. What a terrible choice I'm being presented with. If we eat, we might lose Barnakilla. If we keep Barnakilla, these people might all starve."

"I don't have any answers for you, Muireann," Lochlainn whispered, trying to subdue the feeling of nausea that washed over him.

This was the end, he was sure of it. Any sane woman would cut her losses and run. There was nothing keeping Muireann here now. The whole thing had been one impossible dream. He had lied to her, tricked her into coming, spurred her on in the belief that he could restore Barnakilla to the glorious days he remembered from his childhood.

His own madness, ambition, and desire for this lovely woman had brought about everyone's ruin, he thought wildly.

Muireann saw the stricken look on his face and hugged Lochlainn silently, drawing strength from his huge frame as he towered over her, wrapping her in his arms as though he would never let her go.

But free her he must. He couldn't expect her to endure famine. He recalled all he had heard from his sister of the terrible events of 1841. It was unthinkable to subject a woman like Muireann to that.

"At least you did try. You made me buy the food in advance," he commented softly, trying desperately to cling to the illusion that they could make it.

"Please, Lochlainn, don't, don't talk, not now. I need you to hold me, love me," she moaned, trying to block out the nightmare of the black potatoes.

"Sharon or Brona could come in at any moment," he gasped, shocked.

"And that would be awful, wouldn't it? That someone might see us, think we cared about each other?" she snapped.

"Your reputation!"

"Liar! That isn't it at all!" she accused. "I saw the way you looked at me the other day when I hugged you. You're ashamed of me. I suppose I can't blame you. I'm a complete failure now, aren't I?"

Lochlainn stared at her in utter disbelief. "How can you say that after everything you've accomplished!" he exploded. "You've done everything you can to restore Barnakilla, to help these people, but even you can't work miracles! You're not God. Neither am I! Do you think if I were I would have let all this happen! How do you think I feel, having to watch you sacrifice everything, while you suffer and slave away day in and day out, barely taking time to even sleep, unless I come to your bed to give you a few hours of mindless oblivion?"

Muireann sucked in her breath sharply. "Is that what you think it is?" she gasped, feeling her gorge rise.

"I'm sorry, I shouldn't have said that," he apologized, reaching for her.

She stalked out of the storeroom and headed for her office.

Lochlainn ran after her, pleading, "I didn't mean it!"

Muireann sat down in her chair, utterly defeated, and put her head in her hands. She could have tolerated more deprivation, but Lochlainn's criticism was almost too much to bear.

"Please, Muireann, I'm sorry. I never meant to hurt you. I'm angry at myself for not being able to do anything about this," he insisted, pacing the floor anxiously.

At last she looked up. "Then why did you call our time together mindless oblivion? I asked you to be honest with me when I first came here in January. I can hardly blame you now for being exactly that."

"All right, you want the truth, Muireann, I'll tell you. I never know where I am with you, what you're going to do next. One minute you're warm and loving, the next minute you shut me out for weeks on end. You never speak to me about the things that really matter, about the death of Augustine, the trip to Dublin. Even worse than trying to figure out what is going on in those dark recesses of your mind is lurching from one crisis to the next, day after day.

"So if you want the truth, then here it is plain and simple. I'm terrified. I'm frightened all the time. I'm convinced that one day I will wake up to an appalling reality that is of my own making, though not always within my control. Does that make any sense?"

She stared at him, appalled at the depth of his anguish.

"I want to do what is best for everyone, but I just don't have any answers anymore. You and I have literally lived from day to day and night to night, never knowing what's around the corner, or even where our next meal is coming from. I feel I've let you down. That I should never have brought you here. Part of me tries to tell myself that we will come through this if we all pull together. The other part says we should just cut our losses now, quit while we're ahead," he confessed.

Then he sighed. "But if we do that we will be letting all these people down. I couldn't bear that either. I know it was your idea to take them in from the colonel and Mr. Cole, but it's my duty to make this work as estate manager, to shoulder the burden with you. But I think we have reached the end of both our tethers now. Perhaps it's time for you to consider selling Barnakilla and going home."

"You can honestly say that to me after all we've been through?" she said, stunned.

Though he knew he was lying, the last thing he could admit to her was that he loved her. Not if he was going to convince her to go home before she got dragged down along with the entire estate.

"I can't trust myself, Muireann, or you. I'm sorry. You're like two different people, one hard and practical, the other soft and warm and yielding. I feel that we went down this road as lovers because I was afraid. I've hung onto you like a drowning man clinging to a chunk of floating debris. I clutch you to me, trying to right my eddying world, in the hope of staying afloat. I'm sorry if that means I've been using you. Perhaps you've been using me as well, for the same reasons.

"But surely you see it will all have to end sometime. It's a miracle you aren't already with child. What I've done to you was wrong, but I couldn't help it. I know it isn't an excuse, any more than saying I needed the release I found inside you to keep me sane. But I do have some scruples, some dignity. It's got to end. I can't go on being a selfish brute any longer. Not after everything you've tried to do for all of us."

"What are you saying? That you want to leave Barnakilla? That you're abandoning me?" Muireann asked tearfully.

"I'm telling you for your own good, Muireann, it's all over. Sell this old pile of rubble, and go. Just go!"

Muireann was stupefied by his words. Certainly the potatoes had failed, but how could he ever think she would give up so easily? Anger welled up inside her, and the ruthless streak she had warned him about suddenly came to the fore.

She rose from the chair and stood chest to chest with him. "I'm sorry, Mr. Roche, but I don't accept your view of the situation at all. Only the potatoes have gone. The rest of the estate is still standing. I won't give in, not even to the forces of nature. I refuse to give up Barnakilla without a fight. I told you I would do anything to save it. You don't know even one half of what I've done to keep a roof over all our heads!" she said, her eyes glittering with unshed tears.

"You gave me a promise when I hired you in January, and I intend to see you keep that promise. We've worked side by side together every day since. I have no intention of letting you break your promise. You swore you would never leave me as long as I needed you. I'm now reminding you of your promise, nay, insisting that you keep it."

Lochlainn scowled and turned away to stare into the fire so that she couldn't see the expression on his face. "Aye, I did promise you that, Muireann. But I thought we were talking about things for your own good. Staying here at Barnakilla is *not* good for you. The two of us being lovers isn't good for you. You would only tire of me in the end, come to resent me being inferior to you."

"I would have thought you knew me better than that!" she exclaimed, piqued at his lack of faith in her love for him. "But this *is* for my good. This is my home and no one, *nothing*, is going to make me leave!"

Her voice softened then, and she looked up at him longingly. "Please, Lochlainn, please don't abandon me now."

Lochlainn soothed her as she broke into agonized sobs, hugging her close and leading her to her bedroom.

He sat against the headboard of the bed, let her recline on his chest and kissed her softly on the temple. "Just rest, dear. It's been a terribly emotional day for us all. Please, calm down. There's no need to decide everything this minute."

Lochlainn struggled to keep his touch light and comforting, but as she wept against his chest, he turned her onto her back and began to kiss the tears away. Soon her snuffling gasps subsided, and she began to moan softly.

Time stood still for both of them as he tugged down her underclothes and stroked her until he felt her press down urgently against his hand. He watched her response to him in fascination, until at last he could bear it no longer and divested himself of his trousers. She climaxed the instant they joined as one, taking him with her along the dark road of passion so compellingly that he thought his soul was being ripped from his body.

Despite his brave attempt to get Muireann to see reason in the face of overwhelming odds, he knew he would have been brokenhearted if she had assented to his suggestion. At any rate, how could he give all this up? It would be like ceasing to breathe. He wanted Muireann so badly, he could barely restrain himself when he was around her.

She had thought him ashamed of her? Nothing could have been further from the truth. He longed to tell her he loved her. His fear of being laughed at, or her interpreting his declaration as an attempt to try to persuade her to stay, even though it might be against her best interests, silenced him.

Lochlainn flipped himself over onto his back heavily and sighed. Muireann snuggled up to him, kissing him full on the lips before resting her cheek against his.

"Please, Lochlainn, let's not fight anymore. I'm so tired," she admitted.

"I know, my love, I do know. I am too," he sighed, holding her close.

"You won't leave me, will you?" she begged softly.

"No, never. I gave you my word, Muireann. Even though I've said many a foolish thing in my time, I have no wish to take that promise back," he said gently, and felt a great burden being lifted from his shoulders.

She wanted him now. It was obvious from her kisses, the way she opened to him like a morning glory seeking the warmth of the sun.

Enjoy it while it lasts, Lochlainn, he counseled himself.

No more worries about the future. There is only the here and now.

Muireann hugged him close and prayed she could one day make him love her as much as she loved him. Surely her class shouldn't be an insuperable obstacle? She didn't care what people thought. She only wanted to be happy with the man she loved.

Lochlainn had advised her to go home, but she knew it was only because he worried about her. That surely was an indication that he at least cared a little, wasn't it? She could make this work, she knew she could. They would have a long rest that night, and face the future in the morning.

Lochlainn drowsily closed his eyes, and vowed he would stop comparing Muireann to Tara. Muireann wouldn't run away. She had never run from anything in her life. They were two very different women, he reminded himself, and began to dream of a lovely violet-eyed woman with raven black hair who enveloped him in a silky cocoon of warmth and tenderness such as he had never known.

Chapter Twenty-two

As the Famine raged throughout Ireland, it was a hard winter at Barnakilla. Despite all of Muireann's economies, the estate continued to be encumbered by expenses and the mortgage, and the food restrictions she had put into force meant privation for everyone. When times got hard in December, some of the original Barnakilla tenants urged her to send the newcomers away, but Muireann adamantly refused.

"By keeping them here, you are ruining our chances of

survival!" old Thomas the slate cutter argued one day after dinner.

"I can't send them away, Thomas. They've all worked so hard trying to help make all my dreams for this place come true. I can't turn them out to die a lonely death on the roads. Don't ask me to evict them again, is that clear?"

"Dreams don't fill our bellies!" he sniped.

She rounded on him furiously. "I never asked you for a penny of back rent. I could have evicted every single one of you and found paying tenants, couldn't I? So don't you dare complain to me again! If you're so worried about your survival, why don't you get up off your arse and go hunting and fishing."

The old man stalked out, and she felt Lochlainn's eyes upon her across the room.

"I'm sorry," she sighed when Thomas had gone. "I shouldn't have scolded him like that. He only had the nerve to say what a lot of the others have been thinking. But I've been out hunting and fishing every day this week in the cold, and all the carters have gone everywhere looking for food to buy, only to come back with nothing."

"You're just tired, my girl, that's all. Thomas has a tough old hide. He'll be fine. It's not your fault nothing is being bought and sold at the markets. People are hanging on to whatever they have. It's too late now for any ship to get through, so we'll just have to make do with the food here until the *Andromeda* comes back again."

"We're going to have to kill some of the livestock, aren't we? If we don't, someone will only do it himself, or try to steal them."

"I know. I've put patrols on the edges of our lands and at the storehouses day and night. People will do anything to get food."

"We'll soon be sick of eating soup, but at least it is warm

and filling. But Thomas does have a point. We have so many mouths to feed."

"Do you have to also give something to every beggar who knocks at the door?" Lochlainn asked.

Her shoulders stiffened and she got up off the bench to pump some water. "The Irish have always been famous for their hospitality. I'm not going to turn them away empty-handed, not when we at least still have a warm home to live in. They have nothing but the rags they wear, and if they are lucky, a barn or loft to sleep in. I'll go hunting on the islands tomorrow to make up for it. I'm sure they won't give a damn that they're eating goat."

"There is another option, you know," he said, taking over the pump to help her fill the cauldron. "Let some of our tenants go to the workhouses. They will be taken in with your recommendation, and they are clean and hardworking."

Muireann refused to even consider the proposal. "Those places are full of filth and disease, and the families are all split up, with the husbands and wives and even the children in separate dormitories. I've seen the workhouse in Enniskillen. It's not a place I would wish anyone to have to resort to. No, I'm afraid I'm going to do the unthinkable. I hate asking my family for help, but if it means saving us, I'll just have to tell my father everything. Make him try to understand why I kept the truth from him for so long."

He could just imagine her imperious old father whisking her away from him forever. "But, Muireann, you've done so well. Why tell him now? Things will get better."

"Because my pride won't fill people's bellies. Maybe it's about time my parents knew the truth, all of it. I'm tired of feeling ashamed of what I've done."

Lochlainn frowned. "Ashamed? Why should you be? You've been marvelous the way you've kept your head all this time."

Muireann hauled the pot over to the fire, then sat down on a kitchen bench heavily. "I've been ruthless and unkind. Just look at how I treated old Thomas just now. I'll try Colonel Lowry first, to see if there is any more money forthcoming from Mr. Blessington and Mr. Henry's ill-gotten gains. If nothing can be released, then I shall consider writing to Father. But who knows? With any luck I might get some very expensive Christmas presents we could sell," she said, trying to sound optimistic.

Lochlainn dreaded her parents seeing her in such desperate circumstances. Surely her father would insist upon her selling Barnakilla and going back to Fintry with him, once he knew.

At the same time, though, Alistair Graham couldn't force her to sell the estate, could he? She could always leave it in his own hands, and then when her father simmered down, she could come home to him again.

He was going to suggest it might not be such a bad idea if she went home for Christmas, which was only a few weeks away. But somehow it seemed so underhanded. He also loathed the thought of even being parted from her for one day, let alone indefinitely.

Muireann went back to the stable block and sat in her freezing office as she sought to balance the books. She tried not to think of her family, the little nephew she still hadn't seen, and Christmas the year before, when she had attended every ball of the season with Augustine.

"Any luck?" Lochlainn asked when he came in that night from hunting, and saw her looking completely forlorn.

Muireann threw her arms around his neck to warm him, and shook her head. "We just have to keep on going as best we can until the spring, unless we get help from home. I'll write to Neil, ask him to cash in all my shares. That is, if there are any left."

"You could always go home. There's your sister and her baby, Michael, and your other cousins."

"No, I'm staying here. This is my home. I'll not leave you to go off to have a good time with my family when you all need me."

Lochlainn kissed down the side of her neck while his long, lean fingers worked at the fastenings of her gown. Soon his mouth was feasting on one rosy nipple. He prayed God they would be given some form of reprieve. For surely He had to know that without Muireann, he was nothing and no one. And the good Lord only knew what would happen to them all if she ever left.

By Christmas, some help had come in the shape of Muireann's many presents from her family, who assumed she hadn't come over because she was still in deep mourning. Much to her surprise, there was also some charitable relief from the Stephenses, who couldn't bear to see Muireann suffering so cruelly. Colonel Lowry also advanced her a small sum, claiming it was from Mr. Blessington's funds, when it had actually come from his son Anthony, in Dublin. The colonel half-wondered if the raven-haired beauty hadn't turned his son's head after all, so angry was Anthony when the colonel had spoken to him of Barnakilla's imminent collapse.

But with the cold winter weather came disease, which spread through the crowded cottages like wildfire. The tenants began to die of fever all over Barnakilla. They were mainly the people from the Lowry and Cole estates, who had arrived in poor condition to start with. But even people from Barnakilla itself began to die of the typhus, which turned the patient's face black as coal before death, and produced the most foul odors.

There was also relapsing fever, which turned the victim's skin a yellow color. Though the patients often started to improve slightly, they would suddenly be struck down again by the mysterious malady.

As the diseases spread, Emma and Sam closed the school, and despite Muireann's ardent pleading, they took to the roads together.

"What you tried to do for us was very kind, Muireann, but once a—" Emma began.

"No, I don't believe that!" Muireann shouted at the lovely young woman. "Please, stay, give it a few weeks longer!"

"What we eat here could go to others. Don't worry, we'll be fine. If things start looking up, we'll come back," Sam promised. "You did your best, Muireann. You gave us a chance, showed us a whole new life that could be ours for the asking. We won't forget that. Don't think you've failed. Only the potato did that."

He hugged her tightly as Lochlainn looked on. Sam and Emma disappeared out of the kitchen door into a swirling snowstorm which coated the landscape in a fleecy blanket.

Muireann's tears began to fall then, and she shuddered.

"You were very fond of them," Lochlainn remarked quietly. "How did the three of you meet?"

"I had an, er, accident in the street in Dublin, and the two of them came to my rescue. They needed work, so I brought them here," Muireann said vaguely, avoiding his piercing steel-gray gaze.

"An accident? Nothing serious, I hope."

Muireann made no reply, but moved over to the scullery sink and began to pump water for the dinnertime soup, unwilling to discuss the matter further.

As the sickness continued to spread, Muireann appointed some of the single women to nurse the patients in a small makeshift hospital she had created after the deaths of several elderly people emptied one of the large new cottages that had been built over the summer.

"At least if we isolate the cases, the fever will have less chance of spreading to the others."

Lochlainn was unwilling to allow Muireann to expose herself to the horrors of the fevers, but she shrugged and said wearily, "What choice do I have? They need to be looked after. Let's just hope I'm one of the lucky ones."

Lochlainn lost his temper at last. She seemed to be daring death, without a care for him or the rest of Barnakilla. "Why does it always have to be you?" he snapped. "Why can't you let someone else do some of the dirty, disgusting jobs around here?"

Muireann stared at him for a moment in amazement. "I have to do it myself. I must lead Barnakilla from the front. These people will never trust me, never go along with my schemes if they see me shirking, or see any sign of weakness. Why are you always trying to protect me?" she demanded, putting her hands on her hips and tapping her foot in exasperation.

"Because you don't belong here, don't you see!"

Muireann sat down heavily then, misunderstanding his words. Despite everything, she had failed. She would never be able to call this place home, she knew that now. Even Lochlainn thought she was wasting her time trying to carry on such a futile struggle.

They had talked about this in October, and two months later, she could see he had been right. She ought to just go back to Fintry before she did any more damage. But how she would miss the lough, the stunning landscape of mountains and forests which swept majestically down to the shores of the Erne. How could she give all this up? Give Lochlainn up?

"Thank you for your concern. Now if you will excuse me, I have some laundry to scrub," she stated coldly, turning away from him.

Lochlainn tried to pull her into his arms, but she wriggled away and declared, "Mr. Roche, I told you to go. Are you deaf?"

She looked at him then with something akin to hatred, and Lochlainn, convinced the day had finally come when she no longer wanted him, simply left.

Muireann sat there dazedly, and in an uncharacteristic bout of fury swept all the empty saucepans clattering to the floor.

What has it all been for? she wondered angrily as she threw her cloak over her navy blue woolen gown. Ordering the dog to stay in his basket, she marched out to the potato pit, which she viewed as one might an enemy. She would have succeeded, if only the blight hadn't come. But now, all of her struggles had been for nothing.

She walked to the edge of the estate, listening to the soft crunch of her boots on the newly fallen blanket of snow. She reveled in the peace and solitude of the woods, admiring the tall trees. Though bereft of leaves, they still looked majestic. She touched the trunks, and the ground, then began walking around the whole estate, taking in the pastures, the quarry, the stable block, the cottages. As she came back around to the mansion and stables, she saw the workers scurrying to and fro, and wondered to herself if she should indeed sell it all and go back home.

It wasn't as if these people were her family or friends. They had all been complete strangers when she had arrived, even Lochlainn. He had just told her she didn't belong at Barnakilla. Maybe it was time to stop trying to fool herself. Her mother and sister had always told her to try to be more womanly, that her expected role in life was to marry a man who could protect her.

She had failed in that regard with Augustine. But why couldn't she find someone else? She never would meet a man her parents would approve of if she remained on a debt-ridden, decaying estate. Yet the beauty, the happiness she had felt there, the golden glowing days, the warm passionate nights . . .

Muireann shook her head then. It wasn't real. Lochlainn came and went like a demon lover from that Coleridge poem. She must look it up again some time, she thought idly, as she wandered into the stable block to see how the weavers were getting on.

Everyone there smiled and greeted her cheerily, but she could see their pinched faces. It was her arrogance that had brought them to this. Surely there had to be someone who was willing to take all of this on, to save these people from certain destruction?

Muireann went back inside her office and wrote to Neil and then her father. In the letter to her brother-in-law she expressed her doubts as to her ability to keep going at Barnakilla any longer, and her intention to ask her father for help on the pretext that the potato failure had resulted in unforeseen financial difficulties for her. There was really no need to tell her father she had been lying to him all along.

She sealed the letter to her father in the one to Neil, and wrote to Anthony Lowry in Dublin, asking him to gather together all the papers regarding Barnakilla with a view to selling it to any interested parties who were willing to match her price.

She calculated that price by looking at how much she owed on the mortgage, how much the businesses would bring the new owner, and how much she would need to pay the workers on the estate a stipend to tide them over in case they were evicted. She then added up the rents, and added that to the figure. Sealing the letter with a heavy heart, she stared at it as it lay on the blotter. She was almost tempted to tear it up, but decided in the end it would do no harm to post it just in case.

She went out and tethered Bran and Misty's foal to one of the carts, and loaded up several live pheasants, rabbits and piglets. She sold the animals in town and bought what few staples she could find with the money. Despondently, she posted her letters, and was just getting back onto the box when she noticed a huge coach and four standing in front of the Horseshoe Inn. She instantly recognized the Caldwell coat of arms, and knew Augustine's cousin, Christopher Caldwell, must have at last returned from abroad.

Her guess proved correct, for the very next day the stately brougham drew up in front of the house, and a dissolute young blond gentleman, a trifle portly around the middle and with a rapidly receding hairline, came knocking on the front door.

Muireann, who just happened to be coming around the front of the house with a huge load of woolens to take into town, saw the man standing on the steps tapping his cane impatiently against one leg.

"Hello, can I help you?" she called over to him.

The young rake took in her appearance, especially her hair tied back in a kerchief, and her apron, and said, "Of course you may, my beauty. I've come to pay my respects to your mistress, compliments of the Christmas season and all that, but no one seems to be answering my knock."

He snaked one arm around Muireann's slender waist, and grinned lewdly.

"Would you be a good little girl and tell the mistress of the house, Mrs. Caldwell, that her late husband's cousin, Christopher Caldwell, is here to see her?"

Muireann tried to step away from his amorous advances, but he continued to cling onto her like a limpet, until at last she stamped on his foot and declared, "Let me go, sir! And before you take another step towards me, I'd like to inform you that I'm Mrs. Caldwell. So before you make an even bigger fool of yourself than you already have, I suggest you keep your distance."

"Hah, hah, capital joke, young miss, but you couldn't possibly be," he sneered. "I mean, Mrs. Caldwell is one of the richest women in Scotland by all accounts. How dare you presume to adopt her identity! I have half a mind to whip you for your insolence, you young hussy," he said more threateningly, lifting his cane.

Muireann dropped her woolens then, seeing red at the threat of violence. She was damned if she was going to let Augustine's brute of a cousin thrash her for telling the truth, or for rejecting his unwelcome attentions.

Unthinkingly she grabbed the stick, and broke it in two over her knee. She was grateful that all her outdoor work had toughened her up, and anger had made her even stronger. She then flung the pieces in his face, and gathering her bundle, she marched to the cart, stating, "That's what I think of your violence, sir. Cousin of Augustine's or not, I want you to get off my land now, do you hear?"

Her fury was matched only by his own, as he shouted, "Look what you've done to my cane!"

He advanced on her menacingly, grabbing her by the shoulders and tearing her gown down the front as she struggled to get away.

Just then, a rifle shot rang out. The dirt three inches from Christopher's booted foot flew up into the air. Lochlainn slung the rifle over his shoulder and cocked his pistol. "I'll give you one second to unhand the lady before I shoot. And this time I'll kill you, Christopher," Lochlainn declared coldly.

Muireann shook Christopher's hand off her and ran over to where Lochlainn was standing.

"Are you all right?" he asked her softly.

"I'm fine. He thought I was a servant girl. He was pestering me, that's all."

Lochlainn laughed sourly. "Bad mistake, Christopher. This is Mrs. Caldwell, as I am sure she tried to tell you. Your charming manners with ladies seem to have slipped since we last saw you around these parts four years ago. To what do we owe the pleasure after all this time?" Lochlainn drawled, still keeping his gun trained on Christopher.

"Well, well, Lochlainn, old man. I would have thought after Tara pulled up stakes and left with her whole family that you wouldn't have wasted your time here any longer. But then, you always did have ideas above your station. Playing Mrs. Caldwell's protector now, are we? Looking after the beautiful young widow, eh?" he remarked suggestively.

Muireann looked from one man to the other and saw the unmistakable mutual hatred etched on their faces, glinting in their eyes.

"I think I've already told you, sir, that you're not welcome here. I'll thank you to leave now, before my manager shoots you for trespassing."

"Mrs. Caldwell—Muireann, if I may make so bold—surely you realize it was an honest mistake. I didn't mean to catch you in the middle of your cleaning or whatever other little chores you were doing in that peasant's garb. I honestly meant no offense. I merely wanted to meet you, to see if I could be of service, and invite you to tea." Christopher smiled like a predator about to devour his prey.

"Where's your wife, then?" Lochlainn asked suddenly.

Christopher smirked. "I never married, actually."

"You bastard!" Lochlainn hissed.

Muireann could see his finger tightening on the pistol trigger.

She hastily grabbed at the weapon and shoved it high into the air, causing the bullet to wing a tree branch above Christopher's head.

"Now, now, Lochlainn, I'm not the bastard here, as you well know," Christopher mocked, opening the door of his carriage and scrambling in before Lochlainn could get time to reload. Once safely inside, he instructed his driver to move on quickly and took off down the avenue, leaving nothing but a trail of dust behind.

Lochlainn stood glaring at the carriage until long after it was out of sight, and then straightened. He began to march away, but Muireann pursued him. Clutching her torn gown to her bosom, she ran after him.

"That was Christopher Caldwell?" she asked, her astonishment evident in her tone.

"Yes, and the same as he ever was, more's the pity. You're lucky you weren't hurt. But you should have let me shoot him. His presence here will only cause trouble for us. I can feel it in my bones. But at least you've had fair warning not to trust him. You've seen for yourself what he's really like."

"I could tell from the moment I glanced at him that he's a lecher, but what I would really like to know is what all that hostility between you is about!"

Lochlainn tried to duck down an avenue of trees.

Muireann charged after him and spun him round to face her. "Stop running away from me, Lochlainn! I want the truth!"

"I don't want to discuss it with you or anyone else. It's private, can't you see that?" he hissed, trying to shake her off.

"Not when you try to shoot visitors on my estate, it isn't!" Muireann shouted back.

She tried to cling onto Lochlainn's arm but he stormed off into the wood so quickly, it seemed pointless to try to follow him in the growing darkness.

Muireann trailed into the kitchen thoughtfully. Seeing Sharon in there on her own, stirring some stew every so often while the other women were working digging up the onions and leeks in the kitchen garden, she mentioned Christopher Caldwell's visit.

Then she declared, "I don't want to pry, but Christopher Caldwell and Lochlainn seemed to hate each other. Can you tell me what resentment there is between them?"

Sharon looked at the door warily, and whispered, "I probably shouldn't tell, but you and Lochlainn seem to care about each other, so I think you deserve to know. Christopher lured away Tara, the girl Lochlainn was engaged to. One night they eloped, and soon after that her family moved away and were never heard from again. Lochlainn had been very close to them all. It was like losing his whole family when they left."

"Christopher said he had never married Tara. He must have seduced the girl and then just abandoned her."

"Well, you'll forgive my saying so, but there wouldn't have been any seduction in the case. Tara set her cap at Lochlainn. When a better opportunity came along, she took it. Lochlainn was too blind to see that. She was the only person he ever trusted, and she wasn't worthy of that trust, though of course Lochlainn was so in love with her he thought she was perfect," Sharon said with a twinge of disgust.

Then she looked at Muireann with something akin to horror. "You just said Christopher was back. Are you all right? I mean, he didn't, er—"

"He did, but I fended him off," Muireann admitted.

"Did Lochlainn see? Because he would have been furious."

"He was angry, right enough, but I think it's just because of their old love rivalry," Muireann said with a sinking heart. *Lochlainn is still in love with Tara, has always been. Where does that leave me?*

"You're looking worried. Or perhaps doubtful. I'm telling you, Lochlainn does care for you. I've known him for years, and he's a good man."

Muireann sighed. "Once we were close, but recently . . ."

Sharon said firmly, "I think this potato blight business has taken its toll on you both. And Lochlainn is a proud man. With Christopher turning up here, looking prosperous and as arrogant as a peacock, it would have dredged up a lot of old memories."

"That's just it, though, Sharon. I feel like I simply don't know Lochlainn sometimes. He never talks much about himself or the past."

"Well, neither do you," Sharon surprised her by replying. "We none of us feel we know you, really know you, though we've worked with you side by side for nearly a year."

Muireann shuddered. Her hand began to tremble so violently that Sharon took it in her own.

"Whatever it is, Muireann, it can't be that bad."

Muireann stood up abruptly and put her hand on the latch of the door. "I don't want to think about it, don't you see?"

She fled from the kitchen and ran out to the weaving workshop, where she spun thread for the rest of the day without so much as five minutes' rest. She tried to calm herself, but all the same, Christopher Caldwell had reminded her of Augustine, and of her time in Dublin. She knew his kind. She had met them before. They used women for an hour or two of pleasure, no more. When Christopher had grabbed her and torn her gown, she had detected the same streak of cruelty that she had discovered in Augustine. Why, why had he come here, now of all times, just when things were the worst they had ever been?

Muireann tried to take command of her breathing, to force herself to relax. She tried to view Christopher's arrival in a positive light. It was true that he was odious and lecherous, but perhaps he was the solution to her problems. As a cousin, he might want to help. Perhaps she should consider his offer of friendship for the sake of the estate? He might even be willing to buy it, and look after all the people there, so that she could go home.

Lochlainn had said she didn't belong there. Perhaps he was right? Of course, with the animosity between Lochlainn and Christopher, there would be no question of Lochlainn remaining at Barnakilla as estate manager. Bút that might be just the excuse she needed to get him to come to Fintry with her. She was sure if her father met Lochlainn, he couldn't fail to admire the man she had come to love beyond all else.

Muireann became completely carried away by this fantasy life she planned for herself and Lochlainn. But he never appeared in her room that night. It was the first time for as long as she could remember that they hadn't spent the night with each other.

Refusing to accept defeat, and willing to do anything to win the heart of the man she loved, Muireann worked long into the night in order to take some time off from her chores the next day, when she would make the opening gambit in her bid to save Barnakilla from utter ruin.

Chapter Twenty-three

At about noon on the following day—a bright crisp Christmas Eve—she dressed carefully in her best sable velvet gown and saddled her stallion, Bran. She rode out to Christopher's estate to the south of her own property. She was charm itself as Christopher greeted her at the door with his crocodile smile.

"Please, I wanted to try to mend fences with you after yesterday." She forced herself to smile up at him as he led her into the foyer, a high-ceilinged affair with two graceful marble staircases curving upwards to the second floor.

"Delighted, my dear, delighted," he said with a leer, clutching at her possessively.

It took all of Muireann's strength of character to prevent

herself from jerking her hand away from Christopher as he practically drooled all over it. She hesitantly accompanied him into the drawing room, which was highly ornate and covered from floor to ceiling with nude paintings. Muireann trembled inwardly. She had seen "art" like this before. There had been plenty of it in the house in Dublin.

Muireann tried to keep her tone neutral as she kept herself from staring at the loathsome paintings by mentioning all that had happened to her since Augustine had died.

His blue eyes seemed to stab into her very soul, so that at one point she remarked, "But I suppose I'm boring you with all this talk of my little enterprises."

"No, on the contrary, I'm very interested in the estate," he said with a gleam in his eye that Muireann misunderstood completely. "All that you've been telling me is most interesting. I know your estate manager would be unwilling to do it, but do you suppose you could give me a tour of Barnakilla right now, to show me how much splendid work you've done?"

"Well, yes, of course." She smiled, delighted with how easy it all seemed to be. Even if the paperwork took some time to go through, she and Lochlainn could still go back to Fintry together soon if Christopher were willing to commit himself this afternoon.

Muireann remounted her horse, and showed him every corner of the property, explaining all of the timber and agricultural schemes, and giving him facts and figures to make the whole estate seem even more impressive and prosperous, with nary a mention of the potato failure.

After all, she wasn't going to sell for just any old price. She wanted to get the best deal possible for herself and the tenants at Barnakilla. She could even redo the rent books, set the tenants' rents lower, she thought kindly. It was a bit dishonest, but if it helped the people of Barnakilla to a better life, who was to know?

Muireann took him all over the estate and highlighted her different schemes for him, then brought him back to her office for tea.

After a suitable length of time had elapsed, she said to him conversationally, "So, are you interested in buying the estate?"

"Buying it?" Christopher spluttered, choking until he turned purple. "Not at all! I wouldn't be in a position to buy it! I'm mortgaged up to the hilt myself! But I think a little merger might be in order, Muireann. You've done wonders with the place. It's been difficult, I know, what with the potato crop failing and everything, but you've built this place up into quite an attractive little enterprise. One I would be more than happy to reap the benefits of."

She stared, feeling a sudden creep of unease. "What sort of merger?"

"Why, marriage, of course," Christopher laughed, flashing his sharp white teeth.

"Don't be ridiculous, I couldn't possibly—"

"Come now, you've been a widow for nearly a year. Nothing is to stop us from getting married in a few more months. You can move into my house. Then we can clear all the young and old people off the land and start making this place turn an even bigger profit once we get rid of the useless drain on your resources. You can have some new pretty gowns and grace my drawing room and bedroom, while I take over the running of all this myself. I'll be only too pleased to send that bastard Lochlainn packing, I can tell you. He always was an arrogant young buck!"

Muireann gazed at him in horror. "Surely you aren't serious! You're the last man in the world I would ever consider marrying!"

Christopher leaned forward in a threatening manner, but at least he didn't touch her. "Then I don't even give this place another six months. What do you and Lochlainn know about running an estate?"

"More than you do, apparently," Muireann said with a haughty lift of her chin. "I haven't beggared mine the way you have! I've started out with virtually nothing, and built it up. I didn't squander it and leave people to starve in the road! If you aren't able to buy it, I'll just have to find a purchaser elsewhere. One who won't try to turn out every tenant as soon as he gets his hands on the place. That is, assuming that I ever do decide to sell."

"An admirable notion, my dear," Christopher replied in a tone which belied his words. "But do try to be practical for once, why don't you? No one will want all those old decrepit people and half-starved children! Send them to the workhouse where they belong! Let them go before they drag this place under."

"I can't do that. I gave them my word I would look after them," Muireann said firmly, looking at Christopher as though he were the devil incarnate as he lounged in his chair speaking of the fate of dozens of people in a manner that suggested that their deaths weren't of the least concern to him.

"Well, you still haven't given me your answer, Muireann, and this conversation is growing tiresome. Will you marry me?"

Muireann laughed mockingly. "I've told you, there's nothing in the world that would convince me to marry you!"

"Not even to keep Barnakilla?" he countered smoothly.

"What are you talking about? I don't have to sell. I have other options to keep it running until the spring, when we can begin planting again."

Christopher twirled his new gold-topped cane casually. "I've heard a lot about this estate ever since I arrived back in Ireland a few weeks ago. I came here to see if the reports were true. Now that I see it's all I've been told and more, I think it's about time I informed you of the real reason for my coming back."

"Real reason?"

"As the closest blood relative to Augustine Caldwell, I have a legitimate claim to this property. So, if you refuse to marry me, I'll drag you through the law courts, and fight you tooth and nail to make Barnakilla and all its contents my own. You may be Augustine's widow, but he didn't leave a will, now did he? That was a small oversight on your part, wasn't it, Muireann? So I shall be claiming title to the place in two days' time. Therefore, I'm giving you two days to consider my proposal, or else you will have this place pulled right out from under your feet."

Muireann leapt up and began to pace the floor. "You can't do that! Not after everything I've done to improve it! You might be entitled to the land and property, but it was worth virtually nothing when I first took it over. It was mortgaged up to the hilt, and the bank was about to repossess it. I sold every gown, every jewel I owned, every wedding present I received! I've done nothing but struggle and toil since I arrived here a year ago. Now you're telling me you're going to take it from me!"

He reclined in his chair. "Let's not get hysterical. I've already asked you to marry me. I shall let you carry on pretty much as before, except that I will be in charge from now on. Lochlainn won't be at your beck and call anymore. I can't trust him, so you can start by sacking him. But all other parts of this estate will carry on as before, and soon we shall have some strapping sons to carry on the Caldwell line."

Muireann looked at him narrowly. "This enmity between you and Lochlainn. It wouldn't by any chance have to do with your seducing his fiancée Tara away from him, would it?"

"I suppose the bastard told you that, did he?" Christopher accused too quickly, thus proclaiming his own guilt.

Muireann answered with a level look, "No, he never said a word against you. But I knew from the moment I met you that you were a dissolute libertine, just as Augustine was. I only made the mistake of thinking you could be used to my benefit, just like you seem to use everyone for yours. But now that I have no use for you, Mr. Caldwell, you can get off my land. I would advise you never to set foot here again."

Christopher turned furious, willing to do anything to break this woman's spirit. "I'll give you two days to change your mind. Then I am going to file the papers. If you say no, Muireann, I'll take Barnakilla apart brick by brick if I have to, until there's nothing left. All your precious peasants will be homeless, instead of only the indigent ones. Is that what you want?"

Muireann opened the door and pointed for him to leave. "You can't frighten me, Mr. Caldwell. This is my home. It will take more than a dissolute rake like yourself to chase me away."

Christopher smirked as he brushed past her. "Brave words, girl. I'll see you eat them one of these days. You'll regret this. I won't have any qualms about taking it out of your hide, highborn Graham or not. I can't wait until we're married, my dear."

Suddenly he grabbed her around the waist and kissed her on the lips. His mouth swooped down over hers brutally, grinding his teeth into her tender flesh.

Muireann tasted blood. She pushed against his chest futilely, trying to end the torture. But Christopher clung to her like an octopus, so that Muireann, summoning all her strength and resolution, locked one leg around the back of his knees and shoved hard, sending Christopher sprawling on his back in the dirt.

She then wiped her mouth with the back of her hand

and spat disgustedly at him as he lay prone on the ground. She stalked off, leaving him cursing as she fled.

A movement at the corner of her vision caught her attention as she ran to the stables to soothe her frazzled nerves by grooming the horses. Oh God, that was all she needed, for Lochlainn to have seen Christopher kissing her.

But it wasn't Lochlainn who came into the stables after her. It was Ciara, and she was carrying a pistol.

Ciara raised her arm and pointed it directly at Muireann's head.

Muireann's knees turned to jelly. For a moment she wondered crazily if her nightmares had somehow returned to haunt her during her waking hours. This couldn't possibly be happening again.

"Ciara, what are you doing?" Muireann exclaimed. "Put the pistol down!"

"I can't let you do it! I can't let you!" Ciara shrieked, advancing towards her menacingly.

"Do what, Ciara? I don't understand!"

"You know what I'm talking about!" she insisted, waving the gun perilously close to Muireann's face.

Muireann shuddered as she recalled the last time she had looked directly down the barrel of a gun, and prayed she wouldn't faint. If she did, she was as good as dead.

"No, Ciara, I don't know what you are talking about!" she said quickly. "Please, put the gun down and explain this to me, step by step."

Ciara stared at Muireann, her emerald eyes rolling wildly in her head. Lochlainn had warned her that Ciara was unstable. What on earth could have made her become like this? Why did she suddenly get the strangest feeling that it had something to do with Christopher Caldwell?

She cast her mind back to the other times Ciara had behaved oddly. Christopher was the only common link. His name, her job, the dog . . .

"Please, Ciara, talk to me!" Muireann begged. "Whatever has been troubling you for so long has everyone terribly worried. Lochlainn is sick at heart not knowing what's changed you since he was last home at Barnakilla. If I can help you, please let me. But killing me won't solve anyone's problems here on the estate. If I die, God knows what will happen to this place."

"Christopher Caldwell wants this place. I'll kill him and then myself before I'll ever let him step across the threshold of Barnakilla again!" Ciara hissed, her hand trembling.

Muireann's eyes widened in fear. Ciara might not mean to shoot her, but she was shaking so much, she might well fire the weapon anyway.

"Why do you hate Christopher Caldwell so much?" Just as she said these words, she smashed Ciara's clenched hand upwards. The gun went off as it sailed out of Ciara's hand into a nearby bale of hay. Ciara tried to attack her with her fists, but by then Lochlainn and some of the other men had come running.

Lochlainn dragged his frenzied sister off of Muireann. "What the hell is going on around here! Are you all right?" he asked Muireann as he noticed her ashen color.

"I'm fine. Ciara and I were having a small discussion, that's all," Muireann replied with as much calm as she could muster.

"A *discussion* about what, for heaven's sake! I heard a shot!" Lochlainn roared, touching her hair and shoulder intimately despite the presence of so many other people.

"Just leave us alone together, will you please, Lochlainn?"

Lochlainn stared at her in utter disbelief. "I won't leave! I want to know what's going on here!"

"And I told you to leave us alone, Mr. Roche. You will do as you are told or look for a post elsewhere."

She immediately regretted becoming so heavy-handed

with Lochlainn when she saw the appalled look on his face. But the damage was done.

"Very well, Mrs. Caldwell, I will obey your commands," Lochlainn replied stiffly, with a mutinous look that warned Muireann that she would have to deal with him later and their interview certainly would not be a pleasant one.

He and the other men withdrew, leaving her alone with Lochlainn's sister. Muireann approached Ciara tentatively, and stretched out a hand. "Come to my room now, please, and tell me what's wrong. Whatever has happened to you, it must be a terrible burden to have to carry alone by yourself all the time."

Ciara crumpled to the floor of the stables and began to weep. "I was trying to save you and Barnakilla! If you marry Christopher, you'll be making the most horrible mistake of your life!"

Muireann knelt down and cradled Ciara against her shoulder. "I already did that when I married Augustine, remember? Fortune hunter that he was."

Ciara's sobs subsided then, but she trembled so violently that Muireann began to fear she was really physically ill.

"What is it? What did I say?" Muireann asked desperately, trying to get to the bottom of this mystery at last.

"I have to tell someone. But you must promise me you'll never say a word to Lochlainn, not one word, do you hear me?"

"I swear, Ciara, I would never break your confidence. But surely it can't be so bad—"

"It is worse than you can possibly imagine, Muireann. I beg you, don't marry Christopher," she pleaded.

"But what would ever make you think that I would?"

"I heard him propose to you through the window here. I know what he's like. He's evil, and evil begets evil. And Augustine, he was even worse. How you must have suffered, being married to him."

"What makes you say that?" Muireann asked, suddenly feeling very uneasy.

"Because I know what he was like, the real man underneath the surface. I know. I *know* . . . And Christopher is no better, though he prefers women instead of young boys. He only wants you for your money and the estate. He's committed all sorts of perversions on his female tenants over the years. He'll do it to you. He'll do it to Barnakilla. He'll come here to do the same thing. He must be stopped. You can't let him!" she warned, with a wild look in her eyes. She clung to Muireann's shoulders and shook her.

Muireann's mouth went dry, and she had to swallow hard past the lump in her throat. Suddenly the barn seemed confined and stifling.

She rose to her feet and urged, "Please, Ciara, we can't stay here. Someone might be listening outside, or come in at any moment. Let's go for a walk. It will calm you down, and we can discuss this further."

Ciara assented tearfully. Muireann supported her as she rose from the ground.

Keeping one arm around her waist, she escorted Lochlainn's sister outside. Ciara continued to shiver, so that Muireann draped her own shawl around her. They began to walk away from the avenue towards the turf bog, certain no one would interrupt them there.

"I suppose I had better start at the beginning," Ciara sighed at length.

"It would help."

"I was the housekeeper here for several years before Lochlainn went away to Australia. It was during this time Christopher and I first became acquainted. It's the age-old story of master seducing servant, though I went along with it willingly enough at first, much to my shame. Christopher flattered me, seemed to be kind, bought me small presents.

He made me all sorts of promises he never had any intention of fulfilling.

"I wasn't the only one, though I was too blind to see it at the time. He had dozens of women, some willing, some not so obliging. He took them indiscriminately. I ignored it because I had been foolish enough to fall in love with the worthless philanderer. He used me the way he used all the other women, for gratification of his every whim, no matter how perverse or disgusting," Ciara revealed, her voice quavering with emotion.

"If he was so awful, why didn't you stop the affair?"

Ciara confessed, "I have one serious character flaw, as Lochlainn does, and that's pride. Well, as they say in the old proverb, pride comes before a fall. Everyone said I was Mr. Douglas Caldwell's illegitimate daughter. Christopher used my own pride to get into my bed. He promised me that I would get all the Caldwell fortune indirectly once I married him. Cousins married all the time, he said. He dragged the affair out for years, always playing upon my hope and pride whenever I tried to deny him and break it off."

Muireann was stunned. Ciara was the lord's illegitimate daughter? How had that chain of events come to pass? But she didn't want to stop Ciara mid-story to ask questions, so she let her press on.

"And I did try to stop the affair, believe me I did. I wasn't totally lost to honor and decency. But he would come to me with his winning ways. Because I loved him even though I knew him to be unworthy, I gave in nearly every time. Those times I refused to give in, he took me anyway and called me a whore for having accepted him back into my bed.

"It was terrible, Muireann. He seemed to be driven by some sort of need to punish, hurt, corrupt, debauch. Women are different from men, they must be. There was excitement, danger, but never any real pleasure for me. I put up with his attentions because I thought he loved me. I thought I could change him. I waited for the day he would set the date of our nuptials, but he never intended to marry me, I know that now. And all the while he enjoyed the degradation he put me through, the fact that I was so in love with him I would literally do just about anything for him. Anything."

"I can imagine what it must have been like, though I thank God it's not within my own personal experience," Muireann said with a shudder.

"Count yourself lucky then. Lochlainn loves you, doesn't he? He would never . . ."

Muireann raised her eyebrows in surprise and was about to deny their relationship was of that sort, but then she shook her head. "No, not Lochlainn, but many men would, wouldn't they?" She shuddered, recalling her terrible trip to Dublin.

"I'm sorry, I shouldn't have mentioned anything so personal. But I'm no fool. He's rarely home at night or in the morning. I'm glad you and he have been happy for a time, but I know it can't possibly last.

"I was a fool back then. I would give anything to turn back the clock and undo the damage I caused unwittingly by trusting Christopher. He used me, and even worse, he used me to get to Tara, Lochlainn's fiancée. He said it was just a bit of innocent sewing for her. The next thing I knew they were having an affair. He even boasted about it, wanted me to watch," Ciara revealed brokenly.

Muireann shook her head. "My God!"

"Tara, too, thought he would marry her. He lied to her just as he had done to me and all the others. I tried to warn her, but she wouldn't listen. Lochlainn never suspected, and I couldn't tell him. I felt so guilty for my part in the whole thing. We began to drift away from each other even further than we already had done. I had neglected him sorely when the affair first started, and for that I'm truly ashamed as well.

"Besides, Lochlainn was involved with Tara back then, though she seemed to spend more of her time fobbing him off with excuses, dangling her charms in front of him only to say, 'Hands off.' Both Lochlainn and I are cut from the same cloth—proud, not easily given to showing our feelings. I couldn't speak to him, warn him. He would never have believed me. Or even if he did believe me, he wouldn't have thanked me for the knowledge. I was afraid he would do something desperate or foolish.

"Anyway, eventually Tara ran off with Christopher, or so it seemed. It was more that Christopher went to the Continent and she followed. Of course it was the perfect chance for Christopher to get even with the bastard cousin he had always loathed and despised. Lochlainn was a hundred times the better man than any of the legitimate Caldwells. It's only a pity our father never chose to acknowledge either of us openly. But he wanted a quiet life, and his wife hated us and everything we stood for.

"Augustine hated Lochlainn as well, envied him. At the end he realized he couldn't run the estate without him. That would no doubt have made him hate Lochlainn even more. If you hadn't come here to Barnakilla, God knows what might have happened. All I can say is, it was a lucky day for us all when Augustine Caldwell blew his brains out."

Muireann barely heard Ciara's last words, so stunned was she. Lochlainn was the illegitimate son of Douglas Caldwell? Augustine had been Lochlainn's *half brother*?

But Ciara continued on with her narrative, heedless of Muireann's astonishment. "I think that's really what motivated the affair in the first place, though of course Tara was also a very beautiful woman. She was ambitious, too. I think she set her cap for Lochlainn at first because he was a force to be reckoned with around here, because of his intelligence and hard work. She never loved him. I'm also convinced she truly believed that the old man would leave him something in his will. She would have bided her time, for Douglas Caldwell was quite frail by then, if it hadn't been for Christopher seeming an even more attractive prospect."

"She sounds as though she would have made Lochlainn's life a misery," Muireann remarked quietly, trying to quell her feelings of jealousy and resentment. And this had been the woman Lochlainn had been pining over for nearly four years? He had loved Tara, while he didn't love her?

"You can congratulate yourself on your brother's lucky escape. After all, what purpose would have been served if he had been told the truth? He would have fought Christopher and been put in prison, or worse," Muireann sighed.

"As it was, I lost him anyway, since he went to Australia to try to forget all about us at Barnakilla. He picked up one day and left without a word to anyone. I didn't hear from him for months. I was lucky enough to have an address to write to when he did finally contact me. Many of the workers in Australia just wander around from place to place picking up jobs wherever they can find them. Lochlainn got himself a good job on a cattle station, so I knew where to write when things started getting really bad here, and all the creditors were banging on the door demanding payment."

Muireann digested all she had been told so far in silence, staring up at the slate-gray sky overhead. Then she rose from the rock she had been sitting upon as the wintry wind whipped through her, and took Ciara's arm to urge her silently back to the warmth of her office.

As they went, she spoke her confused thoughts aloud. "But Lochlainn told me that you changed from the time he left until the time he came back. Forgive me, I know it sounds as though we were gossiping about you behind your back, but really, Lochlainn has been so worried about you, and he wanted my advice as a woman. I had hoped you would tell him in your own time, but . . ."

Ciara began to shake again. "There are some things you can never speak about," she whispered.

Muireann stared at Ciara for a moment before insisting, "You're going to have to tell me. I need the whole truth. It can't just be what Christopher did to you before, and his affair with Tara. I've seen the way you behave when Christopher or Augustine are mentioned. And you've said some things to me which suggest you knew Augustine very well also. You've been very disapproving of me and my relationship with Lochlainn, and you've admitted you know of the nature of that relationship. So please, Ciara, tell me all of it. I need to know if I'm ever to help you."

"It was so awful," Ciara wept, nearly breaking down again in Muireann's arms,

She had to half-carry her back to the stable block, and at last slumped her in a chair. Muireann poured Ciara out a measure of Augustine's vile brandy, and waited.

"People will think I deserved it!" Ciara choked, the tears streaming down her face in rivulets.

Muireann reached over and took her hand firmly. "I can't speak for other people. But surely nothing you could have ever done would make you deserve any of what Christopher did to you, or anything that would make you like this."

She stroked Ciara's disheveled hair back from her face and raised Ciara's hand, palm flat against her own callused one to show Lochlainn's sister that she was trembling like a leaf in the wind.

"I have to tell you, because if you marry Christopher it will be a disaster. You married Augustine. Thank God you didn't have a child by him! And I'm terrified of the danger now that you and Lochlainn are lovers!"

"What danger? What are you saying!"

"About six months after Christopher had run off with Tara, he returned to Fermanagh. I was still working as housekeeper here, though with so little money there was little to do. Then Augustine decided to have a huge gambling party here at the house, and Christopher was invited. Christopher dared Augustine to try me out, as he put it, to see how a woman compared to the boys he preferred. They were drunk, of course, but not so drunk they didn't manage to attack me," she revealed in an agonized whisper.

"God, no."

She nodded. "Christopher treated the whole thing as a joke, told Augustine how well he had trained me in the arts of love. He didn't even care that Augustine was my half-brother. But even worse was to come, for I soon discovered I was with child." Ciara choked, and the tears began to fall again.

"My God! Did they hurt you?"

"Yes, but not in the way you mean. It was the crushing sense of my own sin as well as the physical illness. It was the natural horror, having committed incest, and the terrible pregnancy. I was dreadfully ill with fear and shock. It was my worst nightmare come true. I was terrified of what people would say. I even went to Christopher to ask for help. The only thing I got was a handful of coins, as though I were some beggar in the street, and a warning to keep my mouth shut about what had taken place that night.

"Even worse than the terrible treatment I received, though, was the birth. I suppose I had hoped, foolishly of course, that the child would be Christopher's, that somehow I would be able to prove it. That perhaps once he saw the baby, he would change his mind and come to care for it at least, and acknowledge it as his own. Lochlainn and I could tell you how hard it is to grow up without a father's love. I didn't want that for my child, not if I could help it.

But after a dreadful pregnancy, the baby was born, and things were worse than I could ever have imagined."

Muireann frowned. "I don't understand. Do you mean you had a difficult birth?"

Ciara nodded, but suddenly added in a horrified whisper, "The baby was born, and it was a monster, Muireann, a monster! Twisted, deformed."

Muireann's eyes widened. "My God, Ciara, what are you saying?"

"The infant was like a gargoyle, hideous to behold. Evil begets evil, don't you see! And we're in the family line! We're all related. What if it's something passed on in our family? What if you have a child by Lochlainn and it's the same—twisted, malevolent . . ." Ciara shuddered, clenching her fists against her mouth to choke back her sobs.

Muireann felt the icy grip of fear clench her heart. She put her hand on Ciara's shoulder and sought to reassure her as best she could. "I know it must have been dreadful for you, but let's try to be calm about this, shall we?

"First of all, as sure as the sun will rise tomorrow, I know you and Lochlainn are not evil people. Perhaps you two Roches are both proud and haughty, but certainly not evil. Still, you haven't told me all, Ciara. What happened to the child?"

"Its little life slowly slipped away. It never stopped bleeding after they cut the cord, though we tried everything. So much blood for such a tiny baby," she wept, scrubbing her hands against one another in her lap.

Muireann hugged her as Ciara wept as though her heart would break, and tried to think of something comforting to say.

At last, when she was convinced Ciara was ready to listen to her, she remarked softly, "You and Christopher are first cousins, and Augustine your half-brother. It is not so surprising for a child born of such a union to have had a defect. The reason for the Church's edicts on consanguinity, preventing marriage between close relatives, is to make sure that those sorts of things never happen. I'm sure the baby's problems had nothing to do with evil, more to do with being close family relations.

"I say that if there's never been anything like this in your family before, there's no need for you to worry about any baby I might ever have. And there's no history of children such as you describe in my family, either, I swear!"

"I've tried to reason these things out as you have, Muireann, honestly I have, but I'm so afraid. Don't you see, none of us can be sure. That's why you can't marry Christopher, and you can't have a baby with Lochlainn. That's why I can never run the risk of having a child again!" Ciara insisted.

Muireann rose and gazed out the window of the small office for a moment before turning to face Ciara.

"Please, listen to me. I understand that everything you've been through has been terrible, but life is all about taking risks. We can't just give up on living because it's dangerous. We can't stop ourselves from being happy for fear that we might end up unhappy. I love Lochlainn, and I'm prepared to take the risk of having a child with him. If I stopped our relationship now because I was afraid of what you've told me, it would be like cutting off my right arm."

"But to have a child like that! It would kill you! It would kill Lochlainn!"

"No, it wouldn't. Lochlainn would be grief-stricken, true, as would I, but that's no reason to sacrifice our happiness now, or whatever happiness we will have for as long as we love each other."

"Please, won't you reconsider?"

Muireann sat down heavily in her chair. "I suppose I've been taking unnecessary risks all along. Sooner or later I'm bound to become pregnant. Perhaps now isn't the most convenient time to have a baby, with things being as they are at Barnakilla. So if it will make you feel better, I'll say that I shall avoid Lochlainn in that way, make excuses, make myself unavailable, maybe even come to your house and share your room, if I may, so he won't get too suspicious. But as soon as I see some light at the end of the tunnel, I want you to tell him the truth," Muireann added firmly.

"What if we lose Barnakilla?"

"I know things are bad because of the Famine, but I'm not beaten yet. This is my home now. I'll do anything to keep it, even if it means swallowing my pride and telling Father everything."

"But Christopher threatened to take it away from you! I heard him through the door. He said if you didn't marry him, he would put himself forward as the rightful heir!"

"I have no intention of marrying him. Nor am I going to give up and run away. My brother-in-law is a powerful man, and Anthony Lowry is an excellent solicitor. I won't give up without a fight, you can be sure of that. And even if Christopher is legally entitled to Barnakilla, it was a bankrupt ruin at the time of Augustine's death, and I have all the ledgers to prove it. I'll still be allowed to sell the estate to reclaim my share of what I put into it, I'm sure, and we can start again somewhere else."

"What will become of me? I couldn't stay here with Christopher, and you wouldn't want me, not after the way I've treated you. Besides, people think I'm mad!"

Muireann ran over to Ciara's side and put her arm around her. "You're not mad! You've kept this secret inside for so long, it's festered there. Once you tell Lochlainn, you'll be free from the past. I know you were abused and mistreated, but please don't think you're destined to have to pay for your foolish error in trusting Christopher for the rest of your life."

"But I loved him, I trusted him, fool that I was! I deserved what happened for having given in to him willingly!" Ciara moaned.

She lost all patience then and shook Ciara by the shoulders until her head snapped back to look up into Muireann's blazing amethyst eyes. "Get that idea out of your head right now! You might have made love to Christopher in the past, but he and Augustine attacking you is a completely different matter. You were Augustine's half sister, for God's sake!"

Ciara squirmed uncomfortably in her seat, and then asked, "Augustine never—"

Muireann shook her head. "No, he never did. He went back to his old ways as soon as the ring was on my finger. I was horrified at first, of course, but at least it spared me any repulsive physical attentions," Muireann admitted with a ragged sigh.

"Thank God for that." Ciara crossed herself.

Muireann straightened her back and suddenly declared, "Come now, Ciara, it's been a long day for both of us. I think it's about time you headed back home and went to bed."

"You won't tell Lochlainn?" she demanded frantically.

"It is up to you to tell him. I just hope no one gossips about the baby before you get a chance to break the news to him gently. Sooner or later someone will let something slip. Even Christopher himself, out of spite."

"You will be careful, won't you, Muireann?"

"I promise, I'll be careful for now, anyway, just until we get over this bad patch. I love Lochlainn, but he's very confused at the moment, what with Christopher coming back and everything else. If we're meant to be together, then that aspect of our lives can certainly keep for a few weeks."

Muireann escorted Ciara to her own door, then walked with a heavy tread back to the office, where she went straight into her small chamber and threw herself on the bed. God Almighty, what a nightmare all of this had suddenly become.

Damn Christopher to hell, and Augustine along with him, she thought resentfully.

And damn Lochlainn, for never having told her who he really was. Was he simply yet another Caldwell man desperate to get his hands on her fortune, on Barnakilla, no matter what?

Chapter Twenty-four

A tap at the door half an hour later signaled Lochlainn's inevitable arrival.

Muireann hastily jumped off the bed and tried to leave the bedchamber, ever conscious of her promise to Ciara and her own uneasiness over all that had been revealed that afternoon.

"Are you all right?" he demanded huskily, pulling her into his arms despite her efforts to resist.

"I'm fine. It's your sister who needs looking after," she replied, managing to extricate herself from his embrace.

She went into the study and poured herself a drop of the vile liquor in the decanter with shaking hands, then lifted Tadhg out of his basket onto her lap to stroke him nervously.

"I don't understand."

"Let's just say Ciara has had a lot of things on her mind recently. She misunderstood something I did and was upset. It's all sorted out now. Nothing for you to worry about on my account," Muireann lied, trying to smile brightly.

"But to fight with you! Ciara is usually so gentle! Has she lost her wits altogether?"

"No, she isn't mad, just upset, I told you," Muireann repeated patiently.

"Did she confide in you what was wrong with her?"

Muireann ignored the question, and lifted a ledger and pen. "Lochlainn, if you'll excuse me, I have work to do."

"What did she tell you?" he demanded.

"Nothing that need concern you now, I promise. Please, Lochlainn, I don't want to fight with you about this. I need to keep all my attention focused upon the farm business. Whatever is happening in Ciara's head will keep a little while longer."

Lochlainn looked at her carefully. "I'm sorry for prying and for being so rude to you yesterday. Can I come later, to explain?"

"No, it wouldn't be a good idea," Muireann said, glancing away from him.

"Why not?" Lochlainn asked, his expression reflecting true hurt.

"Er, you know," Muireann said evasively, blushing.

Lochlainn began to get the distinct feeling that Muireann was lying to him, but he said nothing, merely scowled and wondered jealously if this was the first telltale sign that Christopher was taking over his position. It had been with Tara, at any rate, he recalled with disgust.

"All right then, I'm going home to Ciara," he said, staring at her lingeringly, making no move to leave.

Muireann nodded. "You do that. I'll see you tomorrow."

Only when Lochlainn had gone did she release her breath and put her head in her hands and weep.

Muireann was able to avoid Lochlainn for the next five days, but by the end of the week, he grew more and more persistent about trying to see her alone. Ciara had taken a turn for the better, at least, but all the same, Muireann was worried about her. She spent several nights with Ciara at the cottage, though it put more of a strain on Muireann because then she had to see Lochlainn, and live in close proximity with him.

But Muireann could see Ciara's fearful looks every time Lochlainn displayed any affection towards her, or whenever she saw a child.

Muireann had a perfect excuse to avoid Lochlainn when Brona went into labor one night, and Muireann went to help out.

"I don't see why you should have to go!" Lochlainn protested, trailing after her as she gathered up fresh linens and a few things she would need for an overnight stay.

"I told you, if anyone needs me, I have to be available."

"I think you're trying to avoid me!" he accused suddenly, blocking her path.

"Don't be silly, I've been staying in your house for the past week," Muireann said evenly, trying to control her trembling voice.

"That's not what I mean and you know it. If you are going to marry Christopher, I think I deserve to be told!"

"Who said anything about marrying him?"

"He wants you. He's of your class!"

"As if those are sufficient reasons for marrying someone!" Muireann said impatiently, brushing past him to search for her cloak, which she had draped over the back of one of the chairs.

"Then he *did* ask you to marry him! I knew it!" Lochlainn rasped.

"Really, Lochlainn, the only reason I was nice to him was to determine whether or not he would be interested in buying Barnakilla to help us out of our difficulties."

Lochlainn glowered. "And is he? Or just interested in you?"

"He's even poorer than we are. And yes, he did ask me to marry him, because he's determined to get hold of this place for himself."

"He wants you, you mean!" Lochlainn sniped. "I knew it! He was after you from the moment he laid eyes on you."

Muireann sighed. "He goes after every woman, Lochlainn, you know that. But because of your old rivalry with him, you're being incredibly obtuse. The problem isn't his lust, it's his greed."

"What are you saying, then? He wants to marry you for your fortune? You haven't got one."

Muireann rolled her eyes heavenward, and sat on the edge of one of the chairs while he towered over her. "Will you please listen? This is important. Christopher says I have no chance of success here unless I throw everyone too old, young, or sick off the land. I have repeatedly refused to do so. Therefore he thinks he's the person to save Barnakilla, though he is bankrupt himself. He has threatened that if I don't marry him, he will challenge my title to the estate and see that he inherits instead, as the next closest in the family line."

He ground his teeth together. "The bastard! He can't do that, can he?"

She shrugged. "We both know we never found a proper will."

He sat down and put his elbows on the table, placing his head in his hands. "I suppose putting it like that, you haven't a choice, have you? Thank you for telling me. I'll start making other arrangements for myself and Ciara."

Muireann stared at him in horror. "You don't seriously expect me to agree to his—his *blackmail*, do you?" she demanded incredulously. She was unable to believe he would give her up without a fight. Had he ever cared about her, or had it only been the estate all along?

"If he's threatened you with legal action, what other choice do you have?"

Muireann rounded on him angrily. "I would never consider marrying him, not if he were the last man on earth!

You of all people should understand that! I thought you knew me. That you were my ally. I believed I could trust you! I'm not telling you this because I'm going to marry him, I'm telling you in order to warn you to be prepared. I'm not going to give up without a fight. These people are relying on me. I'm the only hope they have!"

"But if he succeeds in his bid, we'll have nothing, can't you see that?"

She rose up out of the chair to her full height and looked him straight in the eyes. "There are some sacrifices I'm not prepared to make. I won't even consider marrying him. I'm stunned that you would accept the idea so easily! Has all the time we've spent together in the past year meant so little to you that you would let me go, let our home go, without a murmur of dissension?"

"It means *everything* to me, you know it does!" he said furiously, trying to grasp her hand.

"What does? What 'it' are you referring to? Our relationship? Or Barnakilla?"

Lochlainn stared at her, stunned. "You shouldn't even have to ask that question."

"You're right, I shouldn't. But I need some answers now. You've just told me to marry Christopher to save the estate. Is that putting *me* ahead of Barnakilla? You never told me the whole truth about Tara. You never trusted me, did you? Not really. You always assumed I was going to leave you one day. Now you're practically driving me into Christopher's arms! Will you be happy once your prophecy is fulfilled? Will it make you feel better about yourself to know that you were right not to trust me all along, when you've driven me away? What's even more unforgivable is the fact that you never told me who you were, not really. Did you drift into the relationship with me because you thought it would be the only way to get Barnakilla for yourself?"

Now it was his turn to sit on the ladder-back chair. "What are you talking about?"

"I know you're Douglas Caldwell's illegitimate son! Ciara told me. So look at me again and tell me that I mean more to you than Barnakilla! Go on, tell me!"

Lochlainn sat at the table in a welter of misery. At length he said, "All of it was too personal, too painful. I didn't want to discuss my family or Tara with you. I just wanted to put it behind me."

"But you never did, did you? I saw how you used to look in Dublin, glum, a million miles away, locked in your own sorrow. But sorrow is a pretty poor companion, isn't it? You shut me out because of it, because you felt you couldn't trust me. And you still don't trust me now."

He stretched out a hand to her, pleading for her understanding. "I'm telling you, it has nothing to do with trust. It hurt, that's all, and I didn't see the point in opening old wounds."

She began to pace up and down in front of him, clutching her cloak against her body like a protective shield. "But you promised me the truth! Then you lied, not by commission but by omission. How can I ever trust you again? You've shut me out all these months. Even when we've lain in each other's arms, when you've been inside my body, there's always been a distance between us! I know you were hurt in the past by Douglas and Tara, but I would have liked to have been given the chance to help. I know how painful those feelings can be."

"You? The fairy princess?" he sneered bitterly.

She put up one hand to stay his mockery. "Please don't start that again. You made it abundantly clear the other day what you think of me. I'm sorry I don't belong here. But if not here, then where do I belong? I certainly don't belong back in Scotland. Not after everything I've been through."

His rigid self-control snapped as he gazed into her

amethyst eyes brimming with tears. "You belong here, in my arms." He pulled her to him, and captured her lips in an all-consuming kiss.

She pushed hard against his chest, and shoved him away. "But you've just told me to marry Christopher! How could you think I would ever even consider bowing to his threats! You don't know me at all, even after all this time!"

"You're right, I don't know you. I feel like you're a complete stranger to me at the moment! I can't even touch you without your shrinking away. I can see you have been avoiding me, keeping things from me, even about my own sister! I thought we agreed to be honest with each other. You have the nerve to demand the truth of me! But what about my getting the truth from you? If you aren't going to marry Christopher, and you know about my past, can't you try to forgive me? I know you're angry about my keeping things from you, but there seems to be more to it than that! You've practically run away from me for the past week. You've just shoved me away as though you loathe me. If you aren't in love with someone else, then tell me what I've done wrong."

Muireann felt herself weakening, and stepped closer to put her arm around his waist. "You're right, I'm angry and disappointed in you, and confused about this whole situation. I want to be able to trust you, and I'm sure I will be able to again in time. Please, my not being with you has nothing to do with what you have or haven't said or done."

"Then why are you doing this, keeping us apart?"

"Because I'm afraid," she admitted at last.

"Afraid of what?"

"We've been careless, Lochlainn. I'm amazed I haven't become pregnant already."

"You're sure you're not now?" Lochlainn asked, worry showing on his handsome face.

She nodded.

"But why now? It never troubled you before! Are you afraid of being tied down to me?"

"I'm just afraid it's not the right time, with the Famine and everything else that has been happening. Please, Lochlainn, it isn't a reflection upon you, or the way I feel about you at all. It's to do with Christopher's threats, and the fact that we're slowly starving. I know things were terrible when we came here together last January, but at least I was certain of a roof over my head, and that I could work hard to keep this place.

"But if I do lose to Christopher, he will get the estate, and I shall have to start all over again elsewhere. It will be hard work, you know it will. I don't want to run the risk of carrying a baby in addition to everything else we might have to face.

"In an odd way, I'm glad Christopher has come back. All of this has made me face the truth about us, clarified things for me. I know all about you and Tara now, and about your father. We've never talked about the future together, or our feelings. In fact, we've never really talked about our relationship. It's sort of taken place in a shadowy fantasy world we've created for ourselves in my little room. But I need to know what you see as our future together. Do we even have one, do you suppose? A few minutes ago you were telling me to marry Christopher in order to save Barnakilla."

Lochlainn sighed. He wanted to declare his undying love for her. But his pride had been stung, and he was still trying to do the noble thing by renouncing her. "I think you're right, we've been careless and foolish. I really can't see five years down the road for either of us. Perhaps it's better to part now before anyone else gets hurt. I can see now too that you can never trust me again since Ciara told you about our father."

He turned to go to his room.

Muireann ran after him and spun him around to face

her. "That isn't it!" she cried, trying to take his hand. She longed to tell him how much she loved him, but how could she when he had just declared he saw no future for them together?

"I need to be honest with you too, but there are some things I simply can't tell you, at least not now. But you seem so willing to give up on us that I wonder if there's any point in trying to keep Barnakilla or even trying to stay here, when it seems as though you've never cared for me."

Lochlainn reached out to stroke her cheek, and hugged her close. "I'm sorry if I've hurt you. I didn't mean to. I wanted to comfort and look after you. I lied to you, I know. I should never have brought you to this crumbling ruin. But I hope you aren't telling me that you only stayed because of me; I know that's a lie. You've worked harder than any man or woman on this estate. But I can't just sit by and let you waste the best days of your youth to slave away in endless labor for very little thanks or return. If Christopher wins, it's all my fault for having allowed us both to live in a fool's paradise. If he loses, I think you should sell."

"But you will come with me, won't you Lochlainn, you and Ciara?" Muireann pleaded softly.

He stood back from her and sighed. "If I had any wealth of my own, I would lavish you with every attention, presents beyond your wildest dreams. As it is, I have nothing to offer you except myself, and that isn't good enough. All I have are the clothes I stand up in and the labor of my two hands."

"It would be enough for me if I were sure you loved me," Muireann said tearfully, grasping one hand and bringing it to her cheek.

"I could be sure I loved you if I could be sure I would be enough for you," Lochlainn admitted. "But I'm too frightened of losing you to let myself love you. Oh, I know you care for me now. But how can I be sure that it won't all turn to hate in two or three years? Or even two or three months. You'd only be disappointed in me. I'd only hold you back. I should have let you go back in August, when you came home from Dublin so unhappy. I don't blame you for missing the big city, but—"

Muireann began to laugh bitterly, and shook her head. "No, Lochlainn, you're so wrong!"

"What was it, then! Why did you shut me out, shun me as you're doing now? Were you afraid of having a baby? You've never really been the same since you got back. You accuse me of lying, of keeping things from you, but haven't you done the same?"

Muireann tried to avoid his blazing gray gaze, but he cupped her chin in his hand and forced her to look him in the eye. Amethyst mingled intimately with steel as he demanded, "If you're so insistent upon the truth, why don't you tell me everything? Everything about you and Augustine, your marriage, about how he died? About Dublin, and about anything else you might have neglected to tell me."

Muireann's eyes widened in panic, and she broke away and went over to the fire to warm herself. She rubbed her arms vigorously as though trying to scrub them clean, and raised one shaking hand to her temple. "I need time to think. Some secrets aren't mine to tell."

"What are you afraid of? Are you in some sort of danger?" he asked, suddenly anxious.

Muireann sighed. "No, not really. I just don't know how you would even begin to react. And with all that's been going on, perhaps this isn't the time to dredge up the past."

"But you do admit you've lied to me, don't you?"

"All right! Yes, I have! I've lied by omission! But don't you see, it was personal, just as your never telling me about your love for Tara was."

His lip curled slightly. "All right, if you want to talk about that now, we will. You might not like the crude details, but—"

"No, Lochlainn, not now, I must go. The baby is coming, and Brona's asked for me. She's been a good friend. I can't let her down after all she's done for me."

"Damn it, Muireann, I need you too!"

Muireann stepped away from him hastily before he could grasp her around the waist. "Not now, please. I must go! I need time to think. We'll talk again soon, I promise, just not now!"

He could see that she was nearly at her wits' end, and raised his hands over his shoulders in a gesture of surrender. "All right, I promise not to touch you, not to goad you. You know where to find me when you need me. I'll be in the carpentry workshop. I shall sleep in one of the lofts there if you're going to stay to look after Ciara."

He went into his room to gather some fresh linens, then slammed out of the door, leaving Muireann alone with her confused thoughts.

She sat gazing into the fire for a few minutes before pulling herself together to go to the confinement.

She was up all night, but glad to help Brona. The birth also helped keep her mind off things. She knew if she had remained in her little room, or at Lochlainn's cottage, she would only have tossed and turned all night.

Just as the sun was coming up, the new baby was at last born. Muireann held the boy in her arms, and wondered what it would be like to have a child of her own. She had been so busy worrying about things on the estate, she had never really had a chance to think about what form her future with Lochlainn could possibly take.

Marriage? Children? The more she thought about it, the more she knew they were the only things she really wanted. Barnakilla, her new family, the tenants, they all gave and took. But what of love? All she had achieved meant nothing without Lochlainn by her side. She loved him body and soul. Why shouldn't they marry and be happy? Once the court case was over, they could settle things between them, couldn't they?

But her life was such a tangle at the moment, it was best to just leave everything alone for now. She couldn't tell him how she felt without risking going back to an intimate relationship with him, and she had promised Ciara she would wait. She had also promised Ciara she wouldn't tell Lochlainn about Christopher. It would all just have to keep until after she knew for certain whether she had the right to Barnakilla or not.

There will be time enough then, won't there? she reflected as she washed the newborn infant, and wrapped it in a blanket.

Chapter Twenty-five

At around nine the next morning, there was a tap at the door to her office.

Muireann looked up dejectedly as Lochlainn put his head around the door, stony-faced.

"I'm not here to argue with you, Muireann," he said directly. "I just came to tell you that there's a ship coming up the lough. It's the *Andromeda*. I thought you would at least want to come down to the jetty."

She tried to disguise her relief at the news. Pray God it had brought food and supplies.

"I'll be right there," she murmured, avoiding his gaze.

She tugged her disheveled hair into a long plait before scrubbing her face and hands in the freezing water in the basin, and dusting off her midnight-blue gown. Then she threw her long black cloak over her dress. Yanking up the hood, she raced down to the jetty as fast as her wobbling legs could carry her. She couldn't believe her good fortune. All of her prayers had been answered! The *Andromeda* was here! What a present for the New Year!

The boat docked and the crew immediately began to unload the stores. There were casks of wheat, yellow meal flour, and oats, as well as bushels of turnips, leeks and beets. If they husbanded their resources carefully, there would be enough food to get them through the winter after all.

She ran down to the jetty, hoping to see her cousin Michael. But there were two figures on the dock, and one of them, a tall man with graying dark brown hair and an amiable expression, turned to greet her.

Muireann blinked in astonishment, and threw herself into his arms with a whoop of joy. "Neil! And Philip! How are you?" she asked all in one breath as her brother-in-law twirled her around, sadly noting her thinness and pallor.

Philip, dapper and brown-haired, blushed at this extravagant display of affection, and remarked shyly, "I hope you don't mind. I wanted to come along for the ride. I've heard so much about your life here that I confess I just had to come and see all you have accomplished for myself."

She took Philip's hand. "Mind? Don't be silly. I'm delighted to see an old friend. And of course, a great deal of this would never have been possible were it not for you giving me the use of the *Andromeda* in the first place."

She blushed self-consciously at the state of her dress, hair, and callused hands, a stark contrast to the well-groomed, worldly gentlemen who stood staring at her as though they would never have known her. She had lied to them about her life just as much as she had to Lochlainn.

"Alice isn't here, is she?" Muireann asked in a worried tone. "I mean, not that I wouldn't be absolutely delighted to see her and the baby, of course, but as you see, I wasn't expecting guests."

Damn it, another lie, she thought to herself as the gracious words flew out of her mouth, and she colored again.

By this stage Lochlainn had seen more than enough. He was certain that Muireann was ashamed of herself and Barnakilla in front of these two handsome men. Moreover, he noted the unstinting admiration on their faces. Though he knew that Neil was certainly no love rival, Philip seemed just the type of man for her. The type of man he could never be: aristocratic, wealthy, and unbelievably handsome with his classical good looks. The fact that Muireann had known Philip since childhood and had never wed him did not even occur to Lochlainn.

By the time Muireann looked around to introduce Lochlainn to the two newcomers, he was already long gone.

She disguised her disappointment behind a wide smile. "Come now, everyone, there's no sense in standing here. You must be frozen. I'll see to some refreshments first, and then give you a quick tour of the estate."

The two men exchanged looks, and each gallantly offered her an arm as she stepped off the boat and led the way up to the house.

She brought them directly into her large cozy kitchen.

Lochlainn tried to slip out unnoticed, but she fixed him with a sharp look and called, "Lochlainn, this is my brother-in-law Neil Buchanan, whom I've told you so much about. This is his brother Philip. Lochlainn is my estate manager, well, my partner, really. Thanks to him, all of this has been possible."

"Now don't be modest, Mrs. Caldwell. You've done everything without much help from me," he said gruffly.

She offered the men some refreshment in her office, and Siobhan took them out the back way so that they wouldn't have to see just how crowded the house was.

As soon as they had gone, she whispered to Lochlainn,

"Where on earth are we going to put them? The houses are all full."

"I'll move out of the cottage for one night."

"No, I couldn't ask it—"

"You aren't asking, I'm offering. Really, it's no trouble. When are they leaving?"

"Neil said he wants to sail again tomorrow. There's some urgent business I heard him discussing with his brother."

"I wonder what it could be."

"He reassured me that my sister is fine."

Lochlainn put his arm around Muireann's delicate shoulder briefly. "Then don't look so worried."

But she noticed when she took in the tea that the two men were looking at each other every so often.

They think I've taken on more than I can handle, she concluded inwardly as their unease became more and more apparent.

"This is quite an enterprise," Neil said with a broad smile after she had filled him in on how successful the timber business was becoming.

"I'm lucky to have a manager like Lochlainn."

"Forgive me, but wasn't he here in Augustine's day?" Philip asked, disapproval evident in his tone.

She shook her head, and looked at him coldly. "He wasn't here until after Augustine had run the estate into the ground, and asked for his help. He never got to see him, though, not for more than a few minutes. Lochlainn had only recently returned from Australia. Augustine was already in Scotland searching for a suitable bride to bail him out of his financial difficulties. Lochlainn met us at the docks, took us to the hotel, and then had his supper in the lounge by himself. He was downstairs when the accident happened," Muireann said crisply.

"I see. So he can be trusted?"

"Implicitly, Philip," Muireann said with a lift of her chin.

"In that case I have to tell you that your father is very ill, Muireann, and I think you should come home now before, well . . ."

"Father? He's never been ill a day in his life," Muireann said, suddenly wary.

But Neil explained, "It was a stroke, several days ago now. He is paralyzed down one side. The doctors say another one would certainly kill him. All his affairs are in order. He may even get better. But I think you'll want to be there."

She stared at him in horror, then nodded. "Yes, yes of course. I'm sorry. It's just that you took me by surprise. I never imagined . . . But how can I leave now, of all times?"

"If this Lochlainn Roche is as reliable as you say, it shouldn't be difficult."

As much as she dreaded to think what would happen once she left, she knew she had to go. Her father needed her, and her mother as well. They would never forgive her if she didn't come. She wasn't even sure that she would be able to forgive herself.

She rose from her chair and began flipping through her paperwork, sorting things into three bundles in terms of their priority. "Thank you for the food stores. They'll come in handy while I'm away."

Neil cleared his throat uncomfortably. "Muireann, if I may say so, you've done a wonderful job here, and accomplished far more than I could ever have imagined. It took a great deal of hard work and courage, but you swallowed your pride and got on with things. You've made Barnakilla as much of a success as it ever will be, but it isn't your home. I really think that you should find yourself a buyer, and come home to your family where you belong."

She shook her head. "This *is* my home. At least, I've tried to make it mine, not something I inherited from Father or any man, but a place I created out of my own hard work and determination. I've been independent for the first time in my life, and it's been a wonderful feeling. You tell me I should sell, but it would be like hacking off a limb if I were to leave. These people are counting on me. If I sold the estate, no one would want to keep so many old and sick people, or so many families with young children.

"And I know what you are going to say. Send them to the workhouses. But you would not dare say that to me if you had ever been inside one of those establishments and seen what I've seen. I can't give up on these people now. Not with the Famine and everyone counting on me to make the right decisions. They trusted me with their lives by staying on this estate to work for me, or by coming here when they were evicted from the neighboring estates. I can't just abandon them."

Neil could see he was getting nowhere with her at the moment. "There, now, please don't upset yourself, child. We don't have to make any decisions this minute. Come back home to Fintry, see your father, and we'll talk again in another few weeks."

Muireann was torn. She knew that Neil was only proposing she sell because he was so worried about her ragged appearance, but she felt trapped, as if she were being manipulated in some way. She definitely did not want to leave in these circumstances, but what choice did she have? She just had to have enough self-confidence not to allow her family to manipulate her once she got home.

Muireann also knew she was reluctant because she hated leaving Lochlainn, even though matters had reached an impasse between them. She needed time to solve that problem as well. She was not about to blurt out her undying love for him as her boat sailed away from the dock. She also knew how upset he would be at her leaving; he would take it as a sign of betrayal. But surely her father's illness had to count for something.

"All right, I'll come. Give me a chance to get some things together, and leave my instructions with Lochlainn. We can sail tomorrow morning on the tide. If I may, I'll show you to your quarters for the night now, gentlemen. I'm sure you will appreciate that I have much to do if we're to leave tomorrow. The tide is at nine, by the way, so I'll make sure you're roused in time for breakfast."

"Nine will be fine," Neil said. He saw that in her current mood there was little point in trying to persuade her to look at things from his point of view. It was best to just stay out of her way until the idea of selling could sink in.

"Please, don't let us keep you. We have many things we could be attending to on the boat, and I'm sure there will be plenty of staff on hand should we require anything."

She bit back a sharp retort, and merely smiled. Really, how could he act as though he were in his own fine drawing room back home? But then, he had never known a day's want in his entire life. Besides, the mark of a proper gentleman was never to show emotion. He thought she was a failure, but he had been too kind to say so.

But Muireann had only failed once in her life, and that had been in her marriage. Despite that failure, she had learned some valuable lessons. She was not about to sacrifice everything she and her newfound friends had achieved to go scuttling back to the old dull spoilt life she had once led.

She conducted them to Lochlainn and Ciara's cottage, where she briefly explained matters and thanked Ciara for her cooperation. Then she turned her attention back to her guests. "I shall leave you in Ciara's capable hands, and see you at the docks in the morning. I'm sorry to be so rude, but we have plenty of time to catch up on everything when we sail to Scotland."

She hurried out of the cottage before they could delay her any further. Once in her office, she flung herself into a chair, and began to write as though her life depended upon it. She issued written instructions concerning all of the work in the various industries, and recalculated the food rations in light of all the provisions Neil had brought with him from Scotland.

"At least they won't starve," she muttered aloud as she sat working at the desk.

"Are they settled in?" Lochlainn asked as he popped his head around the door at eleven that night. He had seen Muireann's candles still blazing as he headed for the workshop loft to bed down for the night.

"Yes, everything's fine. Thank you for letting them stay in your cottage."

She wondered if he knew she was leaving; he didn't seem to be unduly agitated. He had left her alone to get on with her work all day. Everyone had. She only prayed she had thought of everything, for once she was gone, she had no idea when she was ever going to come back.

"I'm glad to do it, I assure you. Well, I'll be off to bed now," Lochlainn said, his gaze lingering on her lovely face for a brief moment.

It was enough of a sign for Muireann to reach out her hand to him. "Please stay, Lochlainn?"

He stared at her, holding his breath, hardly daring to hope. "But I thought—"

"No, don't think. Just hold me, love me, Lochlainn."

"I do, Muireann, I do," he moaned, as he began to smother her face in kisses.

Now who was betraying whom, she wondered with a sick pang. She hadn't told him she was leaving the next day. She had issued all the instructions by letter. She was creeping away like a coward. But she needed him. She couldn't leave without spending one last night with him.

She planted hot molten kisses all over his face and throat, stroking him to a fever pitch of excitement.

"Muireann, slowly, slowly, we have the whole night," Lochlainn gasped as she flipped him onto his back and joined with him in a fluid movement of her supple hips.

"I need you now, please!" she urged, gripping him with her powerful inner muscles, and alternating soft and languorous, with hard and quick strokes.

"Muireann, no, don't!" he nearly shrieked as she stroked his tender inner thighs until he completely spiraled out of control. He almost impaled her as he grasped her hips and pushed upwards with one mighty stroke. Muireann cried out her love for him, and collapsed onto his chest, sweat-soaked and trembling.

Lochlainn couldn't understand the change in her. He sensed her inner struggle between wanting and needing him, and keeping her distance because the differences between them still hadn't been resolved. But never once did he suspect that she was planning to leave after all. He was merely stunned at her ardor and grateful that she seemed to have forgiven him.

He made the most of her uninhibited mood to experiment with her, entwining their limbs in all sorts of impossible positions, which even Muireann had to laugh at, despite the secret weighing down her heart.

"I saw it in a naughty book once. It looked like a good idea at the time," Lochlainn laughed.

She stared at him and stroked his cheek tenderly. "You know, I think that's the first time I've ever heard you really laugh since I've known you," Muireann sighed as she snuggled against him, and noted once again just how perfectly they fit together. "It's been hard for you looking after me and the estate. I never meant to be a burden to you."

"You haven't. Just the opposite," he said softly, looping

her arms around his neck to draw her closer to him. "To tell you the truth, the house has always been like a millstone around my neck. I wanted to leave a thousand times when I was younger. But my father or my aunt would persuade me to stay. I resented him like mad, but he was my father, even if he refused to publicly acknowledge myself or Ciara. I suppose he never loved my mother, just used her, though Aunt says she was a fine woman, lovely, full of life and joy until she died having my sister. Aunt said we look like her. She had dark hair and green eyes. Mine have a certain greenish tinge if you look at them in the bright light."

"It must have been a very lonely childhood."

"It was, a lot of the time, though as I got older at least I was given a good education."

"But it doesn't make up for the lack of love. I ought to know. My father was always so strict with me. I know he was doing it to protect me, but all the same . . ." Muireann sighed again, trying to push such thoughts away. She was determined not to be gloomy on the last night she would spend with Lochlainn for a long time. Perhaps forever.

"And your mother?"

"Strict as well, more strict with me than Alice, the ever-dutiful daughter."

"Do you look like her or him?"

"A bit of both really," Muireann replied after a time.

"They must both be very handsome then," he said, planting a kiss on her rosy lips.

"My sister is the gorgeous one in the family, blonde-haired, statuesque. I could never compete with her."

He stroked down the long length of her back and cupped her to him even closer. "My dear, you wouldn't have to. Every man in the room looks only at you whenever you walk in."

"It's kind of you to say so."

"What do I have to do to convince you that you're

lovely?" Lochlainn asked as he kissed her eyelids and cheeks.

"I could think of a few things, but only if you're up to it," she said with a grin, moving her hand down lower.

"You do have the most wonderful ideas sometimes, Muireann," he growled, as she stroked him from head to toe, kneading and massaging.

I want to remember this always, every inch of flesh, every movement, every gesture, she reflected as she caressed Lochlainn.

But soon he took control of her body, of their incredible passion, stroking her until she couldn't hold back any longer. She reached her ultimate fulfillment while he watched.

"Lochlainn please, come here," she panted, opening to him like a flower.

"Gladly, my love, so long as you come with me again."

Much later he remarked quietly, "I wonder if it will always be like this between us. Even when I hold you in my arms, even when I fill you, touch the very core of you, I still want you so desperately. Sometimes I feel as if I'll go mad without you, but at times it gets even worse when I'm inside you.

"I don't have the words. I don't know how else to describe it," he added when he noticed her frown.

She kissed him softly. "Then don't even try, just feel."

As she settled against him, he asked, "Can I stay all night?"

"Please, if you want to."

He smiled then. "No ifs about it, my love."

But all too soon the gray winter sunlight began trickling in through the window. Muireann eased herself from his side and washed herself quickly with her flannel and a basin of water. She got dressed hurriedly, putting on several layers underneath her burgundy woolen gown. Then she tied her cloak around her shoulders.

She placed the small bag she had packed the night before on the step outside, and went back in to see Lochlainn for one last kiss. He wrapped his arms around her and kissed her warmly. Only when his hand strayed down to cup one rounded breast did he realize that she was fully dressed.

"Damn, another day at work," he sighed, opening his eyes drowsily.

"Not quite. Lochlainn, I hate to have to do this to you now of all times, when things are so confused, but my father is ill. He's had a stroke. I've left instructions for you on the desk, but I have to go."

"What! Your father? Wait, I'll come with you!" He began to swing his legs out of the bed, and reached for his clothes in an instant.

She shook her head sadly. "But I need you here."

"You need my support. I know how hard this must be for you."

She stayed him with her hand. "No, Lochlainn, I don't need you with me. I'll have my sister and mother. I'll be fine. I'll get through this one way or the other. I need you to look after things for me here, do you understand?"

He scowled at her, and she could see his anguish just under the surface of his grim face. She had never seen him look more handsome, or more dismayed.

"I suppose I should be grateful that you told me at all, and didn't simply slip away. You knew last night. You knew and never once told me! Now who is the betrayer, who the betrayed? You used me, didn't you, for you own selfish pleasure!"

Her own anger boiled over. "I beg your pardon, but I

seem to remember giving you more than your fair share when I—"

"No! Don't say it!" Lochlainn held up a hand, and shook his head.

Then he tugged on his shirt and sat on the edge of the bed, staring at the floor, his elbows on his bare knees, his hands clasped as though praying, a picture of abject despair.

Finally he raised his head and looked at her. "I'm sorry. I know you have to go. I don't want us to fight like this. But be honest with me, Muireann. Do you ever intend to come back?"

She knelt down beside him and took one of his hands. "Lochlainn, believe me, I want to. But I'm so tired. I can't make any decisions right now, because I don't know what's going to happen in the court case, with my father, anything. The only things certain in my life are that the mortgage has to be paid, Christopher is greedy enough to try anything to get Barnakilla, and Neil and Philip think I should cut my losses and sell. I don't want to, but if they withdraw all the support they've been giving us, we're done for."

He cast aside her hand impatiently, and began to pace up and down in the tiny room like a caged panther. "That's all about the estate. I'm talking about *us!*"

She blinked up at him in surprise. "You know how much you've meant to me all these months. I thought that all we shared last night proved that. Please don't let us part quarrelling. I don't want to fight you. I'm tired of fighting. I don't want us to end up saying things in anger that we might one day have cause to regret."

"I don't want you to go," Lochlainn suddenly declared, pulling her up to him for a passionate kiss.

"I must! My father! I have to go, Lochlainn. They're waiting for me. But I'll come back, as soon as I can. I will see you again, I swear," she reassured him, stroking his cheek.

She extracted herself from his tight embrace gently and turned towards the door to go.

"Wait a moment. At least let me get dressed so I can walk you down to the dock."

"No, don't, please. It would be far too difficult. Just say goodbye to me here, without a hundred other people staring at us."

"Because you're ashamed of me!" Lochlainn accused bitterly.

"No, because it is no one's business but ours. I don't want anyone to spoil things by criticizing the feelings we have for each other," Muireann said, gazing up at him lovingly.

Lochlainn kissed her upturned mouth, and she clung to him like a drowning woman.

"I'll be back," she whispered against his questing lips. "Wait for me?"

" 'Til all the seas gang dry, my dear.' "

She smiled at the quote by Burns. "I'll hold you to that promise when I next see you, Lochlainn."

"And you, Muireann?" he asked gently. "Will you wait for me?"

"Poor man, I'm beginning to think you never should have laid eyes on me at the Dun Laoghaire wharf," she tried to joke lightheartedly before she kissed him one last time, and fled from the room.

Grasping her valise, she ran all the way down to the dock. Only as she stood squarely on the deck and they lifted the gangplank did she dare to look around.

At the top of the hill she saw Lochlainn standing, his hand raised in a farewell salute. Muireann raised her hand high above her head and waved back. She kept on waving until the house was a mere speck on the landscape.

Then she turned to the prow with a sigh.

Her brother-in-law looked at her closely, and she shrugged. "It's been my home long enough. I shall miss it."

"You're coming home now, Muireann," Neil insisted, placing an arm around her shoulder.

She withdrew from his embrace and shook her head. "No, I'm not. Barnakilla is my home, Neil. Lochlainn and the people there are my family. No matter what you say, I shall fight until the last breath in my body to save them."

Chapter Twenty-six

Despite Neil's fears of wintry storms, the *Andromeda* made good headway, reaching the coast of Scotland in four days.

For the first few days after Muireann arrived home at Fintry, all of her time was taken up in nursing her father. He had suffered cruelly from the stroke. He was paralyzed on his right side, and unable to speak. He had to have all his needs tended to day and night, and Muireann did all the chores the nurse indicated to her without complaint.

Certainly her mother and sister noticed the huge change in her. Muireann was no longer the rounded, rosy, cheerful young girl they had last seen on her wedding day. She was more serious and sober now, with a wiry strength and determination that actually made them slightly in awe of her. She was as lean as a whippet, and twice as sharp.

At first Muireann was convinced her father would get better, and she did everything to make his life more comfortable, and to help him recover. She read to him, chatted with him, and though he never did anything other than move his eyes, Muireann was certain he understood her.

Always on hand to help were Neil and Philip. Philip in particular seemed to follow her around everywhere like a lovesick puppy, so that even Muireann, preoccupied as she was with Mr. Graham's illness, couldn't fail to notice his attentions. But since he was such an old friend, she did not feel any great alarm. It was mild admiration, nothing more, she told herself. Surely he couldn't think that she would ever . . . No, the thought of marrying Philip was too absurd, and she shuddered with dread and prayed she was wrong.

The few hours that Muireann did manage to get to herself were spent either sleeping, or writing lengthy letters to Lochlainn about the estate. She tried to keep her letters polite and formal, though she longed to pour her heart out to him and tell him how much she missed him. But it was impossible. How could she be sure he loved her for herself, not for her wealth? She had been sadly deceived with Augustine, hadn't she?

One day about a fortnight after Muireann arrived, her father took a sudden turn for the worse. His breathing grew ragged, and he began to foam at the mouth. He thrashed about for a few moments, and then lay still. Muireann held his hand as it gradually went cold.

The rest of the family, tired of being cooped up in the house for so long, had gone out for a short drive in the carriage. They returned several hours later to find her still sitting by the body, dry-eyed and silent.

"It's all over. He's gone," she whispered.

Her sister Alice immediately swooned, and Neil carried her away to her room. Her mother, silver-haired and rigidly dignified, went over and kissed Mr. Graham on the forehead, and then took his other hand and sat with him, stroking it gently, as her tears silently fell.

Muireann was surprised at her mother's response, for she had never seen her parents exchange any affection in public. She suddenly blurted out the question she had been wondering ever since she had been so cruelly deceived by Augustine.

"Did you love Father?"

Her mother blinked her damp eyes in astonishment. "Of course I did. He was the whole world to me. In our social sphere, marrying for love is considered the height of folly. But I did love him. We may never have shown it. He wasn't an affectionate man. But we admired and respected each other."

"But aren't affection, hugging and kissing, the er, physical aspects of marriage, important?" she asked with a blush.

"Really, Muireann, I thought I explained all this to you, about men and women!" her mother exclaimed impatiently.

"No, that isn't what I mean. I understand the physical aspect. I've seen enough horses in my day, haven't I? I've been married. What I mean is, how do you know when someone really loves you?"

Her mother frowned, suddenly worried by Muireann's persistent questions, her distraught expression. "Why on earth would you ask that? Surely you and Augustine were happy before he died?"

Muireann was tempted for a brief second to lie automatically. But even though this was not the best time to choose, it was her only chance to confess the truth to at least one other person in the world. The secret she had kept bottled up inside her for so long just had to come out.

"He never loved me, Mother, nor I him. It was all an act. He pretended to be the besotted swain in order to get his hands on my wealth. He used me cruelly. He was debauched, drunken and dissipated. I hadn't spent ten minutes alone with him on our wedding trip to Ireland before I realized what he really was. He deceived us all."

Her mother stared at her, appalled. She had always been

stern with Muireann, thinking her too headstrong and hoydenish, but now her love for her daughter came bubbling to the surface like a fountain. "My dear child, is *that* why you look so thin and wasted, because he was cruel to you?" She sat down next to Muireann on the low couch and put her arms around her lightly.

Muireann shook her head. "Not really, though that was part of it. No, the estate was foundering and I was too ashamed of my own stupidity to admit what a mistake I had made. Perhaps I've compounded the mistake by staying in Ireland, but the people on the estate needed me. I just couldn't turn my back on them. Now we're on the brink of starvation because of the Potato Famine. I just don't have any more answers. And it isn't just the Famine. It's Augustine's cousin Christopher, determined that I shall marry him so he can get his hands on the estate. Else he shall take me to court to try to get himself declared the legal heir. I think I'm about to lose everything, and I don't know how I shall bear it." The tears began to fall at last.

Mrs. Graham felt a small burning of indignation that her daughter had obviously been keeping a great deal from her, but she tamped it down hastily. It was all too apparent that the child was at her wits' end if she was now confessing what she had taken great pains to conceal for almost a year from her beloved family. She did not inquire into Muireann's motives for having done so, as she longed to, but instead asked, "Why don't you tell me about it, so we can see if I can help? It is what your father would have wanted me to do."

Muireann patiently explained all she had done at Barnakilla, mentioning Lochlainn once or twice as someone very important in her life, and recounting to her mother the horrors of the Famine. She left nothing out, even telling her all about her fateful trip to Dublin and her bargain with the devil, as Muireann referred to it the rare times she ever allowed herself to think about it.

Anger gave way to disappointment and dismay. Mrs. Graham wished she could turn back the clock and offer her daughter whatever support she might have needed before she had come to such a pass. But deep in her heart Mrs. Graham knew as well that she and her husband would have insisted upon her coming home. Would never have supported the hard decisions she had made for the people of Barnakilla.

At last, Muireann concluded, "I know how ashamed of me you must be, and I've hated every minute of the lies and deception. But what choice did I have? Those people would have died without me. They're good people. They deserve better than absentee landlords who are interested only in milking their Irish estates of every last penny so they can indulge themselves at fashionable resorts on the Continent while their tenants live on nothing but a handful of potatoes.

"I know you and Father would never have approved, but I make no apology for the way I've chosen to live my life, only the way I've had to stoop to evil means to do so. I'll never forgive myself for that as long as I live, so even if you don't forgive me for what I have done, I don't care. I would do it all over again to save Barnakilla."

She stood up to leave, but her mother grabbed her arm and forced her to sit back down beside her. "I'm so sorry it hasn't worked out, after all your efforts," her mother sighed, pushing a stray curl back from Muireann's brow. "Perhaps it's time to come home now? To admit you were wrong and let someone else take over?"

Muireann stared at the older woman uncomprehendingly. "After what I've just told you, you can ask me that? I can't do it, Mother. I love it there. It's my home. I miss it every day that I'm here. There's nothing left for me here. Alice is married. You've always favored her—no, don't deny it. She was always the obedient daughter, lovely, accomplished in all the ways it counted for a woman to be. I don't blame you, Mother, I'm simply stating a fact. I would always be a disappointment to you. And after having known such independence, I couldn't bear to have my wings clipped. I need to use my intelligence, my skills, to be fulfilled. Marriage and society are fine for women like you and Alice, but I need and want something different.

"And then there's Lochlainn, of course. This isn't his world. He would never fit in. I couldn't ask it of him. He has too much pride to ever accept any charity. We've tried our best to make a good home for ourselves and the tenants at Barnakilla. I can't give that up. Not without trying every means at my disposal to defeat Christopher and protect what Lochlainn and I have built together."

"But *this* is your home. Your father left it to both of you girls. I am to have the dower house, though I had thought to go live with Alice and Neil so I can see more of my grandchildren. She is expecting again, you know. So there's no need for you to go back to Barnakilla. Sell it, and you can run your own estate here without any interference. Your uncle would be so delighted. He and the boys were also thinking they might go to Alice and Neil's to help them, now that the shipping industry is really beginning to expand and he needs a good manager, but . . ."

"But what would I do here, apart from wait for the next fortune hunter to come along?" Muireann asked bitterly.

Her mother shrugged. "Philip loves you. He hasn't stood by you all this time, done all the things you've told me to help you, for nothing."

"But I didn't love Augustine, and I don't love Philip."

Her mother continued to stroke her father's cold, limp hand. "Love, mutual respect, regard, they're all good foundations for marriage. Philip is of your class and breeding. You could do far worse, as I'm sure you realize."

"I did realize that, once I had married the husband of my worst nightmares. But I don't love Philip. My heart doesn't leap into my mouth every time I see him. Do you understand?"

Her mother was about to deny that she did, but at last she admitted reluctantly, "Yes, I think I do understand. I met someone at a ball when I was sixteen. I had just come out. He was the most handsome man I had ever laid eyes on, but not as wealthy as myself. I mistrusted him, thought he was only after my fortune. Everyone told me he was, and in the end, instead of listening to my heart, I followed the workings of my head and told him I never wanted to see him again."

"Oh Mother, I'm so sorry."

"So am I. I ruined his life. He ended up bitter and disappointed, for he had truly loved me. The hugs and kisses. I've never known anything like them. But by the time I realized what a fool I'd been, he was dead. He'd neglected himself, died of a broken heart as the expression goes. I would give anything to have been able to make it up to him. It was a long time before I ever contemplated marriage again."

Her mother sighed. "So while I will not say that you should encourage Philip in his pursuit, do at least think about all he can offer you."

"But you lost your love. Shouldn't I be allowed to find mine without having to settle for second best?" Muireann demanded. "Think how lucky you were to have got a second chance with Father. Now I have one as well. I'm determined to take it. I love Lochlainn, Mother, *love* him. I'm sure of it now, though it all happened so suddenly, I didn't believe I could trust my feelings.

"You see, I fell in love with him from the moment I laid

eyes on him at the docks, when I was still wed to Augustine. I've been telling myself ever since that it was impossible, absurd. But it isn't. Nothing is impossible if you truly love someone. I know you'll say that we're worlds apart, that he is only my steward, and a bastard at that. But I love him all the same. None of that makes a particle of difference. I've given up worrying about what other people think of me. What does that matter when we're talking about happiness, true love? It's a rare gift. Now that I have known what it is like to be truly loved, I could never give that up, not for anything in the world. Even if I lose my estate to Christopher Caldwell, I'll find some way for us to be together, and to support my tenants. But at the end of it all, I'll do whatever I have to do to be with Lochlainn. I need him like the air I breathe, the food I eat. I'm sorry if this shocks or disappoints you, but you did ask me for the truth."

Her mother knit her fine silver brows. "No, I'm not shocked, though I'm so worried for you, my child. The problems in Ireland, they might be insurmountable, you know, even if this Christopher Caldwell doesn't win the lawsuit against you. You're a very fine woman, brave, clever. I'm so proud of what you've achieved, even if it's not what I would do. But the Famine might well be the end of it all. You can't fly in the face of nature."

"There are things that can be done with money and goodwill. The Quakers and other religious organizations are setting up soup kitchens, collecting donations. The wealthy people of Ireland simply have to stop their selfishness and think of their tenants a bit more before they depopulate the entire country. And the government will just have to stop exporting food from Ireland. I know they're doing it because they want to make it seem like there's a good balance of trade. Lochlainn and I have discussed all this at length. But the fact of the matter is that all that corn, wheat and oats could be feeding people back home. I will do whatever I can to convince the officials that that is true. And I'll need money to buy food, to make donations."

"You shall have it, Muireann, as much as you need. You're right, charity begins at home. To export that food is a sin."

They sat in silence for a few moments, until Mrs. Graham asked, "If all this is settled in your mind, why do you look so worried?"

"There's one problem that I need to solve, but I do think you have just given me the answer, by listening to me and not judging me too harshly. There can be no love without trust. That's the one thing, perhaps, Lochlainn and I have never given each other unreservedly, though we have shared everything else it's possible for a man and woman to share."

She ignored her mother's shocked look as she rose from the sofa.

"And now, if you'll please excuse me, I'm sorry to have taken up so much of your time with my problems and worries, when you have so many of your own now. I have a letter to write that just won't wait. And I'm sure there are some things you and Neil must see to now that Father is gone. I shall come and help you later, if I may, once I'm finished writing to Lochlainn."

Her mother rose and opened her arms, enfolding her daughter in a tender embrace. "You take your time, my dear. Neil and Alice can help. It is about time she started learning to shoulder a few responsibilities. I dread to think what would ever happen to her without Neil. At least I don't ever have to worry about what will happen to you. With or without your Lochlainn, you'll do well for yourself."

"You don't mind about him, then, Mother? I can tell him we have your blessing?" Muireann asked hopefully.

Her mother kissed her. "Completely and unreservedly. Be happy, my dear. Your father might have blustered and been a bit shocked, but in the end, he would have said the same thing, I know. We've always loved you, even if we've always been stern because we wanted to protect you. I see now that we failed. We didn't protect you when it mattered most." She sniffed.

Muireann embraced her. "Please don't blame yourself. I was the foolish one."

"No, we were all deceived, but you haven't wallowed in self-pity, or used your family as a crutch. I know you've told me some terrible things, child, but never have I been more proud of you. And if this Lochlainn Roche is as wonderful as you say he is, then he will simply have to understand and forgive you, as I do."

Muireann kissed her mother on her wrinkled cheek before going back to her room to write her letters to Lochlainn, telling him the whole truth, sparing no details which might put her in an unfavorable light. Now that she had told her mother, it didn't seem so bad. In the first letter, she explained the nature of her marriage, and even the trip to Dublin and all that had happened there. The only thing she left out was the chain of events leading up to Augustine's death. That was still too painful to recollect, and something she would only tell him if he was able to forgive her for the rest.

In the second letter she turned to business matters, sending him a bank draft to cover expenses, and telling him she would be home as soon as she could manage.

Muireann endured the wake and funeral over the next three days, and the huge number of callers coming to offer their condolences. All the while she kept thinking about Lochlainn, wishing she were home with him. Philip stuck to her throughout, always guiding her in and out of the room possessively as though she were some mindless automaton.

Muireann said nothing for the sake of her family. She didn't want to cause any upset while everyone was grieving for her father. Moreover, she did not dare risk a confrontation with the two Buchanan brothers over her future until she had spoken to her brother-in-law about the disposition of their property, all of their holdings at Fintry.

At last, on the fourth day after her father's death, she asked to speak to Neil and said, "I want to sell my part of the house as quickly as possible. I need the money to go back to Ireland and save Barnakilla."

Neil sighed. "Muireann, please think before you decide to act so rashly. This has been an emotional time for us all. I would not have you think you have to go back there, when you have a perfectly good home here. I know Philip would like to speak to you, but respect for your mourning has prevented him."

Neil would have continued to press his brother's suit, she knew. She interrupted him with a vehement shake of her head. "It wouldn't matter when he asked me. I would still have to say no. I don't love him. He's not the man for me. Barnakilla is my whole life now. I need to go back.

"I *love* Lochlainn. I love him so much it hurts when I'm separated from him even for an hour, let alone days on end. I couldn't live my life without him. Not after the past year. We've been everything to one another, do you understand?"

Neil scowled. "Yes, I think I do."

"Please don't start moralizing."

Neil sighed and sat down heavily in his desk chair. "It's just that I can't help thinking he's taking advantage. I've been making some inquiries ever since you told me about the court case Christopher Caldwell has brought for the possession of the estate. Did you know Lochlainn was the old man's illegitimate son?"

"I do, but I don't care. He loves me for me, I'm sure of it

now. If he didn't, he never would have done all of the things he has in the past few months, big things like always supporting me even when he thought I was wrong, and little things like giving me a puppy for my birthday. He is a good man, kind and tolerant, free from superstition, bias and ignorance. I've never known anyone with a warmer heart, though he has little enough reason to be kind to people when they've done nothing but use him cruelly. Augustine was the fortune hunter, not Lochlainn. And now Christopher wants to do the same thing. Marry me to get his hands on Barnakilla, since his own estate is falling to wrack and ruin."

Neil stared at her, appalled. "What do you mean, Augustine married you only for your money?"

So Muireann once again found herself confiding the whole truth about her appalling marriage, with the proviso at the end, "But you must make sure you never tell Alice one word of this, not one word, do you hear? Or Philip either."

"Who else knows?" he asked in a shocked whisper.

"Only Mother, and you. And Lochlainn, once he gets my letter."

Neil rubbed his hands over his eyes, feeling himself close to tears. Here was a shining example of what love should be. He was touched beyond words. After what Muireann had endured, she deserved every chance of real happiness and true love, and he was determined to get them for her.

"You told me about your desperate finances when you first wrote to me, but you never once let on about your terrible marriage. I don't know how you could have borne it. But now, tell me everything about this Christopher Caldwell again."

She shuddered.

He noted her reaction, and said, "Go on, you can tell me. After all you've just revealed, I'm sure it will be mild by comparison."

"No, it isn't. If anything, it's worse. But it isn't my secret to tell, it's Lochlainn's sister Ciara's secret."

"I give you my word, my dear, nothing will ever go out of this room. But you must tell someone. Bottling up all of these worries and fears for so long has worn you down to almost nothing."

"All right, I shall tell you everything I know of Christopher, but if one word of this ever gets back to Lochlainn . . ."

"It won't, I promise."

She revealed all Ciara had told her, and then went on to tell her brother-in-law about Christopher's threats. "But I won't let him do it, do you hear? Even if he wins the case, I shall buy the house from him, no matter what he asks, before he gets a chance to do any more damage to people, to women, than he already has with Ciara and Tara. He and Augustine were monsters. I can't believe the two of them and Ciara and Lochlainn share the same blood.

"But I know what Augustine was like when he was desperate. I know it will take a lot to buy Christopher off. To get him to go away and never trouble any of us again. But it's a price I am willing to pay if it means we don't have his shadow hanging over us for the rest of our lives."

Neil rose from his chair and paced up and down in front of the window for a few moments. "I wish you had told me about this problem with Mr. Caldwell sooner. I would have had more time to look into the matter further myself. I'm not sure when the court case will come up, but I think we still have a few weeks. Give me the name of your solicitor and I will see what I can do."

"No, you're so busy already, I couldn't ask you to . . ."

"My dear girl, I'm offering. There's no need to ask. But I agree with you. This all has to be put right somehow. The sooner Christopher leaves Ireland, never to return, the better. And something should be done for those two women he abused as well. Leave everything to me."

"But it's my problem, my responsibility."

"Dearest Muireann, you'll have enough of a fight on your hands when you get back to Barnakilla and have to battle the Famine. Save your strength for that fight, for you will most certainly need it. I brought Augustine into this house, introduced you, took him at face value without inquiring too deeply into his affairs. I blame myself for what happened. And no one as vile as Christopher should be left to prey upon unsuspecting people."

"But surely you are not going to have him arrested, have the truth come out about—"

"No, but there are other ways to make him pay," Neil said with a small smile.

Muireann allowed herself to grin back. "What have you got in mind?"

"All in good time, my dear girl, all in good time. But first we have to get you Barnakilla."

In the end, Neil proved to be a tower of strength to Muireann as she made plans for her future. She sold all of her remaining possessions for the best prices she could get, keeping only her most plain and serviceable gowns and under things, and some of her books. Even all of her jewels went to her sister, who pleaded with her to take at least one ring or brooch as a memento of her family and her past life.

But in the end Muireann adamantly refused. "I don't want to look back anymore, I want to look forward."

"But all of your lovely things!" Alice exclaimed with a pettish toss of her golden ringlets.

"They are only things, Alice, not people. What need have I of gowns and jewels when I am surrounded by love?"

"Love doesn't put food on the table," her sister replied with a hint of her old hauteur.

Muireann smiled at Alice and shook her head, unwilling to quarrel with her sister now that she had proven herself a tower of strength to her mother after a good talking to from Neil.

"In five years' time, you and the children will come and visit me, and you'll see the best-run estate in Ireland," Muireann declared, before turning back to pack her trunk.

When she finally admitted what she was doing, going back to Barnakilla to try to save it from the Famine, all of her family from far and wide had turned out in full force to lend a hand, showering her with all sorts of useful items for the house, plain but serviceable.

Muireann did try to point out that she didn't own a grand house any longer, not in the sense they imagined, but her elderly aunt Martha waved away her objections.

"Every married couple needs a house. You'll get one soon, mark my words."

"But Aunt, who said anything about getting married?" Muireann asked, puzzled.

Her aunt tapped her nose with her forefinger, and scuttled away.

Soon everyone was talking excitedly about her owning Barnakilla, marrying the man she loved, and living happily ever after as though it were a foregone conclusion. Muireann gave up trying to argue with them, or even curb their lavish gift-giving, which was rapidly filling the *Andromeda* from bow to stern. Only the livestock had yet to be loaded, and that was only because Muireann kept protesting that she didn't want to strip the Fintry estate of every four-footed creature it possessed.

The rumors of Muireann's impending marriage weren't long in filtering back to Christopher, who had some friends in Neil's social circle. With Muireann married in Scotland, he was convinced he would win his court case. But just to make sure of Barnakilla, he thought he ought to remove Lochlainn from the equation entirely. He rode over to his neighboring estate with the gossip about Muireann's forthcoming nuptials as fast as his horse could carry him, and positively gloated as he told Lochlainn the news.

"Why don't you clear out now, while you still have some dignity intact? This place will be mine soon enough, and you'll be traveling the roads like the beggar that you are in no time!"

"I told Muireann I would wait for her, and wait I will," Lochlainn said stubbornly, though deep down he was in agony. *How can she be planning to marry?*

"You're not wanted here, don't you see that?"

Lochlainn rounded on the blond man furiously then, letting his emotions bubble over. He clenched and unclenched his fists at his sides, praying he would have the strength to resist throttling him. "You're the one who's not wanted here, Christopher! Do you think even if you do win this estate, that these people will work for you? They won't! They stayed because they had faith in Muireann, came to love her. Even if you do win, what are you going to pay these people with?

"Look at these wages books. This is how much you owe to all these people before you can discharge them from your service, or they decide to leave. They will demand their payment, and I will make sure that you give every penny you owe every one of them, even if you get dragged through the courts for years. You'll have to file for bankruptcy, will go to debtors' prison. I'll make sure of it!"

Christopher harrumphed. "Impossible. You don't pay wages to peasants!"

"But that is where you're mistaken. They aren't peasants! They're workers. They worked these many hours at that rate, and after deducting food and laundry and rent, this is how much they are all owed."

Christopher stared, horrified at the huge sum at the end of the long column of figures. "But that's impossible!"

"Don't think your nearest neighbors will do any trading with you for wool and suchlike, as they have done with Muireann all these months. They don't like your blackmailing her, threatening to take everything away from her, any more than I do.

"There won't be a person in the country who will work for the likes of you once they learn the whole truth. Everyone has always thought you completely dissolute and unreliable. Everyone now knows how financially desperate you are! No one will give you credit anywhere! It's you who have lost everything, Christopher, even if the magistrates do decide to give you Barnakilla!"

Christopher raged, "It's not true! None of it!"

"It's all here in black and white. Before you think about trying to destroy the books, they are only copies. I sent the originals to Muireann's solicitor in Dublin, along with a few other important official papers."

"It still doesn't alter the fact that rumor has it Muireann is marrying. That can only mean Muireann is staying in Scotland," Christopher countered.

"You said it yourself, Christopher. It's only a rumor, not a fact. I shan't believe a word of it until I see her wed with my own two eyes, view the license and the man she is marrying. Muireann will come home to me. To Barnakilla. She promised," Lochlainn said simply with a certainty he wished he really felt.

"So *that's* the way of it," Christopher said with an evil leer. "You tricked the poor girl into thinking you cared about her so you could get your hands on the property yourself. She isn't stupid. She'll figure it out in the long run."

"Whatever she believes about me," Lochlainn said with a sigh, "she's still coming home to Barnakilla."

Christopher let out a snort of disgust. "Then she's an even bigger fool than you are!"

"You know, I've never forgiven you, Christopher, for what you have done to me and my sister all these years. But at the end of the day, the only person you've really hurt is yourself. You tried to get the big prize of Barnakilla after you had run your own estate into ruin. Now people know you for what you really are, a dissolute drunkard and gambler with no loyalty to anyone but yourself, and no money to call your own.

"As for the incident with Tara, my pride was dented, but you really did me a huge favor there in the end. I never loved Tara. It didn't take me more than five minutes in Muireann's company to realize that. I love Muireann. She's the air I breathe, the beat of my heart. And, I think she cares for me too. No matter how long it takes, I'm going to prove my love to her somehow, and spend the rest of my life trying to make her happy."

"Love! There's no such thing. It's just people using each other, taking whatever they can get, and moving on to the next person!" Christopher sneered as he put on his top hat and strode toward the office door.

"In a year's time, you'll see you're wrong," Lochlainn vowed, and prayed silently for God to grant him his wish.

Christopher stormed out of the office and got into his carriage without a backward glance, though Ciara tried to catch his attention.

As he drove away, she knew beyond a doubt that it would be the last she ever saw of him. She had wanted to rub salt into the wounds she had overheard her brother inflict upon him, to tell him she was finally free of him. But in the end, she no longer cared.

Augustine Caldwell was dead, and Christopher had no

power to harm Barnakilla any longer. Not with Lochlainn there to protect them all. Lochlainn and Muireann. For Ciara was certain that if Muireann was planning to marry anyone, it would be her brother, and that she would be home soon to tell them so.

She felt a pang of envy for their love and happiness, but only a brief one. She knew how much they had both suffered in the past. They deserved to be happy, and so did she. If only the right man would come along for her one day . . .

She sighed and returned to the kitchen, thinking with bitter regret of how she had chased away a far better man than Christopher Caldwell just because she had been in love with the idea of being the mistress of a great estate.

Yet Muireann was the mistress of a great estate, and wanted nothing except Lochlainn.

Fate was indeed strange.

Once Christopher had finally taken his leave, Lochlainn sat down heavily with his head in his hands. He knew he ought to go out and do some carpentry. He had more orders now than ever before, despite the Famine. But he took out Muireann's small pile of letters and began re-reading them until the paper was almost in tatters, trying to see if there was anything he had missed. Was she really going to marry someone in Scotland, perhaps Philip Buchanan?

He thought about traveling to Fintry to find her, but it was impossible. They had to get ready for the spring planting. Lambs, calves and horses were being born continually, and though Ciara tried to help with the paperwork, she certainly wasn't nearly as good at it as Muireann had become.

"I promised to look after things while she was away. I can't go back on my word. I can't go to Scotland. Besides, she promised she would come back. She promised," Lochlainn sighed, and put her letters away in the drawer with an air of resignation. There was nothing he could do except wait and hope.

He hugged his arms against his chest, and wondered why he suddenly felt so cold.

Chapter Twenty-seven

Early on a bright March morning about two months after Muireann had gone home to see her father, a small two-masted clipper pulled up beside the dock at Barnakilla. Muireann, dressed warmly in a fur-lined traveling cloak and a heavy royal blue woolen dress her mother had insisted upon giving her as a present, skipped down the gangplank gracefully, and began to run up to the house.

As the tenants, including Ciara, began to move down to the dock to see what the *Andromeda* had brought, they at last recognized the well-dressed, bright young woman who had disembarked, and all crowded around her. Some of the young men and women even hugged or kissed her, and Muireann was overjoyed at the warm reception she received.

"I'm so glad to be home," she said with a broad smile.

"Not as glad as we are glad to see you," Colm and some of the others replied almost in unison. "It's been a hard winter, but the weather bodes fair for this year. There will be much to do."

"Please God it's better than last year," she said, and they all crossed themselves devoutly.

Then she turned to Ciara. "I'm glad to see you looking so well, Ciara. Much more like your old self, I'm sure."

"It's good to see you, Muireann. I can't tell you how glad I am to have you home now."

Muireann could see the shadows of the past no longer hung over her like gloomy storm clouds. Perhaps in time, with some small share of happiness of her own, Ciara's terrible ordeal would fade in her memory.

Muireann hugged her and asked, "Where's Lochlainn?"

"Up at the house, I should think, getting his breakfast."

"I'll see you all later," she said with a smile, unable to conceal her burning desire to see him again.

"Welcome home, Muireann!" they all called as she stepped away from the crowd.

Muireann lifted her skirts and ran up the rest of the way to the house. Lochlainn was just coming out of the carpentry shop with a newly finished baby's cradle when she came around the corner.

"Lochlainn! Lochlainn!" she called.

"Muireann!" he gasped, almost dropping the cradle. He set it down hastily, and ran towards her.

"I'm home, my love, I'm home," she cried, flinging herself into his arms, all doubts and reservations having disappeared forever for her.

He clasped her in his arms and kissed her hungrily on the lips before smothering her face in kisses.

"Muireann, my love, you're back. Oh, thank God. All my prayers have been answered," he whispered, shedding a few joyous tears. "And now that you're here, my darling, I'll never let you go again."

"You won't have to, Lochlainn. I'm here to stay, forever and ever if you'll have me."

Lochlainn put her down then and stared into her eyes deeply. "But I don't understand. I can't believe you're really here! Christopher said you were going to marry . . ."

"Shush, my love. Whatever he told you was all a pack of lies. How could you ever think I would leave you, leave Barnakilla?" Muireann laughed tearfully. "You're in my veins, in my heart, Lochlainn, you and only you. This house, this estate is my life's blood. It would be like killing my first-born child to abandon it.

"And even if I didn't love you so much, how could I ever leave the people here to fend for themselves, or allow Christopher to lord it over them?" she chided him, as she held both his hands tightly.

"What did you say?"

"I said I love you, you silly man. How could you ever doubt it?" Muireann declared as she began to smother his face in kisses.

Lochlainn picked her up and spun her around, giving a huge whoop of joy.

"You love me, Muireann? Really?"

"I always have, from the moment I met you," Muireann revealed.

But now Lochlainn's face closed up, and he put her down gently on the ground once more. "Now you're mocking me, Mrs. Caldwell."

He headed into her office then, and Muireann could only follow, bewildered at his response.

He entered the office and poured himself a sizeable measure of brandy, which he threw back in one gulp without even choking, despite its vile quality.

"What's the matter, Lochlainn? What did I say? Or is that you don't love me after all? Have I made a mistake by coming back?" she asked, nearly in tears.

"No, not at all. I'm thrilled to see you, of course I am. But you don't need to lie to me about your feelings. How could you possibly have loved me all that time," he mocked. "You loved Augustine!"

Muireann stared at him, stunned. "What on earth do you mean, I loved him?"

"I know we've never mentioned him, not that aspect of your relationship, anyway, but he was the first! You must have loved him to have married him. Don't bother trying to spare my feelings. I saw you that night at the Gresham Hotel with my own eyes, remember? You were beside yourself!

"So don't lie to me and say you've always loved me. Augustine has stood like a shadow between us ever since we met. I fell in love with you the minute your hand touched mine. But damn it, you were wed to him, of all people! But I don't care anymore. I've tried to restrain myself, out of respect for your grief, but I couldn't help making love to you. I suppose you were lonely, and I guess maybe in the end, because I've tried so hard, you've come to love me in return. But I know I'll always be the second love with you, not the first."

Muireann started to chuckle, and continued until her sides were nearly sore, though there was little mirth in her laughter.

Lochlainn glowered at her. Slamming the snifter down on the table, he went over to her and shook her by the shoulders. "Damn it, Muireann, stop it, stop it now! Do you really think my suffering is so funny?"

"I do, actually. I've told you, I love you. I suppose it might have been better to tell you this sooner, but I had too much pride. You obviously didn't get my letter, did you? It makes it harder, since I don't know what you will think of me, if you can still love me after what I have done, but you need to know the truth. The whole truth, Lochlainn, however horrible. It was something I didn't even want to admit to myself because it was so awful. I'm sure I shall be damned for it. The truth is I hated Augustine. I was glad when he shot himself, do you hear me? Glad!"

Lochlainn stared down at her. "I don't understand. What is it you're saying?" he whispered incredulously.

"I've tried to block out the terrible truth, but I think it's about time I exorcised the ghosts of the past," Muireann said as she poured a glass of sherry for herself and then sat on the small sofa. She indicated for Lochlainn to sit beside her, which he did reluctantly.

Taking his hand, she confessed, "I never loved Augustine, not ever. I married him for all the wrong reasons. Because I wanted a home of my own, free from my father's prying and domineering ways.

"I had been pursued for my fortune before, but in Augustine's case he was such a plausible liar, I genuinely thought he was captivated by me. In the end I thought I could do worse than marry a man who seemed completely enthralled by me, with a huge estate in Fermanagh. But it didn't take me long to realize he was a man of dissolute habits, drinking, gambling, and that he was attracted not to women, but to men. I heard his lovers comparing notes. It was disgusting, disgusting." She shook her head.

Lochlainn stared at her, appalled.

"He never laid a finger on me, well, not in that way, anyway. He said I was far too refined and ladylike to be worth bothering with. Besides, he had just married me as an ornament. With a well-dressed and well-connected wife, he could keep the debt collectors at bay, and secure credit at all the gambling establishments he planned to parade me through. When he won, he was in fine form, but when he lost, he would take it out on the nearest person, namely me. At least he was very careful to ensure that none of the bruises showed," Muireann whispered, trembling slightly.

"So those bruises I saw at the hotel . . . You never fell on the ship!" Lochlainn practically choked on the words.

"I'm sorry I lied. It was pride. I couldn't bear to be an object of pity. The situation was already bad enough anyway."

"But I don't understand. If he had married you for your fortune, why did he shoot himself? And where did all the money go?"

She took a deep breath to steady herself. "He lost all the

cash my father had given me when he went gambling in Liverpool. He was furious with me because my father had proved to be much more careful with my dowry than he had imagined, investing much of it under Neil's care. He hoped to get rid of me somehow, claim my money, and find another rich wife," Muireann revealed. "And in the meantime, he loved to torment me.

"It was meant to be some sort of a sick game. One loaded pistol, one empty. The thing was, he forgot that though he had taken the ball out of one of them, he hadn't removed the charge. Augustine fired the first gun at me. The powder sparked off, and something nicked the wall. He was so drunk he thought that was the loaded pistol and the second one was empty, so he stuck it to his head and pulled the trigger as a joke. But it was no joke."

"My God, Muireann, I had no idea!" Lochlainn gasped, rubbing his eyes and temples with one hand while he gripped hers convulsively with the other.

At length he said, "But you were begging him not to leave you. I thought you loved him."

"I was terrified, Lochlainn. I was hysterical after coming so near to death. I didn't know what I was saying. I was alone in a strange country without a friend in the world except a surly land agent who looked daggers at me every time I opened my mouth," Muireann said with a small smile. "I was also horrified by seeing Augustine die in such a horrible way. Can you really blame me for being so distraught?"

"No, not at all," he said, putting his arm tightly around her waist. "It all makes sense now, now that you've told me the truth."

He held her close for a minute, then murmured against her hair, "And to think I believed you could never love me as you had Augustine."

"There's only ever been you. And not just because of

your kindness to me, either. There was always some sort of spark there between us, wasn't there? I noticed it every time we were alone together."

A light dawned in his eyes. "Then I was your first."

Muireann smiled up at him. "In every sense. I have the sheets still, if you don't believe me."

He began to plant a trail of molten kisses down her ivory throat. "My God, I can't believe how lucky I am. You really love me."

"I do, Lochlainn, with all my heart, though I haven't always shown it. But before we get too carried away by our reunion," she cautioned, holding him at arm's length, "there's something else I have to confess to you, something I'm truly ashamed of. You know that house in Dublin I sold to support us here at Barnakilla?"

"Yes, and you came back so withdrawn and unhappy. What of it?"

She looked at him and colored. "It wasn't just any sort of house. It was a whorehouse. Sam and Emma were two people I tried to rescue from prostitution. That was what Augustine had done with a lot of his money. He was taking a share of their earnings, using those people, profiting from others' vices."

"Good God, I don't believe it! Did they hurt you?" Lochlainn demanded furiously, stroking her cheek.

She shook her head. "No, not physically, but mentally. It was awful. I thought I was a woman of the world, knew about such things, but I had never imagined . . . The things I saw, Lochlainn, were too terrible for words.

"And I hated taking the money for the sale! Hated it! I loathed the idea of having to profit from those unfortunate souls. But what else could I do? We were all desperate for the money, and the madam and pimp were all too eager to buy the place from me so they would no longer have to share the profits with Augustine or his widow.

"I did offer the prostitutes a home if they chose to leave. I talked to them, I saw what their lives were like. But for many of them, it was all they knew, that life, and life in Dublin. They didn't want to come to Enniskillen to try to work on the land, only Emma and Sam. In the end I could see I really had little choice. My scruples over taking money earned in such a way wouldn't have saved them, and certainly wouldn't have helped the estate here. But for a long time after that I was very depressed, wishing I could have done more.

"It also made me conscious of our own sin. Loving you out of wedlock, well, it's wrong, isn't it, according to what the Church teaches us. Only every time I looked at you, felt you in my arms, I couldn't help myself. I didn't want to reject you, believe me. I was just confused and afraid, about my life here, you, the nature of love, oh, so many things."

"But you're not confused anymore?" he asked softly.

She came over to sit on his lap and snuggle up to him. "Not anymore. Love is a rare and precious gift, and I for one am not going to spurn it. I know you better than any other person in the world, and I do trust you. I also know that Barnakilla is very important to you. I needed to be sure you weren't staying with me because you loved it."

He held her hard to him. "I am staying with you because I love you. Wherever you want to go, whatever you want to do, I'll be at your side always."

" 'Til all the seas gang dry?"

"Aye, my love."

"Then you forgive me for Dublin?" she whispered.

"There's nothing to forgive. I don't blame you for being horrified by what you saw. I think I would have been, too. I saw the prostitutes in Cape Town and down in Sydney when I was getting off the ships on my journey to Australia and back. It isn't the sort of life I would like to contemplate for any woman, or man. But you did what you had to do to save the estate. To save the people here from one day having to resort to that sort of existence to survive. How could I ever judge you harshly? I love you, Muireann. Whatever you do, I will try to be understanding."

"Really? Because there's one more thing I'm going to have to confess, before we decide what we want to do with the rest of our lives, well, two things, actually."

He gave her a tiny smile. "All right, I'm listening. But I hope it isn't going to be too shocking. I don't think my heart can take much more."

"I hope the shocks will be pleasant ones. The first thing is that with part of my share of my father's estate, I've bought a new estate. Christopher's, in fact."

Lochlainn's mouth dropped open. "But how? I never thought he would give in so easily."

"Neil put pressure on the debt collectors to call all their bills due, and got them calendared to go through the courts at once. It was either sell or go to prison. So he sold to me, and I discharged his debts."

"That's wonderful news! Now we can really make Barnakilla great again, without having to worry about the wolf at our door. I know you can succeed with both estates, Muireann."

She shook her head. "I can't, my dear, because Barnakilla isn't mine anymore. It never was, not really. There was a problem with the will, you see."

Lochlainn put one hand up to his brow and groaned, "Oh my God, you're not telling me Christopher is legally entitled to it after all? Think of all the money, the hard work, the sacrifices you've made! He can't take what you've invested . . ."

"No, my love, it isn't Christopher's at all. Father Brennan found papers in the parish records in Dublin. The will that your father left said the estate had to go to his eldest living son. Eldest living son, not eldest living legitimate son. It was only Blessington and that horrible crooked lawyer who allowed Augustine and his mother to seize control while you were so far away in Australia. Barnakilla never belonged to Augustine or me. It's always been yours."

He stared at her for a moment before hugging her close. He cradled her in his lap as though he would never let her go. "Thank you, my love, thank you. If you hadn't come to save Barnakilla, to save me, I don't know what would have become of us all."

She stroked his hair back from his brow tenderly. "There's no need to thank me, my love. I did what anyone would have done. I had to. I had no choice. So now we'll be neighbors, and friends. Equals. You don't have to make any decisions right away."

"Yes, I do," he said, rising from the sofa to swing her up into his arms. "I love you, and I'm going to wed you as soon as I get the chance."

"In that case, it's a good thing Father Brennan has come with me to pay his respects," she giggled as he brought her into her bedchamber and laid her down gently on the mattress.

"We will need to make preparations, invite everyone—"

"I don't care about any of that. I've already had one fancy wedding, and it was a nightmare. When I stand up with you, Lochlainn, I don't care if we're the only two people there."

Lochlainn's long fingers worked deftly at the buttons of her gown, while she untied his stock. "We will need a couple of witnesses. But that's fine. Best not to make a fuss with things so hard at the moment."

"They're not anymore. We have food and clothes and everything else I've managed to cram into the *Andromeda*. Neil will help too. He's promised to support me, no matter what. He wants us to be happy, with no more struggles and worries here at Barnakilla. He wanted me to stay in Scotland, but I convinced him in the end that this is where I belong, here with you. I sold my share of everything, and my mother was happy to move to Neil's home along with my uncle and cousins. Neil and Philip are spending so much time with their ships, they need good men to look after the estate. So it's all settled. I have a new home and I can't wait to get started building it up."

"Oh no, you don't, my girl," he said, shaking his head. "Now that we are to be wed, we'll restore Barnakilla to its full glory. We can use Christopher's manor house and his cottages to clear out all of the people who have been living in the big house for so long."

"Whatever you like, dearest. I've also found an excellent blacksmith for our new horses. Robert—I think you know him?"

Lochlainn paused in untying the tapes of her voluminous petticoats just long enough to gaze into her eyes. "My old friend? Ciara's old beau? But why—"

"I think he might be just what she needs if she's ever to be happy and leave the past behind her. She loved Christopher, you know."

He stared. "No, I didn't, but now it all makes sense."

"And Tara. I've sent her some money, but I'm afraid she's very ill. She has consumption. I've said she can come home here if she wants to see her old home and friends, but Neil tells me that she sent a letter to the lawyer saying she's gone to the south of Italy. Christopher has headed to the United States, to seek his fortune, with one of Neil's shipping agents to keep an eye on him, and disburse his funds, which he will continue to receive so long as he stays away from Ireland for the rest of his life."

He bared her bosom and then began to roll down her warm woolen stockings with sensual sweeps of his hand. "You certainly do think of everything, Mrs. Roche."

"I do try, Mr. Roche."

Neither could hold back any longer, and tugging the last of their clothes off, they gave in to the thrilling sensations which only the other could give. Their frenzied lovemaking, though brief, revealed more than mere words the depth of their love for one another.

"My God, Muireann, it gets better every time I'm with you. I'm sorry I couldn't hold back," he panted, rolling onto his back and pulling her close to his side.

"I don't want you to, Lochlainn," she reassured him, planting kisses all over his face. "There have been too many reservations and uncertainties in our life together. I want all the secrets out in the open now, no matter how unpleasant or shocking they may be.

"As for being ashamed of your being my lover, I've told everyone my feelings for you, and they wish us joy. I can't help myself either. Every time you touch me, it is like a spark to powder, and I just ignite."

"An apt description," he laughed. "I feel like I'm on fire."

"I know I am," Muireann said as she snuggled up against him with a grin.

Then she sobered. "But there is one other thing I have to tell you, and I'm not sure how you're going to take it."

He chuckled. "After all you've told me today, anything else will be an anticlimax, but come on, let's hear it."

"We're going to have a baby."

Lochlainn simply stared at her for an eternity, before swinging his legs out of the bed and tugging on his trousers.

"I'm sorry, Lochlainn. I was hoping you would be pleased," she said in a hurt tone, as he presented a granite face to her.

"Aye, of course I would be pleased if I were certain you were. But you have so many plans, things you want to do with your life, and now I've tied you down. Now you'll have to marry me as soon as I can arrange it. Well, I suppose it explains why you came back now of all times," he sighed.

She sat bolt upright in the bed. "I beg your pardon! Are you saying I only came back because I needed or wanted you to be the baby's father, or that I am going to demand marriage of you? How dare you! I love you! I want to be with you every day and night for the rest of our lives. I'm not some coward who can't face up to my mistakes or responsibilities. If you don't want the baby, we'll manage on our own."

She tugged the sheet up over her bare bosom and turned her face to the wall.

Lochlainn reached over and grasped her chin, turning her head so that she could look him straight in the eyes. "How long have you known? Or maybe I should say, how long have you been keeping this other piece of information to yourself?"

"I was so busy with my father's funeral arrangements, it never even occurred to me. It was only on the trip down from Fintry, and especially when I got to Dublin, that I realized. I had been really sick on the boat across, you see, but put it down to simple *mal de mer*. It was only once I was on dry land and kept getting sick in the mornings, and then did some mathematical calculations, that I knew for sure."

Lochlainn sat down on the bed and hugged her to him. "So you were already on your way back to me?"

She stroked his cheek softly, trying to allay his last doubts and fears. "Please, Lochlainn, I know we've had a hard time, and the road we've traveled together has been a rocky one, but please believe me when I say I love you. Please trust yourself enough to be secure in our relationship. I love you. You make me so happy, I can't even begin to find the words. I would love any child we had together unreservedly, whether we're married or not. I hope that any children we may have will bring us even closer together than we already are. Please, no more ghosts from the past to haunt us. I want to start all over again, with no more doubts and misunderstandings."

He sighed and got back into the bed beside her. "Then I have to confess something as well. I wasn't looking daggers at you when we first met because I resented you. I was staring at you because I fell in love with you from the moment I first laid eyes on you. I hated myself for even thinking of you in that way, with you so young and married to my half-brother. I deliberately tried to think ill of you. I tried to convince myself that you were a woman of the world who deserved everything you got for marrying such a dissolute wretch. But one look at those incredible eyes of yours, and I would melt. I've been such a fool. I just can't believe my luck, can't be sure I can trust it or you."

She snuggled against his lean, hard frame. "You can, Lochlainn. I've told you all there is to know. I love you. Nothing else matters, nothing, not even Barnakilla. So long as we have each other, what else do we need?"

"Oh Muireann, I've felt for so long that I've ruined your life, taken advantage of your predicament, by not having told you the whole truth. I was the one who had you come to Barnakilla, and I've been so scared that you might one day resent me for that, and for all we've shared. You've given yourself so generously. Too generously. I've tried to hold back, to give you your freedom. But the number of times I just wanted to kiss you, to—"

"You were saying?" Muireann sighed as she stroked him boldly, and left him struggling for control.

"You little vixen," he purred, rolling her underneath him.

"I don't want my freedom from you, not now, not ever. I love you, Lochlainn, always."

"And I you, my darling girl. But are you sure, really sure, about staying here? We've had such dark days with the Famine, the poverty—"

"But such glorious nights. Really, dearest, I'm sure this is my home, just as I'm sure of our love for one another," she breathed as she moved against him seductively. "Can't you feel it too?"

Lochlainn kissed her then, knowing mere words were not enough to tell her how he felt. Lifting his lips, he vowed, "Wherever you are, my darling, that's where I belong."

"And wherever you are, that's my home, my dearest love."

Muireann kissed Lochlainn tenderly, an unspoken promise that they would never again be parted.

Author's Note

All the historical details about the Potato Famine are accurate. For those interested in learning more about this period of time I recommend the following:

Edwards, R. Dudley and T. Desmond Williams, editors, *The Great Famine: Studies in Irish History, 1845-1852.* The Lilliput Press, Dublin: 1994.

Smyth, Cecil Woodham, *The Great Hunger*. Hamish Hamilton, London: 1962.

Whyte, Robert, *The Famine Ship Diary, 1847.* Mercier Press, Dublin: 1994.